THE STONE WITCH OF FLORENCE

ANNA RASCHE

Legend Press Ltd, 51 Gower Street, London, WC1E 6HJ
info@legendtimesgroup.co.uk | www.legendpress.co.uk

Contents © Anna Rasche 2024
The right of the above author to be identified as the author of this work has been asserted in accordance with the Copyright, Designs and Patents Act 1988. British Library Cataloguing in Publication Data available.

First published in Canada by Park Row Books in 2024 | 22 Adelaide St. West, 41st Floor, Toronto, Ontario M5H 4E3, Canada | ParkRowBooks.com

Print PB ISBN 9781917163033
Print HB ISBN 9781915643100
Ebook ISBN 9781915643117
Set in Times.

Cover Design by Mary Luna and Art Direction by Kathleen Oudit. Ring Illustration by Allan Davey (based on reference images courtesy of the Metropolitan Museum of Art) and Interior Illustrations by Marisa Aragón Ware.

All characters, other than those clearly in the public domain, and place names, other than those well-established such as towns and cities, are fictitious and any resemblance is purely coincidental.

All rights reserved. No part of this publication may be reproduced, stored in or introduced into a retrieval system, or transmitted, in any form, or by any means electronic, mechanical, photocopying, recording or otherwise, without the prior permission of the publisher. Any person who commits any unauthorised act in relation to this publication may be liable to criminal prosecution and civil claims for damages.

Anna Rasche is a historian and gemologist who has previously worked in the jewelry collection at the Metropolitan Museum of Art and as a curatorial fellow at the Cooper Hewitt, Smithsonian Design Museum.

Anna's debut manuscript is based on original research she conducted on the uses of gemstones in medieval medicine at the Cooper Hewitt Museum and on site in Italy.

She lives in Brooklyn with her husband and infant daughter.

Follow Anna on Instagram
@by_annarasche

and visit
www.annarasche.com

For Will & for Bea

FIRENZE
– 1348 –

1. SAN MINIATO AL MONTE
2. PORTA SAN NICCOLÒ
3. CONVENT OF SANT'ELISABETTA DELLE CONVERTITE
4. TRATTORIA ALLE PANCHE
5. TORRE GIROLAMI
6. SANTO STEFANO
7. PALAZZO TORNAPARTE
8. SANTA TRINITA
9. SAN PAOLINO
10. SAN PIER MAGGIORE
11. THE STINCHE
12. PALAZZO DELLA SIGNORIA & RINGHIERA
13. SAN PAOLO
14. APOTHECARY AT THE TWIN JANUS
15. SANTA MARGHERITA
16. SANTA REPARATA
17. INQUISITOR'S RESIDENCE
18. BISHOP'S PALAZZO
19. THE BAPTISTERY
20. SAN LORENZO
21. SANTA MARIA NOVELLA
22. SAN BARNABA
23. PORTA SAN GALLO
24. LUDOVICO'S PALAZZO
25. PALAZZO ALDOBRANDINI

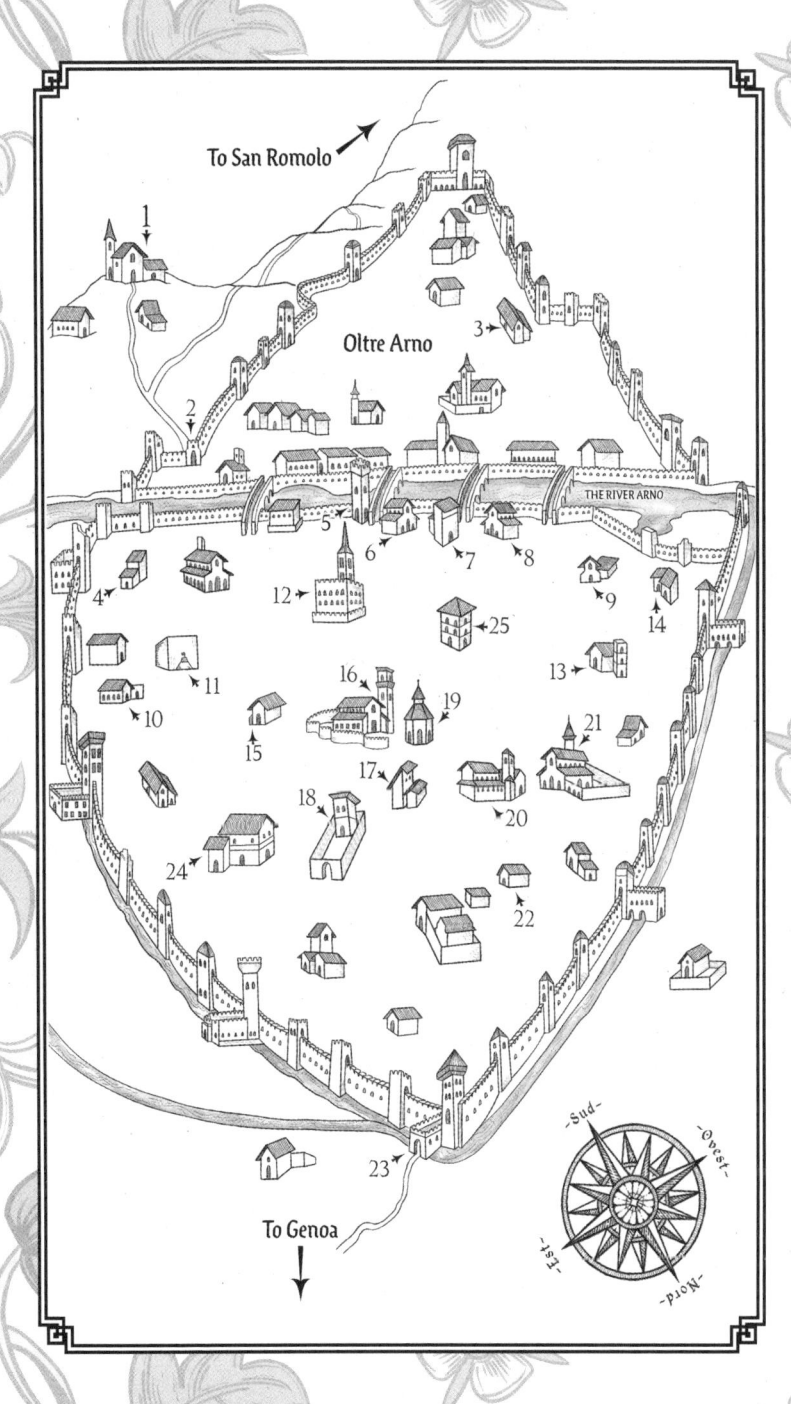

PROLOGUE

Summer, 1348

One wicked July, a boy approached the ancient archway of the Porta di Santo Stefano. Squinting into full summer sun, he saw the heavy wooden doors shut tight. Although it was midday and the normal time for business, no guards stood outside, no people sought entrance. The year before, the scene would have been very different.

In happier times, any traveler arriving with honest purpose could enter Genoa for a small fee. But now cities detested strangers, and the boy was afraid of being turned away. He stepped off the road and into an untended vegetable garden, concealing himself in the overgrown arbor. A feeble breeze stirred the wilting vines, carrying with it the nasty scent of burning hair. There were hard green grapes just starting to grow, and the boy plucked and ate them eagerly. When his sour little meal was through, he settled down in the hot dirt to wait for an opportunity. He peered through the leaves, his eyes following the dirty stones of the city wall southward to where they met the Ligurian Sea.

The squeaking wheels of a cart brought his attention back to the road. It was loaded with dusty sacks, once filled with flour, now to be used as shrouds. In spite of the punishing heat, the cart's driver was wrapped up in a heavy cloak, his hood ringed with salt lines from drying sweat. Cracked leather gloves covered his hands and yellowed linen covered his face.

None of this was strange to the boy. He crept out of the arbor as the wagon rolled past, jumped up lightly, and burrowed into the empty sacks. The driver continued on, oblivious, and when he reached the archway, the gate was pulled open without question.

Once inside the walls, the boy slid off the cart and followed the sloping streets down toward the port, his own footsteps the only sound. The places of mirth, commerce, and worship were now empty. Except for the rats – grown bold in the absence of men and women, the rodents ignored their natural hours and left their holes even in the bright daytime. The few remaining residents, the ones too poor to flee, hid themselves indoors, shuttered against afternoon heat that radiated off buildings in visible shimmers.

When the boy reached the third street from the waterfront, he turned left as instructed and walked until he came to a low house discreetly marked with the image of a serpent slithering up a branch of coral. He might have cried with relief at locating his destination, but he was twelve now and trying to be manly about things. He took a shuddering breath, smoothed his hair, all full of muck from sleeping outdoors, and knocked. A woman of about thirty came to the door. She had the coloring of the region, with dark eyes and light hair that was twisted in plaits around her head. On her left hand she wore a ring set with an orange stone. Her nose looked crooked. The boy saw that a thick white scar hooked up her left nostril.

"What are you doing out now, little one?" she asked, looking down at him. "Has your mama sent you for something?"

The boy remembered the speech he had been told, and said it quickly: "Excuse me, Lady, are you Monna Ginevra di Gasparo, called Ginevra di Genoa, who walks through pestilence but will never be ill?"

"Who has said this of me?"

"The ones that sent me, who said they have seen this to be true with their own eyes."

She nodded slightly at his answer but did not seem pleased to be found. The boy smiled.

"Good. Then I have a letter for you."

The woman ushered him across the threshold, and bade him sit at a small table in the center of her single room. As the boy's eyes adjusted to the indoor darkness, he saw the walls were lined with dozens of neatly arranged blue-and-white ceramic jars. Above his head were ceiling beams strung with ropes of garlic, the feet of little rabbits, and lots of other lumpy dried-out things he did not recognize. Monna Ginevra wiped the dust from his face and hands with a damp cloth and placed a pitcher of cool water and a wedge of yellow melon before him: a feast for the boy. He became completely distracted by the sweet, glorious fruit. Monna Ginevra gave a little cough to remind him of her presence.

"Oh!" he said through a mouthful of melon. "Sorry! I am Piero di Piero Cazzola, and I have a letter for you all the way from Florence. It comes from Signore Ludovico Acciaiuoli. I don't know what it says, but I'm supposed to bring you back with me right away and then he'll pay me." He reached inside his smock and triumphantly pulled out the much crumpled (and now slightly sticky) document. It bore the *lion rampant* of the Acciaiuoli family, stamped assertively into a seal of bloodred wax. Monna Ginevra's eyes widened, then narrowed, and the faint lines between her eyebrows became deep furrows.

She broke open the seal to the letter and scanned the page, surprising Piero with an incredulous "HA!" when she reached the end. She read it again out loud, as if requiring a witness to confirm the absurdity of its contents:

> *In the name of God, Amen. It is June the Twentieth, 1348.*
> *My most esteemed and darling Ginevra, your Ludovico has thought of you often in these terrible times and still laments our unfortunate separation.*
> *I have entreated my dear uncle, Fra Angiolo*

Acciaiuoli, on your behalf. In your absence, he has been appointed most holy bishop of our city, and he is willing to reverse your exile. We believe your – unusual – talents may be useful in resolving a small problem for the city.

It is different now, in all things, except that you remain locked within my heart.

For your Ludovico, I beg your swift return to Florence. In the name of God, Amen.

Ginevra smacked the letter down upon the table.

"You were exiled?" exclaimed Piero. He was impressed. "What did you do?"

"Nothing," she said through gritted teeth. "Tell me, what has happened that the great Acciaiuoli family places such a message in the care of a beardless boy?"

Piero was stung. He thought they were friends, because of the melon, and cast his eyes to the floor. "They sent me because I was the only one they could find that would not die."

"What do you mean *the only one that would not die*?"

He began to tear up a little, in spite of all his efforts, and said in a whisper, "My whole family got sick and they died, but I became well. They say if you survive, you will not catch it again. That's why they sent me, because another might fall ill and die along the way, and you would never even know they sent you a letter."

Ginevra di Gasparo was ashamed, then. Having forgotten, in her own frustrations, to show compassion to a most unfortunate creature. The walk from Florence was seven days, at least, for one who knew the way, and with things as they were, there would have been any number of ghastly sights and dangerous persons along the road. She saw Piero now as he was: a child sent when grown men were afraid to go. She cursed her short temper – a lifelong failing – and went to him and patted his head and said she was sorry. She dried his sniffles, and gave him more good things to eat until he felt well enough to ask if she would come back with him as the letter requested.

Ginevra picked up the document again. For Ludovico to write her after so long was strange. She did not trust it. The seal on the letter looked real; it was the contents that rang false. *It is different now, in all things, except that you remain locked within my heart.* Tender words, which once would have been a balm to her, now offered lamely from years and years and miles away. Did he mean it could be different, between the two of them?

"Tell me, Piero, would you go, if you were me? At such a time as this?"

"Well," he said, "what would you do instead, if you stayed?"

The question stuck. What *was* she doing? She kept her business at a discreet address, her deals small-time. The full extent of her talents hidden. It was safest that way. But there had been years, now, of doldrum days and lonely evenings. The sharp edge of her fear was dulled by boredom. Perhaps, Ginevra thought, she had removed herself from the world more than necessary. Here was an invitation to rejoin it. All she had to do was solve a "small problem." She closed her eyes and searched her secret heart and found in it a tiny flame that still burned with hope for a full and visible life – a life rich with love and with friendship.

The flame grew large and bright, consuming worries of personal danger and questions about the letter's meaning. She turned back to the boy.

"Yes, Piero, I will return with you. I will not make you go alone."

PART I

THE GOLDEN STRINGS OF THE UNIVERSE

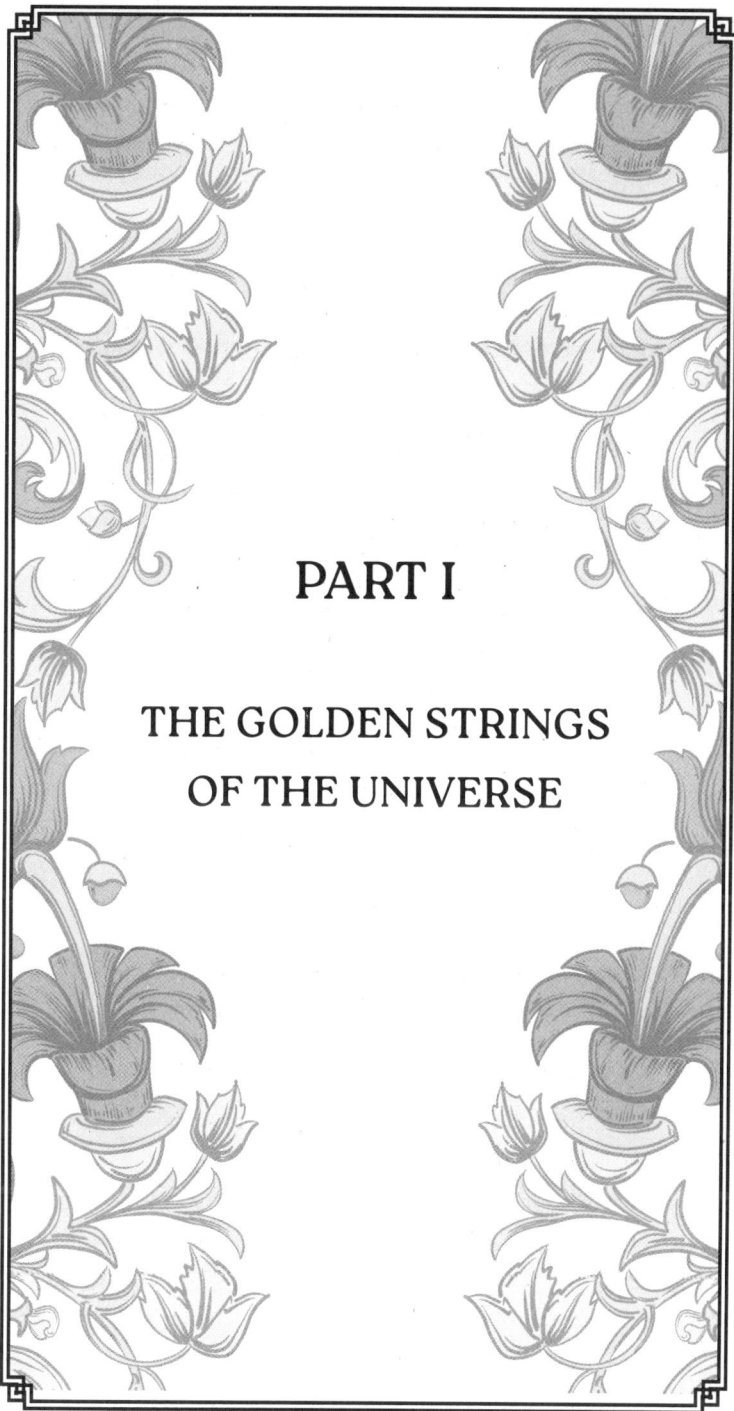

Excerpt from the Lapidary Book of Ginevra di Gasparo

*MS. M.419, The Morgan Library & Museum.
Italy, Florence, ca.1340*

We are told
That the powers of stones are various and wonderful
When invoked by one who is tied to the invisible golden strings

Here is the green crystal called smaragdus, carved with the sacred words of the Arabs. Look upon it when your eyes are weary and you will see with fresh perspective.

Here is the shimmering black obsidian, made by the heat of volcanoes. It is good against fevers.

Here is the hyacinth, which will take your place in death.

And here is the red coral, petrified blood of the Gorgon. It is part plant, part animal, part stone. It is good for all sorts of things.

ONE

HER OWN SELF

About 1330, City of Genoa

In the very old days, before even Rome was great, there were many doctors and witches in Italy who used stones and plants and odd bits of animals to make things happen that wouldn't otherwise. They might, for instance, pound pastes to banish madness, or arrange amulets on women's beds to ease their labor. They could build a charm to warn a prosperous lord when his food was poisoned, and read the future in birds' guts, folding them inside parchment packets to seal the prophecies. Powerful magi hoarded precious gems with secret words engraved upon them, and old women mended broken hearts with bundles of parsley tied up just so.

As Christianity spread, overtaking the ancient religions, the princes and priests of this new church became greedy in their power. Jealous and afraid of the old ways, they condemned any miraculous event with roots outside of Christian ritual. Those who remained artful in the ancient secrets, who remembered how to coax magic from stones and potions from plants, found it prudent to become quiet in their practices. The ones who were brash lost their livelihoods, and found themselves prodded with all sorts of unpleasant and spiky things.

It was into this fraught time that Ginevra di Gasparo was born, to parents of no great importance, about the year 1320.

Her city of Genoa was built right up against the sea inside a large and beautiful harbor. It was filled with sand-colored buildings topped with red tile roofs, all jumbled up with one another and pressed out against concentric rings of stone defense walls. Every day, vessels arrived, sitting low in the water with holds full of treasure from Africa or Britain or some such place. And each year, the Genoese trade routes stretched out farther, like the fingers of an eager hand, poking their way through to Crimea, Antioch, and Tripoli. Merchants returned with gold-threaded tapestries from Flanders, blue lapis lazuli from Kabul, cotton gauze from Egypt, and perfumed woods from the forests of Ethiopia.

From an early age, Ginevra knew about the luxurious cargoes and important transactions taking place in her city, but as a daughter of poor fishing folk, her life was generally devoid of fine things. The pungent scents of fermenting fish and pitch boiled by shipbuilders permeated the district where she lived, so Ginevra's light hair and undyed wool dress always smelled of dockside industry. Her father, Gasparo, made his living fishing for the red corals that grew in sharp crags on the sea bottom. From the time she was very small, Ginevra's father would take her out onto the water to help him with his work. Instead of a net, they would drop a sort of wooden cross from their little boat and drag it across the reefs to crack the corals from their rocky bases. The slick lava-red branches were hauled into the boat and laid out to dry, and Ginevra would watch the tiny white polyps who lived in the coral pulse and writhe about as they suffocated in the air. This filled her with sorrow, because she did not like to see living things suffer. After the harvest, Ginevra's mother, Camiola, would break the dead corals apart. Eventually the pieces would be sent to nimble-fingered orphan girls who polished them into beads to be strung as rosaries, mounted in monstrances, or made into pairs of bracelets that were put on babies to keep them safe.

The corals processed by Gasparo and Camiola were pledged, at deep discount, to a merchant who built his own fortune at the port long ago and now used violence to ensure no others could follow the path he took for success. But, in defiance of the cartel, Gasparo made an arrangement with an old woman called Monna Vermilia, reserving a small portion of his coral for her each week.

To avoid attention from the merchant's agents, Gasparo sent his daughter to the old woman's dingy abode to deliver the parcels of tiny red twigs hidden inside a round of stale bread. Vermilia needed the corals because she still knew the old ways of healing and made her living from them. She said special blessings over the branches and put them on cords, then sold them cheaply to couples who could not afford polished bracelets but were still afraid for their babies. She sold them also to sailors to protect them from drowning, and shopkeepers afraid of losing their inventory.

Ginevra did not know it, nor did her parents, but she had, through her mother's side, the blood of a priestess who could talk to oak trees. And through her father, she was descended from a long line of gentlemen soothsayers, who were shunned after auguring that a young viscountess would betray her husband with a servant (she did). Neither Gasparo nor Camiola had inherited enough magic to amount to anything unusual. But because Ginevra possessed a bit from both of them, she was born with an *aptitude*. And when she walked, the invisible golden strings of the universe were plucked and caused the faintest vibrations in the air, and it was through these strings that the old magic could flow.

Though eccentric in appearance, Vermilia was no fraud. She was attached to a few of these golden strings herself, and when Ginevra delivered the first loaf of clandestine coral Vermilia felt the vibrations. In the blackest morning of the month, she killed a little sparrow and spilled its blood and saw in the drops that the child could be capable of great things if she was correctly guided. Monna Vermilia went to the girl's parents and asked if she might have her as help. Gasparo balked at first, but his wife told him he'd be a fool to refuse a woman like Vermilia.

So, it was agreed that for two weeks out of every month the girl would spend her days with the elderly healer. Ginevra was nervous about this new arrangement. Her parents had never given her to another person before and she wasn't sure what bad thing she had done to deserve it. On her first day as helper, she squeezed through Monna Vermilia's narrow door, marked by a tiny carving of a snake crawling through a coral branch. Inside, she observed a woman with a face so ancient it practically disappeared beneath its wrinkles. Vermilia wore a black dress and tight hood as if she were a widow, though she had never married, and frizzled gray strands stuck out of it, framing her face like the tentacles of a sea anemone. On her left hand, she wore a ring set with a large orange stone carved with a winged figure. Ginevra felt oddly drawn to the jewel and stared hard at it, forgetting her manners.

"Do you know why you're here, child?"

Ginevra's gaze snapped back to the weathered face and she shook her head "no." She looked around and then shifted and hunched her shoulders inward to avoid the sticky pots of goo, lichen balls, and stacks of dead crabs that leaned up on walls and lay in piles upon the floor.

"Close your eyes," commanded Vermilia, "and listen. And tell me what you know."

"I know that Mary is the Mother of God, and all the saints are to His glory—"

"Don't tell me what you've been taught, tell me what you know."

Ginevra was frightened and stepped backward toward the narrow door. With the agility of a much younger woman, Vermilia darted behind her and pulled it closed.

"Now, make your mind dark and quiet like this room. And tell me what you know."

Ginevra decided that to start talking was her only chance of escape. She closed her eyes. "I know… I know that there are seeds in the dirt waiting to grow if we would stop packing it down with our feet. I know that the oysters in the harbor can never love each other because they love only their pearls. I know that there are many people who feel very itchy, and twice as many over who are worried about…about going bald?" She clasped her hand over her mouth, shocked at her strange babbling.

But Vermilia smiled. "Do you understand how you can know these things?"

"I don't know why I said any of it. Please, don't tell my parents – please, can I go home—"

"You know this because you are tied to the strings that are tied to everything else. To the past and the future, to other people, to creatures and to plants and to stones."

Ginevra fanned out her fingers and wiggled them but she saw nothing, felt no pull. She looked back, bewildered at Monna Vermilia.

"They are invisible to us, but they have always been there," offered the old woman. "There used to be more of us that could feel their pull. Now, not so many. But you are special, like me. It is in your blood."

Ginevra looked again at the blue veins in her hands, which seemed so normal, so like everyone else's. Vermilia clasped her own gnarled hand over Ginevra's. "And because we are special, it is our duty to help those who are not."

Ginevra tried to pull away but Vermilia's grip was firm. "Close your eyes."

She struggled and a pot of goo fell off a shelf and shattered on the floor. "Close your eyes, I said!"

The girl obeyed. She knew that the city walls had secrets they would never tell. That the favorite food of fishes was beautiful stones. That the shade of a strawberry plant was the thing held most precious by worms. And she knew – she knew – that Vermilia was a friend. Her fear gave way to a most exquisite joy. She opened her eyes. The room appeared bright now. The balls of lichen seemed to shimmer, the stacks of dead crabs emitted rays of light. She was more than a helper on her father's fishing boat. She was her own self; a conduit through which the secret powers of the earth would be concentrated into visible good.

TWO

SO YOU WILL KNOW

About 1330, City of Genoa

In the center of Vermilia's chaotic room was a small wooden table where a sliver of light came in through the doorway. It was here that clients were received. Ginevra's first duty was to sit in the corner, fetching things as requested and quietly observing.

She observed how Vermilia would nod her head as people whispered their troubles in her ear. They would complain about a quarrel with their neighbor or show their sore foot or brazenly lift their robes, modesty erased by desperation for a solution. Then Vermilia would flit about the mess of her room, pulling leaves from bundles on the ceiling rafters, telling Ginevra to get a scoop of powder from the orange pot painted with black warriors, a stone from a specific bridge, or a hair from the tail of a dog. Sometimes these things would be ground into a paste or rolled up in a pill. Other times Vermilia would tuck them inside a pouch or embed them in clay, and tell a person to wear it around their neck or bury it under a tree and then say a special prayer over it. As soon as the patient went away, questions exploded from Ginevra:

"What were those leaves?"

"Why a stone from that bridge?"

"How will burying it under a tree help?"

And Vermilia answered all of them:

"The leaves are from an oak and will fix his digestion."

"Because she was walking over that very bridge when the argument began."

"Because the tree will appreciate the gift and so make their child well."

Although nearly everyone in the city visited a healer like Vermilia at some point, nobody liked to admit it, and they all kept their hoods up until they were indoors. This was because Vermilia's practice walked the fine line between acceptable and heretical, allowed and illegal. And nobody wanted to be associated with a witch on the day someone important decided her work was more on the heretical, illegal side of things.

"This is why you must always be discreet in your abilities. Only help those who seek you out. Never offer your services unsolicited," Vermilia warned her young pupil.

Ginevra, buzzing with joy at the discovery of her natural talents, chafed at this restriction and did not respond.

"Are you listening, Ginevra?" asked Vermilia as she crunched snails beneath a pestle. "Women like us must be careful not to interfere with the profit of the physicians' guilds, of the licensed doctors. Do NOT flaunt your gift for treating hopeless patients – the ones that doctors pass off to a priest. *That* is how you get the wrong kind of attention."

"Ah!" Ginevra perked up. "So if you're a proper doctor, then you don't have to keep your magic a secret?"

Vermilia shook her head. "You listened to the wrong part of what I said! The point here is to make yourself invisible. If you don't, then sooner or later, the priests will hear rumors of a maid in the harbor who claims to cure people with witchcraft, and you will be sorry. Besides, it's practically impossible to receive a physicians' license as a woman. So don't go thinking you can get one."

Ginevra had already gone and thought it. "What do you mean *practically* impossible?"

Vermilia sighed. "I mean, if you were the richest woman in Genoa and your father and his father were physicians, then *maybe* they'd let you attend university, take exams, make an exception. But for you, illiterate girl from the harbor, none of this."

Ginevra nodded, but inside her head the plan was formed – *I must be rich, and I must be in a physician's family. All I have to do is marry a man who is both of those things. That is not impossible.*

"Anyway," said Vermilia, "you would not like what you learned at university, after everything I'll teach you. We have our own methods. The things we do can't be done by just anyone, *especially* by a man of today. They are too wrapped up in themselves to see what's right in front of them. They become angry when we expose their blindness, jealous when we have success."

Ginevra was quiet at this. Even at her young age she understood that men, even her own father who loved her, had a limited view of what women could comprehend and accomplish. But she also knew from observing her kind mother, her wise Vermilia, and the industrious coral-carving orphan girls, that men were wrong.

"But your remedies actually *work*," she said eventually. "Many men have seen that! Instead of bothering witches, priests should punish the doctors who take money for useless cures."

Vermilia shook her head. "The miracles of saints are the only sort of God's magic the church appreciates. We threaten its power by providing alternative remedies, by reminding people of the magic that God has placed in all things of the earth."

Here, the old woman paused to scrape the mashed snails into a jar. She picked up the container, then walked around the table and with her free hand tapped Ginevra on the forehead. "So you will keep both eyes open, yes? You will learn to see *all* the places in which magic resides. You may find it living in the church – but let me tell you something – true magic can hardly ever be pulled from the dead finger bone of a saint."

Ginevra sighed and took the snail-jar from Vermilia to put away. This part of the speech was familiar to her: relics – finger bones or otherwise – were something of a pet grievance for her mentor. These mortal crumbs of saints were scattered by the *thousands* all over Europe, in grand cathedrals, humble parishes, and personal collections. Relics were believed to have the power both to grant the prayers of the faithful, and to cause trouble for those who failed to show them proper reverence.

"It's NOT that I take issue with praying to relics," Vermilia explained.

"It's just that saints are exhausted and overworked," finished Ginevra dutifully.

"*Exactly.* And who could blame them? Their earthly bodies broken into a jumble of tiny pieces, shipped off to dozens of places, hundreds of miles apart. They are too scattered, too putupon, to answer the volume of prayers sent their way. Nobody, no matter how holy, can be everywhere at once. And THIS is why even devout persons come here for help. They come after faith and physician has failed them."

Ginevra pondered this conversation the next day as she bored little holes in coral branches so they could be worn as amulets. She realized there were also those who came to Vermilia first, because their troubles were not the sort they wished to share with a physician or a saint. Many were women, needing help either to have a child or to not have one. But really it seemed to Ginevra that the whole population of the city was represented in miniature in Vermilia's clientele. Fancy lords and lowly peasants all crept in with problems of love, health, and wealth. The realization that all men were governed by common worries made Ginevra feel equal to those who were in fact far above her station, and gave her confidence in her lofty marriage plans.

As Ginevra was lost in her thoughts, a young woman slipped through Vermilia's door and looked around nervously. Ginevra glanced at her, and without even pausing her coral drilling, she blurted out, "If you anoint your tongue with honey and butter every day for a week, your mother-in-law will become amenable to your request."

Vermilia stared at her, white eyebrows raised. The young woman thanked them both profusely and slipped back out the door.

"That was good, Ginevra," said Monna Vermilia, "but next time remember to ask for payment."

After this, Ginevra was graduated from observer to assistant. She felt pride in herself as never before, and wished she could share all that was happening with her parents, but Vermilia forbade it. "It's for their own good," she said. Whenever they inquired about her day, Ginevra simply told them she did the chores Vermilia required. But it was so much more exciting than that! She boiled cucumber seeds in ash for gout, cut the heads off slippery eels to harvest their blood, and gave rose-flavored comfits painted with gold to rich clients who had nothing really the matter with them, but still liked to have something prescribed, just the same.

In Monna Vermilia's family, the traditions of magic had not died out as in Ginevra's, but remained secret and whole for generations. But the best secrets, these she got from an old monk at San Columbano where there was a precious library. She fed him an intoxicating liquid that rendered him madly in love with her. In order to prove his devotion, Vermilia made him take books from the monastery and translate them aloud from Latin into the vernacular. She remembered almost everything he told her, a skill common among those who cannot read. She said nothing of this to Ginevra, because in general she did not approve of love potions. But, when no clients were present, Vermilia would repeat to Ginevra the myths recorded by Ovid about the pagan gods, and how they had lived in the sky or in hell or under the ocean and caused trouble for humans.

As practice, the two would walk through crowded streets and Vermilia would ask Ginevra to notice what was wrong with people and whisper how she could fix it. On one such outing, they passed a man whose magnificent robes of vermilion silk still failed to distract from an aggressive facial rash. Ginevra saw an opportunity. *This is the sort of man I can use – a rich man we can place in our debt, who could sponsor me and support my entry to the guild.* He had not escaped Vermilia's notice, either.

"What do you think?" she asked Ginevra quietly. "What is his cure?"

She answered immediately: "I would make him a paste of clay and ash from a wormwood, and tell him to put it all over his head and stand outside until the sun had baked it hard. Then he should say he was sorry to whomever he had wronged, then he should wash it off with seawater and he would be better."

"Very good," said Vermilia. "That is what we would tell him if he came to us and asked."

"*Or* we could tell him anyway – he would be very grateful, don't you think?"

"I do not, foolish child. Come." And she turned away.

But Ginevra did not come. Her boldness had grown with her skills. She knew just enough to think she knew everything, and was tired of holding herself back. So when Vermilia turned back around, to her horror she saw Ginevra had approached the gentleman and was making him a proposition. Vermilia hobbled over and smacked her on the side of the head, mid-sentence.

"Forgive her, sir, she is simple."

The man muttered something about crazy *puttane*, and hurried off, a flurry of dandruff in his wake.

"I am not simple!"

"Oh? You will have to prove it after *that*. We have a new lesson today. See if you can take its meaning." Vermilia grabbed Ginevra's arm tight and led her to the stone piers that jutted out into the harbor. They walked to the farthest one, and Ginevra saw that there were no boats tied to it this day. Instead, a large bonfire burned at the end, tended by soot-blackened men stripped down to only their breechcloths. Vermilia pulled her into the crowd that gathered around it. The people spoke quietly and jostled each other for a view of the flames. Soon a group of men arrived, led by a friar in a black pointed hood. Upon their shoulders, they carried a wooden ladder with a woman tied along it. They propped her so she was upright in front of the fire, on view to the crowd. The onlookers' murmurs grew louder until the priest lifted his hands for silence:

"We are here to pray for the soul of Monna Caterina D'Augustino, who calls herself a witch and is an unrepentant heretic."

A few of the people mumbled prayers but most said nothing. The priest continued: "In 1332 she was summoned to court when she claimed to remove vile spirits from a young girl. She paid her fine and promised to cease performing such rituals, but she was a liar. Later, after being shown every mercy by the court, she gave a woman a stone amulet carved with symbols and told her this would make her pregnant, and she did this without the knowledge of the woman's husband. And so she was brought before us a second time and became angry, and was heard to say in the presence of several witnesses that she could remove diseases with methods unknown to physicians, and claimed she possessed other skills over which only God has domain."

The crowd hissed. Ginevra looked at Monna Vermilia, who just inclined her head toward the spectacle, indicating that Ginevra should keep watching.

The priest was now recounting how the woman had repented in the end, admitted her sins. But Ginevra and anyone close enough could see that all her fingers were bent at the wrong angles and that the spirit of God perhaps was not the only thing that inspired her confession. The priest made the sign of the cross over her and nodded to the men who held the ladder. They let it tip forward so she dropped face-first into the glowing coals and was consumed by flames.

A flake of ash landed on Ginevra's cheek and she slapped it away, suppressing a gag. "Why did you bring me here?" she choked out.

"So you know," said Vermilia. "So you know what happens if you do not keep your secrets."

THREE

MILKSTONES

July of 1348, Between Genoa & Florence

Ginevra and Piero were on the road in no time, walking toward Florence under the hot sun, a crooked-nosed woman and a child. Ginevra wore a large straw hat and Piero, who had no mother to help him dress, kept his sun-browned face deep in the folds of his hood. Ginevra walked quickly, eyes forward, observing the empty world. She had not left the city walls in… Had it been years? A jolt of panic. One letter from an ex-lover and here she was, answering the call of the same priest (no – he wasn't just a priest anymore, he was *bishop*) who once ordered her tortured and banished. What did Bishop Acciaiuoli want with her, anyway? Ludovico's letter mentioned only *a small problem*. It *must* be for curing plague – though that problem was hardly small. But, what if it was something else? What if the bishop had sent out dozens of letters just like this, in the care of dozens of orphans just like Piero? What if the Florentines were just coaxing back criminals to burn them; a desperate plan to appease an angry God with offerings of witches and heretics? But even after everything that had happened, she could not believe Ludovico would do something so vile as that.

So maybe the best was true, the hopes so wild that she was self-conscious of them even in the safety of her own mind: that

Ludovico missed her, that he would make amends by using his influence and his fortune to restore her name; his patronage would ensure her application to the physicians' guild was taken seriously. But even if this was Ludo's intent, Ginevra knew she would first have to work some extraordinary magic. And, the truth was she did not know how to cure the plague. At least, not *yet*. Her hand reached into the purse tied around her waist and, for the thousandth time, confirmed that the two hemispherical stones were still there.

"Hey!" said Piero, trotting to keep up with her adult strides. "Slow down."

"Hmmm?"

"We have to go slow. You didn't – you didn't let us get hardly any water. Or food. Or anything at all. We must go slow and stay in the shade or we will die of the heat."

"Here, take water from my flask."

He shook his head. "I told you the next well is a day from here at least—"

"Take it," she said, thrusting the flask into his hands. "We'll find what we need."

But he shook his head no and held it back to her.

Ginevra shrugged, opened the flask, and drank fully. Piero gaped at her in anguish. "Now, Piero, you will have a drink. As you say, the sun is strong and we must be careful."

To his surprise, the flask handed to him was just as heavy as before. He held it to his ear and it sloshed around. He took a cautious sip and the water was cold and bubbled with minerals, as if from a spring in the mountains and not the cistern under Ginevra's gutter, which is where he knew it was filled. And filled it was. And as much as he drank, this did not change. He looked at Ginevra with questioning eyes. "It will last us our journey, I think," was all she said, and returned to her thoughts.

On the second day, they arrived at an orchard. The ground was sticky with fruit that had ripened and rotted unpicked. The air hummed with flies. "Here we will find something to eat," she said.

But Piero hung back. He had passed this place before, and knew that farmers lay dead amongst the dropped harvest. "We are too late in the season," he said. "The trees are empty."

"Come," she said, taking him by the hand.

They walked between rows of trees, leaves curling and wilting in the heat. Air heavy with the smell of molded apricots and something else, sweet and stinging. She stopped at a tree where the trunk split in two and grew in opposite directions, and placed her hands on the spot where the trunks came together.

"I told you," said Piero. "There is nothing here."

She removed her hands from the trunk and smiled at him, tucking something back into her purse. "You must look up, not down. See in the branches? On the left, there are apricots, on the right are figs. Climb and gather as much as you can."

"But – how could they both grow on the same tree?"

Ginevra shrugged. "Trees do what they want," she said, and then began to pluck figs from the low-hanging boughs. They filled their bags and walked until dusk, when they came upon a dry haystack to sleep in just as Piero began to feel tired.

On the third day, there were dark clouds that made the loose hairs on their heads stand out straight. They left their haystack for the safety of a small thatched hut, doors open and black, both afraid of what they would see inside. At the doorway, they jumped at eyes that gleamed at them from a dark corner, like a cat's at night. But the eyes were human – two boys a little older than Piero. One clutched a brand-new baby. Piero stood shy in the doorway but Ginevra walked right in.

"Is it only the three of you left here?" she asked.

The taller boy nodded. "Can you help our sister?" He held out the listless baby.

Ginevra took the infant. "Who has been feeding her?" she asked them gently.

The smaller one began to cry. "We have a goat. But she has given no milk since yesterday." He nodded to the other side of the room.

Ginevra turned and watched a goat lick salt out of the earthen walls. To the boys, she said: "Go into the fields and bring me back a horn. I saw a dead buffalo out there. Quickly, before the storm starts. Piero will help you."

But Piero lingered in the doorway. He didn't like the idea of leaving his traveling companion alone, after he had gone through all that trouble to fetch her. He watched quietly as Ginevra ran back and forth after the goat, who leaped easily away from her grasping hands. The swaddled baby lay on a single bed, staring at the roof beams.

"What are you doing?" Piero asked eventually.

She jumped at his voice. "I am trying to catch this goat!"

"Why? The boy said she is dry."

"Piero, please. Just, help me catch this damned goat and hold her still. I will explain to you later."

So Piero helped her and pinned the goat in a corner while Ginevra pulled from her purse a smooth white disk, opaque and shiny like a tooth. She offered it to the goat, who considered it a moment and then took it on her pointed tongue and swallowed it. The animal shook Piero free and began to pace back and forth, bleating.

Ginevra sighed with relief. "Piero, go ask the boys for a bucket."

"Why?"

"So we can milk this poor goat! Don't you hear her? She's ready to burst."

Piero turned to the goat and then back to Ginevra, who had somehow gotten a fire started in the few moments he looked away.

"Bucket!"

When the three boys came back, she made them boil the horn and scoop out the inside of it so it was hollow, then they poked a hole in the tip and filled it with milk for the baby.

They stayed like this through the storm, eating figs and apricots and feeding the baby until she was pink again. Ginevra and Piero left in the morning.

"How far to the nearest well?" she asked him. "Do you remember?"

"I thought you said your flask would last us the journey?"

She said nothing.

Hours later, they came to another orchard. "Look, Ginevra, these are peach trees. Do you think we can find fruit?"

She shook her head. "No – the trees are barren. I have prunes I brought from Genoa, but we must not eat too many. We have several days' journey ahead of us."

Piero stopped. "TELL me what is going on! First, you don't let us get any provisions because you say you can find them, now you tell me we have hardly anything after we give all our figs and water to those strangers – and why did you make their goat eat a rock?"

Ginevra sighed. Now was the time to stop hiding. "That rock is called a milkstone. It is very old and its presence creates abundance when there is none. This is how I kept my flask full and made trees bear fruit past their season."

"And you fed it to a goat?"

"The baby would have starved, Piero."

"Now WE will starve."

"No. We will not starve because we are clever. Surely, you can see they needed our help? They would have perished without it."

"So? Everyone else has already died. My mother and father and sister – all gone! And nobody helped them."

"My parents are dead also, Piero. I know what it is to ache for family, but you must not be cruel." She reached out to touch him but he jerked away.

"You are old! Your parents are supposed to be dead. Everyone who ever lived along this road is dead besides you and me and those wretches in the hut. You think one goat will save them? All you've done is stretch out their suffering a little longer!"

"Piero, you are too young for such evil thoughts."

"You care more for them than you do for me! Me, who brought you a letter all the way from Florence."

"Shhh. Do not be jealous. The *malocchio* hears such things. It will come and make it worse for you."

"The Eye is not real," he said, though more quietly, unsure of himself. "It is a story women use to scare children."

Ginevra said nothing.

"It's not real, is it?" asked Piero.

"It is real, and I have felt it and you must be careful or you will, too."

FOUR

OCCHIO MALOCCHIO

1333, City of Genoa

Ginevra remembered vividly. The golden strings pulled her, connecting her back to her past self. She was no longer twenty-eight, a woman of advanced age. She was thirteen and her mother had made her a new dress to replace her old one, which was so worn-out it wasn't any good even for a poor girl.

"Keep it clean," her mother said. "It'll have to do until you're married." Ginevra vowed to be careful, and then went away, beaming, to show off her new garment to the world. Her reverie was shortly interrupted by a tug at her hem. It was a beggar girl whose lip was twisted up so her front teeth showed. She held on tightly to Ginevra's dress and thrust out her empty bowl.

Another day, Ginevra might have run home and found an old piece of bread – but today she fretted that her dress would be soiled by the girl's dirty hands. She pulled it away pointedly and kept walking, casting a curious glance over her shoulder at the girl sitting in the dust. Their eyes locked. Ginevra's breath caught in her chest. She looked away and continued onward.

Early the next morning, Ginevra put on her new dress and found it unbearably itchy. So itchy she regretted her old one had already been torn into rags. Doing her best not to scratch all over, she began her daily journey to draw water from the public fountain. At the little square where it burbled, she stubbed her toe so badly that the nail broke in half and bled.

"Porco Dio," she muttered, and then clasped her hand to her mouth. It was an extremely rude curse that only sailors would say. She'd never dared to blaspheme even a little before. She looked around to see if anyone had heard, then carried on with her task, filling the heavy water jug and limping toward home.

On the way, dogs that normally kept to themselves chased her, and she only just escaped by throwing her jug at them where it shattered on the ground. Camiola, displeased that a perfectly good jug was ruined, let alone that she had no water for the day, combed Ginevra's hair so roughly that the comb caught in a snarl and a whole lock was pulled out.

Clutching her head, and squirming around inside her clothing, Ginevra hurried to the home and shop of her mentor in search of solace. She huffed her way into Vermilia's room, expecting her immediate sympathy, but the old woman was hunched over a low fire in the hearth and appeared to be muttering at the orange stone on her ring.

"A-hem," coughed Ginevra.

"You are early," said Vermilia, not turning around.

"Tell me what you are saying to that stone!"

"It is I who give directions here. Get to your work and leave me be!" Vermilia went back to her muttering.

Cowed, Ginevra tried to focus on her chores – preparing nettles to be boiled in wine for men who could not satisfy their wives. But she was so clumsy that the plants' vicious hairs stuck all into her hands. She fanned them in the air for relief, but then her stomach itched and she jerked quickly to scratch it, knocking a cup of wine down the front of her new dress. Tears welled up in her eyes as a purple stain spread across the gray fibers.

Vermilia finally stopped muttering and hid the stone

among her robes. She turned to her pupil. "And so what's wrong with you today?"

Ginevra's bottom lip trembled with the effort of keeping a neutral face. "Since this morning, I have lost my toenail, my mother's water jug, and a chunk of my hair. I was chased by vicious dogs, and now I have stained the only new dress I have ever gotten, which has grown tight and coarse overnight. Have you ever heard of a more terrible day?"

"Yes," said Vermilia. "Is that all?"

Ginevra turned away brusquely. As she moved, the palm of her hand caught on a rough spot of the table, and a large splinter broke off painfully in her flesh. "You see!" she cried, brandishing her new stigma. "I have been *cursed*."

Vermilia looked at the wound and pressed a thoughtful finger to her lips.

"Ginevra, tell me what you know."

She closed her eyes, the exercise now familiar. "I know that bad people are rich, though I, who am worthy, remain poor. I know that I am beautiful in my new clothes but uglier girls receive praise—"

"Enough." She picked up a shallow wooden bowl and filled it with water, placing it on the table between them. "Ginevra, go and dip your fingers in the olive oil."

Ginevra stopped sniffling. She knew this ritual. It was requested by those whose livestock sickened and died for no reason, whose gardens would not grow – young men who became suddenly impotent, women whose hair fell out after they argued with a neighbor.

"You think it's *that*?"

"Shh. Just do as you're told, girl."

She dipped her stinging and bloodied hand in the oil jar, and then let three golden drops fall from her fingertips into the water. The two of them peered into the bowl, and saw the spheres of oil sink to the bottom and join together, a distinct globule intact under the surface.

"Porco Dio!" said Ginevra again.

Vermilia sucked in air through her teeth. "The drops sink and do not spread." She lowered her voice: "Someone has set the *malocchio* on you…"

"The Evil Eye? How did it find me? Is it here now?" Ginevra jerked her head around the room, straining her eyes to see into the dark corners.

"It is here and it is not," Vermilia answered. "This you know. It roams the earth and takes jealousy and pride as its bedfellows. It is everywhere, it is nowhere."

"Why do you mock me by speaking in riddles?" hissed Ginevra. She tried to pick the splinter out of her hand but her efforts only dug it in deeper. "Did you hear me, old woman, or have your ears grown too hairy?"

"Be quiet, rude thing! The *malocchio* makes you speak so. Which means we must make you laugh. Are you ticklish?" Vermilia reached out with both hands and poked her under the arms.

"Don't touch me, Crone!" shouted Ginevra, recoiling. "You become senile in your unnatural age." Vermilia only rolled her eyes in response.

"And *you* become stupid in your anger and forget what I've taught you."

Some small corner of Ginevra's mind shook itself free of the bitter swirling cloud and she remembered her lessons: laughter could deflect the Eye's gaze, scare it far away.

"Tell me a joke, then, so I can laugh," she managed, "but do not touch me again."

"There's a good girl. Unfortunately, the only ones I know are about fornication, and you're too much a virgin to find those funny. But let me ask you this: have you recently purchased fish from Casoli Paracrotti?"

"…is this the beginning of a joke?"

"Well, have you?" repeated Vermilia.

"No! Why do you care what my family eats for supper?"

"Because: that man is a *jettatore*."

The awful word caught Ginevra's attention. "You mean, Ser Paracrotti who always has the big pink shrimp?"

"Yes. The shrimp are a trick – *jettatore* are almost always charming, successful in business. So your guard is down. But misfortune comes to all who go near him. A *jettatore* looks at you and you feel a cold that seeps into your soul, into your bones—"

The Eye itself was not so uncommon, Ginevra knew. It could be thrown by anyone who felt spite, anger, jealousy – people were always coming to Vermilia, putting their fingers in oil, and then being told the excellent jokes about fornication until the Eye ran away.

But a *jettatore*? This was a person *born* inhabited by the Eye, and whether they were angry or not, anyone caught in their gaze was plagued by greatest misfortune. No simple trick of laughter could send away the Eye if it came from a *jettatore*.

"So, Ginevra, if you haven't visited Ser Paracrotti, then have you made somebody jealous? A neighbor?"

She started to shake her head, but then remembered the girl with the twisted lip. A guilty pang poked through her anger and Vermilia felt it.

"Tell me."

"There was a girl – her face was disfigured – all I did was look at her."

"You know better than to stare at somebody's misfortune. At least, did you look at her with kindness? Offer a bit of food? A prayer?"

Ginevra looked down at the floor.

"Wicked girl! You have made it worse for yourself. This we cannot solve with jokes. What would inspire your gentle heart to provoke a deformed child into throwing you the Eye?"

"I didn't *mean* to provoke her. I was just surprised by a dirty beggar!"

"There you go again. You, who eats farro soup on earthen

floors. One frumpy new gown, and you speak badly about one who has even less. Keep it up, that's what the Eye wants—"

But Ginevra was barely listening. She was trying so hard to hold back the vile things she wanted to say and do that she was overcome by a fit of hiccups that convulsed through her body in painful spasms.

"Please – HIC – please, I cannot – HIC—"

"Porco Dio," said Vermilia this time. "If we can't chase the Eye away, we have to puncture it, and it does not forget a stabbing so easily…"

"I do – HIC – n't care, get it *away* from me!"

"Very well, if that is your choice," said Vermilia gravely. She picked up two large needles and handed them to Ginevra. "Poke one through the hole of the other and repeat:

"Holes through Sight
Eyes against Eye
Envy Breaks
Eye Burst and Die."

Through her ghastly hiccups, Ginevra repeated the verses and after pricking her fingers numerous times, threaded one needle through the other. Vermilia took the needles from her and stabbed them three times into the water bowl. They watched together as the large drop of oil floated to the surface and dispersed. Vermilia muttered a prayer of thanks. Ginevra vomited all down the front of her dress.

FIVE

MANO FIGA

1333, City of Genoa

The next thing Ginevra knew she was waking up on Vermilia's little cot. The light was fading and she felt sick and thirsty as if she had swallowed seawater. She tried to sit up but her vision shrank to a pinpoint and she froze, midway up, waiting for the blood to come back to her head. Vermilia heard her stirring and came over to the bed.

"Ah! Good. Welcome – here you are again."

"How…long have I been asleep?"

"Through last night and a whole day besides."

"What?? My mother—"

"It is well, be calm. I sent word to your parents. They know you are here. Come, now."

She helped Ginevra prop herself up and handed her a steaming brew of fennel fronds in a wooden beaker.

"Drink this. It will make your mouth feel clean after all the filthy things it said."

Ginevra clutched her face and groaned.

"It's alright, dear girl, you are not the first and you shall not be the last to catch the Eye."

Ginevra looked at her friend's face, lined all over from the decades of kind smiles and understanding eyebrow raises she gave her clients, free of charge. Her friend who had plucked her from a fish maid's daily drudgery and shared with her secrets and stories nobody else knew.

"Your ears are not really so hairy," she offered.

Vermilia laughed. "You know, you were right about that one. I plucked them while you slept."

"Still, I should not have said it. I will *never* give another person reason to throw me the Eye. I'll always be humble, and never care about my clothes and never think badly of anyone."

"A nice promise, but one impossible to keep even for the worthiest of hearts. For you, it will be even harder. The skills you possess – the Eye covets them. And it will not forget how you punctured it... It will always be looking for you."

"How do I stop it from finding me, then?" Ginevra said, afraid and exhausted.

"Hush. Breathe deeply of the fennel and I will tell you a story while your head clears." Ginevra put her face down close to the top of the beaker and sneezed at the spicy steam.

Vermilia began: "In the time of the pagan gods, there was one called Phorcys, who lived in the sea and ruled over the monsters of the deep. Instead of legs, he had two spiny fish tails. Instead of hands, he had two slippery fins. Phorcys had a beautiful daughter called Medusa, whose finest feature was her hair, which she tossed about in everyone's face, showing it off and always seducing men with it."

Ginevra touched the spot where her own hair had been pulled out the previous morning and found it still tender. She pushed it harder, accepting the pain as punishment for her vanity.

"Eventually," continued Vermilia, "she decided she wanted to lie with a god, so she went to Neptune, who was king of the oceans, and showed him her beautiful hair. He desired her so greatly that he took her to the closest place with some privacy, which happened to be a holy temple, and there they enjoyed themselves for many hours. But it was not so private as they thought: the goddess Minerva, who owned the temple, saw them. Minerva was a famous virgin and was furious to see such lewd behavior. So, to ensure Medusa would never again lie with man or god, Minerva changed her wonderful hair into writhing snakes, and made her lovely face as ugly and frightful as any demon from hell you see painted on the ceiling at San Lorenzo. She became so ugly, in fact, that any man who looked at her would turn to stone."

"And what of Neptune? How was he punished?"

"He was not, because he was also a god, so could do as he wished."

"That seems dreadfully unfair."

"I agree. But this is not the point of our story. After Medusa was transformed into the hideous monster, she went and hid in a dark cave at the bottom of a mountain because she could not stand to see herself. Many men tried to kill her, but she turned them all to stone with her gaze. This went on for some time until a half god called Perseus decided to try his luck. He crept into Medusa's cave while she was sleeping, and carried a shield with him, polished shiny like a mirror. He walked up backward to Medusa and only looked at her reflection in his shield, and this way he was able to cut off her head. This is how the *malocchio* was born. When Perseus cut off her head, he released her evil gaze out into the world, and that's why it's everywhere now. But – he also gave us a way to protect ourselves from it. On his way home, Perseus saw a woman chained up to some rocks in the ocean, about to be gobbled by a sea serpent. He went to rescue her, but to make sure his Medusa head was not ruined, he put it on a bed of soft seaweeds for safekeeping."

"Did he save the maiden?"

"He did! And they got married. But that is not the point of our story, either. The point *is* that while Medusa's head was sitting on the seaweed, blood dripped from its neck and the plants became red and turned to stone. And sea nymphs saw them and were delighted and planted their seeds all over the ocean, and this is how coral was born, from the blood of the Medusa."

"So, corals are the blood of Medusa?"

"Exactly. And this is why I buy coral from your father and why it helps to keep the Eye away from things it might want to curse, like babies or sailors or successful businessmen. The Eye is drawn to coral, but then cannot stand to see its own blood and ugliness. It flees when confronted with its own reflection."

"I need to wear a coral now," said Ginevra, understanding. "I can do that. Lots of people do that. It's so much easier than never thinking ill of anyone! I'll fashion it in the shape of a cross, and this way Christ will protect me as well."

"Ah, Ginevra: the Eye is *older* even than our God. It's not intimidated by Christian symbols. The chantings of clergy are not relevant to it. This is why my business is always constant. People become ill, they pray to Saint This or Saint That. But after, they sneak here late at night or early in the morning to make sure the matter is attended to by someone who does not ignore *other* methods. What I mean to say is, instead of a cross, what you really need is this." She pulled a small package from the purse on her belt and handed it to Ginevra.

Ginevra untied it carefully and drew out a long black cord. Dangling from the end was a piece of fine coral, red as oxblood, carved into the shape of a tiny hand clenched into a fist. The thumb was shoved between the pointer and middle fingers – it was the *mano figa*, a notoriously rude gesture representing intercourse, an instigator of tavern brawls for thousands of years. The *mano figa* hung from the cord so its phallic thumb pointed down into the earth. The wrist was capped with a gilded bezel embellished with symbols Ginevra did not know; shells, nuts, and fruits, delicately traced by some ancient engraver. She held up the strange and wonderful object. It was now quite dark inside Vermilia's house, but the coral pendant seemed to emit its own light. Ginevra saw each finger was capped with a perfectly carved nail, tiny veins webbed the back of the hand, covered by wrinkles and folds of flesh so exquisitely wrought that it seemed a real living hand and not a carved jewel that swayed, pendulumlike, at the end of its cord.

Vermilia broke the almost-holy silence. "Like I said, the Eye can't take a joke. Now, when it goes after you, it will instead be drawn to the red of the coral, but once it sees you've tricked it into looking at the rude *figa*, it will be very offended and leave."

Ginevra was captivated by the pendant's precise beauty. "Where did you find it?" she asked.

"A goldsmith owed me a favor. I visited him while you were sleeping, and lucky day, this is what he had. A drunk pilgrim pawned it and never returned."

"This is for me?" Ginevra said, in complete disbelief that someone of her low station might claim such a jewel as their own. "The goldsmith must have owed you a *really* big favor."

"Yes, yes he did." Vermilia beamed. "He lived bloated and puffed up like a toad for two years until I managed to deflate him. Now, put it on and listen to me." Here, she gripped Ginevra's face with both of her hands. "This is a true amulet, you can see how it glows – the power is potent. It is stronger than the new corals your father fishes, than anything I can make. It was blessed by spells that are long forgotten, secret words, sacred strokes of the graver's knife that modern hands cannot imitate. But there are three things you must remember about this amulet. First: while you wear it, you are safe from any mischief the Eye might wish to cause you. It cannot reach you, not even when cast by a *jettatore*. Second: so long as you wear this, disease cannot enter you. Third and most important: nothing is infallible. Do not attract the ire of men and women – they do not need the Eye to be evil and may harm you the same as they harm anyone else."

Ginevra nodded solemnly.

"Good. You understand. You will pay attention to it – how its color and its temperature change. When other magic is about, or when it is protecting you from something unseen, like the *malocchio* or an illness, it will glow hot and red.

When there is danger it cannot deflect, it will become pale and cold and you should know to run away. And for all this, you must wear it always, even when you sleep. Now that you pricked the *malocchio* with your needle, it will be waiting for its chance at revenge. So keep the coral tucked under your clothes, against your skin."

"Under my clothes, against my skin. Always, always," she said, still staring, transfixed. She placed it over her neck and realized that her life up to this moment was "before" and now it was "after," and it could be glorious if only she stayed within the benevolent light of this magnificent jewel.

When Ginevra was fully recovered from the *malocchio*, she went back to where the girl with the flawed face had been, hoping to make amends. But she was nowhere to be found. She had missed her chance to be kind.

SIX

THE WISDOM OF THE PEAR TREE

July 6th of 1348, Outside of Florence

Ginevra pondered these early days – the terror of her encounter with the Eye, the ecstasy of Vermilia's precious gift of coral – as she wandered through the disease-ravaged countryside with the orphan Piero. The more she thought about it, the more disappointed she became in herself. Vermilia had invested so much in her potential. So had many others. And what had Ginevra made of their gifts? Nothing but to become a mediocre and lonely woman. She looked over at Piero, who trudged beside her. He caught her glance and smiled, picking up his step. *Never mind the past, never mind these black thoughts*, she told herself. *You are going to make it all right now.*

Motivated by the unexpected lack of provisions, the pair had made good time and were close to their destination of Florence. Now, an acute anxiety invaded Ginevra's mind: she was about to see a man who had made love to her and then left her to rot in prison, and there were a few things she needed to say to him. She began to invent entire conversations in her head in which Ludovico, astounded by her wit, begged forgiveness for his transgressions. She wondered (for the hundredth time) if his wife had died, and if that was what all this was about. She wondered again why a powerful man like Bishop Acciaiuoli was begging for an audience with *her*. Especially after he'd so carefully orchestrated her exile. So when they reached the river Arno before the city proper, she told Piero to make camp, even though the Porta San Gallo into Florence was just another hour's walk. She needed one more night to think.

"Please, Ginevra, can't we go on? I'm sick of sleeping on the ground and eating only old prunes."

"Be grateful for those prunes, Piero," replied Ginevra, who was just as sick of them. "It's best to wait for morning. The gate might be closed for the day already, and we'd have to walk all the way back to avoid sleeping next to the rubbish piles outside the wall."

Piero harrumphed off into the surrounding brush to find sticks for a fire in the gathering dusk.

Ginevra sat against a tree and watched the brown waters of the Arno swirl past them. A body bobbed by and she shut her eyes against it. She opened them again and saw a beautiful pear tree growing out of the rocky riverbank that she had not noticed before. It was covered with white buds tipped in pink. She breathed deeply and a light perfume filled her with calm. Pear trees were wise; they knew the answers to women's troubles. She walked to the tree and the buds opened into fragrant blossoms. She touched a branch and the delicate petals closed, swelling into golden pears. The tree was speaking to her, of love that ripened over time: Ludo had asked her back to Florence and she came. They were bound to each other, still, by the golden strings. What joy! What relief! The sound of water drip-dripping on rocks pulled her attention. The corpse she had seen earlier crawled out of the river and stared at her pear tree. She yelled at it to go back in the water, but her voice came out as only a faintest whisper and the corpse did not listen. Instead, it reached into the branches and plucked a golden pear and swallowed it whole. It did this again and again until every single fruit was gone, and then it took the branches in its mouth and sucked the leaves off them until they were barren sticks. With a bloated belly, the corpse slid back into the river and floated against the current, toward Florence.

She awoke to Piero shaking her. The sun rose red. There was no pear tree on the riverbank and no corpse had crawled from the water. But the dream's message was real enough: however he may have felt about her, Ludo was long dead and Ginevra was a fool for thinking otherwise.

She grabbed Piero close and wept bitterly into his shoulder.

SEVEN

THE BELOVED RELICS OF FLORENCE

May of 1348, City of Florence

Several months earlier, at first news of plague, the Florentines did what they had always done in moments of great peril: they organized an emergency procession of the Virgin of Requisiti – the holy statue that served as protectress of the city.

Time and again, in exchange for gifts and prayers, the Requisiti statue had saved the people of Florence from famine, floods, and invaders. But this time she did nothing. Unmoved by the procession of the faithful, she allowed disease to enter her city, potent and unhindered. The Florentines began to die in heaps, the same as everywhere else. They put the Virgin back in her cupboard. They must have asked too much of her, over the years. It was only fair to give her a rest and cast their hopes toward the next holy object.

And so, with stubborn optimism, the people of Florence turned their attention instead to the left arm of San Filippo Apostolo. A gift to the city from the Queen of Jerusalem, this exceptional relic was a forearm and perfect hand with two fingers pointed skyward. It was housed inside a precious reliquary casket of silver and enamel and stored in the main altar of the octagonal church known as the Baptistry of San Giovanni.

The Florentines *adored* their Filippo Arm because, once, a sick goldsmith touched it and instantly became well. Normally, pilgrims flocked into town on San Filippo's feast day, bringing a cash influx much appreciated by local businesses. But in the desolate spring of 1348, those few who came from the countryside were stopped at the city walls.

By then, the gates of Florence were closed to all foreigners: a late and feeble attempt to halt the contagion. The poor pilgrims – who had traveled so far for nothing – could only place their hands on the wall's exterior and hope the prayers of the Florentines would be sufficiently pleasing to Filippo.

The pilgrims were uneasy about this arrangement because Florentines were not exactly known as the most pious of peoples. For all their churches and priests, really they were a city of bankers and merchants who were not hesitant to indulge in luxury. They wore velvet robes embroidered with silver pomegranates, and pinned pearls into the hairdos of their brides. The sexes bathed together in public bathhouses, naked except for fancy hats. Men who could not govern three snails were admitted to the highest offices through bribes and nepotism. Women wore two colors at the same time. Worst of all, they lent money with terms of accrued interest. This was probably why their Virgin statue was ignoring them.

Still, on Filippo's day of May the First, those Florentines who remained alive processed toward the Baptistry – and the Filippo Arm – for a communal confession of sin. They walked in small groups, standing far apart and casting angry glances at one another when a member of a different household stepped too close.

In normal times, this important mass was led by the bishop of Florence himself, a position now held by Angiolo Acciaiuoli, uncle of Ginevra's former lover, Ludovico. But today, the bishop was preoccupied: the king of England had declined to repay his loans to the Acciaiuoli bank. The amount the king owed was, itself, ruinous. Worse still, word had spread of these royal defaults, and the other powerful (and often violent) account holders of the Acciaiuoli bank had demanded the immediate return of their funds. The bishop's father and brother promptly died from the stress of it. Now, the heavy burden of saving family honor and fortune rested solely on the bishop's holy shoulders.

In this way, the pestilence had been a gift to Angiolo Acciaiuoli. As Death rode through Europe, disrupting all rhythms of daily life, the bishop finally had time to *think*. His full focus was now trained on refilling his coffers before the disease ran its course – and before his creditors returned their attention to their bank accounts.

With the bishop on hiatus, the Mass of Filippo was led by a newly ordained priest who until recently made his living as an olive oil salesman. (The best substitute the Church could get, what with all the qualified clergy being dead.)

The whole thing was awkward from the start. The priest spilled the wine. He dropped the Host. And when he held San Filippo's reliquary aloft, he couldn't get it open. A cantor came forward and helped the anxious priest pull it apart. Something fell out and both men gave a little yelp.

Instead of the gilded forearm of a saint, a small glass bottle lay upon the altar.

It was the size and shape of a spring onion, the cork sealed shut with wax and filled with a violet liquid. The astounded cantor picked it up and held it out for all to see. For a moment, the sanctuary was silent. Then distressed shouts of "Where is the arm?" and "He has abandoned us, just like the Virgin!" echoed through the sacred space. Everyone rushed out of the church, and many citizens who meant to stay in Florence left that very night. As they fled through the gates, they told the wall-touching pilgrims what had happened, and they, too, ran away, telling everyone they met the terrible story of how a sorcerer had transformed San Filippo's arm into a small bottle.

Those Florentines who did not – or could not – flee were left in even greater terror, and cast their desperate hopes toward the upcoming Feast of San Zenobio. If no miracle was delivered after that? *Well,* they whispered, *then we are truly cursed above all other cities, and forsaken by God.*

In life, San Zenobio was the very first bishop of Florence. Now his skull was enclosed in a gilt-silver case, fashioned in the shape of his head, hat, and shoulders. And surely, *surely,* he would intercede for Florence in her darkest hour. A sparse crowd of Florentines, faces wrapped in vinegared cloth, gathered at his altar inside the crumbling cathedral of Santa Reparata to ask Zenobio to make the plague go away and tell the Virgin they were sorry and get San Filippo to come back.

Notable among the attendees of the ceremony were the Lord and Lady Girolami, who were rich as Croesus and claimed Zenobio as an ancestor. As was tradition, the Girolami family had processed to the cathedral from their imposing tower home in order to receive the saint's head on a gilded tray.

Again, the Bishop Acciaiuoli excused himself, leaving the ceremony in the charge of an inexperienced replacement (this one a notary public, by training). And when the nervous young priest removed the silver head reliquary from its locked altar, the two halves cracked apart in his hands like a walnut. Instead of Zenobio's skull, out fell a small glass vessel, closed with a cork and filled with liquid of palest sage green.

The priest stuttered with fear. The people fell on the ground and wept. The Girolami ran away and locked themselves up in their tower. Somebody went to the *ringhiera,* the stone platform in the central piazza, and yelled out that the saints of Florence had abandoned the sinful city to plague. Only one or two people were there to hear him, but it was enough.

The terrible news floated with the poisoned miasmas through shuttered windows and sequestered courtyards until it reached the newly appointed papal inquisitor, Fra Michele di Lapo Arnolfi.

The previous Florentine inquisitor had taken to his role

of eliminating heretics with a *bit* too much zeal, and Bishop Acciaiuoli had lobbied the Pope personally to secure the nomination of the younger, more-easily-managed Inquisitor Michele.

A native Florentine of strong faith, but delicate health, Inquisitor Michele was afraid of disease even in normal times. Terrified of stepping out of doors, the new inquisitor plunged into research, obsessively going through records of old trials, looking for anything that mentioned the stealing of relics, of sorcerers turning them into glass bottles.

However, bad news soon overwhelmed his task: every day, it seemed, new and awful crimes were shouted from the central platform by...by somebody, nobody was really sure who, since most citizens remained locked inside their homes.

But to the inquisitor's ears, the yelling voice was authoritative – and well-informed. It shared that the altars inside San Lorenzo, San Paolo, and San Pier Maggiore had been emptied; how at Santo Stefano al Ponte a shrine was broken open; how, in all cases, sacred bones were taken from crystal caskets and switched for tiny bottles of unholy potion.

Determined to end these foul crimes, but unwilling to risk his own health, the new inquisitor sent man after man from his personal retinue to investigate the thefts in his stead. But so potent was the plague that each of his deputies dropped dead before he could gather any helpful information. Down to his last man, Inquisitor Michele changed tactics and hired a disposable peasant to deliver dispatches to the fifty or so parishes of Florence, commanding each of them to conduct inventories of the precious relics within their charge.

The peasant messenger did his best, but really, he could hardly find any people to deliver the letters to. Nearly everyone was dead, it seemed, and those left alive refused to leave their apartments. The peasant abandoned his fruitless task without a word to the inquisitor, who waited in vain for responses that never came.

When summer arrived, hot and deadly, the city canceled

all future processions. The people were afraid to be near their neighbors, afraid another relic would disappear. The Signoria – the group of wealthy men elected to lead the city – ceased to meet, and municipal services were suspended indefinitely. Most churches stopped holding mass altogether. The sickly sweet stench of decay was everywhere, the taste of it stuck in the back of peoples' throats.

But the shouts from the *ringhiera* did not abate: word continued to spread that a wicked thief was plucking the relics of Florence from their golden boxes and leaving strange glass charms in their place. And to heap misery upon misery, it was now apparent that if a parish was robbed of its saintly protection, its *entire* population would soon after be decimated by plague. The people of Florence began to call these unfortunate places "dead parishes," and nobody would cross into those cursed neighborhoods for love or money.

EIGHT

FIRENZE DI NUOVO

July of 1348, Gates of Florence

Ginevra and Piero arrived at the Porta San Gallo early in the morning of July 7, 1348, several long weeks after the fiasco at the Feast of San Zenobio – and only a few short hours after the pear tree intimated that Ludovico was cold and dead. Normally, there was a long line of Florentine gentlemen standing in front of the gate at daybreak, each waiting to pass back into the city after an evening of revels in suburban brothels. But today, Ginevra and Piero were the sole applicants for entry. The gigantic nail-studded doors were shut, and it was only with much shouting that they were able to attract the attention of the keeper who sat in his room atop the gate's tower.

"Move along! The city's closed to foreigners!" he yelled down once he saw them.

"We have business here with His Holiness the Bishop!" called up Ginevra.

"Where is Old Antonio?" called Piero. "He let me out of this gate two weeks ago and said he would watch for my return!"

"Old Antonio is now Dead Antonio, may his soul be at peace. I'm the new gatekeeper, Young Antonio, and I'm not supposed to let anyone in."

"But we have a letter from the Acciaiuoli family, inviting us to Florence!" said Ginevra.

Young Antonio paused, uncertain of the correct action.

"Please," continued Ginevra. "Can you have your man open the door?"

"Man?! I have no man. It is only me at this post! You're lucky you came to this gate and not another, where there might not even be anyone there at all!"

"Well, we are sorry to trouble you, Young Antonio. But please have a look at our letter! We come at the urgent request of the bishop's nephew. Piero here is the son of a Florentine and is a resident of this city."

Young Antonio squinted down from his perch. Even from the height, he could see a big official-looking seal on the letter. He did not want to interrupt the business of the bishop.

Nobody was around anyway to see that he let them in, a crooked-nosed woman and her child. They seemed harmless enough.

"Alright, alright, hold on."

The keeper climbed down the long spiral stairs from his tower, opened a little door that was cut out of the big door, and for the first time in eight years, Ginevra saw her adopted home.

She stepped through the doorway, eager to experience the same elation she had when she first entered Florence as a young girl so many years ago, but O – desolate place! Never had Ginevra felt old before, but nothing shows time like a place once gay and full, now going to dust and shadows. Instead of the giddy excitement of her youth, she was overtaken by deep dread. She was now absolutely certain that her dream had been a portent. It was not just Ludovico who was gone. The city was so quiet she could hear the ringing in her ears, hear the plaster upon the walls. As if all its inhabitants had disappeared into the air.

Gone were the fumbling customs agents, the stoic soldiers, the peddlers of trinkets looking to part you from your coin as soon as you arrived. Gone was the pastry man who sold you hot fried bread that he plucked from a cauldron of bubbling lard with his bare fingertips.

Gone were the merchants' wives, flouting sumptuary laws in their striped purple gowns and ridiculous red turbans, and the country mendicant who shouted at them. Where were the vegetable sellers, with their lettuces and garlics spread on clean blankets on the cobbled streets? And the new kittens who sat on the garlics and mewed for their mother cats? Gone, gone, gone.

"Piero," she whispered, for it seemed strange to speak loudly in this empty space, "was it like this when you left?"

"Not quite," he said with a shiver. "There were still some people walking about when I was last here. Half the city must have died while I was away. Come, I will take you to Bishop Acciaiuoli now. Let's hope he's still alive."

NINE

SOMEBODY LIKE AN INQUISITOR

June of 1348, City of Florence

At the beginning of the summer, in the days just before Piero would be sent on his errand to Genoa, a June sun blazed down onto the rooftops of Florence. The plague settled in, as pervasive and relentless as the heat, finding its way into the cracks of walls and the pores of the Florentine people. Not a drop of clarity had fallen on the mystery of the missing relics, nor a drop of rain on the parched city.

During these steaming nights, the Inquisitor Michele kept his lamps burning late, flipping through records and panicking. At the suggestion of a physician, he drank only strong Spanish wine from a silver ewer, and kept his room filled with perfumed smoke from a flaming brazier. Together, the alcohol and lack of fresh air pushed the normally astute man into a constant mild delirium, and in this fragile state, Bishop Acciaiuoli came to pay him a visit.

"It is seven relics missing now," said the bishop from the doorway. "San Barnaba's thigh bone is gone as of his feast day, June 11. Stolen and replaced with *this*." He walked forward and dropped a small bottle on the inquisitor's desk. Grass-green liquid swirled inside its bulbous base.

"Ahhh," said Inquisitor Michele, pulling his skullcap from

his head and holding it over his face. "I was so engrossed in my work I didn't even see you come in."

"The citizens are distraught. Waiting for more thefts to be shouted from the *ringhiera*."

"Who keeps *doing* that?" said the inquisitor. He fingered some of the many loose parchments on his desk, as if the solution was misplaced among them.

"I come to speak with you," said the bishop, losing patience, "because, as the world crumbles around us, infected riffraff knock upon my door at all hours. They ask me where our relics are – and more precisely, what is our inquisitor doing to get them back?"

"Many things! First, I sent my men out to gather clues. But they all died, besides Giuseppe. So now I await responses from parishes. And also I read! And research! I can't leave my home, you understand. I was ill as a child—"

"Doing research. Waiting for letters. Is that really all?"

"I could do more if you would help me, if you would lend some of your hired guard to watch over our churches until the thief is caught. I have no one—"

"What good would that do? My men would die the same as yours, sitting outside in contaminated places. Look, Michele, these are hard times. Everybody is frightened."

The inquisitor said nothing, only continued to stare at his papers.

The bishop sighed. "If I'm being honest, it's not just the doorknockers: I've received a concerned letter from His Holiness on the matter, and I wasn't certain how to respond."

The inquisitor looked up from his desk now. "Word has reached the Pope already?"

"Indeed," continued the bishop. "And it seems we haven't much to tell him. But I suppose I can explain your efforts, reassure him that you're doing all you can, given the circumstances. He'll appreciate hearing some good news, no matter how slender. He wrote in some distress, you see – so many of his cardinals have died. Most of them French, of course. So no great loss there. But now I hear our lone Italian cardinal is dead also. We must pray for our departed brother in red, mustn't we?"

"Of course, may his soul be at peace, in Christ's name, Amen." The inquisitor made a few more appeals to God on behalf of the Italian cardinal before stopping abruptly, mid-devotion. "But – why did the Pope not write to me directly, if he has concerns?"

"Because, as you know, it was *I* who requested your appointment after his last appointee turned out to be such a tyrannical disaster. He wants to make sure I chose well. But you've been doing your best, and you'll continue to do so. I'll let him know." He turned to go.

Even through the warmth of the wine, Inquisitor Michele felt like a failure. The bishop was right: it was his responsibility to track down heresy, and there was no greater sacrilege than stealing relics.

"Wait!" he cried, rather more loudly than necessary. "It is clear to me: we must hire an investigator, someone familiar with sorcery, who can track the thief, interpret the little bottles."

Bishop Acciaiuoli gave him a bewildered look. "You mean… somebody like an *inquisitor*?"

"Yes. No. I mean, somebody who can go into the city without succumbing to disease."

"No man is safe from pestilence, you know as well as I. God takes whom He pleases."

"No *man*, but look! Look here…" Once again, the inquisitor rifled through his papers.

"Aha! Here it is: Do you remember the rogue ward of FraSimone da Cascia? She was exiled after the water sickness of 1340."

The bishop shook his head incredulously. He knew what Michele was proposing. This was not what he had intended – having two annoying people to deal with instead of just one. All he had meant by this visit was to make sure the inquisitor was doing his job.

"You would entrust a woman and a convicted heretic with such an important task?"

"Don't you recall?" said the inquisitor. "She moved among the sick without ever becoming afflicted."

"It's true, it was unnatural, but—"

"She kept a book of secret spells, too – it's recorded here in her sentencing. *Exactly* the sort of person who could explain these strange bottles."

"I can't see how any of this matters," said the bishop, examining his fingernails. "We punished her rather severely, as I recall. Why would she travel now, in these times, to help us?"

"Lord Bishop, wasn't she in love with your nephew?" asked the inquisitor quietly.

The bishop's silence answered the question.

"Well, let's have him write to her, then?"

"He is already dead, along with his father. I am the only one left."

"My condolences, Bishop, but does the lady need to know that before she gets here?"

Acciaiuoli opened his mouth to argue further, but stopped. If this was how the inquisitor wanted to handle the matter, fine. The woman was probably dead anyhow. And he did not want the Pope to hear he was standing in the way of an inquisitorial investigation. The relics would return, God willing, when the time was right. He had faith. So what did it matter to him who Michele hired in the interim? The bishop had more immediate problems requiring his focus.

So, he obligingly forged a letter in the hand of his late nephew, and hired a boy, Piero di Piero, to go and fetch Ginevra. The plague had taken both the child's parents, and Piero had been moping about the piazza of Santa Reparata ever since, weeping and begging for food. It would be good for him to have something to do. He was a bit young for such a journey, but he was the only one the bishop could find that would not die along the way.

TEN

FRA MICHELE DI LAPO ARNOLFI

July 7th of 1348, City of Florence

And, just as the bishop predicted, Piero did not die. Still, nobody *really* expected Ginevra to show up, from such a distance, with only a boy as an escort. So when the pair arrived at the bishop's residence just a fortnight after Piero was dispatched to Genoa, the Swiss mercenaries guarding his doors regarded them with suspicion. They conferred among themselves in their native tongue, and after a few minutes told the travelers to go meet with the inquisitor first.

A tight knot formed in Ginevra's gut.

"But the bishop said he'd find a position for me if I delivered his letter!" Piero explained.

"After you drop her off," said a soldier gruffly, slamming the palazzo doors.

Piero shrugged. "Come on, Ginevra. The inquisitor's palazzo is just around the corner."

"We are not expected. Someone has tricked us," she said.

"I *swear* it was the bishop who sent me. He promised he would place me with a good family in exchange for delivering you. Come, let's do what his man says."

"No. Something isn't right here."

"Please, Ginevra, I can't be alone anymore!"

She let herself be dragged to the inquisitor's door. The lintel was inscribed *let no man commit error in word or deed* and painted in with gold foil. The gold was peeling.

"I'm going to knock," said Piero.

"Wait – I need to think for a moment!"

He knocked.

"I told you to wait!"

The door opened. A neatly dressed servant stared at them.

Piero looked at Ginevra and then back at the servant. Neither adult said anything, so he announced their purpose. He made Ginevra take out the letter from Ludovico. The servant stepped aside to let them in. The knot inside Ginevra wound tighter. She'd so dearly wanted the letter to be genuine she had ignored her instincts. Now she'd walked into a trap she did not understand. Piero ran back toward the home of the bishop, stopping to wave goodbye before he disappeared around a corner. She moved to follow him, but the servant pulled her by the arm into the dark interior, then shut the door.

"Miasmas," he said by way of apology. Her heart began to flump in ways it shouldn't.

She found herself at the shorter end of a rectangular room, the interior wall pierced by three windows that showed a central stone courtyard. Narrow blocks of light shone through, giving just enough illumination for Ginevra to see the walls were painted with panel scenes of the apocalypse: towers toppled by earthquakes, famine riding fast on a skeletal horse, sinners packed into a flaming kiln tended by beasts.

"So, the boy, he actually found you, then?"

Ginevra jumped. Straining her eyes into the gloom, she saw a tall, slender figure pacing at the far end of the hall, his soft leather slippers making faint slaps on the green tile floors.

"He did. But he ran away, just now."

"Incredible. Monna Ginevra, I am Fra Michele di Lapo Arnolfi, Inquisitor to His Holiness Pope Clement VI." He paused briefly, awaiting platitudes, but Ginevra only studied him intently.

He was not so old, a few years more than herself, at most. But he had the pale skin and darkly circled eyes of one who spent too much time reading by lamplight, and his narrow frame was lost in the voluminous black-and-white robes of his order. A black niello pomander hung from his silk belt, the size and shape of a crab apple. If Ginevra had been closer, she'd have seen that silver letters spelled out prayers to San Sebastiano around its circumference. The trinket emitted a pervasive musky odor and he jerked it compulsorily up to his mouth and nose every minute or so.

Ginevra saw she was being observed just as closely. Automatically, she touched the scar on her nose, and then was annoyed she had pointed to the very thing this loathsome man was searching for. Her gesture broke his silence.

"Er, our deepest apologies, but Signore Ludovico died shortly after he wrote you."

Ginevra's heart panged, but she kept her face stony. This was why the pear tree had warned her. So she did not have to learn of her Ludo's death from this sickly skeleton of a man.

"Ser Ludovico wrote that the bishop had particular need of my services, that I was to be welcomed back into the city."

"Yes, well. Is it true that in the year 1340, when so many died from the water sickness, you went into infected houses and parishes and never became ill yourself?"

"It is true."

"And is the same true with this new and vile plague?"

"It is, so far as I know it."

"And I am also of the understanding that the nuns of Sant'Elisabetta taught you to read?"

"Sister Agnesa did, yes." Ginevra realized she had not said that name aloud in years. Another pang of heart.

"And that with these skills, you became familiar with certain books on sorcery and unnatural arts?"

Ginevra stiffened. "I was accused of such familiarity, as you clearly know. But that does not make it true."

The inquisitor took a nervous inhale from his pomander and spoke: "Well, it's close enough," he said. "What we require is a person impervious to the effects of the pestilence, who is also intimate with practices and writings of charlatans and sorcerers." Another sniff.

Ginevra almost turned and fled right there. She expected to be asked about her healing skills, not interrogated about sorcery. Again.

But then she remembered the lone guard at the *porta*, the absent bishop, the empty streets. If ever there was a time a woman might rise above her born station, surely this was it. She must be steady, make her demands. If it did not work, she could leave whenever she wanted. There was nobody to stop her.

"So," she said, "what would you have me do, then?"

The inquisitor left Ginevra's question hanging in the air and called out to the lone servant, who was named Giuseppe. The fashionable young man reappeared carrying a small slant-top desk and set it in the center of the room. Atop he placed a ceramic beaker painted with green and purple grapevines pecked by golden chickens. Ginevra realized she was desperately thirsty, and began to say her thanks, but the inquisitor walked to the beaker and drank its entire contents himself.

He wiped his mouth delicately, then removed from the desk a little row of bottles, filled with liquids in varying shades of violet, sage, plum, and emerald. He placed them on top of the desk, then retreated to his far side. He indicated Ginevra should come forward and examine.

"In your work with necromancers and witches, have you ever seen anything like these?"

"I never worked with – never mind – no. Flasks filled with liquid. It could be anything." She grew impatient. "Why are you showing this to me?"

"*Because*: someone is stealing the relics out of our churches."

"Stealing...relics?" Ginevra was not sure she'd heard correctly.

"And whoever it is, he leaves these behind. One bottle for one relic. We thought with your background, you might recognize them, which is why, aside from your fortitude against illness, I – er, rather – *Ludovico* suggested that we write to you."

"Ser Inquisitor, I do not follow."

"With so many gone," he continued, "our holy spaces are not watched as they ought to be. Seven of our most precious relics are now gone. And once the relics are taken, so die the residents of the parish. I myself am one of the very few left in the parish of Santa Reparata."

"So...you did not ask me here to heal people?"

"Oh, no, NO, no, no, Monna," he said, pulling at the pomander. "As we all unfortunately know, this plague is the wrath of God—" *sniff* " – manifesting itself on earth. The only escape is to pray for intercession from the saints—" *sniff* " – but we can't do that because our saints keep disappearing." The inquisitor's voice broke and his cheeks became flush. Was he about to *cry*? Ginevra decided it must be the wine.

"Ser Inquisitor, are the relics not crusted in gold and jewels? It is not sorcerers who are interested in those, but ordinary men. You have no need for one with specialized knowledge—"

"Ha! You've a mind for inquisiting, just like me." (Ginevra did not appreciate the comparison.) "The golden reliquaries remain intact, in position. *Only the relics were taken.*"

Ginevra shivered. A pall hung over the city; she felt its suffocating drape when she crossed through the gate. Who would choose to be closer to such a wicked crime? But, if this was the task she must accomplish to begin life anew, so be it. "What happens if the thief is not caught?"

"He *will* be caught. This condition must be met if your exile is to be rescinded."

"Reversing my exile is a start. But it's not enough to secure my help. You ask an extraordinary thing."

"Name your price, then, bold woman."

"I wish to join the Florentine Guild of Doctors, Apothecaries, and Grocers," she said, finally voicing aloud what she had wished for a thousand times in silence.

"You wish to be a grocer?" he asked in all seriousness.

"*No.* I wish to register as a doctor, of course."

"But you are a woman."

"I am aware. And yet, I still wish to be admitted to the guild as a doctor. So I can practice my trade without persecution. I know it is unusual, but women *may* join, if they pass the exam. I'll need the patronage of someone important – I thought Ludovico might... Anyway, I suppose you will have to do." Ginevra was terrible at flattery.

"Monna, that is not in my control. The guild decides its own members."

"Are you saying the guild doesn't value a recommendation from the office of the Holy Inquisitor?" (She was better at insults.)

"It's just, this is a highly unorthodox request..." he spluttered.

Ginevra shrugged. "These are unorthodox times. And I should think, judging by the emptiness of your streets and the stink of the air, that perhaps the good doctors of Florence should not turn up their noses at offered help. No matter where it comes from."

"Fine, then. This deal is in my favor, anyhow, as it will never come to pass. If you recover our relics, I will request your admittance and provide requisite funding to the Guild of Doctors, Apothecaries, and Grocers, which they will decline, as neither your father nor your grandfather was a member. Now. Is *that* all?"

"Yes. *That* is all. Plus expenses. And it must all be in writing." The obstacle of patronage was not a surprise to her, but never mind. She would sort that bit out later.

"Very well, then," said the inquisitor. "But it shall also be put in writing that while engaged in my services, you will not perform any doctoring, and that you must appear at my place of residence to report on progress at intervals of no longer than three days, the first meeting being on July the tenth. You will note my generosity in giving you the rest of today to recover from your journey. Any deviation voids our agreement, and you will face immediate criminal charges for violating your exile."

Ginevra nodded curtly.

"Then we are in agreement. Giuseppe, come here." The inquisitor wrote up the terms, and he and Ginevra signed their names, with the servant acting as witness.

Then the inquisitor gave her a modest sum for incidentals. He also gave her the first small bottle found in San Filippo's reliquary, and a list he had drawn of the robbed churches and the dates the thefts were first noticed.

Ginevra examined the parchment: it was decorated with massive borders of flowers, rats, the crest of the city, and what looked like a procession of saints walking along the bottom of the page.

"This is very...formal, Ser Inquisitor."

"Thank you," he said blushing. "The beauty illustrates the importance of the words."

L ❦ Left Forearm of San Filippo, from the Baptistry. Seen Easter, March 31. Theft reported May 1.

❦ Head of Zenobius, from Santa Reparata. Seen Easter, March 31. Theft reported May 24.

❦ All seen at the Rogazione Procession, April 25: Right-Buttock of San Paolo, from San Paolo. Left-Buttock of San Paolo, from San Lorenzo. Torso of San Piero, from San Pier Maggiore. Left foot of Santo Stefano, from Santo Stefano Al Ponte. Thefts reported May 31.

❦ Thigh of San Barnaba, from San Barnaba. Seen Pentecost, May 20. Theft reported, June 11.

She squinted to read his perfect handwriting, the tiny names of churches cramped inside colorful borders. No *wonder* Florence needed her help. Their inquisitor spent all his time drinking wine and making art.

"Fine," she said, tucking the list and the contract into her belt. "I take my leave, and will return soon."

"In three days," pressed the inquisitor.

"In three days."

"I pray for your success, and for the soul of your friend, Ludovico. I shall inform the bishop of our arrangement."

Before she could respond, Giuseppe ushered her through the front door and locked it. She did not see Piero outside. She called out his name, but there was no answer. She started toward the bishop's home, intending to ask the boy if he'd like to continue as her partner. But then she stopped herself. Perhaps it was better this way. Piero would be sent to live with a family, with other children. She would not force him to accompany her on her crooked path. She put him in the place in her heart she kept for things she had cared for and lost, along with Ludovico, Monna Vermilia, and her original left nostril.

Now, in the street alone, she was struck by the reality of her decision. She did not know how to hunt a thief. She took out the inquisitor's list, with its lush illustrations and scant information, and then put it away again. She looked around the empty piazza, a place once lively and familiar, now distant and strange. Again, her mind went into the past, back to the circumstances of her first arrival as a girl, to the city of her heart.

ELEVEN

A GOOD GIRL, SO TO SPEAK

1335, City of Genoa

Quite a bit of time had passed since Ginevra's first encounter with the *malocchio*, but in those years, the coral *figa* stayed bright red and kept Ginevra in health and safe from the Eye, just as Monna Vermilia promised it would. No longer did she have to close her eyes and concentrate to know how the strings connected one thing to another. She had become fluent in their silent language of cause and effect. But at fifteen, for the first time, her attentions and desires were not wholly devoted to her work with Monna Vermilia. Now when she walked down the little streets along the harbor, she was noticed by the sailors and loaf-abouts. And sometimes she noticed them back. Vermilia listened every day to Ginevra recounting their unoriginal and libidinous comments as if they were rare poems penned by a courtier.

The older woman saw that soon Ginevra would want to marry one of these fools if nothing more interesting happened. This was a treacherous time of life for a young woman, when she was susceptible to finding worthy qualities in men who had none. The time had come, she realized, to push Ginevra toward her full potential. Vermilia went to Ginevra's father, Gasparo, and said, "Look here – you haven't any money, and your daughter is a good girl, so to speak, and does not deserve to become a slave wife to whatever miserable rope-maker will be content with the public dowry."

"What should I do?" asked the poor Gasparo, concerned in earnest for his child.

Vermilia patted his hand sympathetically. "Don't worry, I will tell you: My cousin is an abbess at a convent called Sant'Elisabetta, operated by the Augustinians as a charity for women who were formerly prostitutes but now are nuns. She could make use of a girl such as Ginevra. There, she may learn and practice the healing arts without causing a scandal. Your daughter will make her own living, and she need not settle on the first circumstance that presents itself."

Gasparo conferred with his wife, Camiola, and they both agreed they did not want their daughter to be married to a miserable rope-maker. So Vermilia went to the monk she had seduced and had him write out the letter of introduction. She then helped Gasparo arrange for Ginevra to travel with a group of pilgrims who were making a southward journey the following week and would stop at the merchant republic of Florence.

Ginevra was not entirely in favor of this turn of events – she could not imagine being apart from Vermilia, being apart from her parents. But even though she wore the coral *mano figa*, she had not forgotten the Eye and was afraid it would come back for her if she was ungrateful. So, she cried her tears quietly into her bed and made no protest as she prepared for the journey.

Camiola noticed Ginevra's despair anyhow and went to her daughter and embraced her as she bundled her few belongings together. Ginevra began to weep and clutched at her mother's sleeve. "Why do you send me away? Do you not love me now that I am grown?"

Tears came also to the corners of Camiola's eyes. "Your absence will be a yoke upon my shoulders. But do not think about us – this convent will be a pleasant place, I am sure – go there and be a credit to them. Learn what the Florentine nuns will tell you, see what is in the wider world. Then when you come back to us, it will be because you chose to, and not because it is all you know."

"But are there not convents enough here in Genoa?"

Camiola hugged her only living child closer to her and spoke slowly or else she, too, would weep freely. "This one must be special. Your teacher, Vermilia, is wise. She knows – and I even in my humbleness know – there are not so many ways for a woman to improve her lot. We must be willing to go farther, to search harder to find how we may realize our truest talents, and to please God with them." Ginevra knew her mother was right and that it was not fair.

To solemnize their farewell, Monna Vermilia invited Ginevra to her home for a last supper of sorts. She had gathered a hundred tiny clams from the shore, and now threw them without mercy into a sputtering pot of lard and garlic. The delicate creatures stood no chance, and opened immediately to release their briny liquor into the frying pan. Vermilia dumped the whole lot of them into a great earthen bowl with much clacking of shells and splattering of fragrant broth.

Ginevra smiled weakly, and dipped a round of saltless bread into the broth. Vermilia did the same. In the silence of the shared meal, the immediacy of departure weighed heavily.

Ginevra put down her bread. "Oh, Monna, I cannot bear it!"

Vermilia reached across the table and held her arm tight. "Tonight we must be glad, we must enjoy each other, because I am old and will die before you return."

"No! You are like Noah and will live to be nine hundred years old!"

"Who says I haven't done that already, eh? God has no great plans for me, I saw it long ago – the morning you came to me with the *malocchio*, I asked the stone in my ring and it told me my time is approaching. So go, my dear, and look only forward, for you have had the best of me."

Ginevra sat stunned. "I do not believe it. Show me the stone that could know such things."

Vermilia sat still for a moment. "Very well, then, if it will make you accept it." She took her ring off and placed it among the clamshells on the table.

"Where did it come from?" Ginevra asked, as if through interrogation, she might discredit the jewel.

"From my friend, the monk," said Vermilia, "who pried it from the bindings of a book."

"How can you believe what it says, then? It's only a decoration, it knows nothing!"

"My poor girl, here – touch it." Vermilia pressed the ring into her pupil's palm and Ginevra knew it had been unearthed at an auspicious moment from a mine now forgotten. That it was blessed with words from a dead language and carved with symbols men stole from the old gods. She knew it did not lie.

Vermilia smiled as she took the ring from Ginevra's still-open palm and shoved it back onto her own finger.

"I will send you letters," the old woman promised, "for as long as I can. And the nuns will teach you how to read them. Here is the first one – give it to my cousin, called Sister Agnesa, it explains why I sent you."

Ginevra took the letter. She wiped her eyes and stood and paced up and down the messy room where she'd spent so many days, and decided that, for Vermilia whom she loved, she would have to accept it. All of it. As best she could. "Death comes for us all," she finally said.

"He does, indeed," Vermilia agreed, still smiling.

Along with the letter of introduction, Vermilia entrusted Ginevra with a small, sealed package for her cousin the nun. Ginevra felt her coral amulet heat up as soon as the parcel was handed to her. "Be careful with this parcel," said Vermilia with a wink, "it's not tied *so* tightly."

A few days into her journey, Ginevra stepped away from the pilgrims with the excuse of relieving herself, and untied the package. Inside was a handful of stones. Each was different – some appearing as common pebbles, others as rare jewels. Some were the color of bricks or honey or deepest green or purple like a drop of frozen wine. Others were striped, a few were speckled, and one or two were carved with foreign symbols. Ginevra suddenly felt very small and very young. Her coral glowed so much that its light showed through her clothing. Though it was a chilly afternoon, she could feel a warmth coming off the gems, as if they had been held tight in a hand. Surely, the nun wouldn't notice if she took just one for herself? She picked out the most ordinary-looking stone: brown and rough. It rattled like a dried-out seedpod. She retied the package carefully, and hid the rattling stone among her things to keep as her own secret treasure.

TWELVE

THE WOMEN'S WARD

1335, City of Florence,
Convent of Sant'Elisabetta delle Convertite

Soon enough, the pilgrims reached the walls of Florence, and Ginevra passed under the studded doors of the Porta San Gallo for the first time, into what felt like a whole new world. She breathed in the odor of crushed pomegranates and rare incense, and as her party wound through the irregular web of streets, she gaped up at pink buildings that shot toward the sky and terraced out over thin roadways, so that in places the clouds overhead were visible only in quick slivers. Genoa was the city of her birth but *here*, she knew in an instant, was the place of her heart.

In the midst of all the churches and shops and palaces, everywhere Ginevra looked, the saints of Florence were manifest as statues and frescoes, as effigies held aloft by processing confraternities, watching over the city they had blessed with growth and prosperity. It was the most congested place she had ever been, and she found herself jostled through crowds of painters, stonemasons, woodcarvers, and goldsmiths.

She saw men of God and base women decorated with bells.
Servants dressed in the colors of their masters, and sellers

of parsley who squatted on corners. One of the pilgrims had been to Florence before, and he pointed out all that he knew to Ginevra as they passed, including the men of great consequence, whose ancestors had been vicious lords of the country, and who now made untold fortunes importing Venetian glass, painted books, and English wool. They squeezed past crowds of the wretched poor, crying out for bread, who came as pilgrims to beg for relief in front of Florence's famous relics, housed in gem-studded shrines. And all along the way, Ginevra spotted the little limps and sores and watery eyes and thought, *I will fix you, and you, and you.*

Her walk ended at the front door of the Augustinian convent of Sant'Elisabetta delle Convertite, set into the street-facing stucco wall that adjoined their modest chapel. The pilgrims handed Ginevra over to Sister Agnesa, the cousin of Monna Vermilia.

After a brief and awkward introduction, Ginevra presented Monna Vermilia's letter and the package of stones. She waited nervously for Agnesa to open the package, but the nun put it away in her purse without a word. Agnesa was not quite so old as her cousin, her face lined but not sagging, the whites of her eyes still clear.

"Walk with me now," she said, her gray habit billowing around her as she stepped quickly down the hallway of red tile floors and striped plaster walls. At the end of the corridor was a large wooden door, which Sister Agnesa pushed open to reveal a long rectangular dormitory lined with small wooden cots.

"Here is the hospital. We are one of the largest in the city, with twelve beds," she said with pride. "Its purpose is to provide shelter for poor pilgrims, who travel far to pray before the city's relics. Your job will be to keep it clean and see to their needs."

"Gladly, Sister, but – I can do more than that – surely in her letter, Vermilia mentioned…"

"Do you find the role of housekeeper beneath you? Hygiene and preparedness are the cornerstones of our work."

"No, Sister, forgive me," said Ginevra, perplexed. "But I thought, I mean, Vermilia implied – that the convent had use for *me* specifically. There wasn't a girl already in Florence that would have sufficed as housekeeper?"

"Surely, there was. Now, if you will hold your thoughts for a moment, so I might tell you mine? Good. The reason I will take *you* and not some other girl is this way, come."

They walked through the hospital and exited the other end into a yard, surrounded by high walls on all sides and filled with the stuff of daily life: vats for laundry, chicken coops, a vegetable garden, a privy. In the yard, three young nuns wrapped wool threads with golden foil, and an ancient nun sat and smiled on a sunny patch of earth. And against the far wall, there was a large wooden lean-to that Ginevra took as a shed for animals. It was here Agnesa led her. *Will they make me a swineherd, too?* she worried. But when she stepped inside, Ginevra gasped at the interior. Instead of piglets rooting in apple cores, a proper brick floor covered in reed mats, and another dozen beds, several occupied with very pregnant women.

"Hello, ladies," said Agnesa.

The women murmured back their greeting.

"Here is the other work we do," she said, turning back to Ginevra. "A place for women to have their babies, when they wish nobody else to know. We do this because we remember our sisters outside the city wall, who must sell their bodies and on occasion find themselves in this predicament. My cousin says you understand discretion, yes?"

A woman tied to a ladder and consumed by flames flashed in Ginevra's memory. She nodded vigorously.

"Good. You will help them as you help the pilgrims, and you will not mention this part of our work to anyone. It's the sort of thing where word is passed to those who need it, and no one else. Understood?"

Ginevra nodded again. Being privy to clandestine activities made the prospect of maid's work much more palatable. She was sure they'd get to the magic and healing eventually.

"Good. Now, the other part of what you'll do here, as a laywoman, is see to our affairs outside the convent. The sisters are not permitted to leave. And if you're representing us, you must be an example of what a decent lady ought to be like and, my dear, being *clean* is one of those things." They went back out into the yard, to the area where the laundry was done. In the middle of all the drying underthings, a small cloth-lined tub had been prepared, filled with warmish water.

"Off with your clothes and into the bath," said Agnesa.

Ginevra looked nervously around for some private corner to undress. She could see gold-spinning nuns sneaking glances her way from across the yard.

"No time for modesty now," said Agnesa. "Every sister here had another life before in the brothels; you think we haven't seen it all and some besides?"

And with that, Ginevra was out of her dusty garments and into the tub.

"What's that you wear on your neck?" said Agnesa immediately.

Ginevra's hand clutched at her coral. "It's nothing! A gift. I have always worn it since I was young…"

Agnesa gently pulled her hand open and observed the carved amulet. "You know, lots of our pilgrims carry their own little charms. Corals, bits of horn, prayers tied up with string… though this one has a presence, doesn't it? But you might take it off now, since you've removed all your other clothes."

"But – Vermilia said I was never to take it off, ever."

"She did? My cousin said that?"

"Yes. It was she who gave it to me…*after I punctured the malocchio*."

A brief shadow passed over Agnesa's face. "How does it feel now? Is it hot? Is it cold?"

Ginevra shook her head.

"Well, if Vermilia told you to keep it on, you'd better do it. We are not so foolish here as to ignore… Just keep it to yourself. Don't go showing it off."

"It's only because I am naked, Sister, that you know of it."

"See that it stays that way. And you still need to say your prayers to the Virgin, even with that."

Ginevra nodded and sunk down into the tub, feeling rather self-conscious. She was used to being helpful (and dressed), not a bother who didn't understand how things were. But the water did feel nice. She decided to enjoy the wash. The air of this new city smelled fresh and clean, and she wanted badly for her person to be as well-kept as its surroundings.

Of course, if you walked along the river Arno that cut the city in two, or the breeze blew the wrong way, you would catch an eye-watering waft of sewage, but this happened in every city in the world. A small price to pay for living inside protective walls.

The real smell of Florence was something else. It came from air that blew in through snowy mountains and valleys full of chestnut blossoms, and when it got to the city, it mixed with the pleasant odors of cooking from the markets and the great houses. Not fish fried in stale lard, like in Genoa, but bread baked with finely milled white flour, fruits boiling in spiced wine, and young chickens, stuffed with lemons and rosemary, roasting on spits. So Ginevra relished the rough scrubbing with stinging lye soap, until she was pink as an apple and her pores empty of the salty Genoese grime. She did not flinch when the nun brushed her hair a hundred times with scratchy boar bristles, turning her brittle plaits soft and golden. The braids were wound back up with ribbons and then covered in a new white linen veil so her hair could stay clean as she went about her work.

And her old gray dress – the spilled wine that had so distressed her years ago was now but one stain among many. This tired garment was given to the rag pickers, and Ginevra was gifted a white linen shift to wear next to her skin, and a brown dress to wear over it with a long apron that tied attractively around her waist. A small purse was suspended from the apron, and it was here she put her pilfered stone to keep safe. On her feet, soft leather slippers that fastened at the ankle and came to points at the toes.

Now it was as if the nun's bath had worked its own kind of magic. Ginevra glowed like a star and any fool could see there was something about her not commonly found in a ward at a convent.

Satisfied, Sister Agnesa brought Ginevra to a whitewashed cell, where she would sleep with another servant girl, Taddea, who was also scrubbed clean and wearing a pretty brown dress. Taddea was directed to show Ginevra around and explain to her the workings of things, and the two young women were left on their own.

Taddea had been born at the convent, and the nuns took care of her after her mother ran away. She looked Ginevra up and down, and then her round face spread into a happy smile and she embraced her, glad to have somebody else share the workload.

"I'll show you everything, don't worry," she said. She took Ginevra first to the kitchen with its huge hearth and glowing embers, where a sister stirred a giant pot of groats. She showed her the dormitory where the nuns had their cells, and then took her back outside and introduced her to the weaving nuns who had spied on her bath.

Ginevra nodded shyly at their friendly greetings, her eyes drawn to the sparkling spools in their laps.

"The silk guild gives us gold to spin into threads for tapestries," Taddea explained. "We make money from this, from our eggs, and from leasing out the bakery across the street." Ginevra tried to absorb it all, amazed that a girl her own age could know so much about business.

"And HERE," said Taddea, taking Ginevra's arm and bringing her back to the other side of the yard, "is the garden where we grow all sorts of herbs and flowers that can't be bought anywhere else." Ginevra looked closer and saw that what she had taken for an ordinary vegetable garden was filled with all sorts of wonderful leaves and blossoms.

"Oh! Is this a…a plantain flower?" she asked, kneeling down.

"It is!" said Taddea. "How'd you know that? It's special for the women's ward."

"I've only seen it dried up before!" said Ginevra, excitedly.

"In Genoa, we'd use it to help with all sorts of things." Here she dropped her voice down. "Mostly for people's bottoms."

"That's what they use it for here, I think," said Taddea, not in the least bothered by talk of bottoms. "Now come with me to the chapel. It's the best part of the whole convent." She led them back through the nuns' dormitory to a discreet door that opened into the side of the sanctuary. They paused to cross themselves at the threshold, and stepped into the cool space, the interior frescoed all over with the tales of Christ and Santa Maria Magdalena.

"There," Taddea said, pointing to a carved wooden cupboard behind the altar, "is the relic for the church. Brought here by our founder, Fra Simone Fidati da Cascia."

Within the cupboard, Ginevra saw a large crucifix, a crystal orb fixed at its center. Something was suspended in the center of the orb.

"It's a piece of bread, soaked in the blood of Jesus Christ *himself*." Taddea crossed herself again and Ginevra followed suit.

"I've never seen such an important relic before, besides from far away in processions," Ginevra said, impressed that Taddea was allowed to just walk up and point to it whenever she felt inclined.

"It was a real, actual miracle. A parish priest put a piece of the host inside a book of prayers to bring to a sick person. When he opened up his book, the bread was soaked in the blood of Christ. He was afraid of it, so he brought it to Fra Simone."

"In my parish in Genoa, we just had a rock that touched a piece of San Francesco's robe once. I don't think it ever did any miracles."

"Well, this one does. All the women about to give birth

– we pray to the bread to keep them safe, and so far no mamas or babies have died, *ever*."

Ginevra looked at the extraordinary communion bread and crossed herself again. No mothers and no babies? This was unheard of. Vermilia must not have known about this relic, or she wouldn't have been so dismissive about praying to them.

"Anyhow," said Taddea, "I have to go help with supper now. Today is porridge day – actually, most days are porridge day, but I think you'll like it – oh! And can you run across the street to Ser Cecchi, the baker? His rent is due and we must collect it. Tell him I sent you. Thanks!"

And with this fragmented introduction to the Convent of Sant'Elisabetta delle Convertite, Ginevra began to settle into her new life. For a while, she worried Agnesa would ask her about the rattling stone in her purse, but days and weeks passed and it was not mentioned. Ginevra continued to wonder, though, why Vermilia thought this place, where coral amulets must be hidden, and where there was a relic that actually listened to healing prayers, was the right place to send a girl with witchcraft in her blood and a package of magic stones.

When Vermilia's letters began to arrive, they contained no answers, only the normal things: Messages of love from Ginevra's parents. A bit of gossip here and there. All this was transcribed by Vermilia's monk, and then Sister Agnesa and Ginevra would read them together – the nun using them as lessons. But in all the syllables and sentences that Ginevra painstakingly sounded out, never was there anything about Ginevra's aptitude for magic, about how Sant'Elisabetta was connected to the golden strings. So, she put questions of this nature in the back of her mind, and focused instead on the pleasant challenges of literacy and of learning to navigate her new city as she ran errands for the convent.

Every day, Ginevra was dazzled. Florence had its troubles, of course, but they were covered over with veneers of parti-colored marble and the nervous hands of its citizens were hidden, tucked into fur-lined cloaks. It was only in the large numbers of destitute women who came to seek help at Sant'Elisabetta – far more than pilgrims who sought lodging – did she notice the cracks in the facade of her new home.

Taddea explained to Ginevra that the women's ward was a bit of an open secret.

"Nobody talks about it, but everyone knows."

Prostitution was not permitted inside the city, but it flourished just on the other side of the Porta San Gallo. And even though extramarital affairs were practically the national pastime, an unwed mother was the most wretched creature in all of Italy, and there were not so many places that would care for them. Women who came to the convent were encouraged to stay and take the vow themselves, but not everyone was meant to be a nun, and many women preferred to return to their old lives. A very few who came were noble, whisked there by their mothers to carry their shame to term. These women paid large sums of money for discretion and private quarters. But rich or poor, no woman in the ward ever saw her man come back to marry her or claim his child.

THIRTEEN

DE LAPIDIBUS

1335, City of Florence,
Convent of Sant'Elisabetta delle Convertite

In the women's ward, as Ginevra gathered up the soiled reeds and emptied chamber pots, she kept a careful eye out to observe the nuns at their healing work. She noted the plasters that eased pain here, and the suppositories that erased discomfort there. She memorized the little prayers said to saints, prescribed alongside the physical medicines. And every time a baby was born, she went with the nuns to give thanks to the Relic of the Blessed Blood that sat inside its crystal orb in the chapel. But Ginevra never saw or heard anything about the packet of gemstones sent from Genoa. She would never ask about it, either, lest there be questions about the rattling rock she'd stolen. As for the common little amulets of stone or bone possessed by the women who came seeking help, there was no hint that Agnesa saw such objects as anything more than harmless superstitions – not quite approved of by the modern church, but generally tolerated for the comfort they brought.

Though she tried her best, Ginevra could not learn everything from eavesdropping. Particularly vexing was that whenever a challenging medical scenario arose, she was sent away and couldn't observe.

"It's not for you to see what happens next," Agnesa would say when a woman could not breathe in spite of the mustard plaster or stop vomiting long enough to get out the correct prayer to San Timoteo. Ginevra felt she was prepared for whatever unpleasantness came, that she was being unnecessarily coddled. After all, hadn't Monna Vermilia trusted her for years to witness important rituals and prepare delicate mixtures? She complained about this to Taddea, who nodded sympathetically.

"It's the same with me. Whenever Agnesa is about to make the most interesting medicine it's always *Taddea, go to the market for this* or *Taddea, go get this pot fixed*, even though the pot had a hole in it for *ages* and nobody ever cared."

One morning, as Ginevra cleared wooden eating bowls from the ward, she observed Sister Agnesa attending a breech birth. The poor mother had labored with difficulty a whole day and night, and now as dawn came on the second day, the leg of the child appeared and nothing more. The mother became still, white with fatigue on top of sheets brown with drying blood. She would not move her gaze to acknowledge her nurse, nor part her lips to receive a sip of water.

"Alright, so it comes to this," said Agnesa. She looked around, and spotted Ginevra. "You – come here a moment and give her your hand. I'll be right back." The nun walked away, as fast as she could without running. Ginevra's chest tightened – there was only one reason she would have left her charge at this moment: to fetch the priest for last rites before the baby was cut out of its dying mother. But Taddea said this never happened at Sant'Elisabetta! The mama must have sensed the danger, too, and through her unconsciousness, she clutched so hard at Ginevra's hand that her fingertips turned white and tingled.

Out of nervous habit, Ginevra put her other hand into her purse and fiddled with the brown rattling stone. As soon as she held it, the coral *figa* on her neck grew warm, as did the stone in the purse. The air around her began to vibrate, and all other sounds became muffled, as if she were underwater. She felt an irresistible urge to take out the stone and put it on the bed. In fact, she could have sworn the stone strained against her tightly closed fist. Ginevra glanced around furtively – it was just the two of them in the ward, her and the dying woman on the bed. She gave in to the strange rock, allowed it to pull her hand out of her purse and onto the bloody pallet, and place it down next to the child's leg.

The little foot immediately withdrew back into its mother. Her swollen belly roiled like a pot of soup, and then out came the head where the foot had been and the baby was born quickly and correctly. A moment later, out whooshed the afterbirth. The mother woke from her stupor, released Ginevra's hand, and asked if she might have a portion of wine. Before the mightily shocked Ginevra could gather her wits and take back the stone, Sister Agnesa was at her side.

"Thank Mary and all the saints! The brave girl managed it on her own." She picked up the baby and slapped it until it bawled. Ginevra tried to surreptitiously grab the stone back, but Agnesa's quick eyes followed her hand and saw the little rock there on the sheets. She gasped and snatched it away, hiding it inside her palm.

"Fool, fool, how long has the eaglestone been lying here??" Agnesa hissed.

"Just a moment…"

"Did my careless cousin give you this?"

Ginevra hung her head, and Agnesa's eyes widened with understanding.

"So you helped yourself, then, to a package meant for me, to a thing you don't understand?"

"But, it *worked*! And, you know what it's called? An eaglestone?"

Agnesa bit her lip.

The new mother again asked for wine.

"Ginevra, go and fetch this thirsty lady a drink. Then come straight away to my cell."

Ginevra left the fuming Sister Agnesa clutching the infant, and went to pour a draft of wine with shaking hands. She was terrified of what she had done. She had stolen something, something that compelled her to use it carelessly. She thought of the thieves in Genoa who became beggars after their hands were cut off for their crimes. Would they do that to her?

She touched quickly her coral to make sure it was still there, that this was not caused by the *malocchio* finally come back for her. The jewel lay at her collarbone, where it always did. Whatever punishment was coming her way, she had brought to her own self. Maybe Fra Simone would excommunicate her, when he was told what she did, and after a miserable, handless life she would go straight to hell and be tortured for eternity. But under these fearful thoughts there was something else: anger. She had saved a woman's life and was in trouble for it.

FOURTEEN

THE GOATS LED ME HERE

July 7th of 1348, Streets of Florence

Ginevra leaned against the door of the inquisitor's palazzo and shook herself free from the memories of her early years in Florence. Right. The sooner she solved the inquisitor's "small problem," the sooner she could fix her own. She looked across the piazza to the messy construction site of the new cathedral, which seemed no closer to being finished than it had eight years earlier. It had been only partially built for as long as she could remember, the massive foundations of this new building enclosing the original, intact cathedral of Santa Reparata. The site was covered with tatty wood scaffolding, and at the top of one platform a stonemason, still holding his hammer, had crawled up to die in the sun. Birds were picking at him, a feast with a view. This was the place from which the relic of San Zenobio had been stolen.

She must start investigating right away, perhaps by examining the cathedral? Three days was not much time. But her stomach rumbled loudly, and she realized that she'd had a long and arduous morning without food or drink, and was now standing in the full heat of the afternoon. Her mind was strained with the loss of Piero. The remembering of Sant'Elisabetta. The death of Ludovico. The empty reliquary of Zenobio would wait until she found a place to settle her own bones. But where could she go? Her internal map of the city was outdated. New buildings had altered the pattern of streets since her departure eight years earlier, and the paths leading out of the Piazza della Santa Reparata were not as she remembered. Without Piero as her guide, she had no idea where she might find lodging.

She sat down on a bit of quarrystone, and looked around to make sure nobody was watching. From her bag of gems, Ginevra plucked a limpid green smaragdus, which was supposed to bring clarity, focus, and guidance. She had never been able to make it work properly, but now was as good a time as any to try. She stared into its minty depths, and willed her mind to empty so the stone could do its work. Her thoughts went immediately to Sant'Elisabetta. She saw Taddea, Fra Simone, and Sister Agnesa kneeling before the blessed bread. But even after eight years, the shame burned hot and she wished to wash her memory like a sheet.

"No!" she said out loud to the smaragdus.

She put the stone away, told herself it still wasn't working properly, and watched as a dusty white goose walked into the square, followed by a herd of emaciated goats who had adopted him as their leader. Ginevra couldn't help but laugh at the band of misfits. She thought for a minute and then walked over to join them – a sight so merry was good luck, in times like these. They must have been sent specifically to get her attention.

She was with them about an hour, twisting through residential streets, seeing no other human soul the whole while. No breeze stirred. The animals let out not a single bleat or honk. Everywhere doors were left ajar to what were recently well-tended and busy homes. Foul odors wafted through open windows, where now-gone neighbors had been too afraid to retrieve the dead for burial.

The sun was directly overhead, casting no shadow, when they arrived at the church of Santa Trinita. At this, Ginevra lost faith in her goose leader. She was familiar with this spot and knew it was only a short distance from where they had started. She began looking at the empty homes with an eye for one that might do for her own shelter when she heard a loud BANG. The door of a fine palazzo flung open twenty yards ahead. A man, welldressed, though quite disheveled, blinked in the sunlight and let out a deep sigh of relief that he stifled when he saw Ginevra and her companions. Before man, woman, or goat could say anything, a piteous cry escaped from a window of the building the man had just exited.

"Come back, come back, my lord!" called the voice, with wheezes and rasps.

The animals jerked their heads in unison toward the sound. The man glanced at the window, cast a pained look at Ginevra, and said, "I'm just…going to find the…thing!" And then he ran away.

The voice cried out again, "Come back, my lord, I'm still alive! Perhaps I won't die! Please, don't leave me all alone!" The goats looked expectantly at Ginevra, who thanked them for their company and shooed them on. She walked through the loggia at the front of the building; in his haste to depart, the disheveled man hadn't locked his front door. She entered into the dark courtyard of a fine home.

"Hello?" Ginevra called up the stairs that ran round the courtyard, blessedly cool against the afternoon heat. "Who is there?"

The cries stopped. The stench of yesterday's death lived in this house. Up the steps to the second floor, through a great hall, the floor covered with rotten salad leaves and old pork bones, she came to a door that was locked from her own side, the key still in its hole. She turned it and the door swung open into a finely appointed bedroom. A young woman lay on the floor next to a bucket of black bile. She was crumpled below the high open window, having collapsed with the effort of shouting after the escaping man. She was pale and her dark hair stuck to her sweaty forehead. At her throat, the swollen nodes of advanced disease. Ginevra looked around the room and saw a foot sticking out from a stained sheet in the corner; the source of the death smell.

She asked from the doorway, "Can you speak still, my darling? What is your name?"

"I am Lucia," she wheezed. "Where is my husband?"

Ginevra had no more tolerance for absent men. "Think of him no more, the worthless fool has fled."

Lucia breathed in to begin a sob, but her throat was so swollen she stifled herself and then lay back down on the floor in exhaustion. Ginevra's hand dipped into the purse at her waist and her fingers were drawn to two bloodstones, recently acquired. They thumped like little hearts at her touch. She'd had no opportunity to use them yet, was not sure if they might cause more harm than good to a sick body. There was another wretched gasp from poor Lucia. She could barely breathe. One thing was certain: the lady was sure to die without intervention.

Ginevra raised her eyes to the heavens. Here she was, just an hour after swearing to a papal inquisitor that she would perform no medicine. But how could she withhold help from this poor woman? *Well,* she told herself, *my mistake last time wasn't healing people. It was being caught.* "I am going to come into your room now, Monna Lucia, do not be afraid."

Lucia said nothing. This woman had clearly come to rob her home. At least she could have waited until Lucia was properly dead! This new woman, Lucia observed, did not share her husband's fear of infection. How greedy, to risk your life for linens and chairs. It would serve her right when her own throat was swelling up like a toad's. But the new woman did not go to the painted bridal chest, where things of value might be stored. Lucia watched with unfocused eyes as the thief moved aside the bucket of vomit and knelt down in its place.

"I am called Ginevra di Genoa. It is within my knowledge to cure you...I think...but you must promise that you will keep my secret."

Lucia wondered if this was the devil, tricking her into bargaining away her soul... Were there any demons named Ginevra? She couldn't remember. But her fear was superseded by anger toward her husband, and she thought of how shamed he would be if she got better and arrived, unannounced and alive, at the country estate (her inheritance), where he had surely gone.

"Listen," said Ginevra di Genoa. "I believe the goats led me to you for a reason. But you must promise you'll keep my secret. Tell no one if I cure you."

Lucia tried to speak but only bloody bubbles came out of her mouth.

"If you promise, squeeze my hand." Lucia did not understand about the goats, but she understood she didn't want to die and with her last strand of energy gave Ginevra's hand the faintest little squeeze. Lucia then blacked out into nothingness.

Ginevra set to work, pulling out the two speckled bloodstones from her leather pouch. They were darkest green dotted with flecks of red iron. A long time ago, they had been polished into smooth ovals and inscribed with runes by the priestess who first blessed them. Like the eaglestone so long ago at Sant'Elisabetta, Ginevra let the rocks guide her hand. She placed the stones against the swellings that protruded from Lucia's throat, willing her own health to flow through them and push out the disease. At least, that's how she hoped it would work. The thrumming sound she now knew as familiar filled the air and the stones' heartbeats went faster, faster until they were buzzing. She held them firmly against the swellings, her fingertips growing numb, her hands cramping from the vibrations. Lucia began to spasm, arms flapping and slapping, back arching, mouth chomping. And then with a terrible, rasping gasp she became still and collapsed flat against the floor. *Oh, God, I've killed her*, thought Ginevra. She took the stones away and broke out in a cold panic-sweat.

"HUNGGGHGHH." Lucia sat straight up and dry-heaved. Ginevra screamed in surprise and jumped away. The sick woman leaned her head forward and a large black glop fell out of her mouth and onto her lap, and she collapsed again onto the floor. Ginevra crept back to her and listened. Lucia's faint and ragged breaths became slow and even. The swellings on her neck shrank into dark purple bruises. A hand on the forehead proved the fever had broken. Ginevra laughed out loud and sat back on the floor, legs splayed in front of her. Lucia would live. The bloodstones *worked*. For the first time in years, she actually felt good about herself.

Now Ginevra finally took in all the details of her surroundings. She was in the town house of a well-to-do merchant. The family must have been without proper help for months, and the palazzo was cluttered with the detritus of daily life. The fireplace was full of ash, dirty sheets were upon the bed. *Right,* she thought, *let's get poor abandoned Monna Lucia off the floor.*

She opened the painted wedding chest. There were sheets inside of very fine Flanders lace, and shifts of transparent linen, trimmed in cream silk. Things that should not be used for a sick and dirty body, but they were all that was at hand. She remade the bed and with some effort, removed Lucia's ruined nightshift and lifted her onto the mattress. Ginevra's head spun with the exertion, and she remembered her hunger and thirst.

With Lucia asleep in her finest sheets, Ginevra went up to the top floor, where the kitchens were located in such homes, so if they caught fire, the house below might be saved. It was a massive room with red tile floors and creamy plaster walls. The unadorned plaster was in contrast to the colorful faux tapestries frescoed on the walls of the living spaces. She went to the three large windows and opened the shutters, letting in sunlight. She was relieved to see there were still a few provisions. There was a bin of barley flour, half a wheel of hard cheese, a box of lard, and a sticky plate of honeycomb (now rather dusty). Hanging from the rafters, a desiccated link of dark red salami, two salted fish, and bundles of rosemary, lavender, and sorrel.

Taking up an entire wall of the kitchen, the great hearth, big enough to roast a boar in, gaped black and cold before her. Among the ashes was a large iron cauldron that in better times was kept bubbling with soup bones. On the wooden table, where the longgone cook had once trussed rabbits and shucked oysters, a rat nibbled at a nub of stale bread.

She shooed away the rat and took the bread, scraping off hard bites with her teeth. The crumbs coated her parched throat and made her cough. Just outside the kitchen, she saw a small cupboard that opened into a shaft, containing a winch to draw up water from a cistern under the house. Ginevra tried to turn the crank, but it did not budge. She didn't want to risk breaking it. So she walked all the way down the stairs, stopping at the dirty dining table on the second floor to pick up a fine painted beaker, laughing to see it was the same pattern favored by the inquisitor – chickens eating grapes – and into the cellar below the courtyard.

In the dim light, among leaking oil jugs and scampering mice, were a heartening number of barrels stacked neatly against the wall. She poured herself a healthy portion from an already-tapped hogshead. A normal sip was quickly followed by a deep draught, for in her thirst it seemed finer than any drink she'd tasted before. In truth it was only *vinello*, the mild "little wine" that everyone drank daily. But it was fizzy and tart and slightly cool from the dark room it was stored in. She dipped the hard bread into her cup to soften it, allowing her to take the first real bite.

Off to the side of the cellar was a cistern that collected rainwater, funneled from roof gutters and a drain in the center of the courtyard. She looked into it and saw it was filled with blind eels, who ate the eggs of mosquitoes that grew in the water, and were also delicious when baked in pies. With her *vinello* and bread, she walked back up to the ground floor courtyard and through a rear door to find an octagonal plot enclosing a now-overgrown garden. A fountain burbled in the center of the space, surrounded by four symmetrical planting beds that contained a good number of onions, savory herbs, and flowering nasturtiums. Gnarled quince trees provided shade for benches placed between the beds. The stone walls of the enclosure were mostly covered by apple trees that had been trained so their branches grew flat like vines against the stones instead of out in all directions. Pecking their way around the onion tops were two peacocks, who remained ignorant of the present chaos, living happily off worms and fallen apples.

In this space of calm and luxury, clutching her fancy new cup, Ginevra felt the mild potency of the *vinello* take effect. For a moment, she forgot to feel anxious about the great tragedy through which she was living. But only for a moment. And then she went back upstairs to drag the dead maid out to the curb for the next morning's body collector. Here she was, among compatriots. One woman living, one woman dead. And herself, feeling somewhere in between. All of them left alone.

FIFTEEN

A TRUE AND ACTUAL SECRET

1335, City of Florence,
Convent of Sant'Elisabetta delle Convertite

After the eaglestone incident, Ginevra sat alone with Sister Agnesa upon a straw mattress in the nun's plain little cell, the intimate proximity at odds with the serious mood.

"Do you know why I picked up the stone so quickly from the bed?"

"No," Ginevra said quietly.

"I took it, because if an eaglestone is left too long, it will pull the woman's womb out along with the baby. Or did my cousin not teach you that part?"

"No! I had no understanding. I wouldn't have – I didn't even know there *was* such a thing as an eaglestone. I've never seen one work before."

"Never?" said Agnesa, scratching under her gray veil. "You mean you got it to work, just like that?"

"Yes, I swear it – it's just something that's always in my purse – it was like the stone *told* me somehow, that it would help get the baby out. I didn't know about the womb part. Please, I thought you were going to cut her all up."

"No, ignorant girl. Such a thing would not happen here."

"I know, I know. The Relic of the Blessed Blood. It protects them."

"No. Well, maybe. I don't know, I haven't pressed it to work on its own."

The nun opened her hand and placed two stones on the bed, Ginevra's and another, nearly identical. The rocks drew toward each other across the rough woolen blanket and settled together with a gentle *snap*. "I went to fetch my own old eaglestone, for in this you were correct: the time had come when there was no other way...normally it requires rigorous training, to work the stone properly, to hear what it is telling you. But you have done it all on your own."

"Sister, will you not teach me? I thought that was why—"

"Ginevra, you arrived here with a letter and a package. We both know you were aware of the contents of the package. But do you know what the letter said?"

The girl's cheeks burned. She shook her head. "You know I could not read when I came here."

Agnesa gave a great sigh. "The letter absolves you from the wicked sin you meant to commit – that of *stealing*. The gems have always been yours, a gift from my cousin. But entrusted to me to keep safe. Until I could determine if it was correct for you to have them."

Ginevra whipped up her head: "So *is* it correct, now that I know about the womb part?"

"Ha! Absolutely not. Letting a *rock* – albeit a magic one – force your hand to action. Shame. But – also it is clear to me that my cousin was right – you have a gift, an ability above others to direct the healing properties. When God grants a person such abilities, it is another sort of sin not to use them."

"Please, Sister. I'll do whatever you say. Only teach me."

Agnesa turned to face her fully and looked at her with hard eyes out of place with the kindly crow's-feet that framed them. "Listen here – the fact that we access methods such as this – this is a true secret. Not like the secret of the women's ward, which everybody knows about. I mean a true and actual secret. If Fra Simone found out—"

"Why are you here, then, at a convent? Why not work on your own, like Vermilia?"

"Because it is the priest's reputation as a holy man that gives us protection. Who would think to look for healing magic – or what many would call sorcery – in the house of such a saint?"

"But sorcerers speak to the dead! They call on demons to do their bidding. The stones, the medicines, the spoken charms your cousin taught me, they work just because – well I don't know why, but I know I never spoke to a demon."

"But you can see how the ignorant believe such things. Do you understand what would happen if others learned that within these walls, nuns make God's magic flow through heathen stones?"

Ginevra understood, but she did not like it. *This* was why Monna Vermilia disguised her talents, and why Agnesa had made her keep the coral amulet a secret. To know of the magic that resided in natural things, to be able to channel and use it – it scared those who could not.

"Now that you know, here is how it will be," said Agnesa. "If you wish to learn the secrets of the stones, and one day take custody of Vermilia's gift, you must never speak of this outside our walls, never in front of any of the women lying in. Not even Taddea, who, bless her, does not have the abilities you do. And NEVER in front of our founder. Do you swear all this?"

"Yes, I swear it."

"And you will never again attempt to use a healing stone without my explicit permission so long as you are here. Do you swear it?"

Ginevra swore it, for what else could she do?

"Good. You may go now. I'll summon you when I have time for lessons to begin."

Ginevra stood to leave, but one last question burned in her

and she couldn't help but to ask it: "Sister... If we can save those who come to the convent, what about the ladies in the rest of the city?"

"Child. Your desire to do good is commendable, but it is naive, and I grow weary. We only help those who seek us out. This is for our own safety. I assume my cousin keeps similar habits? You must accept that my counsel is correct if you wish to stay."

Ginevra nodded and hurried away, not wanting to push her good fortune any further.

From then on, while the rest of the convent slept, the two of them worked together to identify Monna Vermilia's gems and make sense of their powers. Their studies were aided by another secret of Agnesa's: a noble lady who once delivered a bastard at the convent donated her dead husband's library in thanks. In this collection were many wonderful manuscripts, including ones written long ago by the Romans and Greeks, on the secrets of natural history. Inside were descriptions of stones and their appearances and useful properties. Properties that modern physicians could hardly ever get to work. Agnesa knew better, and kept the manuscripts for herself, hiding them beneath loose tiles under her mattress.

"These books are the real things, the sources of truth," said Agnesa, lovingly tapping a moth-eaten volume of Theophrastus. "The old information, not messed with or misinterpreted by some self-important monk who couldn't feel the vibrations of a golden string if it were tied to his prod—"

Ginevra stifled a laugh.

"Enough of that, tell me – what is this?" The nun held up a round stone, nut-brown and shiny like a leather button. Ginevra reached for a volume by Pliny, ready to plow ahead with the rudimentary Latin Agnesa had been teaching her along with her reading lessons. But Agnesa pushed the book out of reach. "No. No. Just hold the rock. Let it guide you, as you did with the eaglestone." Ginevra pressed the strange stone between her two hands so it looked as if she were praying. It became warm in her palms, and so did the coral upon her neck. She stood up and looked out the doorway, then crept through the dark hallways toward the kitchen, Agnesa following her with a rush light. In the kitchen, Ginevra's hands went like a dowsing rod to a barrel of rye flour. "My hands...are so *sweaty*," she whispered.

"Are you sure? Open them."

"Aha," said the pupil, "it is the *stone* that sweats."

Agnesa nodded. "Now I will tell you – this is the toadstone, it comes from the heads of old toads. It sweats when brought near poison so, if you'll take the lid off that barrel..."

Ginevra lifted the lid and sure enough fluffy white mold had spotted the surface of the dark flour.

"Very good," said the nun. "About the toadstone, I mean. You clearly need a different lesson on how to properly store food."

Back in Agnesa's cell, she picked up the Pliny, looking for more information about toadstones; as she leafed through, a small thin volume fell out from the pages.

"What is this?" she asked Agnesa. The binding crackled and flaked under her fingers as they traced golden letters. "*Liber Iuratus Polydorus* – who is Polydorus, Sister?"

"Ginevra, do not—"

But already she was flipping through the pages. Upon papyrus sheets, she saw strange symbols, circles inside stars, lists of names with Latin letters spelling guttural syllables, strings of words arranged into triangles. Agnesa slapped it from her hands.

"What *was* that??" asked Ginevra.

"Shhh. An evil thing – for men who believe they can summon demons to do their bidding. Books like this give our work a bad name, Ginevra. They lure the ignorant into chasing base and selfish desires by placing pins into dolls, baking hair into bread, writing chaotic arrangements of letters and numbers."

"You mean – the spells in this book are fraudulent?"

"Probably. But who can know? For only a saint could perform them, and no saint would ever try. Books like this are all the same, look here—" she said, pointing to a page " – it dictates months of fasting, of chastity, of punishing the body with scourges and hair shirts as prerequisite for a spell to obtain a thousand armed soldiers! Here I am in agreement with the priests: to attempt these rituals is surely a crime against God."

Agnesa tried to stuff the book into the little clay brazier she kept burning in her room for warmth, but no matter her angle of approach, it would not fit, and not even a corner of it became charred. The nun sighed and tucked the book carefully back into the hidden space under the floor.

"Now," she said to Ginevra, "let us return our attention to Theophrastus: he says here the antipathy stone may be worn at the wrist to absorb unpleasant memories – I think we have one of those somewhere – and here he discusses the lyngurium stone, which is the crystallized urine of a lynx. Lyngurium has many virtues – but, unfortunately we do not have this stone. In fact, I've never known anyone who's seen a lyngurium, for the lynx buries her treasures…"

When Ginevra was good enough at writing, Agnesa had the parchment of the convent's earliest records scraped clean and bound together into a blank book so her pupil could keep her own notes. *Here is the green crystal called smaragdus, carved with sacred words of the Arabians. Look upon it when your eyes are weary and you will see with fresh perspective.* Or: *Here is shimmering black obsidian, made by the heat of volcanoes. It is good against fevers.*

Ginevra was grateful for the lessons, but still, beneath it all, there was that tiny current of skepticism that most young people have, that her elders were *too* cautious. That if she was just given the chance to try things openly, then Fra Simone and the physicians' guild and everyone else would understand that there was nothing sinister in women's use of healing stones.

This sense of lost opportunity was even more acute on days when the stones called to Ginevra and her fingers tingled to use them. But unless it was a matter of life or death, Agnesa insisted on standard herbal remedies, on prayer and patience. What might be resolved in an instant with a hematite rinsed in rainwater instead took weeks of drinking tea made from agrimony and oak leaves. Ginevra found the whole thing maddening. It went this way for some time. In the middle of the night, Ginevra and Agnesa explored the mysteries of striped agates and red carbuncles. In the daytime, they pretended these treasures did not exist. Only when Agnesa decided a patient was beyond the help of prayers or of plants, did she reach under the loose tiles in her cell.

SIXTEEN

A LOVING SPIRIT

1340, City of Florence,
the Kitchen of a Great House

When Ginevra was twenty, she fell in love. It happened when she was making a delivery of eggs from Sant'Elisabetta to the kitchens of the Acciaiuoli family, who were such important bankers that they lent money to the king of England, or so they bragged. Ginevra disliked this particular errand. Every week the bankers' cook condescended to her how the Acciaiuoli only bought from the convent out of charity, how the eggs were not any good and that was why his custards never turned out properly. This was very frustrating to Ginevra. She knew their chickens were the finest in Florence, because Agnesa had found a piece of Sardinian pink granite that was just the exact shape of a hen egg and buried it in the floor of the coop. Ever since, each of their hens laid two perfect eggs, speckled and pink like the granite, exactly as the sun rose. Of course, she could not explain this to the cook.

On one of these occasions, Ginevra looked with exasperation past the grumbling chef and was startled to meet eyes with a young man, his smooth face brimming with suppressed laughter. Ginevra looked to the floor, embarrassed. For this young man was not a servant of her own station. He wore a flocked doublet woven in blue checks. His hat matched it perfectly.

"Gentiluccio, if you go on harassing vendors like this, we're all going to starve."

The cook turned around to face the young man. "Signore Ludovico! What are you doing here? You'll get your nice hat all smoky."

"I just wanted a—" He looked at Ginevra again and stopped speaking.

"A what?" asked the cook.

"I – I've forgotten somehow. Introduce me to your friend."

"Who, her? She works for the egg nuns. Don't worry about it, she's gone."

And Ginevra was, as fast as she could go.

But Ludovico Acciaiuoli could not forget her. Because it is true that the eyes are a window to the soul; it is therefore not just the *malocchio* that may use them as a portal, but also Love. So when Ludovico and Ginevra had locked eyes, her invisible golden strings became tangled with his plain strings of cat-gut or whatever type of string the universe attaches to ordinary men. And when she hurried out of the room, their strings stretched and twisted further round each other, and bound them in sweet longing.

For Ludovico, this manifested as the overwhelming and immediate urge to impress Ginevra. It was not something he was used to feeling. As the eldest son of an important family, he was used to women trying to impress *him*, and he was all but immune to the chemically whitened necks and carefully plucked foreheads of his young lady peers. But Ginevra – to his eye, she needed no sculpting, no bleaching, or other artifice. He concluded a donation of provisions to the convent would be appropriate. When Ginevra came with Taddea to accept the gift, he remained unnecessarily involved in the transaction. He was polite to Taddea, of course, but upon Ginevra, he heaped an embarrassment of attention. As his father's servants filled a cart with luxurious foodstuffs, he gazed deeply into Ginevra's eyes and asked her hundreds of mundane questions, nodding intently at her answers and repeating them aloud as if to commit her words to memory.

"And where is your family?"

"Genoa, sir."

"Genoa. Yes. And what does your father do?"

"He...he fishes, sir."

"He fishes. Of course. The sea. It's there, isn't it?"

Ginevra, doing her best to ignore the pull of her golden strings, was cautious in her answers. She felt not only the gaze of Ludovico but also of Taddea, whose own eyes were wide with disapproval.

With provisions loaded, Ludovico offered Ginevra a formal goodbye, extending his arm in a low bow. As a result of the gesture, his hand touched hers. Just a tiny bit. The slightest little brush, really. Barely a fingernail. So quick it might not have happened at all. But she knew it had happened. She knew because she felt it from the tips of her toes to the hairs on her head.

The two women walked back to the convent in stiff silence, afraid to speak a dangerous thing into existence. A cart loaded with salami and peaches followed behind them.

As soon as they left, Ludovico locked himself in his studio to write Ginevra a poem:

Your dress is brown
Your skin like down
Your friend is just fine
But you must be mine

Ludovico at least had the good sense to be embarrassed of his poetry, and threw draft after draft into the fire until he decided it would be much easier to just borrow a few lines from Dante. Impatient in his task by this point, he modified them hastily, sent the note out with his servant, and devoted himself to pacing anxiously until Ginevra replied.

Knowing he couldn't approach Ginevra at the convent, the servant went to the bakery across from Sant'Elisabetta and waited. To pass the time he stuffed himself with bread and flirted with the good wives who came to have their clay-potted suppers cooked inside the bakery's giant ovens. At last, the bread-bloated servant saw Ginevra exit the convent. He gave the baker a look so he knew to busy himself at the oven, and then went and pressed a letter into her palm. "Read it here," he said, "and give me your reply straightaway."

With trembling fingers, she unfolded the note, eyes flying over the words – could this all really be for her?

My Dearest,

That day in the kitchen I felt a marvelous trembling that started on the left side of my chest and spread rapidly throughout my entire body. I raised my eyes and saw that most gracious of creatures, Beatrice. My spirits were overcome by the force of love.

"But this is not for me," she cried. "This is for some Beatrice!"

The clever servant read the note and realized at once what had happened – in his haste, Ludovico forgot to switch out the name of Dante's beloved Beatrice for Ginevra.

"Dama, be assured! I would not misdeliver a message of this importance. Beatrice is…a pet name! That's right, a pet name Ser Ludovico has bestowed upon you, Ginevra, the object of his affection."

"You swear it?"

"Of course." The servant already had many lies he must confess; this one did not bother him.

Ginevra's earlier resolve gave way to the delicious pull of mutual connection. She cut a blank page from her notebook – the notebook Agnesa scraped clean for her to record the magic of the stones – to write back that she always brought eggs to the house on Thursdays, and perhaps if Ludovico requested more custards from his cook, she could come on Mondays as well. He wrote back right away and said that custard was his favorite dish.

And then it was ritual. Twice a week, they would flirt in the Acciaiuoli kitchens, as the long-suffering cook boiled custard after custard between them. Ludovico would ask egg-related questions, and call her his Beatrice. She would laugh every time. But it was clear to the both of them (and also to the cook) that this was not enough. With the help of Ludovico's bread-loving servant, they arranged clandestine meetings in ancient chapels where nobody came to pray anymore. They stood close to each other on cracked stone floors, clasping hands and whispering their secrets.

"My family would not be pleased to know of the time I spent with you, a poor person, but I am my own man," Ludovico would say.

"Well, I'm not just an ordinary peasant," answered Ginevra, so eager to please she forgot to be insulted.

"Really?" said Ludovico, so eager to please he forgot to sound incredulous.

"Really." She explained all that Monna Vermilia told her, all that was meant to be her own particular secret – about her blood being special, and how she could work healing wonders with stones.

"Is that what has happened?" he teased. "Have you put a love charm on me?"

"No! No, that's not the sort of thing – I would never do that to you…"

He put his hands upon her waist. "It's alright, even if you did, for I have never been so happy."

Soon they were sneaking out in the gray dawn to make love against the walls of forgotten gardens. Ludovico wasn't very good at it, but Ginevra didn't know any better and luxuriated in his rough pressings, his eager hands. She did know, at least, how to avoid becoming pregnant. A mixture of pomegranate seed and alum, applied at the correct time. The compound must have made up half of Monna Vermilia's business. Now the alum, bought from an alchemist who winked at her, took up more than half her meager salary.

"Taddea," she asked her friend one day, "do you think you would like to have a husband and children?"

"No, I would not," said Taddea without blinking.

"I think it might be nice."

"Once you are married, you work like a slave cleaning up after your man while he lazes about waiting for you to cook him supper."

"Of course – but – what if you married a *rich* man, who had his own cook?"

"That's a foolish question – no rich man would ever marry me – or you, for that matter. They need to marry a woman who's rich also, or at least one of noble family. Otherwise, they won't stay rich. Is this to do with Ser Ludovico?"

"No," Ginevra lied. "I was just wondering."

"I know how often you go to the kitchens in his palazzo."

"They are our best customers!" she retorted. "In fact, I am going there today, right now." She shook her straw-filled basket in Taddea's direction.

Her friend rolled her eyes. "And why do you think they're such loyal customers? Do you know how many women come here, disgraced by the greedy men of that family? The Acciaiuoli buy from our hens as a favor for the *many* services rendered to them by the nuns of Sant'Elisabetta."

"You are jealous, Taddea, that Ser Ludovico spoke more to me than to you." She hated how awful she sounded, but could not help herself.

Taddea looked back at her, hurt. "Nothing good will come of it, I'm telling you."

"And what would you know of such things, speaking only to nuns your whole life?"

"Yes, but before they were nuns, they were prostitutes."

Ginevra hurried away from the conversation, toward

Ludovico's home, as if she could outrun the truth her friend had spoken. She knew Taddea was right, that for *most* women this would be a dangerous situation. But she was not most women. She was one of the lucky ones. Had she not been told since she was a child that she was privy to the wisdom of old? To knowledge not accessible to ordinary women? Besides, had she not dreamed up this very situation? For a man of Ludovico's station to raise her up? If Taddea only understood how deeply Ludovico was devoted to her, she wouldn't be so skeptical. So what if other men in his family were typical scoundrels? Ludo was different. He had given her a pet name, after all, and once, when they were up against the garden wall, he said he loved her with the gentle and spontaneous tone of one who truly means it.

"Beatrice?"

Startled, she saw the man himself in front of her. Lost in thought, she had already arrived at his doorstep.

"Is everything alright?"

She did not answer, for how could she say that it was his own hypothetical misdeeds that furrowed her brow. Ludovico took the basket from her hands.

"It will rain soon," he said, looking up at the gray sky. "I know – I will take you somewhere to be dry, and there you will tell me what bothers you."

He took Ginevra by the hand and guided her through a maze of alleyways she had never explored, until they arrived at what appeared to be a disused shop. Ludo opened the door with a key, and led her through the empty storefront, up a long staircase, and into the most beautifully appointed apartment she had ever seen. "We keep this place for business associates who are visiting from out of town," Ludo said by way of explanation.

Ginevra looked around in wonder. The walls were dove gray, burnished to a satiny glow and accented with elaborate moldings of vermilion plaster. Beneath furniture in polished woods and soft peach velvets was a flocked carpet woven with flowers that bloomed in every color of nature's palate. The ceiling was painted blue with gold stars, and the shutters were decorated with patterns of green parakeets that stood, jewel-like, upon a gilt field. Above the shutters, round transoms paned with fine slices of alabaster bathed the room and the two lovers in an ethereal gold light. Ludo opened the shutters to a view of the rooftops of Florence. "Come stand by the window – I want to see all that is mine together, you and the city."

"You are greedy," she teased, obliging him and leaning on the sill.

"I am a rich man," he said, placing his hands around her waist and pulling her close. "So I am greedy, but also I am generous." Raindrops began to pat against the alabaster panes. Ginevra closed her eyes and they fell into each other, and when she opened them again, the gold light had faded into purple dusk.

After, as they lay intertwined upon the colorful carpets, he asked again, "What was it that troubled my Beatrice this afternoon?"

She thought for a long while, her head resting upon his chest, her mind replaying the conversation with Taddea.

"I know," she said, finally, "that I am not the sort of woman that would – excite the admiration of your family."

"Which is precisely why I am excited about you."

"You are excited here in this dark room, when nobody is around to know about us."

"Yes, very," he answered, and began to let his hands wander anew.

"Please, I'm being serious—"

Ludovico squeezed her tight to him and kissed the top of her head. "I know, I know you are. You are my life. Do not doubt it. I will find a way."

Ginevra curled into the crook of his arm, afraid to utter another word, afraid to show her happiness, for it was so great she was sure it would scare him away if he knew the extent of his powers.

* * *

She slipped back through the gate of Sant'Elisabetta just before the city's curfew began, and nearly jumped out of her skin at Taddea standing by the door, wringing her hands.

"What are you doing here?" asked Ginevra, still angry from their earlier conversation.

"Waiting for you – I'm supposed to tell you to go to Sister Agnesa's cell straightaway."

"What for? What has happened?"

"Ginevra, don't be upset – I was worried about you – I told her how you and Ludovico Acciaiuoli have become... particular friends—"

"How could you?? This will ruin everything—"

Taddea turned red in the face. "It is for your own good." She walked away toward their shared room and, fuming, Ginevra went to Agnesa's cell.

She knocked and entered. "Taddea knows not of what she speaks—"

"Ginevra – you're a fool if you've allowed an Acciaiuoli to charm you. But I cannot chastise you tonight. I don't have the heart – child, bad news has found its way to us. My dear cousin, your teacher..." She covered her mouth with her hand and held out a letter. Ginevra knelt beside her and read:

For my Ginevra,

Your mother and father send you their love and say they pray for you daily and look with joy toward the day you may be reunited. And I, Vermilia, say to you what you have long known – dear one, my time is now, as the stone told me, and you shall not hear from me again. Be glad for me; I am curious to know the broader reaches of God's kingdom as I have known His earth.

I send you the ring, which told me of my hour. It is the last gem I kept, but I need it no longer. It has diverse powers, only a few of which have been revealed to me. Perhaps you may divine more. What I do know is that each of the stone's powers may be used but once. So do not bother asking it for your death date – I have already drained it of that ability.

I have saved the ring for you for another reason: because you are prone to act on instinct, without considering consequences. If you find yourself in danger after offending the wrong person, this stone can help. It has the power to change even the most stubborn minds. This is my last gift to you, who has been so willing a pupil, when I had no daughter of my own.

The letter ended with a note from the monk, saying he would not be transcribing any further correspondence from Ginevra's parents, as he could not bear to be reminded of his sweet Vermilia. Ginevra held the parchment in both hands, staring at it, willing the letters to rearrange themselves into any other message. All the years she had been in Florence, she had never once tried to go home. The letters had tricked her – they had kept coming and given her a false security that – that what? That Vermilia would live forever?

Into her hand, Agnesa placed Vermilia's ring, set with its orange gem, engraved with a winged woman atop a wheel. Ginevra knew now, from her studies, that the stone was jasper, and the winged woman was Nemesis, pagan goddess of retribution. She turned it over and saw a Greek spell carved on its reverse, where it would touch the flesh of whoever wore the ring. She placed it on her left hand, as Vermilia had worn it, and left the room. Agnesa, face buried in her hands, did not try to stop her, though she still closely guarded the rest of Ginevra's inherited stones.

In her own room, Ginevra lay down on her stomach, shoved her face into her bedding, and sobbed. Taddea came over and apologized profusely for snitching about Ludovico; Ginevra did not bother to correct her by explaining the true meaning behind her tears. Her time with Ludo in his beautiful room seemed a thousand years past. How could one day contain such joy and such sorrow?

SEVENTEEN

LUCIA, TORN APART

July 7th of 1348, City of Florence,
the Palazzo Tornaparte

Lucia awoke, alone in her room. A sinking sun cast long shadows through her narrow window, shutters open to the outside for the first time in many weeks. She wondered if she was dead, but if that were so, she'd be in hell since nobody had heard her last confession, and surely hell would be worse than her own empty room. Slowly, her brain separated the weird fever dreams from reality. She remembered her husband's cruel departure and her wordless promise, made earlier that afternoon, to a woman who listened to goats. Was that stranger still in her house? She touched her throat. The hated swellings were gone.

She found she had strength to prop up onto her elbows, and noticed several pleasant changes had occurred while she slept. Most obviously, the body of her maid and bucket of vomit were gone. Poor Antonella! She was a hopeless cook and a worse maid, but she had been kind and well-meaning. Lucia looked down and saw she was sleeping in her wedding sheets.

"Monna Lucia! It is so pleasant to see you awake."

It was the stranger – Ginevra? – back with a brew that

smelled of honey and rosemary. "How is your throat? Do you find it comfortable to speak?"

Lucia gave it a try: "Ahemmm. Hmm. I... Yes...yes, I do."

"Good. The stones worked perfectly. I wasn't sure they would, but either way, since I have saved your life, I am bound to you as your devoted friend. You must tell me everything about yourself and how you came to be a lady in charge of her own palazzo."

Everything was so strange that Lucia did not know what to do besides agree, and found herself telling a very personal story to a woman she did not know, who was sitting on her bed.

When the pestilence first arrived, Lucia was invited to go with a group of friends to their country home, but her husband would not allow it, preferring her to stay with him as he kept an eye on business affairs. So, Lucia resigned herself to some boring weeks while she waited for the disease to pass.

As was not uncommon in her social class, Lucia's husband was some twenty years her senior. But since she was only sixteen at the time of their betrothal, he was not yet such an old man as to be completely unpleasing. He was born very poor in the country, but through luck and scheming, had become so rich that nobody cared he was born to farmers who lived in the dirt.

Lucia descended from a noble clan; however, her family had become impoverished when her father, accused of supporting the wrong political faction, was beheaded by the Signoria. But the merchant was in no need of money, and what Lucia lacked in dowry she offered in her youth and impressive lineage, so the thing was arranged.

Lucia was excited for her wedding to the rich merchant. She was brought up her whole life for this purpose, and selecting items for the trousseau became a passion. Her gown was crimson silk embroidered with gold (103 florins). Around her waist, a silver girdle with enameled scenes of Tristan and Isolde (20 florins), and on her head a jeweled brooch (also 20 florins). She also ordered five other fine gowns (one of white brocade with a long train, one of rose-colored silk, one lined with cat fur, one of embroidered taffeta, and one of forest green with long sleeves), eight plain gowns for daily wear, twenty shifts of gauzy linen, and the aforementioned bedclothes (now ruined). The marriage feast was as magnificent as Lucia's wardrobe. To feed the multitude of guests, the merchant ordered 406 loaves of bread, 250 eggs, one hundred pounds of cheese, half an ox, four sheep, thirty-seven capons, eleven chickens, and a number of seabirds, along with eight barrels of fine Provençal wine and two dozen more of cheap Tuscan Chianti. Lucia touched none of the food herself, of course. It was gauche for a bride to eat at her own wedding.

Ginevra yawned a little at this point and Lucia realized she ought to move on from the details of her nuptials.

The marriage started out pleasantly enough. The merchant was eager to impress his bride with a lavish lifestyle, depositing her in the fine palazzo where they now sat. But, after several months went by and Lucia was not pregnant, the merchant became frustrated. He knew the issue was not his, on account of all the bastard children he paid for, and informed Lucia so.

She wished for children as strongly as her husband, and purchased an ointment that was guaranteed to result in a pregnancy. But it smelled so terribly that the merchant refused to come near her and made her throw it out, so she never found out if it worked. The months became a year, and the merchant grew bitter. Lucia was a bad investment, but he couldn't extricate himself from the situation as he would have normally. He also informed Lucia of this fact. No longer did he have a kind word or loving touch, but criticized her every movement.

This imperfect domestic life was further exacerbated by the departure and deaths of the household servants as the pestilence took hold. Lucia tried to ingratiate herself to her husband by taking charge, but really she had not much experience in running a household. She was used to telling her wishes to her maid and having them carried out. So their grand palazzo quickly became disheveled. Lucia's one small victory was in securing Antonella, who was available only because she was too poor to flee the disease. She was untrained, however, and did not do much to improve the general order and appearance of things.

With her home such a miserable place, and her hired help so unhelpful, Lucia, for the first time in her life, began to personally run errands and pick up food. Her husband would not have approved, but he stayed shut up in his studio all day, working and reworking figures, writing correspondence nobody would read, looking for the magical calculation that would leave his wealth intact even when every single one of his clients had closed their own shops.

In normal times, when Lucia went out, it was always with a companion. But now nobody stared if she was alone. Nobody cared what anybody did, really, so long as they kept their distance. For the first time, she walked without worrying if she was too fast or too slow, and could choose the route she liked best. She had always loved the streets of Florence, many just wide enough to fit a man's shoulders. The city felt close and safe to her, the high exterior walls impenetrable to enemies, the gates a welcome port for friends.

But soon the food vendors vanished, and in their stead *flagellanti* wandered the barren markets, beating their backs raw and screeching at the sky. Then even they left. The friendly streets became dikes through a fetid swamp, their narrowness and crookedness holding the putrid air in place. Lucia imagined she could see the miasmas, puffing out around her skirts like fog, every step she took stirring up the sick like dust that clung to her clothing and her face. So she went back inside her house, and decided they would make do with what was stored in the larder.

One night, Lucia woke in the pitch-black of their shuttered bedchamber, covered in sweat and trying to discern if anything was actually the matter. She thought she detected the first faint beginning of nausea, and focused on it, waiting for the feeling to dissipate, the leftovers of some anxious dream. But the dull ache tightened into sharp waves and she knew she would vomit. She leaped naked out of bed and ran to the chamber pot, clutching her mouth, retching violently.

"What is it, wife?!" cried her husband.

Lucia was throwing up and could not answer. But she did not need to. He gathered his things and locked her in the room. Still, she would not believe it was *that*. It must have been the old salted fish they had for dinner. Had she put it to soak the night before or in the morning? Perhaps she was finally pregnant? She dragged the pot back over next to the bed, and waited to feel better but only kept feeling worse. The relief from the vomiting lasted only minutes before her stomach cramped anew. She spent the rest of the night like this alone, growing weak and thirsty. In the early morning, the door was unlocked and Antonella pushed in, looking sweaty and wan herself.

Then the dreadful buboes grew on her throat and in her secret places and Lucia could deny no longer that the pestilence had found her. All the other worries of her life, past and present, became trifles. In between bouts of vomiting, she bargained with God, offering her most weak and painful moments, to be experienced a hundredfold over again in exchange for deliverance from her current plight. Antonella became too weak even to put a tepid rag on her mistress's brow, and curled up in the corner where she expired. This was when the merchant locked the door for good, letting the body molder in the same room where his wife lay bedridden. It took a few days, but with his entire household (almost) dead of the plague, he finally knew it was time to abandon the inventory in his Florentine warehouses and flee.

"And that is how I found you?" said Ginevra.

"Yes, that is how you find me."

"Monna Lucia, I'm very sorry... I know what it's like when a man leaves you all alone."

"I had heard of this, this terribleness where family abandons family. But to hear these things is not to believe they will happen to oneself. But we were not such good friends, my husband and I."

"It is monstrous all the same, for him to flee from you."

"How many times I prayed he would go away, but I meant on business. Not like this."

She teared up, and began to mutter over and over, "What shall I do?"

"Lucia – now you are free to do as you wish."

Lucia sniffled and thought this over. What *did* she wish? It was possible, once her tale was heard...people would sympathize with her taking a vow of chastity. She could become a nun in some comfortable convent with nice gardens. Or! Her husband could die of plague, in which case she might inherit all his properties, if she could keep the knowledge of his death from the bastard sons for a bit. She smiled a little. Ginevra saw it.

"And another pleasant thing: if you are cured of pestilence once, you are cured forever."

"May it be so, God willing," Lucia said. "*That's* the thing to think about, not my stupid husband. Blessings upon the Virgin for sending you, dearest Ginevra, to – uh, why *did* you come into my home?"

Ginevra didn't really know how to explain it herself. "Well, I was summoned here by the bishop, from Genoa, to catch the thief who has been stealing relics and switching them for bottles."

Lucia frowned. "I have heard of the missing relics. But I thought the saints abandoned the city because we're all such awful sinners. The bishop really asked *you* to help?"

"Not directly, I suppose, but his nephew who was once my… friend wrote to me on his behalf. And this morning, I spoke with the inquisitor, Fra Michele di Lapo. He gave me a contract that validates my being here. Here, you can see the documents. I do not lie."

Lucia looked skeptically at the cramped writing and large seals presented to her.

"Well, it all seems very official…" She read a bit of the letter. "Ludovico Acciaiuoli is *your* friend?"

"Was. He died before I arrived." Ginevra winced at her own statement, as if she had just uttered the curse that made an awful thing permanent. "Did you know him?"

"Just a bit, his wife is a friend of mine, though – do you know if she lives?"

She shook her head "no," and felt a fool for mourning somebody else's husband.

"And so… I'm sorry, but still, why you? All the way from Genoa?"

"Because," Ginevra said, forcing herself to focus on the present conversation, to hold in her grief a little longer yet, "they know I will not get sick. That I can go investigate the places where other men fear to go. And now, you could, too, if you like?" She said the last bit hopefully, timidly.

"Me???" said Lucia, sitting up too quickly, making her head spin. She lay back down in the pillows. "How strange my life has become."

"I'm sorry. Let us stop here, you need more rest."

"No, it's just… I'm not sure how helpful I can be. If you wanted money, or a place to stay…"

"A place to stay, I would not refuse."

"To that you are most welcome. I will be glad of the company."

Ginevra felt a little wave of happiness. It had been years since anyone was glad of her company, besides of course Piero.

"As to your other task," Lucia continued, "it does not seem right for we two women to interfere."

"Why not?"

"Well, I don't know about you, but my education has only been in the realm of ladies' business. This seems a very complicated and delicate matter, more than women can comprehend."

"Trust me, Lucia, if there were any man for the job, they would have taken him. But you will see when you go outside again, there are no men for any job at all. So we can decide for ourselves what we may do and what we may not."

Lucia was terrified and intrigued by this statement. No one had ever trusted her with anything more important than party planning.

"But aren't you afraid? The thief might not even be a man but a demon." She thought for a moment. "Or, maybe it's like others say, and the relics can only be found by the right person."

"How do you mean?" asked Ginevra.

"Well, you know, like San Marco in Venice."

Ginevra looked at her blankly.

"I thought *everyone* knew that story. The relics of San Marco that went missing? No? Well – they disappeared. For years. Nobody could find them until their bishop prayed in just the right way and then – a miracle! They tumbled right out of a column and into his arms, in front of all the most important people in the city. So maybe our relics are just waiting for that. For somebody worthy enough, and then they will return." Lucia stopped speaking, out of breath.

Ginevra leaned over and wiped beads of sweat that formed on Lucia's brow. "Hush, hush. You're still weak from thirst and hunger. Open your mouth, I'll help you."

Ginevra thought about what Lucia had just said as she spooned honey-water into her mouth. "Or perhaps it is simple," she said, tipping the last of the drink into Lucia's mouth, "the thief steals only for earthly profit."

"No, no," said Lucia faintly, still lying down with her eyes closed. "Why not steal the jewels, the gold? And why leave behind those bottles so the crime is obvious?"

"Aha...see. You have sought out the details. You are at least a little bit intrigued."

Lucia made a face, annoyed at how she had been pulled in.

"Look, Lucia. This is not a situation I would normally interfere with." Ginevra sighed. If she was going to convince Lucia to help her, she would have to be honest about the entirety of her circumstances. "I only agreed to do it because it is required to reverse my exile and start my life over again. This contract guarantees that if I find the relics, the inquisitor will supply funds for me to start my own business here and to support my application to the physicians' guild."

"Ginevra," Lucia said, fortified enough by the drink to sit herself up, "if it's money you need to start your business, I will lend it to you. You'll have all the business you want and more besides, when I tell how you cured me."

"No! You promised. You must tell no one. Do you remember the water sickness of the year 1340 – you would have been a child. I lived here then, and did my healing as I liked, and was banished because of it."

Lucia was unfazed. She stopped caring about such things after her own father's execution. "This is why you made me promise to keep it secret?"

Ginevra nodded.

"Why not go anywhere else besides here, then? People are dying the whole world over, you know."

Because every night, I have terrible dreams; because I cringe with guilt and shame when I think of Sant'Elisabetta; because this is the place I felt most myself and also the place where I was robbed of that feeling; because if I am accepted again in Florence, perhaps these sorrows will go away. "Because living safely has left me sad and lonely. So I am here to do good in a dark hour. And you could, too, if you wish it. In three days, I'm supposed to deliver news of progress to your inquisitor… I could use your help."

Lucia lay back and tried to imagine herself as a sort of saint, frail and glowing from fasting, demurring humbly from those who asked her to recount how she had rescued the stolen relics of Florence. Perhaps Ginevra's arrival was a message from God, her true purpose, when she had failed as a wife.

Ginevra took her hand. "Kind lady, lie down and rest now. In the morning, you will begin to feel your regular self. We can talk of these things later."

"Thank you," said Lucia, relieved. "When I am better, the first thing I must do is visit Santa Maria Novella and light a candle in thanks that you were sent to me. There is a shrine there to San Tommaso D'Aquino, who keeps special watch over me. It must be he who sent you."

"I would be grateful," said Ginevra. And she meant it, though she had never heard of San Tommaso D'Aquino.

EIGHTEEN

GHOSTS IN THE RIVER

1340, City of Florence,
A Romance Interrupted

During the spring of Ginevra's love and grief, a terrible flood came roaring. Bridges were washed away, shops crumbled into the river, and houses filled with mud. Many hundreds drowned and when the waters receded, their ghosts climbed up over the banks and followed people to their homes and sat beside their beds all night. "It's in your head," said their friends and neighbors who hadn't seen the ghosts. "It's been so hot, so sad. You're stressed, you're tired. You need to eat something, you need to rest." But then the people who had seen ghosts were covered in red spots and consumed with fever and soon they died. And then anyone who had touched them died also.

Physicians were called, summoned for cures or at least explanations, but as soon as they said somebody would recover, he died, and as soon as they said somebody would die, she lived. Then the doctors themselves began to die. They refused to see patients anymore. Told the priests it must be something to do with God's wishes, and perhaps the ghosts came from purgatory to warn the living.

The priests did their best, told citizens of the commune

to stop being so lazy and self-indulgent, to redouble their attendance in churches and shrines and pray for deliverance. They held emergency processions of the ancient statue called the Virgin of Requisiti, who was helpful in times of crisis. Held aloft on her gilded palanquin, the Virgin was paraded through the streets, surrounded by clouds of incense and nuns dressed all in white. The procession ended with the Virgin placed upon the *ringhiera* in the central piazza, and presented with flowers and candles and money.

But once they crowded together, they realized the sickness moved from one person to another, and those gathered in front of the Virgin in the piazza were made ill there by their neighbors.

When the priests realized the prayers were not being heard by the Virgin, they knew then that the ghosts had come to deliver punishment, not to warn about it. They locked themselves in their quarters, but this did not protect them and many clergy still died on their fine sheets behind shuttered doors.

Fra Simone declared Sant'Elisabetta closed to pilgrims. He ordered the nuns and employees to stay inside the walls and spend hours kneeling before the Relic of the Blessed Blood. Agnesa made them boil all the water with a silver coin before they drank it, but still a few of the nuns caught sick and died.

Markets closed, and no farmers entered Florence. Porridge days at the convent became watery gruel days. And Ginevra, for the first time in her life, was lonely. She felt the absence of Vermilia like a wound that would not heal. Cut off from her parents now, as well, she realized it was these far-off supports in Genoa that had allowed her to stand tall and go with confidence in Florence. Agnesa was too busy for her, and her relationship with Taddea remained strained – her friend rarely left the chapel, kneeling to pray disease away, and Ginevra was still upset by her betrayal, too wrapped up in her own grief to reach out and make amends. What she really, desperately needed, was to see Ludovico. He alone might provide solace. But his letters, too, had stopped. Fear crept into her heart that he would die of the current fever.

"Agnesa, let me go out," she begged when she could stand it no longer. "Let me collect our golden wires from the silk guild. Let me get back what flour I can from our tenant the baker, who is dead. You know this coral that I wear is special – Vermilia told me, as long as it hangs from my neck, no disease can enter me."

Agnesa pulled the black silk cord at Ginevra's neck until the amulet was visible. She looked at it closely, examining the carved fruits on the golden bezel, placing her own thumb end to end with the perfectly carved miniature. She closed her eyes and whispered words Ginevra did not understand. She nodded and tucked it back into Ginevra's dress.

"Go, then. Get the wire and any food you can. We cannot pray all of the day and all of the night. We must keep busy and we must keep fed, or the sisters will go mad. Be discreet." Ginevra flew out of the doors as fast as she could, desperate to reach Ludovico.

Outside, she saw no one and the air smelled of the black mud that still coated the streets and hid all sorts of rotting things. She went and threw pebbles at Ludovico's window, but he did not come, though she was sure she saw him moving around behind the tiny panes of glass. She comforted herself with the knowledge that, at least, he lived. She went next to the merchant with the gold wire, but he would not open his door for her. There was nobody selling any food. Somebody had already taken the flour from the dead baker. Indeed, there was nobody walking about at all besides her. No sounds besides grief wails and death rattles behind shut windows. She remembered what Vermilia told her as a child: to keep her ears and eyes open for all things. She did. And though she returned to the convent empty-handed, that night she dreamed.

She was floating above the river, her toes skimming the surface as if she were a bird. The water was black, except for glittering streaks of gold that swirled and disappeared. Ginevra reached out and touched a streak with her finger. It was burning hot. Her finger glowed white and then fell off and sank into the water. She woke up sweating and gasping in her room, using her fingertips to count each other in the complete darkness of early morning.

At first light, she checked in her notebook, to be sure. *Here is shimmering black obsidian, made by the heat of volcanoes. It is good against fevers.* She ran to Agnesa's cell and shook her awake. "Sister, look." She shoved her book in Agnesa's face. "I had a dream – the fever came from the river. Something in it, stirred up during the flood. Agnesa, we *have* an obsidian stone – black and streaked with gold—"

"Stop! Stop. Have I not been clear? Have I not been direct? *No* magic outside these walls."

"But people are dying and the priests cannot stop it."

"Exactly," she said, putting on her habit over her nightshift. "This is the worst time to attract attention. If we have success, we will make the priests look ridiculous, and it will go badly for us... They will say we have conjured demons. And *he* will say we have made terrible sacrifices in exchange for this cure."

Ginevra understood immediately that *he* referred to the recently appointed papal inquisitor, Fra Andre di Perugia. Before the flood and sickness, the unusual zeal with which the new inquisitor approached his position had been the talk of the town. How he had hired two hundred men to his personal retinue, granting them the unusual permission to carry weapons inside the city walls. How these men slunk about, shouting "Heretic!" at anyone from whom they might extort a fine. Most extreme, how an academic was whipped through the streets for wondering whether earthquakes might occur separate from God's intervention. The poor man was put into the *stinche*, the city's jail, and all his possessions confiscated. He was fined 200 florins and his left hand was amputated when he couldn't pay it. But Ginevra was not to be deterred. Her dream had been so clear.

"Healing sick people is no heresy, Sister. Even the inquisitor must know that. You have not seen as I did, walking about yesterday. There are many thousands—"

"Enough. You must bear it," Agnesa interrupted. "This thing will leave us in a few months, but poor women are a constant in this world. Do not draw attention to yourself. We must still be here to care for them when this is all over. Now get out, it's too early for this."

Ginevra left, resolved to act as she saw fit. Agnesa might be afraid of the inquisitor, but she was not. She paced ruts in the courtyard all morning, waiting to cross paths with her mentor and continue the conversation. Finally, she stopped her as the old nun was crossing to the women's ward. Ginevra knelt before her, hands clasped.

"Please, Sister, I beseech you – our people are dying when they may live. We will be subtle, we will be quick. Nobody will know that magic happened. Except for us, who will know we have done right by our fellow man."

"Get UP. Get up, you make a scene. Come with me. Now."

Ginevra followed Agnesa back to her cell. The nun shut the door. She pried up the tile under her bed, and took out the obsidian – black and streaked with gold. She placed it in Ginevra's right hand. "Speak of this to no one. Tell me not what you do with it." She left Ginevra standing alone in her cell.

Ginevra opened her left hand, where she'd twisted Vermilia's ring around on her finger. The orange stone had been so tightly pressed into her flesh that the goddess Nemesis was imprinted in her palm.

She left the convent, quietly triumphant, and did what the obsidian told her: drop it over the side of a bridge, into the Arno. She wondered if it was very expensive or if it would be hard to find another one. The stone called out from the river and told her not to worry about all that, but to bring a wineskin to the banks and fill it and bring it to those who thirsted.

Ginevra did as the stone said, and then brought the full wine-skin to the poor crowded quarters, where people were desperate enough to drink river water offered by a stranger. Some were too sick and could not get better. But others saw their spots fade, felt their fevers cool. Ginevra rejoiced, and went again to the home of Ludovico, throwing handfuls of rocks at his window until a pane cracked, and he finally gestured that they should meet in the kitchen of the palazzo.

"Didn't you see me at your window yesterday?"

"Ginevra, it's not the time for visitors."

"I know, but I come with the best news."

He did not respond, nor did he reach out to take her hand or touch her waist, nor had he called her his Beatrice, but just plain *Ginevra*.

"I've found it, My Heart," she said quietly, and pulled out the wineskin. "Drink this and you will be safe from disease."

"Really?" he said, his voice suddenly imbued with emotion.

"Yes, really, I promise you."

He took it and drank, and then smiled at her and put his hand on her shoulder. She relaxed a bit at the touch, but still, her shoulder was not her waist.

"There's enough for your whole household," she said.

"Thank you, Ginevra, I will not forget this. But now you must go, it's not a good time for us to visit."

"But you'll write to me, when it is?" she said, hearing her own desperation.

"When it is a good time, I will write." He kissed her on the forehead and then walked through the doors that led to the palazzo of his father, where Ginevra was not allowed to follow.

It was not long before she was noticed. Florence was not so big and people peeked out through their shutters and saw her going from house to house when nobody else was about.

Whispers spread as the poor became well while the wealthy

still wasted away: there was a woman who was not afraid of the disease, who was not afraid to touch the ones coughing and spewing out vile humors. People began to leave their shelters to seek her out, and if they found her, she would not turn them away, but followed them to their homes where their children lay dying to administer the enchanted water.

She went into every parish, into places where the disease was thickest, and walked out again unaffected when all others who tried to do so were struck with the illness themselves. Soon, so many people said things like "bless you" and "God protect you," and gave her food from their own meager stores, that she forgot all about discretion, all about Agnesa's warning, about the woman burned to death on the ladder and the man whose hand was cut off for wondering about earthquakes.

NINETEEN

Bones, Bones, Bones

1340, City of Florence,
Palazzo Aldobrandini

One day, as the water sickness was still flourishing among the wealthy, a messenger interrupted Ginevra on her rounds, and said her services were required at the home of the mighty Aldobrandini clan. The master of the house was desperate to cure his son and heir.

When Ginevra arrived, however, she was greeted by the lady, a small woman who could barely walk under the costly textile draped about her person. "Signorina Nun-Helper," Lady Aldobrandini cooed at their introduction, "I am pleased you are here as it soothes my vexed husband. But, woman to woman, I must tell you your presence is redundant." She inclined her head toward a flabby man in velvet physicians' robes. He was picking at a lunch of roast piglet with bejeweled fingers. "You see, I have already engaged the exclusive services of Maestro Ficini there, who is attending his every medical need. He has been diligently applying the most scientific remedy, and we are only waiting for it to take effect."

Ginevra was taken aback. In all her house calls, she had not seen another physician, and in truth she was a bit disappointed. She'd hoped that treating such a high-profile patient might finally allow her to practice her healing arts in the open – but she had not grown *so* bold that she would interfere with the work of a licensed doctor. Perhaps, though, she could prove herself a useful and clever assistant to the maestro, so he would speak kindly on her behalf later.

"Of course, Dama," she said, bowing her head. "Maestro, with your permission, may I behold your illustrious work?"

Lady Aldobrandini nodded her acquiescence, pleased that Ginevra so readily deferred to the carefully selected and outrageously expensive Maestro Ficini. The maestro reluctantly put down his greasy knife, and the three of them went to the bedchamber where the child lay. When Ginevra saw him, it was all she could do to hold in a gasp of horror, for the little thing was wasted away almost to bone, and his skin had a strange and sticky sheen Ginevra had never seen before.

"Ahh, Maestro, here is a patient in dire need of your help if I ever saw one," said Ginevra leerily. "What causes the appearance of his skin? It is something unfamiliar to me."

Lady Aldobrandini looked quickly to the doctor.

Maestro Ficini rolled his eyes, annoyed that he had to explain the complexities of his methods to the women. "It is an ointment of lard and exotic oils that is much too subtle for a midwife to mix. It does not surprise me that you do not know of it."

"Of course, and, forgive my ignorance, but what is its purpose?"

"The child is too dry from the fever; it helps to keep him moist. But really it is only for his own comfort, because not an hour ago I fed him a Venetian theriac and he will be well in the morning – provided he does not fall asleep at all tonight, in which case the healing effects of the drug will not be able to manifest."

"A Venetian theri— what?"

"Theri-*AC*. *Ack!* It is the most potent of medicines, a precise mixture of all sorts of rare and wonderful compounds."

"It is the most effective cure for any disease, the maestro

tells me," interjected Lady Aldobrandini. "It is only through his extensive network that he was able to procure it."

"Quite," said the physician, "and I was most grateful for the opportunity to be of service to your family, Dama."

Lady Aldobrandini smiled. "You see, Signorina, my husband has been overly eager in calling for your help. You'll stay here the night because my lord expects it, but we have no need of your direct assistance. My maid will take you to the kitchen for refreshment and a place to sleep."

Ginevra allowed herself to be led away. She had never heard of the pill the maestro mentioned, but it did not look like it was working. What she saw was a little boy white with fever, his discomfort increased by a coating of lard. But the lady was satisfied with the current treatment and it was, after all, her own child. And the doctor did seem awfully confident that he was going about things the right way. Ginevra spent a fretful night on a mat in the kitchen of the great house. She dreamed she was walking through a field, but her feet became stuck and she realized the field was lard and at the other end was the girl with the twisted lip holding up her bowl for bread.

She was awakened roughly in the morning by the maid: "My mistress calls for you, her son has worsened." They hurried back to the bedchamber, and there found the maestro pacing back and forth, muttering confused and panicky things about how he had been given the child's incorrect birth date and therefore the medicine had been administered on the wrong day. It seemed he had found himself in the professionally embarrassing position of the boy having remained conscious through the night, but the wonderful theriac pill still had not worked.

Lady Aldobrandini was now ignoring the physician's presence, on her knees at the bed of her son. She had placed relics, little bundles of bones wrapped in ribbon, on his forehead, and was repeating a healing prayer so long in use that Ginevra's mother had said it when she fell sick as a child:

Bones, Bones, Bones
Keep him from death
As Christ conquered death
Bones, Bones, Bones

Then she saw Ginevra. "YOU – you will cure my son now with your remedies…"

"But…the maestro, surely he is—"

"PLEASE, you will help him. You would not let a child die?"

Ginevra looked down at the bed and saw the little boy was barely strong enough to breathe.

"…I…I am sorry, Dama…he is so sick…it is too late for my…" Just then the Lord Aldobrandini, who was a man used to things going his way, entered the chamber fully expecting a merry scene of recovery. Instead, a room full of chaos with the maid now crying, his wife staring angrily at Ginevra, and the expensive physician talking to himself. In the midst of this was his dear little son closer to death than even the day before.

"Wife! What is this? The girl could not help?"

"Who knows, Husband. She has done nothing! Refuses to apply her remedies."

Ginevra looked, hurt, toward Lady Aldobrandini, who averted her gaze. The wife could not admit she disobeyed her husband. Certainly not when it involved the survival of their child.

"Ungrateful girl," spat Lord Aldobrandini, "did you think I brought you here to enjoy a meal and a warm place to sleep at my expense? Do you know how much money I send to Sant'Elisabetta every year? You would not have a home or a wage were it not for me!"

She wanted to respond that she would have much preferred her own bed and Taddea's porridge to his kitchen floor. That she knew he only gave money to the convent because more than one of the bastards born there were his own. But she looked instead at the lady's desperate eyes, and stood silent as he threatened to ruin her if she did not save his son. When his anger was spent, the lord assigned his clerk to remain in the chamber and make sure Ginevra did not leave until she had done what was expected. He then stormed back to his studio, where he could sob in private.

Ginevra knelt down by the boy on the opposite side of his bed from where Lady Aldobrandini was crouched in prayer. She placed her hand on the boy's chest: his breath was slow, but his heart raced. She did not know how to cure him. It was too late for the river water. How stupid of her to come here. She looked across the room at the maestro's wringing hands, now at her eye level. She hated him for the money he extorted from desperate people; wearing fine rings to attend a sick person just showed he never intended to lift a finger himself. *Rings.* On his pinkie, there was a blue-violet stone, transparent and deep, the color of the sky just before the sun has risen. She took out her book of notes and flipped through:

Here is the hyacinth, which will take your place in death.

Agnesa would be furious if she found out. But Ginevra was frightened of the Lord Aldobrandini. Trapped between the opposing wishes of two people, both with very real control of her fate, Ginevra made a choice. "Maestro – Maestro, give me your ring please?"

"My *ring*?" he sputtered with indignation. "It is a precious thing, delicate—"

"GIVE IT TO HER or I will see that you are cutting boils out of the assholes of beggars on San Pancrazio Street," shrieked Lady Aldobrandini. The shocked physician handed over his jewel. Ginevra rested it on the child's navel. She closed her eyes and placed two fingers on the gem, focusing all her energy toward it. For a minute, nobody said anything; the air in the room became completely still as though a window had just been closed. Then, vibrations, inside, outside, everywhere. Their teeth buzzed as if a lute were being strummed deep inside their bellies. The boy began to shiver and the relics fell from his forehead.

"Leave them, it's alright," said Ginevra when Lady Aldobrandini reached to replace the fallen bits of bone. "It's better to not interrupt the stone."

"What are you doing? What is that *book*?" asked Maestro Ficini, eyeing her notes.

"I am trying to remove his disease," said Ginevra, not looking at him, not wanting to break her concentration.

"Such arrogance! To claim you can do things that only God can control."

But Ginevra was not listening. All her efforts were focused on holding on to the ring. It shook now, so wildly that it sprung out of her hands and clattered to the floor.

The mother, the maestro, and the two servants all gathered round it: the stone had turned to black. The doctor let out an indignant gasp that turned into a screech of horror when Ginevra took it and threw it into the fireplace where it broke in half with a loud CRACK and evaporated, leaving the empty gold ring behind. The child sat up and looked around, confused by the gaggle of distressed adults that filled his room.

Ginevra was the first to notice him. Everyone else was still staring in amazement at the fireplace where the hyacinth exploded. "Hello, little one," she said. "Welcome back."

Lady Aldobrandini whipped around.

"Dama," said Ginevra calmly, "you will have a bath made for your son, and then he will be like he was before and will not be sick again."

The lady flew to her son and embraced him.

The maestro opened and closed his mouth like a dying fish. "My ring!" was all he could say. "My ring, my ring!"

Oh, no, oh, no, I have gone too far, Ginevra thought.

"Maestro – we will compensate you for the loss of your miraculous jewel," said Lady Aldobrandini, wiping tears of relief from her eyes. She picked up the relics from where they had fallen, and made the sign of the cross over them.

"How, how, how??" yelled the maestro, crossing to

Ginevra. "I have worn it for years and never has the stone performed thusly!"

The lady stood up between them. "You must be tired, Signorina Ginevra, you'd better go. Now." She looked at her pointedly. Unspoken gratitude flowed between the two women.

The clerk stepped forward and took Ginevra's arm, guiding her toward the door.

"I will ensure a proper payment is sent to Sant'Elisabetta," said Lady Aldobrandini.

"Actually, there's no need—" called Ginevra. But the clerk had already steered her out of the room.

TWENTY

SMARAGDUS

July 8th of 1348, Palazzo Tornaparte

While Lucia slept the deep sleep of the recently ill, Ginevra tossed and turned in a bed in another room. The comforts of a proper place to sleep after weeks on the road were lost on her; the first part of the night was spent weeping tears for her dead lover and her disappeared Piero. Eventually the tears were supplanted by the sort of neurotic and futile plotting that only happens in the middle of sleepless nights. How on earth was Ginevra to find seven bits of saints in a city of infinite rooms?

Sleep eluding her still as dawn rose, Ginevra decided to get the house in order as best she could. She opened the windows of turpentined linen to let in cool air and cleaned up the spoiled food from the dining hall. She shooed the rats from the kitchen and mice from the cellar, then sifted weevils out of the flour and started a dough, so they might have bread in a few days' time. She took the dead wood from the garden and managed to begin a fire in the hearth that produced good hot coals that could be stored for days in the ash. She untangled the kink in the well's chain, and filled the sinks and basins. She caught one of the well eels and baked it in a pie.

With her current abode made as orderly as it could be, Ginevra felt ready to turn her mind to the problem of the relic thief. She sat down at the long rectangular table in Lucia's dining hall. How strange to be in such a grand room all by one's self. She put the inquisitor's overly illustrated report upon the boards, to see if it made any more sense now that she'd had something to eat. Seven stolen relics were listed, chronologically in the order of their disappearances. Also written were the last dates the relics were seen in their places. *Alright,* she thought, *so here, at least, we have the windows of time when the thefts occurred.*

The cathedral and its baptistry were robbed first. Their Filippo Arm and Zenobio head were taken in April. The next month, May, the four churches of the Rogazione *were pilfered sometime after the annual procession along their cruciform axes. Lastly, San Barnaba's relic – taken about a month later again, near the start of June.* Was the thief making monthly visits to Florence's churches? What would be the point of that? And today was July 8 – if Ginevra was correctly reading his cadence, he might be robbing another church this very minute! But which one? There were dozens within the city walls. It seemed possible he was targeting relics with upcoming feasts or processions. Or were those events simply when the thefts were noticed? Ginevra rubbed her eyes, overwhelmed.

Again, she took out the green smaragdus and focused her vision into its depths, concentrating on the question "Where must I go first?" A puff of air, like a little sigh, came from the gem and again the convent of Sant'Elisabetta appeared in her mind's eye. She shook the jewel and shook her head and asked it the same question once more, disliking its answer. But still, she could not get her one-time home out of her head. Very well, then, if that's how it was. She must go to Sant'Elisabetta and face those she had wronged.

TWENTY-ONE

TRAFFICKING OF NECROMANTIC BOOKS

1340, City of Florence

After being turned out of the Aldobrandini sick room, Ginevra walked back to Sant'Elisabetta, her head floating with a poor night's sleep and a deep sense of dread. She'd used a magic gem to cure the son of a noble. Or, as others might put it, she had stolen and destroyed an expensive jewel that belonged to an important physician. It was all well and good, giving enchanted river water to peasants. But this was further than she'd intended to go.

Still, she *had* saved the son of one of the most powerful men in the city. And she had Ludovico on her side. Ostensibly. By now, it was a week, at least, since their last visit and he had sent no word. Perhaps nothing would come of it. Perhaps the physician would be ashamed. The Aldobrandini would be grateful and discreet. Soon the city would be well again, thanks to her. She tentatively decided she'd done nothing wrong.

However, the next day Fra Simone, founder of the convent of Sant'Elisabetta, called Ginevra to his studio for the first time ever to ask why Lord Aldobrandini had sent him sixteen cured hams and a gilded reliquary containing the toe of San Silvestro.

"Oh, did he?" she said with rehearsed nonchalance. "That

was kind of him. Their son was sick, and...I have been helping sick people a little bit on my errands."

"The Aldobrandini are clients of the physician Maestro Ficini di Salerno. Was he not available?"

"Oh, yes. He was there, too. Only he had this – theriac pill – it wasn't able to help the child, so I did," she said, omitting the bit about the destroyed ring.

"You should not have made a fool of that man. He is friendly with the inquisitor."

"He made a fool of himself with no help from me," she said before she could stop herself.

Fra Simone shook his head. "For these hams and this toe of Silvestro, you have put our convent in danger. You must always remember who holds the bridle, girl, or they will rattle the bit against your teeth! Agnesa has given you too much freedom. You will cease your work in the city and stay cloistered with the nuns."

"But—"

He put up his hand. "That is all we will speak on the matter. Your stupidity pains me too greatly."

Ginevra walked out, furious that he wouldn't acknowledge the good in what she had done.

"Ginevra!" called Agnesa, hurrying to catch up with her. "What did Fra Simone want? Why are there so many hams here? Does he know about...*it*?"

"What? No. It's nothing, a donation. We needed food, didn't we? I have to go lie down, my head aches."

Ginevra just wanted to be alone. She was very upset. So upset, in fact, that she did not notice how her coral *figa* grew pale and cold, a warning sign of danger it could not deflect.

The danger was the Maestro Ficini, who was not just a bad doctor, but also a bad man. Instead of rejoicing that his patient lived, he was consumed with jealousy, humiliated that he'd owned a magic ring for so long and never even noticed. So, as soon as he left the home of the Aldobrandini, he wrote a letter to his friend the Inquisitor Perugia detailing how Ginevra di

Genoa had let holy relics fall onto the floor and consulted a strange book.

When the sickness withdrew at the end of summer and all the frightened clergy unlocked their doors, the inquisitor walked straight over the fresh graves of fifteen thousand Florentines to have a talk with Fra Simone. What was the Fra thinking? Harboring the likes of Ginevra, letting her run unsupervised throughout the city – he was supposed to be saving souls, not corrupting them! The inquisitor still had to think what he would do with the girl, but as a first step, a massive fine was levied against the convent. The amount was staggering, disastrous. More than a year's worth of eggs and gold thread for tapestries. More than the entirety of the secret donations of the noblewomen.

Agnesa found Ginevra sitting on the floor in the corner of the empty women's ward. Sighing, she crouched down next to her pupil and took the girl's hand in her own.

"Do not blame yourself, Ginevra. I was a fool to let you take that stone. I don't know what I was thinking."

Ginevra crawled with guilt. "It is my fault, not yours. I convinced you. How can we pay that fine?"

"Shhh." Agnesa studied their clasped hands before she spoke again. "You are young and in my charge, which means I bear the responsibility. But – there is a way to fix it."

"There is?"

Agnesa smiled. "One more act of magic. Give me your Nemesis stone – I am sorry – I know it was left for you but it's the only way to save this place. Give it to me, quickly. The man is here!"

Ginevra blanched. "I… I don't think it will work."

"Of course it will work." Agnesa took the ring from Ginevra's finger. "Vermilia understood these sorts of things."

Ginevra buried her face in her knees.

"What is it, girl? Oh. Oh, no. You – Ginevra you haven't used it *already* have you? You know it only works the once!"

"People were dying," she whispered, her head still buried. "You wouldn't give me the obsidian—"

Fra Simone burst through the door backward. "You CANNOT just come through here. The sisters are not used to strange men—"

"My brother in Christ, I can do whatever I want," said Inquisitor Perugia smoothly. "But do not fret – that's the girl right there, isn't it? Come, child, I have questions for you." He snapped his fingers and hired soldiers peeled her from the floor as Fra Simone held a weeping Agnesa. The parting came almost as a relief for Ginevra – never had she seen Agnesa shed a single tear. The inquisitor put her in the *stinche* where the one-handed academic still languished, and in short order convicted her of "heretical depravity," the full charges consisting of "the trafficking of necromantic books; possession of notebooks containing witchcraft; destruction of property; practicing medicine without a license; and, finally, disrespecting a member of the Guild of Doctors, Apothecaries, and Grocers."

In her hot cell inside the prison, she awaited sentencing and pondered the awful possibilities alone in the dark. This could not be happening to *her*. She bribed the jailer with shameful favors to send word to Ludovico (*Dear Heart, It is your Ginevra (Beatrice). Surely, you have heard how it is for me…*). But days of silence turned into a week, her coral *flga* was white and cold, and she eventually understood he would not come; that no help of any sort would come. Her mind stopped looking for ways to escape, and instead fixated on what terrible things they might do to her. She looked at her fingers and imagined them smashed. Imagined her ankles as stumps. But try as she might, she could not imagine what it was like to be killed. With these thoughts, she was left alone, and they sunk into her until she wished for nothing more than the moment to come, whatever it was, so she would be afraid of it no more.

Though nobody was talking to Ginevra, many were talking *about* her. The matter of her sentencing was fiercely debated in the ecclesiastical court. On the one side was the inquisitor's cohort, who wanted nothing less than to burn her. On the other, a number of sympathetic individuals, members of the Signoria and other powerful men, who not only supported the convent's work, but had also benefited from Ginevra's cures. There was Lord Aldobrandini, of course, and also the leaders of the powerful wool merchants' guild, whose workforce had been preserved in large part thanks to her river-water cure. Her death would weigh heavily on their souls. So, while no one could defend her directly (one must always respect a guild doctor), they made it known to the court in subtle ways that they did not wish to see her burned up for it.

During this time, Ludovico paid a visit to his powerful uncle, the priest Fra Angiolo Acciaiuoli, who sat on the ecclesiastical court. Eyes brimming with tears and cheeks hot with shame, Ludovico launched immediately into a confession of his great love for the nuns' servant convicted of witchcraft, and wasn't there anything his dear uncle could do to save her from an awful punishment? Ludovico pushed Ginevra's last letter, written from the *stinche*, toward his stunned relative.

Fra Angiolo read the letter carefully, keeping one eye on his distraught nephew. Really, the two men were not so far apart in age, both with the same dark hair and elegant profiles. A few silver strands at the temples, and faint lines around the eyes, were all that distinguished the older from the younger. But while Ludovico carried himself with an arrogance that was easily dismissed, the priest's dignified manner left no doubt he was one of those rare men whose intellectual abilities matched his lofty position.

"Why does she call herself Beatrice?" he asked at last.

"It was a pet name!" wailed Ludovico.

"A pet name – Ludo, have you shown this to anyone else? Does your father know?"

"No, of course not, do you think I'm a fool?"

"Yes. That is exactly what I think you are. If word of this spread – you know what's at stake for our family, the long plans we've made for you that are soon to bear fruit."

"I know! I know! It is front of my mind, every day."

"And yet, you allowed this affair to go so far that this girl – this convicted criminal – thinks she may write to you with such familiarity?"

"Uncle, you would not understand. I could not help myself!"

"You think a priest doesn't know what it's like to be with a woman?"

Ludovico said nothing for a moment, then, "I come here only to ask that she is shown mercy. I could not bear it otherwise." Ludovico sat upon a velvet stool and wept.

Acciaiuoli looked down at his nephew and sighed, placing a hand on his head. Personally, he was not terribly bothered by Ginevra's brand of heresy. If it were up to only him, a punishment of one thousand paternosters and a barefoot pilgrimage sounded more than sufficient. Those in favor of burning her were nothing but a chorus of simpleminded zealots, he thought. But now, the priest wondered if it might actually be to his advantage to allow this contingent to have its way. Ludovico's affair could not continue, and there *was* a certain finality to an execution. And yet – if he went along with burning a woman who cured sick people, he risked being labeled an extremist. Fra Angiolo had his sights set on the Florentine bishopric, and it wouldn't do to align himself with the vicious fringes.

"Go with God, nephew," he said. "Speak of this to no one. Burn her letters. And if you do this, I will see that she does not come to any great harm."

In a very clever move, that gained him the reputation as a reasonable and civic-minded official, Fra Angiolo proposed a compromise in the form of *cave a signatis* – a mutilation that would mark Ginevra for life as a dangerous heretic and warn others to stay away. To be certain Ludovico was dissuaded from further bouts of ardor, his uncle suggested they ruin the girl's face, rather than cut off an ear or something that might be overlooked by a zealous lover. This they would do with a large notch taken out of her nose. They would also banish her from Florence. The Signoria agreed, their tender hearts appeased by the reduced sentence.

So, at last, Ginevra was taken from the *stinche* and held down upon her back by four men, one at each of her limbs. Her head was placed between two wood blocks so she could not move it while a fifth man sliced her up with a stubby iron knife. She let out such a shriek that they let go of her almost immediately. She clamped her hand over the wound. Blood spurted through her white fingers, and she stared up at her assailants in horror but none of them would look her in the eye, especially the one who held a triangle piece of her nose in his hand. With gazes cast down, they tied Ginevra up in a cart and rolled her through town for all to see, a winding route back across the river to Sant'Elisabetta to collect her belongings and be gone from the city. As was tradition, people came out to see and yell things at her. Many supported her and shouted kind things like "Bless you, Sister" and "Pray to God for us!" But most had no idea what was going on, so they threw wilting vegetables and other trash at her because that is what you do to people in criminal carts.

Ginevra had intended to stand proud and tall, in case Ludovico was there to see her, but when her mutilated nose was smacked by a cabbage, the pain sank her to her knees and she did not get up again. They dropped her at the gate of the convent, her face wrapped in a dirty rag the jailers gave her. The nuns were all in the chapel, forbidden by the inquisitor from saying goodbye. Ginevra was glad that none would see her shame. She found her small possessions already bundled for her on her bed. A tiny parcel with a note pinned to the top – her heart leaped – but it was in Sister Agnesa's hand, not Ludovico's.

Go with God, but go far away from here.

It will bring me joy to hear you are well, but far away. Taddea wishes to provide the parting message that she will pray to the bread for your salvation.

Inside the parcel – the collection of gems left to her by Vermilia, including the Nemesis ring, which she placed back upon her finger even though its powers were spent. The jewels, which she had so long desired, at last in her possession, but O, at what cost! The guards then escorted her to the Porta San Niccolo, the towering gate on the city's southern wall, and registered her with the keepers as a *persona non grata* before shoving her out into the world. Like this, she walked back to Genoa, where she had not been for five years.

The nose notch was not so severe a punishment as Ludovico's uncle had intended, for the healing magic of the coral did its best and eventually only a thick white line, an asymmetry that gave her a quizzical look, would be left of what was meant to be a gross disfigurement. The banishment was much worse. She was distraught over her Ludo, who hadn't even come to see her being wheeled around in the criminal cart, and now she had no way of meeting him to learn why he'd abandoned her when she was in such dire need of a friend.

When she arrived at Genoa, she learned the water sickness had also infected that city's drinking fountains, and her parents were among the dead. This loss struck her as a blow strikes one already beaten to the ground. She curled further inward upon herself, unmoored from everything but the misery of her current situation. *This is how it is*, she thought. *This is how everything is and how everything will be forever, now. Loss upon loss upon loss.* But – even with all this – still she could not lay down and die herself. The golden strings wove a net to catch her in her free fall; some hidden part of her could not shake the instinct of self-preservation. In a dreamlike state, she put her small savings from the convent toward a little room in the ugly part of town where she was born. It had a hard dirt floor and a soggy garden plot, good for growing nothing but mosquitoes.

Then the strings tugged at her and made her take up the old reed mats on the floor and burn them and weave new ones. They told her to dig trenches in the garden to drain off the water, and coax what medicinal plants she could from the brackish soil. When she was finished, she painted a little symbol of a snake in coral outside the door, a tribute to Vermilia. Vermilia, who knew how it was, how to appear quiet and poor, and how to be left alone.

Gone were Ginevra's lofty plans; the hopes of marrying rich, of moving outside the realm of her sex, of helping the world on any grand scale. She just wanted to lick her wounds in the dark. *But you still need to eat*, the strings reminded her. So, she opened her door and it was not long before the curious housewives of the port began to visit her with their problems, their little coins and barters of bread sustaining her. In this way, Ginevra resigned herself to a future as a local healer and permanent spinster.

TWENTY-TWO

WE DIE, WE FLY

1340–1348, City of Genoa,
Ginevra in Exile

Some months after Ginevra's forced return to Genoa, a letter arrived from Ludovico. Immediately, she closed her shop and with shaking hands drank wine straight from its jug. She had spent many nights wishing for such a letter – it would say how Ludovico was physically restrained by his father during her trial, and had only now escaped to send word to her. But when she broke open the seal and read, here was the truth written out in fine walnut ink on smoothest vellum: her Ludo had always been promised to another, since he was a small boy. His intended – the only child of a very powerful family – had just come of age. It was his inescapable duty to marry her. This alliance of two great houses was the cornerstone of the Acciaiuoli plans for the future.

Ludo was sorry for keeping this from Ginevra, but he didn't want to ruin their precious moments together, the memories of which he would always treasure. He explained how even though he could not visit her in prison, he had intervened on her behalf with his uncle, the priest, and convinced him to cut up her nose instead of something worse. It had been a large humiliation to admit their affair, but he did it anyway because of his great love for her. Now that some time had passed, could they not be friends? It would bring him great comfort. His new wife would never inflame his heart as Ginevra had.

Ginevra threw the letter into the fire and watched the red wax seal turn black and sputter away into nothing. A small bit of the wine came back up into her throat, and she lay down upon the floor. There, sideways, she took from her bag of gems a stone called antipathy, a dense black bead the size of a hazelnut. Agnesa had taught her it would absorb unpleasant memories. She tied it around her wrist and sat up, but her troubles were too heavy and the yarn it was strung upon snapped and the stone fell to the ground. She tried to pick it up, but its heaviness was extreme, and she could not. So there it stayed in the middle of her floor, where she stubbed her toe upon it daily.

Now, the strange dreams that began during the flood were her constant companions. Dead things and peculiar creatures visiting with messages she could not understand. She was held down in her bed, and she opened her mouth to scream but could produce no sound. Cruelest of all, she was back in Florence, Taddea telling her she was a lady in the Acciaiuoli household. When she woke and reality was once again manifest, for days after she sunk into an even darker depression. She learned to get by with as little rest as possible, preferring tiredness to the places her mind journeyed in sleep.

She kept to herself, besides modest dealings with clients: people who needed their rashes or toothaches cured, or vendors, sellers of lavender, and fishermen who brought her broken bits of coral or special sea snails. Occasionally, individuals came to her with greater troubles than toothaches. Business was done between Florence and Genoa, and word of her special abilities spread. A noblewoman who had miscarried five times and was pregnant with a sixth child. A merchant who lost all his ships because of the *malocchio*. But Ginevra turned away these people, referred them to the shrines of the saints. The court of the inquisitor had done its work well. Like Vermilia, she shied away from the use of stones, from grander gestures of magic. She provided simple herbal remedies, fixed minor wounds, built small charms for small problems. She was cured of the delusions of her youth, that the good results of her work would excuse its unorthodoxy. On the frequent nights when she could not sleep, Ginevra spent the dark hours experimenting with her healing stones, counting and re-sorting them, learning what she could without the use of a human subject. She put out subtle inquiries with merchants who had taken her help in sensitive matters, so she could be sure of their discretion, and took as payment unusual stones from their travels. In this way, her collection and knowledge grew, though it remained unused, theoretical. This much she allowed herself of her former passion.

She lived this way for seven years, when, late in the year 1347, a sailor came to her with a large swelling on his neck. He was home from a long journey, he told her. Part of a Genoese merchant contingent, trapped for years by the Tatar army at Kaffa. They had been under siege in their citadel, living off cockroaches and shoe leather toward the end. Ginevra gave him a cup of undiluted wine and tilted his head; this was to get a good look at the lump, but also to make him be quiet. Such were her own troubles that she did not like to hear others'.

"Oof," she tutted. "This thing is as big as a pigeon egg! Surrounded by water all that time and you never thought to take a bath?"

"Monna, there was no time for baths. Once we were to sea, away from that foul place, we just wanted to be home as quick as we could."

"Fair enough, though a layer of dirt is what you have to thank for your twin that's growing here."

"Really? You're sure?"

"Unless it is something I've never seen before, I'm sure."

"Good. This is good news."

"If you say so. Look, I'm going to lance it and then you must scrub your neck so you don't get any more. Ready?"

He drained his wine. "Ready. I've pricked enough women. I suppose it's only right to have the favor returned."

"Well, as they tell us ladies in such situations: close your eyes, it'll be over soon."

"OWWWW!!! OW, OW, OW, STOP! For the love of Christ!! *Dio cane*, is it supposed to hurt like that??" Ginevra withdrew her probe. It was not supposed to hurt like that. Purple veins began to spider out from the point of her needle, like stripes on an unripe eggplant. Shaken, she gave him a poultice and sent him on his way. She was not used to hurting her patients. Later that week, she heard that the sailor and a lover had been found dead together, black swellings at their necks and other places. Ginevra's coral *figa* glowed red. Her dreams were filled with rats and beetles.

Soon, she knew the whole story of the ill-fated expedition to Kaffa, told to her in bits and pieces by clients who came to buy something, anything, whatever she had that might keep away foul disease and evil spirits. It seemed that the only reason the Genoese had escaped the siege was because the Tatar army became very ill. So many of their soldiers died, in fact, that they were forced to abandon the fight. And as a last spiteful act, the Tatars flung the infected corpses of their comrades over the citadel walls, as many as they could, until there were not enough left alive to load the catapults. This was how the Genoese escaped, stepping gingerly around their exploded enemies.

So eager to be home, were they, that they all agreed to keep this unpleasantness a secret lest they be denied entry to the port of Genoa. They would not mention their comrades who died on the journey home, their bodies covered in black spots. They said nothing as they spilled forth from their ships, into the arms of loving wives, eager mistresses, and sympathetic courtesans. The young ones made no mention of death in the dimly lit taverns where they leaned close to impress strangers with tales of their adventures. The old ones omitted disagreeable details as they dined gratefully in the homes of friends.

By the time it was realized what a mistake all this had been, by the time the truth came out, death was on every man's doorstep. Coffin makers were out of inventory, graveyards were full. Genoa blockaded the port, the source of their livelihood, but it did not matter. The insidious pestilence had gotten down into the blood of the people and no longer needed passage on ships to reach its doomed destinations.

Now Ginevra woke every morning to a line outside her door of sick people begging for help. But she had none to give – her shelves and jars were bare. Her garden was plucked down to the earth. No dreams came with messages of magical cures, and midnight experiments with gems yielded no answers.

"Go to church," she said, not knowing what else to do. "Pray to the rock that once touched the robe of San Francesco."

"We have already! Look," cried a desperate woman, holding up a small glass vial. "It is holy water, poured over the rock you speak of. The priest is giving it to anyone who asks. But it is not enough! Look also here." She stuck out her tongue and it was black as ink.

"Oh, Sister," said Ginevra, "I am sorry, but I have no antidote. You must find another saint, and pray to them. Maybe it will work better than San Francesco's robe's rock."

Now came panic. All who had the means fled. Toward rural estates, holy shrines, or just into the country, preferring open fields to their own poisoned beds inside Genoa's walls. Those who, like Ginevra, had nowhere to go hoarded food and stuffed their shutters with rags. Families shunned members who fell ill. Friends and neighbors refused to touch the sick, and when they died, their bodies were poked into the street with long sticks, where the poorest of poor, who had no shutters to close anyway, made a business of collecting them for disposal.

This pestilence felled those who were young and healthy as if they were old and frail. Mercurial in its nature, it eluded the logic of physicians by manifesting differently from one patient to the next. It might appear as tumors in one person, but a rash of black spots on another. In some people, the disease showed itself not at all until they coughed up blood all over their bedchambers and then expired.

Within months, all of Genoa and its surrounds were covered with bloated bodies, and every corner turned risked the ghastly sight of some poor human decaying without the dignity of burial.

In the springtime of that year 1348 a traveler came to Ginevra's door, the first in many weeks.

"I am told you pay good money for old rocks?"

She looked at his travel-worn clothes. "Come in," she said, "and tell me what you know of the world."

He was, it turned out, a son of Genoa returned home.

"I have gone everywhere, Monna. The whole of Italy is ravaged with disease. We flew, this way and that, to the shrine of Saint Whoever-Can-Stop-the-Plague. None of them helped. I went even to Avignon, the Holy City of the Pope – but there, too, the city is like a sepulchre."

"And what does the Holy Father say of this pestilence? What does he say we should do?"

"He wrote a special mass, made everyone in the city hear it, and then said we all had to keep a candle lit for three days... Maybe somebody couldn't keep their candle lit, I don't know... but it didn't work. And now their Rhône river, they use as a graveyard because the earth is full, and the Pope calls it a punishment for our sins."

"But if it *is* punishment, why is it that priests who are good, who attend the sick at their deathbeds, die in the greatest numbers?"

"Monna, I do not know. Even the Pope's cardinals are all dying, and they are supposed to be the best among us! Did you know the only cardinal from Italy is dead? The Pope is sure to fill the empty spot with another one of his bastard French nephews, to heap misery upon our misery."

Ginevra shook her head. "Well, at least show me the old rocks you brought, then."

She bought a pair of stones from him. Dark green and speckled red, carved with ancient writing. She added them to her collection and resumed her lonely vigil. She watched her city empty, her people gone, saw all tenets of civic life crumble, for lack of living to operate or enforce them. And so it was, soon, all over the world, from the dark north of Scandinavia to the citadels of Egypt. But as is always the case in times of great turmoil, there are certain individuals who remain immune to the chaos that surrounds them, and instead hide within it to conduct their nefarious business without scrutiny.

PART II

THE RELIC THIEF

*...Oh, happy people of the future,
who have not known these miseries and
perchance will class our testimony with
the fables.*

–PETRARCH

TWENTY-THREE

SANT'ELISABETTA DELLE CONVERTITE

Morning, July 8th of 1348,
City of Florence, the Start of a Very Long Day

Though Ginevra had years to prepare something to say, then a day since she'd returned to Florence, and then a good half hour as she walked over, still no words came to her as she approached the Convent of Sant'Elisabetta delle Convertite after her early morning cleaning of Lucia's palazzo. Thoughts passed through Ginevra's head in rapid succession. She would come humbly, with an apology. Or, better to be proud and show no shame. They should apologize to her! They would embrace her. They would weep. They would shut the door in her face. *It will bring me joy to hear you are well, but far away.* She forced her hand to lift the knocker. Its heavy *thud* rang out against the walls that lined the narrow street. A nun opened the door and peeked out with a scowl that turned quickly to surprise.

"Taddea?" said Ginevra, stomach aflutter.

Taddea reached out her hand and touched Ginevra's scar. "Is it *you*?"

"It is me," said Ginevra shyly. "Um. How are you?"

"How *am* I? The world is swallowing itself whole. Come inside. I need your help right away." She pulled at her arm.

Ginevra gripped the door frame. "Wait – Agnesa, Fra Simone – will they accept my presence?" Now Taddea pulled with all her might, and Ginevra tumbled through the door.

"Fra Simone is dead since yesterday, and if you will not come help me, Agnesa will follow him."

Ginevra's mouth went dry, her ears rushed, and her limbs felt floating. How stupid, how blind she had been. When every person had dropped dead, how had she not considered this possibility? Is this what the smaragdus had been trying to tell her? That her healing abilities were needed desperately at Sant'Elisabetta?

"Come," said Taddea. And then, head still swimming, she was in Agnesa's plain little cell. The white walls and tiles and pallet on the floor, and her dear old friend, so frail as to be almost transparent, delirious and covered in black spots like insect bites.

"Agnesa! Sweet Agnesa, here is somebody who will help you. One of our own."

Agnesa looked at Ginevra with wild eyes. Ginevra was ashamed at the relief she felt that there was no recognition in them.

"What are you waiting for?" whispered Taddea to Ginevra. "Do you have – *do you carry magic stones, still?*"

"How did you know—"

"Agnesa told me everything, after you went away. *Do you have them?*"

Ginevra nodded, all thoughts of inquisitorial contracts gone from her mind, and knelt down beside the pallet, wondering what on earth to do. Lucia's disease had been contained in tidy swellings. Here it was spread throughout Agnesa's whole body. Tentatively, she placed her bloodstones on two of the spots on her chest, over the heart. She waited for the vibrations to start but the stones stayed cold and still in her hands. Still, when she lifted them, to her immense relief the spots had disappeared.

"Is it working?" said Taddea, who hovered, wringing her hands.

"It is. I think it is!"

"Thank God you have come. Thank God."

As Taddea flitted back and forth behind her, Ginevra touched the bloodstones to every spot she could find, methodically starting at the fingertips on Agnesa's left side, working her way back to her shoulder until her entire arm was clear of them.

"That feels nice, what is it?" said the faintest, tiniest voice.

"It is working!" said Taddea. "She has not spoken since yesterday!"

Ginevra could have cried with relief. "It is bloodstones, Sister. They will make you better."

"Oh, is that all?" Agnesa closed her eyes. "They will not. I've tried it all; nothing will make me better."

"These stones are rare, they came from far away. Don't be worried."

"I'm not worried. But I could not save my sisters, and you cannot save me."

Ginevra looked at Taddea.

"We are the only ones left, we two," Taddea said.

"It's alright, Sister, it's not your fault. This plague keeps its secrets well."

"I tried everything, but this disease – it is old, it is evil. It has not come for many thousands of years. The knowledge was lost. I am old, too, my golden strings grow thin and snap. The magic does not flow through me as it used to."

"Do not speak of yourself so," said Ginevra, doing her best not to cry, to focus on the task at hand.

"I put strings of corals around their necks, but the corals were unripe and they held no power."

"Hush, Sister," said Ginevra. She guiltily tapped her own coral amulet, warm and red in the presence of Agnesa's disease.

"I placed red carbuncles upon swellings but it caused fits of apoplexy and they died."

"I will say a prayer for them, Sister."

"I ground pearls into dust and fed them the sparkling powder. But all of them died."

"But you did not have bloodstones, Sister," said Ginevra, touching the speckled jewels to the spots on Agnesa's shins.

"Bloodstones. Hmmph." She spoke animatedly now. "You do not listen to me. For those who are young and strong, perhaps those rocks will work. But even your bloodstones cannot draw out what is already deep, what is already spread. If you had a lynx, you might use its urine to extract the essence of your jewels. Then the patient could drink it down – and the stone's powers could reach into all the various folds where plague has taken hold."

"A lynx, Sister?" Ginevra was onto the right arm now.

"Yes, a lynx. Like you, she possesses wonderful powers. But the animal is cleverer than you. She buries her urine, guards it jealously because she knows it is magic and that men will steal it from her. But you walk around an open book so all may know your secrets and use them against you."

"Lynx urine? She is going mad," said Taddea.

"No," said Ginevra. "She is remembering from a book."

"You will never find the lynx's treasure, so your stones will not work and I am dead," said Agnesa.

"Sister, please. I have seen them work. I am *watching* them work."

Agnesa smiled a wicked smile. "Look again." She held out her shaking left arm: the splotches Ginevra had erased before had bloomed again, large and angry.

Ginevra moved the stones frantically from spot to spot, but now where one disappeared another came back to take its place.

"What is happening?" said Taddea.

"I'm not sure – this worked before, I swear it!"

"Try something else!" said Taddea.

Ginevra, not knowing what else to do, began to fumble with the loose tile on the floor. If the books were still there, maybe they held an answer. The passage about the lynx.

"It is empty, empty!" cried Taddea. "We sold everything, sold those secret books years ago to pay our debts. Try something else."

But Ginevra did not know what else to try.

Taddea ran away.

Ginevra knelt back next to Agnesa and panicked. The bloodstones worked so easily before. She should have come yesterday, before the disease was so advanced. Right when the smaragdus had first conjured the image of Sant'Elisabetta in its green depths.

"Please, Agnesa. Oh, please, oh, please. You will be well, and I will tell you how sorry I am and we will talk and be friends as we used to be."

"Don't fret, girl," whispered Agnesa. "You arrived exactly when you were meant to."

Taddea returned with the Relic of the Blessed Bread from the chapel, and laid it atop Agnesa and prayed:

Bread, bread, bread
Keep her from death
As Christ conquered death
Bread, bread, bread

Agnesa began breathing very quickly.

Ginevra grabbed her hand. "Please, Sister, I am here. I have come back."

Then she breathed not at all.

Both young women, who thought they had no tears left, sat down on the floor and clung to each other and wept until their eyes puffed and they could not breathe through their noses. And then they tripped over each other to apologize, through their tears, for how they had been apart and for how it took the most awful thing God ever wrought upon the earth to bring them back together again.

When they were spent of crying, because eventually you must be spent, they carried Agnesa's frail body through the convent, and Ginevra experienced the strange and immediate recall of details – floor tiles, icons painted on the walls, even little chips in plaster, all as it was when she left. The place had not been flourishing.

When they reached the courtyard, they bathed the body of their friend and teacher, and laid her in the shallow pit Taddea had scratched out of the dirt, next to the shrouded thing that was once Fra Simone da Cascia. The rest of the yard was studded with mounds of freshly turned earth and crosses made of sticks. They sat down on the ground then, for a while, in shocked silence. Too stunned to feel the full weight of grief. That would come later, Ginevra knew.

"Taddea, come stay with me – this place is filled with pestilence. I am at the house of the Tornaparte, in Santa Trinita. The master has fled, there is room for you."

"I can't go."

"You can't be the only one here by yourself."

"But I am not by myself." She gestured to the relic of the bloody host, which had overseen the funeral services.

"Bring the bread with you, then."

"No. Fra Simone built our chapel for it, and here it shall stay – I pray to it daily for the plague to leave. It's important. It won't be as powerful outside of its reliquary."

"I suppose you're right."

Taddea looked over. "You look like you could use a meal. I'll be right back. Today is porridge day."

She returned with a bowl of cold groats. Ginevra spooned it into her mouth mechanically.

Taddea watched her as she ate. "Why are you here, Ginevra?"

Ginevra ate several more spoonfuls before she answered. "It is so strange, I fear you will not believe me."

"Just now, I would believe anything."

She started at the beginning, the message supposedly from Ludovico on behalf of the bishop, the contract with the inquisitor, the relic thief that eluded them.

"So you have been in town since yesterday, and only now you come?" Taddea said quietly, trailing her fingers through the dust of the courtyard.

"I was afraid Agnesa and Fra Simone would not forgive me for the trouble I caused. And my fears have come true, for they are dead and I cannot ask them."

"I will not deny you brought us trouble – the loss of funding. We had to close the women's ward."

Porridge stuck in Ginevra's throat as she was told what she already knew – she was the reason why the plaster was chipped in all the same places.

"But I don't believe Agnesa held any of it against you. Bringing your healing magic to so many – you did what she would have liked to, but she was too afraid."

"She said all that?" asked Ginevra, hopeful, desperate.

"No," Taddea admitted. "I just assume that's how she felt." The two sat in silence for a moment before Taddea sighed and continued, "So. The disappeared relics. It's bad, isn't it? Without their protection, the whole city will die."

"You keep your holy bread locked up, don't you?"

"Yes – in its crystal case, in its cupboard in the chapel, which I also keep the key for. And I visit it many times a day because there are so many people dead so quickly, I must pray constantly for their souls. Their ghosts come to me every night, complaining of purgatory."

"You have done better at protecting your relic than the priests in the grand parishes." Ginevra scraped to the bottom of her porridge bowl, and saw it was made of fine earthenware, decorated with grapevines in purple and green, surrounding a gold chicken.

"I see this style everywhere, with these colors," she said absently.

"Hmm? Oh, that. It's really too fancy for everyday use, but what's the point, now, of saving nice things? It was a gift from the man who bought Agnesa's books. A rich potter in San Romolo. His workshop is the only place that paints this way…"

Ginevra looked up from the fancy bowl, saw how out of place it was in the dusty graveyard garden. "If only I had never left, Taddea. I could have still been here, and when the plague first arrived, Agnesa and I, together we could have found a way to save the sisters."

"Don't flatter yourself, Ginevra. No matter what happened, you would not still be here."

"What do you mean?"

"I *mean*, you said it yourself: the only reason you came back is because of a letter from stupid Ludovico Acciaiuoli."

"That wasn't the only reason. I wanted to come back for… for myself. To clear my name and make amends and make a life here, again. Anyhow, he is dead now, and I was dead to him long ago."

"You were not *so* dead to him."

"What do you mean?"

"I mean, there is something he left for you. Years ago. He said you never wrote him back, and he thought we might be in touch with you."

"What is it? Let me see," Ginevra said, too quickly.

Taddea rolled her eyes, but left the garden and returned shortly with a small leather case. Ginevra opened it. Inside was a gold brooch set with a honey-colored stone at the center – amber, frozen sap from the forests of the north. The amber was encircled in a pair of arms, with hands clasped. She turned it over, and saw an engraved dedication:

"'Not my wife/But my life?'" said Taddea, reading over her shoulder. "What's that supposed to mean?"

Poor, dense Ludovico. So cruel in his kindness – he meant the jewel as a token of affection, this Ginevra understood. But to think this would be enough for her, to be a lonely secret while he lived his own lonely life at the side of another poor woman who undoubtedly would be lonely as well. She held the jewel out to Taddea.

"You take it. Sell it for the convent."

"I will not. Sell it for yourself. You really think the inquisitor will pay you? He is a frail man. Even if you find the relics, he won't live to fulfill his obligations."

Ginevra put the jewel away in her purse, distraught. She must have misunderstood the smaragdus. What did it send her here for? To see someone she loved die? So she could be humiliated anew by an old love affair? She couldn't stand to be at the house of her failures any longer.

"Taddea, I must go. Now. I have business to attend. Please, are you sure you won't come with me?"

Taddea just shook her head. "Go, Ginevra. And help in your way. I will stay here, and help in mine. And if God allows us to survive this, we will both know we have done what is right."

TWENTY-FOUR

THE BECCHINO

*Morning, July 8th of 1348,
City of Florence*

That same morning Lucia awoke late and famished. She went to the kitchen to find Ginevra, but was distracted by the eel pie her new friend had left on the kitchen table. She ate with relish, tasting each crumb and bit of eel jelly. She went to the open window with the pie in her hand, and looked out to greet the world with the true joy of one who almost had to leave it.

Joy immediately tempered at seeing the shrouded corpse of Antonella, lying stiff on the piazza. This saddened Lucia, who wished some dignity for her loyal employee. She decided she would see to it that she was properly buried before she went to give thanks for her salvation at the church of Santa Maria Novella. Lucia finished her pie, licking the crumbs from her fingers, dressed in her plainest green gown, and went outside to sit next to the body. It was here she sat when Ginevra came, returned from Sant'Elisabetta.

Lucia waved with a smile but saw something was wrong.

"Why are you sitting here next to this moldering body?" asked Ginevra by way of greeting.

"I'm waiting for the *becchini*, the gravediggers, to make their rounds."

"Ah, of course. I'm sorry she's still here. I thought the city would pick her up."

"Perhaps they will, eventually. But I'll need to be here and pay them, or they'll just dump her in a ditch around the corner."

"It is hard now to find places…"

"It's not just that. These *becchini* are terrible men. They are lowborn and charge exorbitant sums, and they sing frightening songs to mock our sorrow. Awful tunes, heard even through our shut windows." She adjusted the shroud that had fallen away from her maid's hand with its blackening fingertips.

Ginevra nodded, and sat down next to her. "I will wait with you."

"So, where were you this morning?"

Ginevra took out the brooch and handed it to Lucia. "Ludovico left this for me."

"'Not my wife/But my life?'" Lucia read. "So he was not just your friend, then?"

Ginevra answered her with silence.

"It's not *so* bad if you don't read the words – it has this lovely jewel in the center."

"It is an amber. Do you know what an amber does?"

Lucia shook her head.

"When put on the left breast of a sleeping woman, she must admit all her secrets – it's used to make adulteresses confess."

"I'm sure he didn't mean it that way—"

"I ruined my life for an idiot," said Ginevra.

"I think you should still wear it – the words are on the back anyhow. It's a pretty thing."

"It is yours, then, if you like it."

"Fine. I'll wear it for you until you want it back. And now the message means something nice… You're not my wife, but you saved my life."

Ginevra managed a faint smile as Lucia pinned the brooch to her shoulder.

"Do you think it would work on a man, too? Make him tell his secrets, I mean."

Ginevra shrugged. "Probably. Whatever man wrote down the amber's powers probably didn't want his wife to know she could turn it right around on him." The women fell into silence, and Lucia busied herself adjusting Antonella's shroud. Ginevra needed to distract herself from the worst possible morning. So she gestured across the piazza and asked, "Do you know this church well?"

"Santa Trinita? Of course. It's where I'll be buried; my husband bought us a chapel inside. Though it's dark and damp now since the last flood. Why?"

"What relics does it hold?"

"The most famous is the crucifix of San Giovanni Gualberto, who spared his enemy after receiving a kiss from Christ. It's supposed to grant wishes if you pray to it correctly... You don't think?"

"Why not?"

"It's been locked for months, since the plague first started."

"Let's go and see anyhow—"

"I'm sure it's safe – I have a wish on it!"

"Lucia, I must see the inquisitor the day after tomorrow, and so far I've found nothing to tell him. Won't you come with me since you know the inside?"

Lucia thumbed the golden jewel she had just accepted. "Alright, but only if we're quick. I don't want to miss the *becchini*."

Santa Trinita was fronted in plain brick, pierced by three arched doors that led into the sanctuary and aisles. All of which appeared quite locked. The women walked up to the central door and Ginevra gave it a gentle push. At her slight touch, the entire door fell inward and slammed down onto the hard floor. They screamed in tandem, but there was not a soul around to hear the noise or chastise them for the damage.

Shaking her head, Ginevra stepped lightly over the fallen door and into the sanctuary, Lucia following timidly. Light poured through high windows onto mismatched murals and cracked stone floors that showed fantastical beasts rendered in black and white. It smelled of mildew, and dark stains crept up the walls – damage from the flood Lucia had mentioned. The flaking eyes of the holy martyrs and their painted benefactors did not appear to welcome them. Lucia stopped at the stone font and filled a small flask with holy water, tucking it back into her purse. "This way," she said, leading them toward the chapel of San Giovanni Gualberto. "Look! It is still here. I told you so." She pointed to a small sculpture: Dying Christ carved in ivory on a cross of gold, the points studded with shining red carbuncles.

"Lucia," said Ginevra, "what is meant to be below the crucifix?"

Upon a velvet pillow was a tiny bottle, filled with a deep green liquid.

"No! That's where the shoulder of San Giovanni Gualberto is kept."

"He must have taken that, then!"

"But why? The crucifix is much better, hardly anyone prays to the shoulder."

"Why take one relic but not the other?"

"Of course, *this* is why I became sick, why we are the only ones here: Santa Trinita is a *dead parish*, Ginevra."

A grumbly voice singing and the rasping wood wheels of a cart on flagstones came through the broken doorway and interrupted them. As the voice got closer, they could make out the words to its song:

> *My passengers are stacked within*
> *And though their lips are taut and grim*
> *With puff of gas and jerk of limb*
> *Your friends and lovers call to me*
> *"As you are now, once was I thee*
> *As I am now, so you shall be"*

A *becchino* had come at last. Ginevra tucked away the bottle, and the women ran out and called to him. The frightful character stopped. Ginevra and Lucia looked at him as they walked across the piazza, shielding their eyes from the afternoon sun with their hands.

It was impossible to tell his age. His posture was crooked from years of manual labor, so that at first he seemed to be very old. But then he had moved his heavy cart so deftly it seemed he must be very young. He was dressed in nothing but his breechcloth and a large rag piled up on his head.

"Good afternoon, rosy maidens," he said cheerily. "I see you've a fresh one for me?" He lifted the corner of Antonella's shroud. "Oof, maybe not so fresh. She smells like Satan's farts."

Lucia's jaw dropped. Ginevra grabbed her shoulder.

"Excuse me, my dear Signore, for interrupting your song," she said. "We were hoping we might acquire your services to take our departed friend to the yard at..." She looked at Lucia.

"I... I don't know her parish, she was poor."

"Well, you'll want San Paolino, then," said the *becchino*. "That's where the poor are buried. And I can take her there for two florins."

"Two FLORINS?" the women shouted in unison.

"San Paolino is not even a mile from here," objected Lucia.

"Ladies, if you can find a man cheaper than I – or, rather, if you can find any other man at all than I – then I shall be on my way and leave you with your fragrant friend."

"Give us just a moment," Ginevra said.

He bowed accommodatingly, and the two women stepped away to consult each other.

"Has your husband left you wanting?" Ginevra asked Lucia quietly.

"For Christian tenderness, yes."

"You know what I mean."

"In his haste to escape me, he neglected to collect a certain strongbox."

"Let us appease the *becchino*'s greed, then, for we have no other alternative."

Lucia nodded reluctantly.

"Good," said Ginevra. "And besides, I have an idea."

She turned back to the *becchino*. "We'll pay, but I'm coming with you to make sure that she is buried properly where you say."

The *becchino* shrugged. "As you wish, Dama."

"Well, aren't you going to put her into the cart?"

"Aren't you going to pay me two florins?"

"Ugh. Rude man. We'll be right back."

He grinned a horrid grin. "I'll wait."

"Are you *sure* you want to go with him?" whispered Lucia once they were inside.

"I'm sure – he is one of the few who still goes about the city. He may know something about the thefts."

"Ah! You are clever. Very well. I'm going to go to Santa Maria Novella to pray. I'll see you back here this evening for supper?"

Ginevra was touched by the hopefulness in her voice. "Yes, I promise. And – since they are on your way anyhow – would you consider stopping in at Santa Reparata and the Baptistry?"

Lucia stiffened. "And what would you have me do there?"

"Just look, that's all. It's where the first two thefts took place, so you might see if there are any signs or clues, any more of these strange bottles…"

Lucia tried to think of an excuse, but really she couldn't see the harm in simply walking into two churches in the middle of the afternoon. "Alright, since you are being so good as to accompany Antonella to San Paolino. I have no desire to see any more corpses."

"Don't look at the scaffolds at Santa Reparata, then."

The women went back outside, embraced, and parted ways. Ginevra pressed two heavy gold coins into the *becchino*'s palm, then habitually felt for her coral pendant to make sure it was securely in place. A plague pit was no place to take chances.

The *becchino* hoisted dead Antonella into his cart with surprising speed, and then rolled along toward San Paolino. He said nothing as they walked, preferring to whistle the tune of his earlier song, including all sorts of trills and flourishy notes that made the melody inappropriately cheerful for the ghastly lyrics it accompanied.

"What is your name?" asked Ginevra, to make him stop whistling.

"You may call me to my face what you call me to my ass: I am the same as all who toil like me. For you, my name may be just Becchino."

"Very well, Becchino. You know, it's hard for some, to accept they are despised. But you do not seem to mind it?"

"Well, it is better not to be, when one has a choice, but I haven't a choice. Because I was born a poor man, my existence was despised before I ever earned it. Now, at least, I do my best to earn it."

"By singing perverted songs and cheating those in desperate situations?"

"Aren't you a lofty one! I do a great service with my songs. Death comes for everyone. Mocking it is the only way to remove its sting."

Ginevra thought about this. Laughter to drive away darkness, as Vermilia had taught her so long ago about the *malocchio*. "Alright, Becchino," she answered. "But how does that explain your exorbitant billing practices?"

"Ah, yes. Well I am a bit greedy about it."

Suddenly, Ginevra became aware of a low humming sound. "What's that?"

"That's the sound of the yard at San Paolino."

"The sound?"

"You'll see." They rounded the corner. "Which spot is good enough for your friend?"

TWENTY-FIVE

SAN PAOLINO

*Afternoon, July 8th of 1348,
City of Florence*

Beetles. The humming came from masses of tiny iridescent beetles that crawled like shimmering waves atop the yard of San Paolino. Ginevra's amulet grew hot. All the people missing from the streets seemed to be crammed into this very plot of earth. Plants had been ripped up, gravestones pulled out and moved to the edges of the yard, and even the street-pavers along the boundaries had been chiseled out to make room. Nobody had received a proper burial here in weeks, though the burying beetles were busy at work, reducing flesh to tidy bone. Adding to this macabre and industrious scene were people, even more wretched than Becchino, picking through the bodies searching for treasures. Ginevra saw one person cut the finger from a hand.

"What is he doing?" she asked, speaking loudly over the sound of the insects. "Do you think he found a ring?"

"Nah, it's the finger he's after."

"The finger? What will he do with it?"

"He'll sell it to a charlatan apothecary, who will sell it to somebody who thinks it can protect them. Of course, the thumb'll be from San Sebastiano or the like by the time it reaches its final customer."

"Of course," replied Ginevra. Maybe this thing was not so mysterious as the inquisitor believed. In times like these, there must be a class of wealthy clientele willing to pay for relics with guaranteed provenance. Perhaps if she followed these false relics taken from San Paolino, they might lead to the genuine articles. She turned to Becchino and asked, "Do you know where I could find such a business as that?"

His eyes narrowed. "Why would you want to know when you could take your pick of any number of fine fingers right now?"

"Oh, um. Not for me. I am fine with my own ten fingers, thank you. I have a friend who believes in these things and needs to be cured of her illusions."

"So long as you don't mix me up in it. Wouldn't want to ruin someone else's business."

Ginevra crossed herself solemnly.

"Right. There is one I know, who was scamming pilgrims long before the plague times. He is old as Methuselah; if something could kill him, he'd have been dead fifty years ago. You can find his shop on the street of the apothecaries, under the sign of the twin Janus head in the old *sestiere* of San Pancrazio."

"San Pancrazio – I think I remember..." Ginevra trailed off, looking past Becchino and noticing for the first time that the entrance to San Paolino was wide open. But not in the welcoming way; the entrance was black and gaping, a place abandoned. She moved toward it.

"Hey, you!" said Becchino, waving his hands in front of her face. "Where should I put her?" He gestured toward Antonella.

"Huh? Oh. I'm not sure – will you put her aside for a moment? I want to go inside the church quickly to say a prayer."

"As you wish. Say one for me, too, while you're at it."

Ginevra entered into the dark sanctuary and paused as her eyes adjusted. No candles were lit, no incense burned. And no Franciscan brothers, who were meant to be the keepers of this place, came forward to entreat her for coins or offer a candle. Instead, garbage and leaves, the refuse of a beggar's bed, and the smell of stale urine. An easy target for a thief.

Ginevra walked up to the apse and paused before the main altar. Grime covered the windows, so it was barely visible in the gloom; a slab of stone over a diamond-patterned iron grate. She knelt down, as if to pray, but instead peered through the grate to view the relics below the altar stone. No carved crystal goblet or gilded effigy. Just a simple glass box, the panes held together with uneven lead solder. There was something inside, something lumpy and bulbous, but it was so dark that no matter how she strained her eyes she could not see. She walked around to the back of the altar, entering the sacred space normally off-limits. "Hello?" she called out cautiously. "Is anyone here?"

But no disapproving priest came out of the shadows to ask her business. The back of the altar was closed with a grate the same as the front. She knelt down again and saw the corner was eaten by rust, and that a hole had been broken through. There were flaky bits of metal all on the floor. Somebody had poked at the hole recently! She looked around again, and seeing no one, crouched down more and stuck her arm through the hole, but the box was too far for her to reach. She strained farther, the rough broken edges of the grate pressing into her shoulder.

"Hey! What are you doing??"

Ginevra's heart lurched into her throat and she jerked her arm back.

"You know you're supposed to pray to the front of the altar, not the back of it, eh?"

It was only Becchino.

"I told you to wait outside! To bury your others first."

"Well, I already did that. Doesn't take so long when you

just dump 'em in a pile. What are you doing, anyway, reaching into there?" he said, crouching down beside her.

"I can't see in the dark but it looks like there is something strange about the reliquary…"

"Uh-huh," said Becchino skeptically. "It's supposed to be San Francesco's shoe."

"My arm is not long enough to reach it; it's very far back. We need a stick or something."

"I can help with that," said Becchino. "Wait here." Several minutes later, he appeared with a withered arm, the hand frozen with rigor mortis in a gesture of pointing.

"Jesus Christ, isn't there just a regular stick?" said Ginevra.

"No. Want to see what's in the box or not?"

She grimaced, and grasped the shoulder socket so that the dead hand looked like an unnatural extension of her own arm. She lay down again on the floor and the grisly tool did its job and soon the box was in her own live hands.

"Here you go," she said to Becchino, handing him back his corpse arm. They walked back toward the entrance, to where there was enough light to see into the box. It was a bundle of red velvet, tied up with gilded thread.

"Well, that looks as it should," said Becchino. "Let's put it back quick before we get ourselves cursed…"

"No," said Ginevra. "Look!"

The fabric was very old, and there were faded lines on it, the ghosts of careful creases that were no longer in their place. The gilded thread was in a loose and messy knot, not a neat bow. Somebody had put this back together recently and hastily. She pulled on the thread and the packet fell open, revealing an old sandal with holes through the bottom. The relic of San Paolino remained in its place.

"The shoe of San Francesco," said Becchino, touching it reverently. "Dama, I've got a friend watching my cart, but he's not *such* a good friend. Please put the shoe back. It's bad luck to steal from the poor."

"Yes, go. I'll be out shortly. Let me just return this." She rebundled the shoe and put it back inside the altar, then took out the inquisitor's list of thefts again. San Paolino was not so far from Santo Stefano, one of the four *Rogazione* churches that had been robbed in May. And the church of Santa Trinita, also, was but minutes away. Had the thief struck all these churches at the same time? But why take the time to break into San Paolino's altar, only to leave his prize where he found it? He must have been looking for something else. The shoe of San Francesco was a worthy relic by anyone's estimation – surely, it had significant monetary value. With lead stylus, she made additions to the list, her crude characters next to the inquisitor's expert flourishes:

> Santa Trinita – shoulder of San Giovanni Gualberto.
> Theft noticed: July 8. Relic last seen: unknown.
>
> San Paolino – shoe of San Francesco.
> Attempted theft noticed: July 8. Relic tampered with, left behind.

It struck her, then – the golden crucifix of San Giovanni, overlooked in favor of the less-valuable shoulder. The shoe of San Francesco, inspected and then put back in its place. *He only wants the relics that are body parts.* Ginevra had the sudden urge to be in full daylight. She tucked the inquisitor's colorful parchment away and went back outside, where her Becchino chatted to another.

"Well, Becchini," she said, "you must be rich men, with business so booming."

"Ha! It's true, the world's misfortune is our fortune. Were they to redraw the guilds, the gravediggers should be placed above the bankers, the physicians, all of them, for we are the only ones who keep to our posts. But even with this good run, I will never be a rich man."

"Why not?" asked the new *becchino*.

"Because! None of us are here for long, so I spend my money as soon as I get it."

"Where does one spend money right now?" asked Ginevra. "Whose business is open?"

"There are people with things. Live ladies and barrels of wine, if you know where to look for them, and anything fun right now costs almost as much as a decent burial." He winked at Ginevra. The camaraderie she was beginning to feel faded.

"You are wise to spend everything as it comes," said the new *becchino*. "I've just come from the dead parish of Santo Stefano; the Lord Girolami has expired."

"See what I mean?"

Girolami... Ginevra knew the name – they were rich enough to be famous even during her youth. "You mean the Girolami who say they are descended from Zenobio, whose head is missing?"

"The same," the second *becchino* said. "He spent all his days being mean, gathering and guarding his fortune. This is why Zenobio cursed him and left."

"Why do you think Zenobio would do that? I thought the Lord Girolami built him the chapel in Santa Reparata, that he paid for the silver head casket."

"Everyone knows the chapel was only because it saved him on his taxes. And the rest – all these things they say they do for Zenobio are only for themselves, to gain the favor of the populace. But all Ser Girolami's grasping has been for nothing. I hear his wife and his sons are sick, too, so his whole pile of gold will probably go straight to the commune."

"The children and wife – they are sick, but not dead yet?" asked Ginevra.

The second *becchino* shrugged. "If they are sick, they are dead. Along with the rest of their parish. It was only a matter of time; the relic was taken from the parish church weeks ago."

Ginevra remembered how the Girolami family were intimately involved with the annual mass celebrating his head relic. If anyone had the opportunity to see something, notice something amiss, it would be them. But already the man was dead. She must hurry if she was to speak with his wife.

"Thank you for the information, Becchini. I must take my leave." She turned to go.

"Hey! Wait a minute, what about your friend here? Where do I put her?" Becchino gestured to the full graveyard with the dead arm, still held in his own.

"Won't you put that down?"

"Nah, I kind of like it. Adds a gravitas to whatever I have to say."

Ginevra looked around the hellscape that was the churchyard of San Paolino.

"Becchino, is there no other option?"

"We could wrap her with stones and sink her in the Arno. It'll keep her from the scavengers, at least."

"Very well, let's do that, then."

"I'll need some money for rope, and for the extra time spent..."

Ginevra took the dead arm from him and threw it back into the graveyard. It landed at the feet of a scavenger, who picked it up appraisingly. "You press too far, Becchino! Do not take me for some girl-child. You have been paid enough to throw ten maidens into ten rivers!"

"Alright, alright," he said, miffed, as the second *becchino* snickered. "You can't blame a man for asking." He took his cart, now empty except for Antonella, and rolled away singing:

> *"A rosy maid in crimson gown*
> *Weds noble youth with golden crown*
> *But lo, their beauty soon departs*
> *See rotten eyes and wormy hearts..."*

Ginevra turned away from the foul place and headed toward the dead parish of Santo Stefano al Ponte and the tower of the Girolami.

TWENTY-SIX

TORRE GIROLAMI

Afternoon, July 8th of 1348,
Torre Girolami

Nobody knew how long the Girolami had lived in Florence, but it might as well have been since the beginning of time. Their tower was in the oldest part of the city, near the Ponte Vecchio. The structure itself was already a relic of another age, built when the magnate families fought openly in the streets and then ran back into their personal fortresses to shoot each other with arrows from the rooftops. Now, though, the city was a place for fat merchants, not hardened warlords. The outdated towers were eyesores, and it was forbidden to build any more of them. Most families had moved on, chopping off the tops of their towers and renovating them into more comfortable modern palazzos. But the Girolami remained in their ancestral home, its archaic form a testament to the longevity of their clan.

Ginevra had hurried past this tower many times during her years at Sant'Elisabetta, but never paid it much attention. Now, as she stood at the locked door, she was struck by the oppressive gloominess of the massive gray stone structure. It was square and narrow, high as a bell tower. She had to bend her head all the way back to see the top. The door was as small as the building was large. She banged on it, then stepped back, afraid of her own boldness. Nothing.

She shouted, "Hello," up at the small windows that perforated the tower in a vertical line.

Nothing.

They are dead already, she thought.

"Hey!! You!"

Ginevra jumped and looked up at the tower, but the windows remained shut.

"Hey! Over here, stupid woman!"

She spun around. It was a neighbor – poking his head out of his own window. "I wouldn't try so hard to get in there if I were you," he said. "The whole family is nearly dead."

"Did you say *nearly* dead? As in, still alive?"

"That's not the part I would focus on. The lord and master is cold and carried away."

"So I have heard – but I have urgent business with his widow and must be admitted."

The neighbor spit out his window. "See to it that you shut the door quickly and open it only slightly. I'll not be made ill by them."

Ginevra returned her attention to the door. It fit so perfectly against its frame she could not even get her fingernails around the edge. She heard a little creak from above, and saw a small child poking her head out some forty feet above the street. Ginevra smiled and waved at her, motioning for her to come down. The child disappeared immediately and was gone for so long Ginevra thought she had scared her away. Of course, anyone inside would know not to open the door for shouting strangers. But fortune was with her, and after some minutes of creaking gears and jangling chains, the door opened a crack and the child peeked out. She was about five years old and wearing only her shift of the finest linen that was very dirty.

Ginevra put her hand into the opening quickly, before the girl could shut it again, and eased her way in. There was hardly any space in the entry, just a small stool where a guard should be sitting and a long staircase twisting up into gloom. Ginevra marveled at how such a young child had managed to open the secure entryway, but remembered that opening forbidden doors is one of the very first skills a child learns. And also, in the same way an adult may receive a surprising burst of strength and endurance when confronted with danger, a child has the ability to become older and wiser than their years, and this poor little one had been waiting patiently for somebody to come see her. Now that a woman her own mother's age was present, she reverted and flung herself against Ginevra's skirts and held them tightly.

"It's alright, little bird," Ginevra said, kneeling to embrace her. "My name is Ginevra, what's yours?"

"Zenobia," she whispered, barely audible.

"Of course it is. Is your mama here, Zenobia?"

She pointed up the stairs. Ginevra put the child on her hip and began to climb. Even though Zenobia curled up like a kitten in her arms, it was a struggle to keep from tripping on her long skirts as she made her way up the narrow spiral in the dim light.

After what seemed like ages, the staircase opened up into a compact salon with low ceilings supported by massive wooden beams, painted with stripes and stars. The walls were lined with real woven tapestries instead of just painted imitations like at Lucia's. On a sideboard, again those ceramics of chickens with grapes, only here the suite was bespoke, the painted vines swirling about the great thick X that was the Girolami coat of arms. A ewer of silver was engraved with the same. There were carpets placed over the red tile floor, and the narrow windows were glazed with crystal panes of Venetian glass. But it was dark and silent, and stank of sick. Ginevra tried to put Zenobia down but she would not let go. Instead, she pointed one little finger toward a doorway on the other side of the room.

Still locked together, the pair crossed over and entered. For the second time that day, Ginevra was shocked by the foulness she saw, and felt her coral grow hotter still as it held at bay the disease that filled the air and coated the walls. Here lay mother and two sons on one mattress, breathing with heavy wheezes. Not one of them was strong enough to acknowledge Ginevra, let alone question her presence in their home. They had lain like this since their father's body was taken away the day before. With the great man dead, none of his friends felt obligated to attend to his family. Ginevra felt the girl's forehead, examined her throat. She showed no signs of infection. Yet.

"Zenobia, I must put you down so I can help your mama and brothers." The child reluctantly loosened her grip and allowed herself to be placed on the floor.

Ginevra went up to the bed and pulled back the cover, damp with unmentionable fluids. Their fevers were so high she could feel the heat rising from them. All were very far gone, the mother, lost in the troubled sleep that precedes death. *I must save the mother first*, she thought. *Her daughter needs a mother.* She turned to Zenobia. "Little bird, go find a cloth and cool water, and put it upon the foreheads of your mother and brothers. Can you do that?"

The child nodded and ran away. After she left the room, Ginevra peeled back Lady Girolami's shift and saw the swellings were on her thighs and in her armpits, too, black and trembling. The same symptoms as Lucia. *Thank God.* The bloodstones had been effective against this manifestation.

"Forgive my familiarity, Dama," she said as she took out her bloodstones and placed them to the swellings. As with Lucia, the stones began to thump like hearts, speeding up until the ill woman spasmed and vomited and the swellings shrank back into dark purple bruises. Ginevra did the same for the eldest boy and his breathing grew calm. But when she turned to the younger boy, he had no swellings. Instead there was dried blood around his mouth, and his breath came out in pneumatic wheezes. *It is in his lungs.* She placed the stones to his chest. His back arched and his mouth foamed and would not stop until she took the stones away. *It is too deep. Shit. Agnesa was right. Shit, shit, shit.*

She turned quickly, afraid Zenobia had seen, but she had not yet returned. She rolled him onto his side so he would not choke. She thought of how haughty she was toward the guild doctors, and now here she was, as unprepared as all of them. With a sorry heart, she pulled from her pouch a Memphis stone, which is white and crumbly, and can take away pain but will not cure a disease. She went to the fireplace set in the corner of the bedchamber, carved with more of the Girolami *X*s, and rubbed the Memphis roughly against the hearth until a bit of powder accumulated. She poured a few drops of water on it and mixed it into a paste, which she put on her finger and then shoved it into the boy's mouth. Ginevra wrung her hands. If he were to get better now, it would be through the strength of his own body and nothing she could provide.

She almost began to weep in frustration but then Zenobia returned with a wet sheet and began dutifully to wash his face. Ginevra's throat tightened into a painful knob as she held back her tears. She was the only conscious adult in the whole tower. And poor brave Zenobia trusted her to help. In the fireplace, Ginevra found an ember still burning in the ashes. She stripped Zenobia's soiled shift and lit it, and then did the same for the rest of the family's clothing, and their lovely bed things. She redressed them in clean shifts, and then she pulled Zenobia to her chest and sat down to wait for what would become of the other three. Death came soon, to the little boy. Ginevra and his sister wrapped him up solemnly. The second time in a day Ginevra had shrouded someone. This was when the Lady Girolami awoke from her stupor. She sat up with a start, her body understanding that it had been asleep while her children needed her.

Ginevra placed gentle hands on her shoulders, explaining all that had happened, how she was a healer, and how Zenobia had gone down all the stairs by herself to let her in. How the littlest one was dead. The lady stared at her, with wide blank eyes. She rose shakily, and walked around the bed to view her child's body, placing both hands upon him.

"Why are you in my home?" she asked at last.

"I am *so* sorry, Dama – I just wanted to help—"

"Nobody *just helps* anymore. We are in a dead parish. What did you come here for, tell me?"

"It is nothing. I would not burden you with it on such a day."

"Woman, look at what has become of me! I struggle to make sense of what is real – state your purpose, do not add to my confusion. Why are you in my home as my children die?"

Ginevra bit her lip, then haltingly answered: "I came because I am tasked with stopping the relic thief. I was going to ask about the missing Zenobio head. I know the relic is of great importance to your family. But, once I saw… I just wanted to help… I stayed to help."

"*Zenobio.* The moment that head was gone our fates were sealed. We should have fled, but my husband made us stay shut up in here, waiting for death to find us. And so he has." She pulled Zenobia to her, and made them both lie down on the bed, nestled between the body and his still-breathing brother.

Ginevra cringed. What had she been thinking, letting the little girl remain in this room? "Dama, your daughter has not yet contracted the disease. We must bury the dead immediately to protect her. I will help you—" She reached toward the body.

Lady Girolami pushed her hand away with unexpected force. "Do not touch him. I will not let you take my boy!"

"I understand it's hard, but we must act quickly. Surely, you have seen—"

A book of prayers struck Ginevra in the forehead. "Get out of my home! My babies belong with me!"

The woman was mad with grief, and what was Ginevra to

her but an intruder upon her most awful moment? An oil lamp whizzed by Ginevra's ear and smashed on the wall behind her.

Zenobia began to cry. She ran to Ginevra and whispered, "Please don't leave us."

Lady Girolami wrenched her daughter out of Ginevra's arms. "I said GET OUT."

Overcome by rage and anguish, she shoved Ginevra out of the room and slammed the heavy door.

No amount of pounding or pleading could convince Lady Girolami to readmit Ginevra into the locked chamber. And so, with heavy heart and leaden legs, she began the long descent back to the street.

TWENTY-SEVEN

SANTA MARIA NOVELLA

Afternoon, July 8th of 1348,
City of Florence

After Ginevra and the *becchino* rattled away, Lucia walked toward the complex of Santa Reparata and the Baptistry of San Giovanni. There she would fulfill her promise to Ginevra by (briefly) examining the altars of San Zenobio and San Filippo. Afterward, she would go to her own favorite saint, San Tommaso D'Aquino, whose blessed finger was kept in the church of Santa Maria Novella.

Picking the correct personal saint said much about a person, and Lucia was very proud that she had developed a special relationship with the exotic, foreign Tommaso *before* any of her acquaintances even heard of him (he had only just been canonized a few decades ago). When the wealthy Strozzi family acquired his finger relic and built a chapel for it in Santa Maria Novella, Lucia thought smugly how it had been she that first mentioned San Tommaso to Jacobo Strozzi at a party. So, although the chapel had not been built with her funds, nor according to her design, she felt ownership of the completed structure and took pride in how it drew pilgrims to Florence. In fact, the finger was so popular it was made part of a new pilgrimage route, "The

Divine Nine," a compact walk featuring the most celebrated relics in the city center.

Free from the pain and terror of pestilence, Lucia couldn't help but be in a good mood at the thought of visiting Tommaso, and the emptiness of the city did not scare her. It was not long before she arrived at the tangled scaffolding that enclosed Santa Reparata. The dead man Ginevra mentioned was still there, and she hurried quickly past him, hoping he would not drip on her. Once through the scaffolding, she stepped carefully over torn-up earth, stone blocks, and abandoned masons' tools to reach the intact facade of the church. Reparata had been enveloped in this confusing jumble of construction since before Lucia was born. No longer a grand enough symbol for the city, the Signoria had broken ground on a new cathedral so large that now, a half century after the project began, only the lower portions of this vast structure had been erected.

The exterior chaos spilled inside the poor old building, and instead of a space of sacred geometry, the interior of Reparata felt cluttered and sad. The scaffolds blocked the sunlight that once glowed through stained glass, and broken tiles made it treacherous to walk. Even the faces carved into marble tombstones set in the floor were worn beyond recognition from centuries of feet stepping all over them. Lucia walked down the dusty aisle toward the apse, where a gilded mosaic of Jesus and his flock, now nearly obscured with soot and evaporated beeswax, decorated the concave ceiling above the altar. This golden Christ was very old-fashioned now, a relic of Byzantine taste, and would be broken apart when it was time to lay the floors of the new cathedral. Even so, Lucia knelt before him to pray for guidance.

Lord Christ, is it correct for a woman to attempt to solve such a large problem as the missing relics of Florence? Ginevra had saved her life, and so she was indebted to her. This she had no problem comprehending. And if she had asked any other favor of her, she would not feel hesitant, but this – to become involved with thieves, with sorcery. *It sounds exciting, but is it allowed?*

Um, Amen, she said, standing up, not really sure if she had been praying or just talking to herself. Lucia walked into the columned alcove underneath the main altar, to where Zenobio's shrine was located. She knelt down and peered through the iron grate on the front of it. There was the emptied head reliquary, staring back at her stern as ever. She thought of all the places a thief could hide a saint's skull and grew overwhelmed.

Standing back up, Lucia noticed her dress was covered with a reddish dust that stained her garment when she tried to brush it off. She became frustrated with her task, with dirty old Reparata. Her whole life, people had removed whatever obstacle they could for her comfort, including the making of all but the most trivial of decisions. Now she was wandering by herself through the unknown and she did not like it.

She left Santa Reparata and crossed the piazza to the Baptistry. Gilt faces glared at her from the twenty-eight quatrefoil panels set into its massive bronze doors. She pushed, but they did not budge. *Here is one building still properly tended, at least.* If the Baptistry was kept locked up, how did the thief get inside to take San Filippo's arm? For that matter, how did he get to Zenobio? The church was open, but the altar itself was kept locked. Lucia suddenly realized she was alone in a place that should be crowded. Just her and the faces on the doors and that dead man on the scaffold. She hurried away toward Santa Maria Novella. What a fruitless afternoon! Lucia knew she wouldn't be a helpful assistant. She would explain to Ginevra that evening – she would have to understand. Lucia just wasn't as clever as her new friend, wasn't cut out to investigate mysterious crimes.

At Santa Maria Novella, Lucia looked around for a Dominican brother so she could purchase a candle for her San Tommaso, but there was nobody. At least that she could see. The church was massive, and the far corners disappeared into darkness. Never mind. She was sure San Tommaso would understand. She would find a candle from her home to bring him later.

The chapel that housed his relic was in the western transept. Often a gilded iron gate kept all the public out, and the finger could only be admired from afar, but today Lucia saw it was open. She took this as a good sign, and went inside and knelt before the rock crystal goblet containing his relic. But as she directed her adoring gaze toward the object, her eyes focused not on the familiar, withered bit of flesh but a small bottle filled with lavender liquid – it could not be! San Tommaso would not have left Florence – left *her* – in her time of need! Somebody took him. Lucia felt violated, as if she personally had been robbed. Never mind her misgivings – she could not let whoever did this get away with it. She knelt again. *Blessed Tommaso. Don't even worry. I will help Ginevra find your finger. And then I will bring you a candle. Amen.* She removed the glass bottle from the reliquary and put it in the purse (embroidered with a scene of Tommaso levitating in prayer) that hung from her belt. She left the Strozzi chapel, shutting the gate behind her, and walked quickly toward the exit, across the empty narthex at the heart of the great sanctuary. A ghostly figure crossed in front of her, out from the shadows of the ambulatory. She stifled a gasp and crouched down, though there was nothing to hide behind. But the ghost paid her no mind and went on gliding through the gloom in its long crimson gown until – Lucia recognized the figure. It was not a ghost, but a friend, the same friend who many weeks ago had invited her to come away to the country.

"Pampinea?" called Lucia. The figure let out its own small cry of fright.

"Pampinea," Lucia called again, "it's me!"

"Oh! Oh, my goodness, Lucia Tornaparte, is that you?? Alive? I heard you were dead."

"Ha! I thought you a ghost as well." She crossed toward her friend, but as she did, Pampinea took steps backward and the space between them did not grow smaller.

"Praise be to the saints," said Pampinea. "And how is your lord and husband?"

"I know not. He thought it best to go to the country. I remain alone."

"I don't know why you should choose to stay. Isn't it true that your parish is all dead? That your Santa Trinita is robbed of its relic?" As she spoke, Pampinea took a few more steps back.

Lucia halted her advance. "How did you know it was missing?"

"Somebody shouted it from the *ringhiera* days ago. Is it not true?"

"It...is true the shoulder of San Giovanni is missing." Lucia was stunned. How could it be common knowledge when she and Ginevra had just discovered the theft hours ago?

Pampinea took another step back.

"Wait, why are *you* here?" asked Lucia. "When last we spoke, you were about to leave."

"The thing has not yet come to pass. It's not easy to organize a party so large, and we heard that the roads were full and one must be exposed to all manner of people in order to travel...as I suppose is the same to go to church."

A new voice called out from the entrance.

"Pampinea, is that you over there? Sorry I'm late – Lucia?!" said the newcomer as she approached. "What are you doing here? I thought you were dead!"

"Well, as you can see, I am not," she said, doing her best to sound cheerful. "Hello, Fiammetta."

"Hello, I suppose. Ah, and look, there is my cousin Filomena entering now."

"Hello, dear ladies," called Filomena as she hurried toward them and then stopped short. "Oh, Lucia! Why are you here? Isn't Santa Trinita a dead parish? Do you not care for us that you come here and expose us?"

That morning Lucia had been excited to become a part of the world again. Now she realized the world did not return the sentiment. "I am not sick, but quite well, and this is the first time in many weeks I have left my house. Is it not natural that the first place I came was to a church to pray?" She meant to keep an even tone, but Lucia's voice was loud now, defensive, echoing throughout the sanctuary. Several other women, who had been praying in their own dark corners of the cavernous space, came forward as they heard the voices.

"See, I was not the only one who still comes to pray! Surely, mine is not the only parish affected by pestilence."

"No, but it is one of the worst. Everyone knows that where relics are taken, the pestilence cannot be held back," said Fiammetta.

But they must not know about San Tommaso yet, thought Lucia, *or they would not dare to meet here. This theft is fresh.*

The newcomers approached and Lucia recognized all of them. "Hello, Emilia, Lauretta, Neifile, Elissa... Elissa! Oh, how are you – how are you all here together? At the exact same time?" (Lucia had barely caught herself from offering condolences – for Elissa was none other than the widow of Ludovico Acciaiuoli. She did not look like one bereaved.)

"We're not here together. It's just a coincidence," said Pampinea, speaking over Elissa. She looked around at the group of women with a pointed stare. Several looked down at their feet.

Now Lucia understood. It was their whole brigade who planned to leave to the country, the group Lucia had once been a part of herself. They were here to finally organize their trip, and nobody had even bothered to check and see if she still might join them. Worse yet, now that they saw she was alive, nobody wanted to let her know she was not too late. First, her husband, and now her friends did not want her. She had only Ginevra, who might have found a house already empty to stay in but instead heard her cries and rescued her. Very well. If these false friends would not give her an invitation, perhaps they could give her information.

"Well," Lucia said, putting on her most genteel smile. "What a very pleasant coincidence. What *are* the chances?"

"It's not so strange," said Elissa, eager now to assist Pampinea. "Everything is closed besides churches. There is not one market open, nor any piazza not fouled by corpses. My home is so dull and silent that prayer sounded like an exciting change of pace."

"You *must* have been bored, Elissa," said Fiammetta, "to have taken to praying."

"You know I have been bored for years," said the widow.

"What do you mean?" asked Lucia.

"She means," said Fiammetta, "that her dear late husband spent his nights pining for his lost *amante* instead of visiting her chamber—"

Lucia subconsciously touched the brooch pinned to her shoulder. *Not my wife/But my life.*

"Fiammetta, don't be unpleasant," said Pampinea. She turned to Lucia: "Please, I can hear in your voice you are hurt, but why should we not believe you are dead, when all we hear all day is this friend or that friend is dead." But still she did not mention the trip.

The rest of the group nodded their agreement and murmured apologies.

Lucia wondered if she'd have done any different if one of them had stopped leaving their home. Even still, she was not ready to forgive them, and focused on her small revenge of manipulating the conversation. It wouldn't be hard. This was a group that thrived in gossip.

"Elissa, you are right. There is nothing to do except go into churches. In fact, this is the third one I have visited today."

"Really? Whatever for?"

"Well, since my own parish was robbed, I wanted to see the altars of San Filippo and Zenobio as well. *Who* could have done such a thing?" she said conspiratorially.

Pampinea shrugged. "Incompetent priests leave doors unlocked and thieves steal treasures. That is why I keep my own relics! You never know when you need a saint devoted just to you." She pulled out a tiny reliquary pouch on a string and kissed it. "Lucia, do you still have the San Sebastiano I gave you? Is that what has kept you well?"

"Oh…mm…yes," said Lucia, working hard to control a sarcastic snort. "I keep it by my bed and pray to it every night! I am sure it has kept me in health." Actually, the cheap necklace gave off a very strong odor, and she had put it in the bottom of a chest long ago. Once she found San Tommaso, she would have to ask forgiveness for lying in his church. She hoped he would understand, considering the circumstances.

Pampinea relaxed a bit. "Lucia, everybody knows all about the missing relics, one after the other for weeks, it's all we hear. It's why we finally decided to lea – haven't you any better gossip, I mean?"

Had she. Lucia thought about the missing saint finger and the bottle in her purse. About the convicted heretic now living in her home, who cured the plague with magic jewels and had a big scar on her nose and who was the *amante* of Elissa's husband. But all of this must be kept secret. For now, at least. She had promised.

"Well, I have been shut up that whole time, and since I missed the processions, I admit I was curious. Santa Reparata is unlocked, though you are right everyone in the parish must be dead. I was the only person in the whole place, I swear it."

The group leaned in, forgetting their fear of contagion in their hunger for a bit of conversation.

"And you went in all by yourself? Is that dead stonemason still up there? What did you find?"

"Nothing, I found nothing. Though I crouched down on the dirty floor to look – the silver head is there the same as before except empty, I suppose. And the Baptistry *is* locked so I couldn't even see where the Filippo Arm is stored. Do you know how to get into the Baptistry when nobody is being baptized?"

They all shook their heads.

"Lucia, why are you doing all this? Do you think you can catch the thief?" Pampinea said incredulously.

"Of course not." (Another lie she'd have to tell San Tommaso about.) "I just find it fascinating. Somebody *must* know. And the fact that relics were stolen from the *church* makes it all the more sordid."

"Lucia," said Pampinea, "this is *hardly* the most sordid crime happening."

The group leaned in again.

"Oh?"

"I mean, it's not a thing to discuss in church..."

With only the slightest bit of encouragement, Pampinea crossed herself and continued:

"I suppose I'll just have to go to confession later. Well: I have heard that many of our fellow citizens are determined to make a good time of what time is left. They do this by entering properties left untended and enjoying their goods. It's a very popular pastime, for a certain type."

"How do you know this?"

Pampinea shrugged. "I have a cousin who's a bit of a rogue. He's in love with me, so he tells me whatever I ask him. You know, it is probably these same shameful people stealing the relics. Some say they are angry at God for not helping us, so they mock Him."

All the ladies crossed themselves.

"But...how would they find each other?" asked Lucia.

"It's easy, because like attracts like. The same as in any time, you can find those vile folks drinking themselves into a stupor at the trattoria Alle Panche."

Alle Panche. Even Lucia knew of that infamous place. "I thought all the drinking houses – all businesses – are closed now. As Elissa said."

"It is true during the daytime, but these thieves need a place to spend what they've stolen, so after dark, the tavern breaks curfew. I mean, who is there to stop them? They run about by torchlight like devils and go to the tavern and drink cheap wine from stolen silver. They show off what they have robbed and trade it amongst themselves. But it is not just common criminals there. Some of our own class – and even the clergy – go, determined to indulge in as many sinful activities as possible. They have no scruples of eating, drinking, and fornicating with whomever they choose. Once they find their band at Alle Panche, they make their wicked plans. Every night, they take over the houses of those who fled, and empty all their provisions and wear their clothes."

Lucia was glad she had locked the door to her house when she left. Silence filled the sanctuary after Pampinea's story. She realized the women were still waiting for her to leave, so they could get on with their planning. Fine, then. She was tired of pretending not to notice.

"I suppose I'll go home, then, before it is too late. The afternoon shadows grow long, and as you said, there are nasty people about."

"Good idea," agreed Pampinea. "Well, goodbye, then."

Lucia turned and went toward the doorway, willing herself not to cry about the missing Tommaso, about being uninvited to their holiday.

"Wait!" called Pampinea as she neared the door. Lucia turned around, hopefully. "Lucia, I know I made it sound terribly exciting, and you seem almost as bored as Elissa, but don't get any ideas about going to Alle Panche – it *really* is too much for one of your delicate sensibilities."

Lucia smiled graciously, and walked out of the church into the dusty, deserted city. Never mind them. Soon she would become a woman so interesting nobody would dare leave her behind. She clutched the mysterious bottle in her purse, certain of one thing: she must visit the trattoria Alle Panche as soon as possible.

TWENTY-EIGHT

RUBY RED CLARET

Evening, July 8th of 1348,
Palazzo Tornaparte

Ginevra walked slowly along the river toward Lucia's home, rubbing the bump on her forehead where Lady Girolami's prayer book had struck her. She didn't blame her. The poor woman had lost so much – and had more to lose, still. The girl, Zenobia, was in grave danger. Ginevra's coral had glowed bright red in the tower, and it seemed only a matter of time before the little one fell ill. *Please don't leave us*, she'd said. Ginevra could not bear it. Perhaps there was a way to protect the child without provoking the mother. Something in the stones. She must find it, and quickly.

In the approaching dusk, a pile of discarded rags rustled ahead of her. Ginevra heard a little cry; it was a kitten, the color of dust and clay, decorated all over in stripes and dots. Ginevra looked around, but saw no mama cat watching from the shadows. She crouched down and reached out her hand. The kitten suckled her offered fingers. The rags smelled strongly of ammonia. Ginevra's mind leaped to Agnesa's deathbed rantings. *If you had a lynx, you might use its urine to extract the essence of your jewels.* That was what she needed: a catalyst to draw out the healing magic of stones, turn it into something that could be swallowed to protect the blood, the lungs. More than a cure; a prophylactic. And what was a lynx but a gigantic cat who lived in the mountains? Ginevra had seen the pelt of a lynx once, at the port in Genoa. This kitten had the same sort of coloring, the same markings. *This* is how she would protect Zenobia. She gathered up the kitten and rags in her arms. "Come on, cat, I will let no more creatures die today." The kitten mewed her thanks.

As night fell, the pair arrived back at the Palazzo Tornaparte, and found Lucia in the kitchen, where she had put together a supper of stale cheese ends paired with a rare ruby claret foraged from her husband's private cellar. Ginevra looked around the kitchen: the eel bones were still upon the table, and her embers had gone out even though she had buried them carefully in ashes. They'd been scraped out onto the hearth to heat a pot containing the remnants of Ginevra's bread dough – now scorched and fused rocklike to the bottom of the tin vessel.

"Sorry about dinner," said Lucia. "I wanted to make you an eel pie like you made me but I couldn't catch an eel and then I realized I didn't know how to make a pie and also the fire went out. So, here is cheese."

"Thank you, Monna Lucia, I'm grateful all the same." And she meant it.

"Tell me, what is that bundle you carry? It smells like cat piss."

"It IS cat piss. And I've got the cat to go with it. Look – here is one even more in need of a meal than we." She pulled the top of the rags away and a little cat head popped up to observe her new surroundings.

"Ohhh, she was left all by herself, the same as me. Ginevra, you have collected us all together. Give her here." She took the kitten from the filthy rags, and fluffed up an old apron inside a basket for her new home. She set down a dish of water and then picked the remnants of dried eel from the rubbish bones and fed her in little bits. The kitten nipped hungrily at her fingers and started to purr.

"Lucia, you are an excellent mother cat."

"It's nice to be needed... I came upon my friends today at church. They all thought me dead, and were not so glad to be wrong."

Ginevra could only shake her head. It had been too much for one day. The numbness was fading, the day's horrors reasserting their dominance over her psyche. She took a gigantic gulp of the wine.

Lucia grinned.

"What?" said Ginevra.

"The wine – my husband reserved it for his most important business partners. They would only take tiny sips and then praise it like it was their lover after each little drop. Pour me some and we'll drain the bottle."

Ginevra obliged, and the women fell into their supper, such as it was, discussing how it had been in their separate days. Lucia told how she had dirtied her knees at the altar of Zenobio, how the Baptistry was locked up. She shared the sad news that the finger of San Tommaso was stolen, and how everybody already knew her Santa Trinita was a dead parish missing its relic. How wicked people met at the tavern Alle Panche to drink and plot. (She tactfully left out her encounter with Ludovico's widow.) Ginevra carefully added the theft of the Tommaso finger to the inquisitor's list:

> Santa Maria Novella – finger of San Tommaso D'Aquino.
> Theft noticed: July 8. Relic last seen: winter 1348.

She then told Lucia of the dead Fra Simone, dead Agnesa, and the dead child in the Torre Girolami, and of how the bloodstones failed her twice. She spoke of the tampered-with relic at San Paolino, and its awful graveyard.

"I couldn't leave your Antonella there, it was not right. There was not an inch of dirt not already filled. And those on top covered with the most meager sprinkling of earth, like cheese on a lasagna."

Lucia pushed away her cheese. "So…where is she, then?"

"We sunk her in the river, that way nobody would come and take her finger or her nose."

"I hope it's alright if you have been buried under water instead of earth. She did not have a confession, either." Both of them thought of poor Antonella, stuck in purgatory.

"I will light a candle for her," said Lucia, adding it to the mental list of candles she'd already promised San Tommaso. "Ginevra, what did you mean, that people would take her finger or her nose?"

"Ugh. Give me some more of that expensive wine." Ginevra explained what she had heard – people making a business taking bits from the newly dead and disguising them as genuine relics.

"No!"

"It's true, I swear it. And there is a man who makes his living buying up these pieces of flesh and keeps a shop where he sells them as true relics."

Lucia turned ashen, and went to her room. She came back with a necklace containing a small bit of dried-up something. "A gift, from Pampinea, who is much taken with that sort of thing. I suppose this is not really a piece of San Sebastiano, then?"

Ginevra remembered Becchino's mention of the current popularity of San Sebastiano and grimaced. Lucia threw it out the window. "Alright. Enough. There is work to be done." Ginevra stood up and busied herself in starting a new fire. She had to keep her mind occupied or the sorrow would take over and she would never be able to accomplish the task the inquisitor set for her.

"What are you doing?"

"Two people died today under my fingertips. I might have

saved them had I been more prepared. There is a girl still alive – for now – the bravest little thing, Lucia. She begged me not to leave her."

"It is tragic to be sure. But, Ginevra, you must—"

"There is a way, I think, I can draw the power out of the bloodstones, so it can be delivered all throughout the body. Protect her from disease before it happens."

"Really? How would you do that?"

"I'm not sure exactly," Ginevra admitted. "I only read about it once, long ago. My teacher Agnesa reminded me of it with her last breath this very morning." *Before you could make amends, before you could say you loved her and you were so, so sorry.*

"Ginevra?"

"Yes. Sorry – there are standard methods for transferring the magical essence of one thing to another. If I am remembering correctly, the first thing is the stones must be steeped overnight with urine from our cat, and I suppose a bit of honey and wine, and tended constantly the whole time."

"The *whole* night?" Lucia had never done anything that took a whole night.

"Yes. Then eventually it will froth up, then you let it rest, and then it becomes clear and that's how you know it's done. The magic of the boiled object – in our case, the bloodstones – will have spread also to the boiling liquid."

"And it has to be cat urine because…?"

"For magic things like this, it's the urine of cats that works the best. Or rather, really it should be a wild lynx from the mountains whose urine works wondrous things all by itself and sometimes even hardens into gems, but for us this regular kitten will have to do. I think it should still work, right?"

"If you say so. What is the honey for, then? And the wine?"

"That's just so you forget you're drinking cat piss."

"Ginevra, I am so very glad you broke your contract to cure me. But deliberately mixing medicines for one of the most famous families in town? You must understand that they punish people most terribly here. It is not so uncommon that someone is beheaded or burned for some trivial-seeming thing... My own father..."

"Yes, I know how it is," said Ginevra defensively. "I used to live here, too, you know."

She pointed to the scar on her nose. "This line that makes my face crooked – this was my reward for stopping the water sickness of 1340. They meant it to be much worse."

"Your face is not so crooked, Ginevra," Lucia replied quietly.

"That's because I fixed it myself – they cut off half my nose to mark me a heretic."

"So you understand better than anyone what will happen if they catch you at healing again."

"That was the problem, the first time I was *caught*. This time I will be quick – by tomorrow morning, this new medicine will be delivered, then back to the missing relics. Nobody will notice. The inquisitor has no retinue. The bishop cannot be bothered. Who is there to see me?"

"Yes, it seems that way now, but you know how it can be. Just when you feel safe, somebody hears something, sees something, and the guard who went away will be back and knocking at your door. *My* door."

"No one will know."

"The Lady Girolami will know."

"I'll tell her it's nourishing broth to aid recovery. I will visit her in the morning and be done with it." Lucia was torn. Of course, Ginevra was right; she should do what she could to save a child. But she was worried about what would happen to her friend should she be found repeating the crimes of her past.

"Ginevra, my acquaintance Pampinea, she said people trade stolen goods at Alle Panche. She said corrupt clergy go there, too – would this not be a good place to investigate? We should go now – it is only open at night."

"Tonight is for saving Zenobia's life. Perhaps tomorrow."

Lucia did not appreciate being discounted yet again. She decided to take a dramatic stance to get Ginevra's attention.

"Fine. I will go to Alle Panche tonight. By myself, while you work. The sooner we catch the thief, the sooner you can get your license and stop this sneaking around." The ploy worked.

"By yourself??" said Ginevra, looking up from the fire she was attempting to rebuild.

"You speak with the same tone of Pampinea! What, am I a baby who can't even feed herself? There is no curfew enforced now."

"I'm sorry, of course, you are not. It's just…have you ever spent time in taverns before?"

"Sometimes when traveling."

"But not by yourself, of course."

"No. Always with a chaperone."

"Don't you think your presence would be obvious, then? What would happen if our thief *was* there, and learned he was being asked after?"

"I wouldn't be *so* obvious. All sorts are mixing who wouldn't otherwise. Look at you and I, for example. I would *never* have invited you here in normal times."

"Exactly, your husband is a man of importance. You don't think you'll be recognized?"

"Well… I could wear poor Antonella's other dress so I'll look like a maid."

Ginevra was about to continue her list of reasons why Lucia shouldn't go, but stopped herself. Who was she to tell an adult woman where she could and could not go? She'd practically begged Lucia to help, and now it was being offered freely. Perhaps it would be good for her, to enact something of her own design. "It's true the light is low in places such as this…and people have had much to drink, as a rule, before they even walk in the door."

"Yes!"

"And, I suppose you could just say you're a new widow

joining in by yourself for the first time, because your husband and all your friends are gone."

"Yes. How depressingly true that is."

"Alright, then, if you are determined, Lucia, you go with my gratitude. Here, I have some things that will help keep you safe." Ginevra pulled her little leather bag from her purse, and carefully poured a colorful pile of gemstones onto the table, selecting a transparent wine-colored disk, about the size of a thumbnail. She held it out for Lucia to take.

"What is this lovely thing?"

"It is a purple amethyst, and a very special one. If you keep it under your tongue or in your cheek, you may drink as much as you wish but never feel drunk. In this way, you may benignly loosen the tongues of others while remaining lucid yourself." She dropped the stone into Lucia's outstretched palm.

Lucia grew nervous as she looked at the amethyst. She hadn't expected Ginevra to agree to it so readily.

"Wait – I just thought of something: Even if I *were* to go to the tavern with the jewel, and speak to rough people, and even if my disguise were convincing enough…to walk the streets alone after dark. It is not wise. Any scoundrel knows he can get away with any crime right now…"

But Ginevra just nodded knowingly. "Don't worry, I have something for that, too." She picked up from the pile a golden hexagonal crystal attached to a silver chain, and put it around Lucia's neck. "This is a heliodor. Hold it in your hand and it will be a torch seen only by yourself and anyone touching you. The light is invisible to all others. It's so dark now, the moon almost gone, that if you are quiet, you can move about unseen."

"Oh – so, that solves that issue, then?"

Ginevra beamed.

"I supposed I'd rather not be here to smell all the boiling cat urine, anyhow… Tell me," she said, stalling for time, "where do you get your wonderful stones?"

Ginevra had never had the chance to show off her collection

before. "The most precious to me were given by a dear friend. She is long dead." Ginevra paused, swallowing hard, waiting for the lump in her throat to leave so she could speak further. Even with all the day's death, the loss of Vermilia still stung like a new cut whenever Ginevra's mind landed upon it. She touched the jasper ring on her left hand. Lucia reached out and squeezed her arm.

"So, as I was saying," said Ginevra, taking a deep breath, "once I learned what to look for, I acquired more gems from merchants and sailors who came into Genoa from their own far-off lands."

"And where do they find them?"

"From all sorts of frightening places. Some grow in the sea, or in the stomachs of animals, like this bezoar." She picked up a shiny brown sphere, about the size of a peach pit and with the look of fine polished wood.

"And what is its magic?" asked Lucia, now enthralled.

"If you grate a little bit of it over a poisoned drink, it will render it harmless."

"You mean, grate it as if it were a nutmeg?"

"Precisely."

"But if you know it's poisoned, wouldn't you just not drink it instead of wasting the bezoar?"

"I hadn't thought of that... In truth, I haven't used this one yet. Maybe if the drink was something really delicious and you didn't want to throw it out? Something expensive like your husband's wine?"

"Oh, yes, then that would be a good thing to have. And what about this one?" She picked up a gem clear as water, the shape of two pyramids stuck together at their fat bottoms.

"Ah, you remain as ever the wife of a wealthy man. These come from far away and are exceedingly costly. I got this one from an heirless merchant on his deathbed, otherwise he never would have parted with it. It is called diamante. When given as a gift between two quarreling parties, it ends the quarrel."

"Even a war?"

"So they say."

"Do diamanti come from inside animals also?"

"No, they come from deep canyons in India where they are guarded by serpents and sharp rocks so it is too perilous for any man to venture down and gather them."

"So how do they get them, then?"

"They throw butchered goats off the cliff tops into the canyons, and the stones stick into the soft meat. Eagles fly down to the dead goats and bring them back to their nests to feed their chicks. Then the merchants scare away the mother birds, and pick through the carcasses to find their treasure."

"Come, Ginevra. This is a story for a child, is it not?"

"Perhaps, but it is what they say! And until we have journeyed to India and seen for ourselves, who are we to doubt such a fine tale? But enough of this for now. It is late already, and if you are to be on your way, you must be on your way."

And with that, she picked up the dirty street rags and threw them into a pot with water, beginning the long process of extracting the healing essence of the bloodstones with the help of a kitten.

TWENTY-NINE

ALLE PANCHE

*Night, July 8th of 1348,
an Infamous Tavern*

With an amethyst in her cheek and the heliodor held aloft like a lantern, Lucia crept through dark and empty streets toward the infamous tavern Alle Panche. It was black as a hole outside the small golden sphere of light cast by the gem, and even with the magic beacon, her mind still played tricks as she hurried past the doorways of dead neighbors. Several times, she heard whispers and pattering steps, a pleading cry ending in a muffled *whump*. She held her breath and pressed against walls, clutching the light, until the silence was full again, and it was as Ginevra said: nobody noticed her. Quickly, quietly, Lucia hurried onward. In her old life, she would *never* have left her home after curfew. Certainly not to visit Alle Panche. But still, she knew where it was. Everybody in Florence knew where it was, either to seek it out or to avoid it.

Alle Panche was the sort of place where naive travelers were robbed of their purses and young men met to realize the grisly ends of familial vendettas. Whenever there was a criminal led through town on a donkey, you could bet the location "Alle Panche" would be yelled out in the catalog of his crimes. But it was also the sort of place that guaranteed an exciting evening, if you could manage to just observe the trouble instead of joining it.

It was with this intrepid thought that Lucia steadied her nerves, tucked away her light, and stooped through a sunken door into the low vaulted interior. It was smelly inside, and dim, and it was *crowded*, and the rumble of conversation was punctuated by real, actual laughs. *Here are all the people with life left in them!* she thought. Instead of the repulsion she was bred to feel, a sense of camaraderie swelled in her breast – and as she observed the dirty crowd, sitting close to one another on rough wooden benches, she almost had to wipe away a tear. She peered through the smoky light of clay lamps and saw a man in a monk's habit perched importantly atop a mighty stack of barrels.

Lucia made her way to him across the sticky floor and called, "Hello... Brother Monk? Are you the keeper of this place? May I have some wine please?"

"Hello, Sister Lady. Are you a patron of this place? May I have some money please?"

"Oh, yes, of course, forgive me. How much?" She pulled her purse out and the monk eyed its heft.

"Two lire."

"Of course, I have that."

"And that is just for the wine," he added hastily. "You must also pay to rent the vessels."

"I see...and what is the cost of that?"

"Four lire for a jug to hold it and a cup to drink from."

"Twice as much as the wine??"

"If you'd rather, you can kneel down and I'll uncork my barrel straight into your mouth."

Though Lucia did not grasp his meaning exactly, she understood well enough she was the butt of a joke. "How dare you suggest such a thing, that I would dirty my dress on this disgusting floor!"

"Oh, come off it, from the looks of it, you've kneeled down in far worse."

Lucia remembered that she was wearing Antonella's old dress – without her own fine garments, she was subject to the crass treatment of a common woman.

"Well, actually, I haven't, so – don't say I have!" she retorted, dropping coins obediently into his greasy, outstretched palm. The maybe-monk stashed them, and passed her a rough earthen vessel filled to the brim. She clutched it to her chest and looked over the crowded benches of strange faces, not seeing any open place for herself.

"Brother, where shall I sit?" she inquired of the monk.

She really was making it too easy for him.

"Right here," he replied, grabbing himself. A few nearby patrons sniggered.

"I do not believe you are a monk!" said Lucia, mortified. The nearby patrons lost all composure.

"Look, darling, you don't want to mess with that," said a disheveled drunk, between guffaws. "I've got a nice straight one, sit on me instead."

Lucia looked around desperately and decided to move back toward the door, the farthest point from the rude men. She spotted a man and woman in conversation near to the entrance. Surely, in the company of a woman she'd be safer from terrible jokes. Also, it was usually easier to get gossip out of couples, since they were always trying to show off to the third party how witty they were. *Right. Forget the monk and his drunks.* She was going to ply this couple with drink, and ask them about the thief once their wits had been dulled. She made her way through the crowd, bumping into everyone and spilling her wine all over.

"Hey, watch it, whore!"

"Excuse me, pardon, I'm so sorry!"

She reached the couple.

"Salve," she said in greeting, interrupting their conversation.

"Salve," said the man warily, eyeing the carnage of winesoaked patrons behind her.

When Lucia did not speak further, the woman asked, "Can we help you?"

"Oh, yes! May I barter some wine for a seat?"

"Certainly," said the woman. Lucia made a move to sit down.

"Providing," she continued, "that you first tell us where you come from."

"From Florence, of course."

"But *where* in Florence?" said the man.

Lucia remembered how Pampinea had been afraid to come near her, and decided a small lie was the best way forward. "In the...parish of Santa Croce. Not so far from here. I heard this was the best place to find others of my own disposition, that is, alive and enjoying themselves."

The lady laughed at the small witticism, relaxing. "Santa Croce, it's still alright there. They still have their relic of the cross. Come, sit. My name is Maria and this here is my man, Lorenzo."

"Charmed," beamed Lorenzo, visibly tipsy now that his guard was down.

Maria moved over to make room on her bench. "What's your name, darling?"

"I am Lucia, it's a pleasure," she said, sitting down and passing her wine jug. Two more men stumbled into the tavern and waved their hellos to Maria and Lorenzo as they unwrapped cloths from around their faces.

"Does everyone here know each other?" asked Lucia.

"A bit. After a while, you remember the faces and, in truth, you're the first new person I've seen come in here in some time," said Maria.

"So...do you come here often?"

"Often enough. But we go from place to place, enjoying food and wine...little pleasures, wherever we can find them." Lorenzo pinched Maria's bottom at this and then looked away innocently. She gave him a playful whack on the head. Lucia noticed that Maria wore a girdle of silver over her rough linen dress, and that Lorenzo's cap was of fine red wool...

the expensive sort of textile her husband always complained about her buying. These were people Pampinea had described! People who stole from the homes of the dead. Just the sort to mingle with a relic thief. Lucia's cheeks flushed with secret excitement at her discovery.

"Are...are there many of you who go around like this?"

"Too much asking questions, not enough drinking wine," said Lorenzo, filling a cup and shoving it toward Lucia.

"Pshh, don't be rude," responded Maria. She turned to Lucia. "At first, there were many, yes, and we would all go around together, but our numbers dwindle as... And, of course, if somebody is from one of the dead parishes, we must shun them for our own safety, though it is a pity."

"Ah, well," said Lorenzo. "More for us." He picked up the wine jug and drained it, then engaged Maria in a passionate bout of kissing that Lucia found quite fascinating.

"Sorry, darling," said Maria, noticing her stare. "What were you saying?"

"I wasn't saying anything," answered Lucia awkwardly. "You were talking about how everyone you know is dying?"

They continued kissing and Lucia sensed she was failing at her mission of making friends.

"I'll go refill the wine!" she said (a strategy used since time immemorial to defuse uncomfortable situations). She tried her best not to engage the lecherous monk and the leerers who sat by the barrels, and managed to get her next jug with only loud squelchy kissing noises from her tormentors. Maria and Lorenzo smiled politely when she came back with the full pitcher.

"I'm sorry," said Lucia, sitting back down. "I didn't mean to be unpleasant. It's just...you see, all my acquaintances are gone, and I've been staying in my house, so I don't know how people are talking of these things."

Maria sighed. "Who knows what to say or to do in times like these? It's supposed to be the Lord's punishment, but I see holy men and women struck down the same as the most abominable whores."

"It is true," said Lucia, thinking of her maid Antonella, who was a poor, devout virgin.

"I am inclined," said Lorenzo, who was slumping lower and lower on his bench as the effects of the wine jug manifested, "to agree with the greatest minds of our day, at the University of Paris."

"*Porco Dio*, here it comes again," said Maria to Lucia with a knowing wink. "There's no stopping him on this one."

"On March 20, 1345," stated the couple in unison, Lorenzo seriously, and Maria in jest. He scowled good-naturedly at her and, with a gracious nod, she allowed him to continue on his own:

"Ahem, as I was saying, on March 20, 1345, the doctors at Paris have confirmed there was a triple conjunction of Saturn, Jupiter, and Mars in the fortieth degree of Aquarius." He attempted to give Lucia a grave stare, but his eyes were a bit out of focus so he looked more fool than wise man.

"I... I'm sorry," said Lucia, suppressing a giggle. "I'm not well-versed in astrology. Tell me, what did this observation portend?"

"It made the earthquakes and floods that have bothered us these past years, it made the famines. And they determined that these shakings and quakings released the poisoned air we must now breathe, and *this* is the cause of the pestilence." He smacked his hand down onto the table, rattling their cups.

Now Lucia was genuinely intrigued. She had not heard anyone, not even Ginevra, who knew so many things, provide a rational answer to the question of why the pestilence had come to them. Of course, as Maria had mentioned, the clergy said it was a manifestation of God's wrath, but they said that any time something bad happened.

Maria saw the impressed look on Lucia's face. "Don't you listen to anything this drunk fool tells you."

Lorenzo swiped his hand disdainfully, too stupefied by wine to provide a more articulate rebuttal.

"Well," said Lucia, "regardless of whether it was earthquakes or floods or something else, I am at least glad to have met the two of you." This was true, not just flattery in service of her secret task. Even though she knew they were robbers.

"Thank you, darling, likewise." The two women clinked cups across Lorenzo. Maria's cheeks were flushed now, and she was on her way to joining her man in his reduced state. Lucia settled more into her surroundings. She remained clear-headed and felt pleasant, and realized that the amethyst was hardly needed. Between her clumsiness and Lorenzo's thirst, she'd barely consumed any alcohol. Even still, she tongued it in her cheek to check it was safe, and decided the time was right to begin her inquiries in earnest.

"Tell me, Maria, who besides myself is the newest to enjoy your company? What other sorts of stragglers have been hiding away in their homes like me?"

"Hmmm…there have not been so many… Actually, most here were known to us before the pestilence. You said you live in Santa Croce? Who is your baker?"

"I was not in the town often, my husband did not like me to go about," Lucia offered a bit too quickly. "He certainly would not approve of me visiting Alle Panche. But! I don't have to listen to him now."

"Huzzah!" Maria clinked cups with her again. "Oh. Sorry. Is he dead?"

"No, just fled."

"Well then, huzzah!"

"Thank you! So, I'm the only stranger you've met lately?" she pressed.

"Well, not the *only* one. Who was that guy, Lorenzo? He wore a rough cloak – definitely not a Florentine. Who knows how he got in."

"All the gatekeepers are dead," offered Lorenzo without lifting his head from the table.

"How do you know he was foreign?" asked Lucia.

"Well, he asked lots of stupid questions, about how to get around the city, which churches were the best—" Lucia's ears pricked up.

"And he *stank* like he was from the country," said Lorenzo from the table. "Awful. Wouldn't look you in the eye. Gave me the chills just to be near him. Could practically see my breath."

"Do you think he was from a dead parish?" asked Maria, crossing herself.

"No – although, did you hear?" said Lorenzo.

"Hear what?" asked Lucia.

"Santa Maria Novella is missing its San Tommaso finger – it was shouted from the *ringhiera* this afternoon. Another relic switched for a bottled potion. Another parish, dead."

Lucia was stunned. How could this be known? When she discovered the theft of Tommaso, she had taken the bottle with her. Had one of the other women seen her take it? "Shouted by whom?" she asked.

Before either could answer her, another man sat down roughly on their bench. The disheveled drunk, from over by the wine barrels. He reached his arm around her waist and pulled her tightly to him. Lucia struggled to keep her face away from his wine breath.

"Hello, Maria, Lorenzo." He grinned across the table. "Why are you keeping such a fine young thing to yourselves?"

"Hello, Bertoldo," said Maria dryly. "You know fine young things need no prompting to keep away from you. Why don't you let go of her? The poor girl is wriggling like a caterpillar."

"Yes, I insist you let go of me!" cried Lucia with as much dignity as she could muster.

"But it is a game. The more she struggles, the tighter my hold! If she becomes gentle and gives me a kiss, I'll set her free."

In Lucia's whole life, no man had touched her besides her own husband. She pushed with all her strength, but he was large and she was small, and she could not get away. In response to her shoving, he squeezed her so hard she thought her chest might crack. He laughed at the little squeal that escaped her involuntarily. Maria stood up to put a stop to it, but Lucia could not take the pain any longer so she did what the man asked and gave him a dry peck on the cheek.

Bertoldo released his grip and Lucia fell onto the floor, gasping. "See," he sneered, "that wasn't so unpleasant, was it?"

"Bertoldo, you slimy goat, say you're sorry," scolded Maria. "You've hurt her!"

But Lucia had had enough for one evening, and gave up her plans of learning more about the stinky peasant and the person who announced thefts from the *ringhiera*. "Goodbye, Maria. Goodbye, Lorenzo," she whispered, and fled toward the door.

"What's the matter, my sweetest heart?" called Bertoldo after her.

Lucia held her tears as long as she could, but when she was far enough away from the tavern, she wept at how such a low man had ruined her plans and gained mastery of her. Overcome by emotion, she forgot to be afraid of the black night outside the light of the heliodor she carried, and her sobbing gave a terrible scare to a few people who were on their way to Alle Panche and could hear but not see her. Lucia tried to compose herself before she reached her home, but her face was still red and puffy and was noticed immediately by Ginevra, who was at the fire stirring her nasty pot.

"You're back so quickly, what happened?" she coughed through the acrid steam. "Are you hurt??"

"Just my pride," said Lucia, who plopped down next to the kitten and relayed her misadventures.

"We should have waited and gone together," said Ginevra. "I knew it."

"I was doing so well, too! I was talking to people, they said there was a man who smelled awful and made everyone cold and asked directions to churches—"

"Cold?" said Ginevra quickly. "This man *made* them cold? In the summer?"

But Lucia was not listening. "Ohhh, what have I done? My brothers would murder me if they knew. I can't believe you let me go there by myself."

"I didn't let – never mind. Lucia: your brothers, be they living, won't find out because nobody will tell them. You've never had to go places by yourself – I'm sorry to say that every woman who does is accosted like that from time to time. But the fact is a lady on her own, as you are now, will inevitably have to fend off a man at some point."

"It was humiliating."

"This Bertoldo is the lowest worm."

"It is unkind to worms, to compare them to Bertoldo."

"He is the mud, then, that worms crawl through. Do not waste your thoughts on him."

Lucia spit the amethyst into her palm and drained the rest of the claret straight from the bottle.

"Ginevra, right before Worm Mud interrupted me, the people I was speaking to…they said that the theft of Tommaso's relic had already been shouted from the piazza. How could that be when we only just discovered it?"

Ginevra stirred her bubbling pot, thinking. "It has to be somebody with prior knowledge of the crimes. The thief must want everyone to know of his misdeeds. The city has stopped the processions, so he spreads the word himself."

THIRTY

THE APOTHECARY AT THE TWIN JANUS

July 9th of 1348, City of Florence

Dawn came and Ginevra decanted her noxious brew into a jar, and dropped in the two bloodstones. The viscous liquid foamed, then settled, and she placed a lid, purposefully askew, atop it. Lucia, too bothered by her encounter at Alle Panche to have gone to sleep, watched her with puffy eyes from across the table.

"Now what?" she asked.

"Give it an hour, maybe less. It will become clear and golden, and then it is ready."

But an hour came and went, and then two, and it was still a frothy, fizzy mess.

"I don't think it's working," said Lucia unhelpfully.

"It must be because it's so hot out," said Ginevra. "It just needs a bit longer." In truth, she was beginning to doubt that her gutter kitten was an effective substitute for a rare lynx.

"Come on, let's go," Ginevra said, tired and frustrated and impatient for progress in any of her current endeavors.

"Where?"

"To the crooked apothecary that Becchino knew. To see if he stocks the relics of Florence on his shelves. By the time we're back, this will be ready and I'll bring it to Zenobia." So they rushed out the door, bringing Lucia's rock-hard bread along for breakfast. Business hours were always ephemeral in Florence, and now finding a shopkeeper at his post could nearly be considered a miracle. Either way, he was certain to be shut up by midday. As they walked, they took the bread from their purses and tried to eat. Ginevra nearly broke a tooth before throwing her piece down in the street. Lucia pretended not to see and ate the whole thing out of vanity.

The twin Janus head identifying the shop was not easily found; they walked past it three times before noticing it carved into a wooden lintel above the partially sunken door frame, steps leading down to it from the street.

"Lucia, let me speak first," said Ginevra quietly.

Lucia nodded blearily. Her head ached and her mouth was dry from the terrible bread. She just wanted the whole meeting over as quickly as possible so she could go to bed. They walked down to the sunken door and before they could even knock, a small peephole, disguised within the grain of the wood, opened and a pair of black eyes with drooping lids appeared. The eyes looked them up and down.

"How can I help, ladies?"

"Ser Apothecary?" said Ginevra. "You were recommended to us by a friend, as one who provides useful articles for pilgrims?"

The peephole shut and the door opened to reveal an ancient man with puffs of white hair clinging haphazardly to an otherwise bald head. His robes were dirty with grease spots of many a meal, and his fingers were crooked with arthritis. There was an odor that reminded Ginevra of the Genoese port for a moment, and she realized the source was an entire anchovy dried into his beard.

She looked over his shoulder and saw the shop was as derelict as the proprietor: dark, damp, and smelling of moldy earth. She saw a few jars of pale powders, the ink on their parchment labels now faded to illegibility. The stacks of comfits had melted into one large sticky mass, and the ubiquitous bundles of dried herbs hanging from the ceiling were now anchors for cobwebs that spanned the width of the room. The decayed condition of the goods ruined their intended illusion; none of them were meant to be sold. They were only a lazy disguise so the apothecary could conduct his true business: the buying and selling of "holy relics."

"Good afternoon, signoras, good afternoon," he said, the anchovy jiggling precariously as he spoke. "What brings you to me?"

"We're new to the city, pilgrims from Genoa," Ginevra said, knowing she could not hide her accent from a man used to travelers. "We'd like to see as many of the Florentine saints as possible. Do our part in getting the pestilence lifted, you know?"

"Genoa?" he asked, raising a dusty eyebrow. "I would not be too loud about that, my dear, seeing as the sick came first to your city, after the earthquake. I myself am not afraid of such things, but it is a surprise that they let you in!"

"All the gatekeepers are dead, it seems," explained Lucia.

The apothecary tutted for a whole minute. "What's the point of paying all these taxes, dealing with all these municipal regulations if they can't even keep the damn door shut?" He stopped talking, narrowing his eyes until they disappeared under the drooping lids. "How did you say you found out about me?"

"Others on the road. They said you are known to help pilgrims like ourselves by providing – guidance – in how best to keep our journey blessed."

"Others on the road, hmmm?" he repeated.

"Um, yes?" said Ginevra.

"What were their names, then?"

"We did not ask," she said.

The apothecary stared at her hard. Ginevra became uncomfortable under his gaze... Had he seen through her lie? She wished she spent more time preparing a story. She had been so eager to brew her remedy, she'd had no time to formulate a plan. Why did she always assume she could make something up as she went along?

But eventually the apothecary just shrugged. "The first thing I must do is consult the heavens, to see what is appropriate for your own individual situations."

"Yes! Yes, please – do my friend first," she said, nudging a reluctant Lucia forward. She felt badly, but she needed the apothecary to be distracted so she could scrutinize the dirty shelves to look for onion-shaped bottles, for any plants or pigments that might tint a potion purple or green.

"Whatever pleases," said the crusty old man. "Come over to my counter, signora, and place your hands upon it."

Lucia resignedly picked her way around the broken ceramics and oily rags that littered the floor. He laid down a parchment that was already covered in writing, then flipped it over. He picked up a piece of charcoal from a cold brazier, and began to draw with it, a spiral from the center outward to the edges of the parchment. He closed his eyes and leaned back his head.

"But don't you need to know my birthday, at least, or…" Lucia began.

"Hush! The stars are speaking to me, don't interrupt them."

This man is a charlatan of the highest order, thought Ginevra, as she walked, in what she hoped was a casual manner, around the shop.

The apothecary leaned his head back even farther, and began droning as if he had swallowed a beehive. As his volume increased, so did the speed with which he drew his charcoal spirals, until he was almost yelling and the whole page filled in. Ginevra stopped her snooping, worried he might actually be having a seizure. But just as she stepped toward him, his head snapped forward and he said to Lucia, "Ah! Signora, it is clear. I would recommend some San Sebastiano *con carne* for you."

"Con carne?" she asked cautiously.

"Yes, meaning, of course, with some of the holy flesh still

attached to the holy bone. It is much more effective that way. And the stars tell me, you require something potent."

"Oh...um..." stuttered Lucia.

"Of course, if you're on a budget, I can ask the stars again to recommend some second- or third-class relics that will also be helpful in their own way."

"Ah. No, it's just how did you – how did you settle on San Sebastiano from that bunch of circles?"

"*Mystic* circles, signora. I would not question your knowledge of Genoa, since your friend says you are from there. And in that way, you should not question my secret knowledge of the planets and stars."

Ginevra intervened. She had come to get information about the thief, not to force Lucia to make up facts about Genoa. "Pardon me, Ser Apothecary, are you sure there isn't something more... local, that would be more powerful since we are in Florence? Is it possible to get a relic of, for example, your San Zenobio?"

"Zenobio, eh? That's not a request I have heard before. The body of San Zenobio was found miraculously intact and unblemished within the foundations of Santa Reparata. Such a man has been kept *whole*, as much as possible, only his head was separated for veneration and the rest still safely buried in his crypt. You might have gone and visited the head at its church, that is, until recently. You must have heard?"

Ginevra continued her play at ignorance. "Heard what? We only just arrived."

"It is the biggest news besides the pestilence. The blessed head of Zenobio has been missing for some weeks now. And then two women show up from far away, asking for a bit of him, thinking I, an honest apothecary, serving my city in a time of great need, might have it."

"No, of course, we would never suggest—" sputtered Ginevra.

"And who is your master that sent you here??" continued the apothecary, sending flecks of white spittle toward their faces. "You with your fake Genoese accent. I noticed it was false the minute you came in. Your friend might be from the north, but not you!"

"What? No, you've – my accent isn't fake," said Ginevra. *Shit.* Lucia looked back at her, panic-stricken, afraid to speak and be discovered as not actually from Genoa.

"Look, Ser Apothecary, I'm sorry I asked about Zenobio, I'm an ignorant woman from a far country… It's so very lucky for us that you have a relic of Sebastiano. We will buy it, of course."

"We *will*?" said Lucia to Ginevra.

"Yes, we will," she said pointedly.

The apothecary smiled and opened his hands, indicating their quarrel was of secondary importance to commerce. "It is a gift, signora. Free with your payment for your star reading."

"How blessed we truly are, by your generosity," said Ginevra.

"Indeed. You *should* count yourselves so. I have been in business for *many*, many years. People know that when a truly rare and precious object is needed, I'M the one who has it. The fact that the two of you have found yourself here at my doorstep, in the middle of the apocalypse, illustrates my prestige among travelers, and the quality of my clientele."

"Your logic is as infallible as your reputation," replied Ginevra. She wished fiercely she could tell him that even the *becchini* found his business unpalatable.

The apothecary bent down below the counter and brought out a dusty wooden box. He opened the lid; it was filled with dried-out fingers.

He rummaged through it a moment before saying, "Aha, here is the one, it is perfect for you."

"How do you know that one's San Sebastiano?" asked Lucia. "They all look the same."

"A true expert knows his wares, signora. That will be two florins for the reading."

"Two florins??" the women yelled, for the second time in as many days.

"Does *everything* in Florence cost two florins?" Ginevra asked, incredulously.

"These days, yes," he said without skipping a beat. "But in any time this would be a fair price for a reading that resulted in the acquisition of such a prestigious relic."

Ginevra bit her tongue. "Of course. You are quite correct. Monna Lucia, you'll hand him the money?"

"And that, of course, is just for the one reading. In order for you each to have your own personal relic—"

"I think the one will do just fine for the two of us. After all, San Sebastiano only had so many fingers. It would be unkind for us to take up two of them," said Lucia, dropping gold coins into his open palm. If she was without a husband, she couldn't go spending her whole fortune on dead fingers and burials.

"How magnanimous of you," he said with slight disappointment.

"So, signore," asked Ginevra, "if we may impose upon you further, since the shrine of San Zenobio is empty, what other shrines should we pray at in its stead?"

Encouraged by the pieces of gold, he continued: "Here, let me show you a book I have, that can be used by pilgrims to know all the places to visit." He pulled a cheap-looking volume from behind his counter.

"Here you go. My highest recommended *libri indulgarium et reliquarium*: *The Pious Pilgrim's Guide to the Most Holy Sites of Florence Including the Best Prayers to Be Said at Them, and Number of Indulgences Granted per Visitor, and Where Best to Stay Nearby to Them*."

"That is a very long title," said Lucia.

"And what may we find in this glorious treatise?" asked Ginevra.

"It details the most prestigious relics in the city, where they are in the churches, and so forth." Ginevra reached out her hands eagerly to take a look, but as soon as she reached, he withdrew it. "But now is not the *best* time to be walking around – you know that miasmas float on every street, even inside churches and monasteries. I'm afraid you will find that our great churches, usually all shiny and carefully tended, will be dark and empty, with saints disappeared, the same as Zenobio."

"Even still, we at least could see where they *should* be and surely that will count for something." She stretched out her hand again and smiled, but he kept the book clutched close to his chest, as if he thought better of bringing it out to show them. Ginevra grew impatient. "I thought the San Sebastiano finger will protect us?"

"Oh, it will, it will. It's just best not to strain it unnecessarily, you understand?"

"We have traveled a long way, and are intent on visiting the shrines."

"Perhaps, if you each had your own relic, I would know you were adequately protected. As it stands now, it would be unethical for me to encourage your journey."

Lucia looked at Ginevra imploringly, but she knew the man was not to be denied his sale.

"Perhaps you have something not *quite* so glorious as the Sebastiano finger? We must mind our funds carefully."

"Of course, signora, I am here to serve. The stars tell me that Sebastian will be good for you as well – and I have a piece of skin from the forearm of the same, half the price would likely recommend—"

"A florin is still more than…"

"Then perhaps signora would be interested in toenail clippings belonging to the blessed San Gregorio. I could part with them for a donation of three lire."

"Fine. The stars said he was good for me, too, did they?"

Lucia pressed three more coins into his palm. "Wonderful. Do the ladies wish me to read it to them?"

"Thank you, but we can read ourselves."

"Ah, wonderful, how things are changing! Here we are." He placed the book on the countertop next to the melted comfits, and noticed the gloom of his surrounds.

"Excuse me one moment, signoras, I think a light might be in order." He shuffled into a back room.

"Ginevra! This place is so *dirty*, I don't feel well—"

"Shhh...let's look at this book quickly and then we'll leave."

They brought the book into the light of the doorway. Each page contained a woodblock print illustration of a reliquary, and a messily written description of how to properly pray to it. The women leafed through quickly.

"Look, Lucia! Santa Reparata and the Baptistry are right here. The first places robbed..."

"Of course. They're the most famous churches in the city. The first stop for anyone."

"True," said Ginevra, "but next there is Santa Maria Novella and the chapel of San Barnaba. Also robbed."

"Yes, and the four churches of the *Rogazione* procession are here, too," said Lucia.

Ginevra took out the inquisitor's list and ran her finger down it. "And from those churches are taken the torso of San Piero, the left foot of Santo Stefano, and the left and right buttocks of San Paolo."

Lucia nodded and continued flipping. "And if all those places are present, there must be... Yes, my Santa Trinita on the opposite page...but Giovanni Gualberto's *crucifix* is recommended, not his shoulder, not the bit that was taken. Ginevra, this is just—"

"Lucia, the thief must have come here and been shown this very book!"

The proprietor returned and placed a lumpy tallow candle on the counter.

Ginevra gave him what she hoped was a charming smile: "What a wonderful and useful treatise."

Lucia brought the book closer to the feeble light.

"Ah, yes! San Paolo's left buttock," said the apothecary, glancing at the open page. "A most worthy and effective relic."

"Ser Apothecary," said Ginevra, "we will buy the book, as well."

"I'm afraid not, signora. It's a *very* rare volume."

Lucia scoffed and the apothecary looked at her.

"Quite rare. The very last copy, I couldn't do without it.

You'll have to make do the old-fashioned way, with what you can remember." He shuffled to put it away in his back room.

Ginevra looked at Lucia.

"No! Ginevra, I don't want to spend any more money here. And besides, this book just has—"

"Alright, fine, there is another way without money – do you have that bottle of holy water? I saw you fill it up yesterday at Santa Trinita."

"Yes…"

"Quick, then – put this in."

"What is it?"

"It is a selenite, whoever drinks water touched by it will become very agreeable for a very brief moment."

She dropped a translucent grayish crystal into Lucia's little flask.

"But does it have to be holy water? *My* holy water? I need it."

"It can be any water, but do you see anything else around?"

"But how will I get him to drink it?"

The apothecary returned. "Signoras, you are still here? It seems clear our business is concluded."

Ginevra stalled as Lucia stood frozen, clutching her flask. "Please, if you won't take money, we have traveled with—" Ginevra cast her mind about to the contents of Lucia's home "—some beautiful cloth."

"The end is truly upon us! A Genoese offering textile to a Florentine! Suspicious women! Hussies! Get out of my shop. OUT!" He picked up a jar of beans and rattled it at them as if they were a pack of stray dogs.

"Get it on him," Ginevra mouthed to Lucia.

Lucia, not knowing what else to do, held the flask up to her nose, then did a gigantic fake sneeze and sprayed her holy water all over the face of the stunned apothecary.

His face quivered with rage. The anchovy in his beard also quivered with rage.

Shit, shit, shit, thought Ginevra. Her elixir was not working.

Agnesa had died under her fingertips. And now this selenite did nothing. She had lost her touch with gems.

The apothecary went over to poor Lucia and grabbed the front of her dress.

"YOU— DID YOU— ah— did you want to see my book again?"

"What? Yes! Yes."

"Actually," interjected Ginevra, pulling her friend away from his grip, "we were hoping to buy it."

"Buy? Oh, no! I couldn't take money from such lovely creatures, please, take it. I insist. As I said, it is my very last copy, but I suppose I can make do."

"Um, thank you, we will."

"How else may I serve you, gentle ladies?"

"Well," said Ginevra quickly (she wasn't sure how long the selenite would last), "actually, we had a few questions – namely, do you know where Zenobio and the stolen relics are?"

"Signoras, look around you at my establishment. Does it look like I'm involved in anything that would be so lucrative?"

"But, do you know where they are?"

"Surely you must realize this line of inquiry is insulting. Perhaps there is another question I could answer instead?"

Ginevra changed her tactics. The selenite was not a truth serum.

"Very well, who else has visited your shop? You said this is your last copy? Who else have you sold it to?"

"Why, a number of pilgrims over the years. They know to come to me for it. It is very rare."

"Did any of them smell badly?" asked Ginevra.

"Of course," said the apothecary. "All pilgrims smell badly."

Lucia nodded in agreement.

"Do you remember what any of them looked like?"

"My sight is not so good for earthly matters. Anything farther away than a book is a complete blur. But my customers prefer it that way. Now, are you quite through taking up my time?"

The selenite was wearing off.

"We're through, thank you! Come on, Lucia."

Blinking in the hot sunlight, the women gulped the rot-tinted air of the city, now fresh and sweet after exiting the apothecary's gloomy lair. They ran away, taking several twists and turns until they were sure the apothecary could not follow them.

"Ginevra, did you see—"

"The anchovy in his beard, I KNOW."

"Oh, yes, that. But I meant how the selenite worked – could we not have given it to him at the start and saved my florins?"

"I didn't think of it, sorry – I'll pay you back when I'm a doctor. But look, now we have this book! Surely, here is the answer.

There are nine relics in here and *all are missing*."

"Ginevra, that is what I have been trying to say! This is not a rare volume. He was just trying to swindle us. This book – the relics inside are famous! Together, they are called the Divine Nine and they sell this sort of guide at the gates, on every street corner."

"The Divine Nine? I never heard of this."

"It's new, since you left, to attract more pilgrims. I was a fool not to see it right away! The thief might have read about them in this book from the apothecary, but he also might have asked anybody where he should go."

Ginevra felt deflated. All this running around and all she had learned was what she should have known right from the start. "The inquisitor should have told me all this! Wine has dulled his wits."

"He certainly should have mentioned it," said Lucia, indignant. "But looking at it laid out like this, do you think maybe the thief is from an enemy city? From some place jealous of the Divine Nine?"

"What do you mean?"

"Well," said Lucia, "last night you said the thief spreads word of his deeds as soon as they happen. He leaves behind these bottles when he could easily keep the crimes hidden for months. This makes sense if he's from a rival city – he would *want* everyone to know that Florence cannot protect its most precious possessions."

"That is brilliant, Lucia! You may have hit upon it. And by the way, your sneeze back there was also brilliant. I'll take the selenite back now."

Lucia took out her holy water flask and shook it. Then she dumped the whole thing out on her hand.

"Ginevra, I'm sorry…it must have flown out…"

"*Damn.* You're sure?"

"I'm so sorry, let's go back and look for it."

"No, no, it's alright. He won't be pleased to see us. It's my own fault for putting you up to it. If I'm being honest, I have no idea how to catch a thief. I don't know why I thought I could solve a mystery that has stumped all the holy men of this city."

"*I* know what we should do next."

"What?"

"Go home and take a nap. We have been awake since yesterday morning. It's so hot right now and the air is heavy like thunderstorms will come. It's unnatural to be awake on an afternoon such as this."

"I can't sleep now. I must go to little Zenobia and then prepare to see the inquisitor. I hope my elixir has settled…"

"I'm sure it will turn out alright. And, Ginevra, please don't be hurt, but I can tell by the circles under your eyes that you need rest as well. It will be easier to think after."

"You sleep, then. I promised Zenobia I'd come back…"

"If you run yourself ragged, you won't help anyone. You've got to keep your wits about you and there's no doing that without sleep. In normal times, I'd rest every afternoon. My mother taught me it's important to retain one's youth."

"Well, we'll see. I suppose if the medicine is still bubbling when we get home, I could try to rest for a moment before going out."

"If it's not done, we'll pray for Zenobia to be safe until it is, which should give you some extra time."

THIRTY-ONE

DINNER AND AN EXPLOSION

July 9th of 1348, Palazzo Tornaparte

Ginevra went to the dark cellar where she had stored her medicine pot. It was still frothing and oozing out from under its askew lid. Not ready. Now she was very nervous it would not work at all. She would wait a few hours longer, and return to the Girolami tower today either way, do what she could for Zenobia with what she had. She would use the time to draft her report for tomorrow's visit with Inquisitor Michele.

She went back upstairs to gripe to Lucia, but Lucia had already gone to take a nap and no amount of heavy sighs or loudly moved plates could rouse her. She sat down at the long rectangular table in Lucia's dining hall. The little cat ran in and burrowed under her skirts to nap on her feet. Feeling slightly better for the company, she pulled out the original list of robberies drawn up by Inquisitor Michele, and looked over the new discoveries she had added in her own rough handwriting.

Santa Trinita – shoulder of San Giovanni Gualberto. Theft noticed: July 8. Relic last seen: unknown.

San Paolino – shoe of San Francesco.
Attempted theft noticed: July 8. Relic tampered with, left behind.

Santa Maria Novella – finger of San Tommaso D'Aquino.
Theft noticed: July 8. Relic last seen: winter 1348.

The dates and letters began to swim before her eyes. The inquisitor was expecting her, and all she had discovered was apparently already known to everyone in Florence.

She shook the cat off her feet and went to the cellar to look at her jar again. Still oozing. An eel made a little splash in the well, and she realized that she hadn't really eaten anything of substance since Taddea's porridge. She could make another eel pie? No, that would take hours, and Ginevra was hungry right now. And she needed to go to Zenobia. She filled her fancy green-and-purple cup with *vinello* again and drank the whole thing. She filled it back up and carried it to the garden, intent on picking some apples. The peacocks gathered round her, hoping for treats. "I could make you into a pie, too," she said to them, already a bit drunk. They took no notice of her idle threat, and went back to pulling worms out of the spaces where dirt showed between flagstones.

She picked up a nice-looking apple from the ground and took a bite. It was sour and made her mouth dry. She sat down fully on the sun-warmed stones. The *vinello* was working its own magic, dulling the thoughts that refused to quit her exhausted brain. Perhaps Lucia was right. She would just lay down for a moment and rest her eyes. She listened to the pecking of the peacocks and burbling of the fountain. A line of cool shade crept over her face as the sun shifted its position behind the tall walls of the courtyard.

A peacock stared at her. "What are you doing here?" it asked.

"I— I'm helping."

"Are you sure?"

"Yes?"

"Trouble follows you. The *malocchio* waits for you to drop your magic jewel."

"I will not drop it."

"Are you sure?"

She felt desperately for her amulet, but her hands became tangled in her clothing until she could not move them. The peacock came forward and snapped at her nose with pointed teeth.

"Ginevra! Gineeevra!!" She woke with a start. A peacock hopped off her with an indignant "scree." The courtyard was all shadows. She had been asleep for hours! She looked up and saw Lucia, waving from the roof terrace of her home. "Did you sleep in the dirt all afternoon? You know we have three empty beds in here, right?"

"Um, yes, it looks like I did... The peacocks..."

"What about them?"

"They – nothing – they ate the rest of my apple!"

"Well, pick another one and get me one, too. Come on up to the roof. It's lovely and cool up here. We'll have supper."

Ginevra brushed the grit off her cheek and went to join her. A much-needed meal, then to Zenobia. Up on the roof, the city was laid out before them, and the waning toenail moon, as if in tribute to San Gregorio, rose in the still-light sky. Lucia had fished down the shriveled salami from the kitchen rafters, and found more of her husband's expensive claret. Ginevra wanted to protest – the salami would keep for ages, and they didn't know when they could get more – but she was too hungry. She took the knife from Lucia, who was struggling to cut into the unwieldy sausage, and sliced them both a generous portion. Dainty nibbles became hearty bites, followed by large draughts of the pomegranate-colored wine. The fat and salt and sugar were restorative. Ginevra felt the fog lifting from her brain with each swallow.

"It almost seems like a normal summer night from up here, doesn't it?" said Lucia.

Ginevra looked out at the bell towers and rooftops that stretched out from the Piazza Santa Trinita. The bricks of the church gleamed yellow and lovely. No sign that inside it was covered in mold and emptied of its relic.

"It makes me ache in a way. When I was younger, I thought I would find my own husband and we would have a house like this, and I would sit on a peaceful terrace as we are now, with children."

"You have to marry a rich man, for that. And trust me, it's not such fun."

"Well, it hasn't been much fun for me without one, either. But – no matter. It never could have been; he did not – he did not need me how I needed him."

"Oh, my dear friend – do not think that. Look, I wasn't going to tell you – I saw his widow yesterday. It was said he spent their whole marriage ignoring her, despondent over some other lost love."

Ginevra didn't know what to make of all this – of the sentimental brooch, now pinned to Lucia, of this purported pining. What good did any of it do for her, except to make it difficult to feel justified in her anger. "Maybe he acted this way after I was gone. But before he missed me and commissioned jewels in my name, he stood to the side so his uncle the bishop could order me mutilated, so the old inquisitor could take away the funds from my convent and leave the women in their charge with nowhere to go."

Lucia sat back in her chair. "Well, it is a bit hard to defend him, when you put it that way."

The pair lapsed into silence.

Ginevra felt badly, then, for ruining the mood when Lucia was just trying to be kind. "Maybe, though, there is still a nice rich man somewhere. Or two, why not? One for each of us."

"Handsome brothers," said Lucia, appreciating the distraction of this new game. "The elder for you and the younger for me. Assuming, of course, my present husband dies."

"Oh, he's sure to, one of these days. Just like my Ludovico."

"Then we can be with good men, and we'll take them up here to enjoy the cool air—"

"And the streets wouldn't be so quiet. We'll hear the sounds again of neighbors returning before curfew—"

A loud BANG echoed up from the interior courtyard.

"What now??" said Lucia.

But Ginevra knew the sound exactly. "No, no, no, no."

She ran down to the cellar with a sinking feeling and a lamp held aloft. It was as she feared: the lid had exploded off her jar and a honey-colored film covered everything. The eels were at the surface of their well, investigating the strange globules that now floated in their home, swallowing and spitting them back out.

Lucia entered right after. "My well! My eels!"

"They'll be fine... I think..." said Ginevra, distractedly. She held the lamp over the jar. "Oh, no, oh, no...there's hardly any left...and the bloodstones... Oh, they're gone! I cannot try another batch. I am the stupidest woman on the earth."

"Ginevra, you're not! Don't say such a thing."

"I shouldn't have fallen asleep. I should have been tending it, sitting by it. I don't understand. I left the opening askew..."

Lucia blanched. "Left askew?"

"Yes – to keep it from bursting. I don't understand."

"Oh. Oh, Ginevra, I'm so sorry. I came down here to get the wine and I saw your jar was leaking. I knew the substance was precious so I refastened the lid... Oh, dear, I've ruined everything, haven't I?"

Ginevra looked up slowly from the jar. "Why would you touch this? You don't even know how to make bread. Why would you assume—"

"I don't know what I was thinking. I feel awful, stupid, just please tell me what to do to make it right. I'll go find more cats, or if you need money to buy ingredients, my purse is yours!"

For a long time, Ginevra said nothing, but clutched at the coral pendant through her dress. It was warm. As the peacock had warned, the *malocchio* hovered nearby, aroused by her anger. She closed her eyes and breathed deeply. When she spoke again, it was slow and full of effort.

"You were only trying to help. I can't make another batch unless we can find the bloodstones. I can't cure anyone else unless we find the bloodstones. I'm not sure where they've gone." When she mentioned the lost jewels, her eyes flashed with the anger her words did not express.

"We'll find them – I'll find them!" said Lucia hastily. "They've got to be in this room somewhere." But after going round on hands and knees, raking over the earthen floor with their fingers and shining their light to the bottom of the well, the gemstones were still missing.

"Oh, God, I'm a useless woman. Any brewer's wife would have known not to do what I just did… Look! There is still a bit that clings to the inside of the jar. Perhaps it can be useful?" She reached out to grab it.

"Don't! Just don't touch it. I'll do it."

"We could go pray to San Antonio. He'll help us find them."

"Just go to bed. You've done enough. I'll keep looking…"

"If anyone should keep looking, it's me. You take what is left in the jar and go to the Girolami. By the time you are back, I'll have found the stones and—"

"I SAID I will look for them," interrupted Ginevra. "Go to your chamber and pray for the little girl. Surely, you can do that properly, at least?"

"Of – of course. I will. I'm sorry. Good night."

Ginevra turned and went back to raking her fingers along the dirt floor, commending herself on restraining her temper. But the little barbs she couldn't resist, about the bread and the praying, worked their way deep into Lucia's flesh and stung terribly.

Any rest Lucia had gotten during the afternoon was wasted as she lay awake praying to San Antonio di Padua to find the missing bloodstones, promising to light a candle for him, too, eventually.

She, then, became worried about all the saints to whom she owed favors. Her thoughts turned to the Divine Nine. How proud she'd been, to once think she was good enough to become a holy nun. She should probably confess about that as well. With these nasty thoughts swirling about her mind, she managed only to fall into a troubled rest as the sun began to rise on the next day.

THIRTY-TWO

O, ZENOBIO

July 10th of 1348, Torre Girolami

Ginevra never found the stones. In the earliest morning, she left without rousing her friend. She was still angry, and did not want delays or distractions. The girl Zenobia could be very sick or even dead by now, and she wasn't sure the little bit of medicine she'd salvaged from the inside of the jar would be enough, or if it even was properly made. After, she would visit the inquisitor. Explain about the Divine Nine and San Francesco's shoe and the man so smelly he stood out even among the patrons of Alle Panche. Surely, all this was not nothing? Surely, she and Lucia had reached a greater understanding in three days than the inquisitor had in as many months!

Now, back in the dead parish of Santo Stefano al Ponte, the streets were silent as midnight, though the sun was full and round and heated the air like a bakery. The door to the Girolami tower remained unlocked from her last visit. Easing her way in, Ginevra realized how tightly her jaw was held and willed it to soften, moving it back and forth with a painful click. Again, she walked up the twisting stairs; again, she went brazenly into the chamber of Lady Girolami, bracing herself for whatever household object would be chucked at her head.

Instead, the lady barely looked up to acknowledge her arrival. She knelt on the floor, with gray face and black gown, slowly folding children's clothing into a chest.

"I never paid you for your services," she said by way of greeting. "You must be coming about that."

Ginevra exhaled with relief. "Where is your daughter?" she asked. "I was worried, with the sickness – I have something that might help."

The lady stared at her hard. "You were right. I should have moved the body sooner but I could not bear it… She is dead now, like him. I have buried them next to their father."

Ginevra sunk onto her knees, shattered. To save this child, with the stones and the secret of the cats, it would have brought some meaning to witnessing Agnesa's death. But again, she had arrived too late to help. The golden strings that attached her to people, to places, one by one they were being snipped and snapped. She felt that soon there would be nothing left to tie her to the earth.

"I'm so sorry, I tried to come back sooner with medicine—"

"If you are sorry for anything, let it be for saving me to witness the death of my children."

"Your elder son – he lives yet, does he not? Let him be your salvation."

The lady softened. "He lives, it's true. Thanks to your interventions. I'm sorry I hit your head. You don't want money?"

"No, Dama. It's as I told you: I only came here to look for Zenobio, to help the city."

"What city? Look around you. Soon there will be nobody. Why attach yourself to such a place? In a year, it will be abandoned to ghosts and grazing sheep."

"It doesn't have to be."

"And why do *you* care what happens? You seek our stolen property out of the goodness of your own heart?"

"Only saints can claim such motivation, and I am not one. I was hired by your bishop, and I work for a fee: the funds to establish myself as a businesswoman here. To gain sponsorship to the doctors' guild."

"After everything they did to you? You would wish to entangle yourself further with Florence?"

Ginevra stiffened. The lady continued. "Don't be surprised. I know who you are, Ginevra di Genoa. We are the same age, you and I. Your trial was the talk of the town, and I remember how it went for you. Wheeled out of Florence as an exile – covered in manure and blood. I can see the spot where they cut your nose. They did not accept your miracles then, and they will not accept them now… Monna Ginevra – I will not tell that you came here and used your magic on us. But I cannot be associated with a heretic, now without a husband to protect my interests."

"I am no heretic, Dama. I just want to help people the only way I know…"

The lady packed furiously now. Crushing beautiful tiny embroidered gowns into an overfull valise. "Then we both want impossible things. I want to tear all the hair out of my head. I want to crawl through the streets until my hands are worn to stubs and my knees are bone, and rub the filth of the gutters on my face and shriek until the voice in my throat has shattered and my mouth fills with blood and I choke to death upon it. But not all my children have died. Just the two of them. So I curb my grief and take the one living away from here to survive in a different way. And for his sake, I cannot follow the desires of which I have just spoken. I say thank you for what you've done, but now you must go and leave us to swallow our sorrow and make what we may of our blackened lives."

"Mama—"

The two women turned. Lady Girolami's son had entered her chamber.

"Oh, my God – Zenobio – forgive me, that was not for your ears." At ten, he was the same height as his mother. She embraced him fully and began to weep, but he wriggled away toward Ginevra.

"Hello, so nice to see you!" he said.

"He is strange, cheerful," whispered Lady Girolami, "since the deaths of his father and siblings."

"It is the shock of grief," said Ginevra. "He will return to himself."

"Mama – Papa would not want us to leave – this is going to be MY tower."

"Go back to bed, child. I am master of this house now." But the boy did not move.

"Mama, this lady said she can find Zenobio, I just heard her! I am named for him," he said to Ginevra. "Can you help about Santo Stefano, too? He is my dead brother's saint."

"Yes, I will try," she answered. "I know he is missing, too, since…" she pulled out the inquisitor's list of thefts "…since the *Rogazione* procession in the spring."

Lady Girolami sat down on a painted chest and put her head in her hands. "We donated a whole foot of Santo Stefano. It went right up to the knee joint! Acquired at great expense. The whole city knew it was gone except for us."

"I'm sorry, Dama," said Ginevra.

"After the fiasco at the Feast of San Zenobio, my husband fell into a very deep depression. He had been *so* sure that if we held the procession correctly, our ancestor saint would intervene, would make the city lively again. But after – he forbade us all from leaving the tower. So we heard no news, we did not know for weeks that the sacred foot was missing, that we had sealed ourselves up in a dead parish…"

"Santo Stefano is my brother's church!" said Zenobio.

"It's not *his* church, my darling. My only darling. We have a chapel there is what he means. Several days ago, my husband went there. Left our tower for the first time in weeks. He knew, suddenly – it struck him in his bones – that the relic of that church would be taken as well. He went to check, though I begged him not to. He brought death home with him."

"Did he see anything in the chapel? From where the foot was taken. Did he tell you anything?"

Here, the lady looked up at Ginevra with red-rimmed eyes. "He said – it could only be dark magic. We kept the foot in a gilded cupboard, studded with lapis and colored enamels, and it was fit with an ingenious iron lock, commissioned at great expense. He said the lock was all taken over by rust. It crumbled at his touch. Who could make such a thing happen?"

Ginevra nodded, but she did not think it took magic to rust a lock. She thought of the doors at Santa Trinita, falling off their hinges, the inside covered with mold. Even the Girolami could not stop mists of the Arno dampening their church, corroding metals and warping wood.

"Monna Ginevra, I repeat my request, for you to go. I am tired, so, so tired."

"Not me," said Zenobio.

Ginevra bowed her head. "I take my leave, and pray for the souls of your family."

The lady said nothing, but went back to her packing. Zenobio waved goodbye as she made her way down the stairs.

Outside she walked out of sight of the tower and then sat down in the street against a building and tried to cry for Zenobia. But she could not cry anymore. She took out the small flask of elixir she had salvaged from the exploded jar. It was probably useless anyhow, even if she had arrived in time. If she was ever to break out of these cycles of death and fear, she must complete her task. She made her way, determined, to the inquisitor's palazzo.

But at the inquisitor's residence, the shutters were closed, the door was locked, and no amount of her shouting and banging brought anyone to let her in.

"Have you seen the inquisitor?" she asked the dead mason on the scaffold. He did not answer. She sat down on the doorstep to wait for his return. She sat there until the shadows grew long, and realized with a jolt that she had never picked up the heliodor from Lucia's kitchen, after her friend's night at Alle Panche. Without the gem, she would have no way of finding her way home after dark – she could wait no longer. She tore a corner from the inquisitor's list of thefts, and scrawled a note saying she would try him again tomorrow and stuck it into the door frame.

Ginevra arrived, disheartened, at Lucia's palazzo, thinking that at least now she would have the chance to make amends with her friend. But when she got back, there was nobody home but the kitten mewing for her supper. In the kitchen, she saw the heliodor and amethyst were both gone from the place she left them. Her anger redoubled, and brought with it worry for Lucia's safety. She had an hour of daylight left, at most. Ginevra ran back out, as fast as she could, to the tavern Alle Panche. But as with the inquisitor's home, as with Lucia's palazzo, the place was dark and empty. Was she the only living person left on the earth? Fretting, she hurried on to Santa Maria Novella, thinking that Lucia might have gone to her favorite church if she was not at the tavern.

Into the vast and empty sanctuary, she ran, watched by the stone eyes of those whose graves paved the floor and lined the walls. From chapel to chapel, she went, peeking in at the effigies and reliquaries that sparkled and winked out from the darkness pooled in their niches. Not one saint had a candle lit before them, when it should have been many hundreds.

At last, she found the shrine of San Tommaso D'Aquino, but Lucia was not there. She examined the wrought iron gate that separated the shrine from the sanctuary. It was shut up again, but there was no lock hooked through. She stepped up close to the gate, and jumped at a quiet crunch beneath her shoes. A smattering of brick-colored flakes dusted the floor. Rust. She knelt down and crushed them beneath her fingers. Ginevra looked around for a leak, but the space was as dry as a bone. She shivered. It was as the Lady Girolami had described at Santo Stefano, a lock ruined prematurely with rust. She thought again, of how the hinges gave way at Santa Trinita, remembered how Lucia had complained of dirtying her dress at Santa Reparata, and how the altar at San Paolino was rusted through.

A low whistling hummed in the striped stone arches of the church – the wind of a coming storm, making its way through the open doors. A man who could turn iron to dust. Who stank and made a room cold. Who announced his crimes as they were committed. Oh, where was Lucia?? She yelled out her friend's name, and got only the echoes of her own voice for an answer. There was nothing to do but to return to the palazzo and hope Lucia had returned already. It was a new moon, the darkest night of the month was fast approaching. Without the heliodor, it would soon be impossible for Ginevra to find her way. She walked back out into the dusk, the growing wind whipping up her skirt and blowing unpleasant trash at her ankles.

PART III

THE PLAGUE SAINT

*It is a matter of humanity,
to show compassion for those
who suffer…*

–GIOVANNI BOCCACCIO

THIRTY-THREE

A FEAST IN THE NIGHT

July 10th of 1348, City of Florence

Lucia had slept until late afternoon, and woke up cursing herself for her laziness. Her friend was gone and left no note. Lucia did not blame her. She went to the kitchen to find food, but instead her eyes landed on the amethyst and heliodor – left in a little dish on the window ledge after they were last used. Lucia remembered the unfinished conversation at Alle Panche. The smelly man, asking about churches and making people cold. Perhaps if she could find Maria and Lorenzo and get *some* idea of who this mysterious individual was... Well, it would be a step to putting things right with Ginevra.

Determined to make this evening one of progress, she changed back into Antonella's old dress, put the heliodor in her pocket and the amethyst in her cheek, and went once again to seek the dubious company of Alle Panche. But when Lucia reached the tavern, out came a dozen or so stumbling persons, Maria and Lorenzo among them.

"Lucia!" said Maria delightedly. "I'm so glad you came back, I wasn't sure you would after Bertoldo—"

"*Salve*, Maria. Never mind him. Where are you going?"

"You must come with us!" said Lorenzo. "Alle Panche has been drunk dry, and we just got word of a party."

Lucia joined in, linking arms with Maria. She gave a few little tries at bringing the conversation back around to the smelly stranger, but they were walking quickly and speaking and laughing with others in the group so she never got the chance. They ran through many twisted streets, across the river, and somewhere in the Oltre Arno district they stopped short. One of their number said, "This is it," and pushed through the front door of a palazzo that made Lucia's home look like a hole in the dirt.

"Whose house is *this*?" she asked Lorenzo, looking up in awe at tall ceilings painted blue with golden stars.

"Ahh, well, this is one of those wonderful parties where the host has graciously made themselves absent so the bounty may be enjoyed without need for boring pleasantries."

"You mean, they've left the city, so we're going to help ourselves?"

"Lucia," said Lorenzo reproachingly, "we're all going to die tomorrow so what's it matter if you drink some rich man's abandoned wine? C'mon."

Lucia had to admit he had a point. She decided, for the sake of investigation, she would commit the little sin of joining the party. Another thing added to her tally of prayers and penance.

When they arrived at the second floor dining hall, Lucia was glad she already decided to sin because this party looked *very* fun. It centered around a massive table, the inlay of ebony and mother-of-pearl barely visible below sweating platters of food that left rings on the marquetry. Somehow, somebody had gotten hold of a pig and the shiny beast was roasting away on an improvised spit in the massive fireplace, which surely had never been used for the dirty task of cooking until this evening. On the table, wheels of soft cheeses wrapped in delicate leaves, plump olives, and platters of crispy partridges with their melty drippings soaking into a bed of yellow onions and ashy branches of rosemary. A gigantic pie topped with a crown of smaller pies, thick brown sauce oozing through vents slashed in the pastry so spiced steam could escape. Rounds of bread, real and puffy, dusted with sugar and stuck with raisins and suet. Boiled eggs dyed pink with beets and yellow with saffron. Bowls of tender, frilly salad leaves dotted with tiny yellow flowers and splashed with vinegar. Trays heaped with long thin strands of macaroni, slippery with butter. Piles of summer oranges, a majolica dish filled with special sweetmeats normally reserved for expectant mothers. And barrels and barrels of wine, being decanted into fine glassware, pewter, silver, even a few of the same shimmering grapevine ceramics she had at home.

Many of the vessels were surreptitiously pocketed by guests after they finished their first cup. Three fellows with flutes of different sizes were tootling along with a tambourine, and a man dressed as a woman sang along sweet as a nightingale. Though dusk was approaching and shutters were closed, the room was ablaze with light thanks to hundreds of candles – enough for a whole year, it seemed, if used prudently (which was not currently the case). The room was as crowded with people as the table was with food, and just like the pig in the fire, the guests were all pleasantly shiny from the warm and fragrant air.

"Who made this food?? Where did the oranges come from?" Lucia asked incredulously, ignoring Lorenzo's earlier advice to enjoy rather than question.

Maria was more willing to indulge her curiosity. "The cook of this house – she came back after the master fled, and took up with a baker. They make a good pair, don't they?"

"But it must have taken them days…"

"A week, at least!" said Maria. "But what else is anyone doing? Might as well make a feast, eh? How fortunate to be among the guests. Now, excuse me for a moment while Lorenzo and I go…explore. We won't be long. Save me one of those eggs, will you? A pink one."

Lucia nodded and went to help herself to the feast. It was all part of her investigation, she told herself, plucking up a large orange, peeling it with as much ladylike restraint as possible. She broke the skin and a delicate spray of oil burst out of the peel, floating into the air and surrounding her with its agreeable perfume. She pulled a wedge from the juicy globe and popped it into her mouth, transported for a moment to another summer when death was not the topic of every conversation.

She put another orange in her purse for Ginevra, filled the nearest glass with wine, and looked around. Now – how should she approach this feast? Should she start with the macaroni? Would the cheeses be gone if she didn't take one right away? As she walked toward the platter where they were arranged, she froze; there was the *becchino*. The same who took away her maid. Not dressed in the stinking rags of his trade, but in a finely embroidered tunic and red turban. He grinned at her. Lucia pretended not to notice, but to her immense horror he came right over.

"And where are you from tonight, eh?" he said, getting close so no others could hear. "Did the invitation extend all the way to the dead parish of Santa Trinita?"

"I don't know *what* you're talking about," she said, mustering false indignation. "I live in Santa Croce."

"Haha, sure, and I live in the Garden of Eden. Don't worry, though, we liars have to look out for another. I'll keep your secret."

Lucia turned away only to see another disagreeable figure – the lech Bertoldo, drunk and hassling other women, who, more used to that sort of thing than Lucia, were snubbing him effectively. And though Bertoldo was, to Lucia, ten times more repulsive than the gravedigger, their reunion was a moment she secretly hoped for. For she had invented, in the aftermath of their first unpleasant encounter, a far-fetched plan for revenge. Her tongue played with the amethyst buried under its soft folds. She stared at Bertoldo.

"Who do you watch?" pressed Becchino. "If it's a ghost, I believe you – the lord of this house is dead, not fled, trust me…"

"Shhh! Go away!" she whispered.

Bertoldo turned from the group of women, and (good for him) remembered Lucia from the tavern. Exactly as she hoped, he lurched forward to continue his overtures. He promptly bumped into the sideboard, which knocked over a bit of crockery that fell and smashed on a flutist's foot so the music stopped and everybody turned to look at him.

"Aha!" he slurred to a silent room. "I see the lady has not been able to forget me! She followed me all the way across the river. Tell me, darling, have I been in your dreams?"

"Yes. I dreamed that you would shut up and leave me alone." The room erupted in laughter, but grew silent quickly to see Bertoldo's response.

"The only thing I'll leave you is begging for more."

"Is that what you want? To please me in bed? Is that what this is all about, then? I'm a married woman. I don't want to sleep with you. I'm just trying to eat cheese."

Bertoldo was tripped up by the straightforward questions, but recovered quickly: "Er...yes, of course, I am a gentleman, and it is my privilege to please a lady." He then made a rude gesture that removed any kindness that may have been accidentally taken from his statement.

With only the slightest bit of pink rising in her cheeks, Lucia played her hand. "Very well, then, what would please me most is for you to accept my challenge *of a drinking contest.*"

The crowd gasped appropriately.

"Drinking contest???" Bertoldo could barely get the words out, so eager was he to imbue them with derision. "What substance, Small Woman, do you think you can best me at?"

"The wine of the house, of course. Whoever drinks the most and keeps their wits is champion." She took a deep swallow from the elegant Arabic glass goblet she adopted as her vessel, and stared him straight in the eye the whole time. The partygoers erupted in cheers and whistles.

Bertoldo hesitated a bit. "Er...come now, it wouldn't be right..."

"If you are too scared to face a *small woman*, then so much be your shame." She finished her goblet.

Such were the hisses and yells that Maria and Lorenzo came down, with red faces and mussed hair, from whatever private corner they had found to see what was going on. The musicians added their flutes to the jeers, and Bertoldo had no way to excuse himself from the challenge. "Alright, darling, if that's your pleasure, then it is mine! And may our granting of each other's mutual pleasures continue onto soft feather beds."

"There is not enough wine in Italy. Come, who will pour us our first?"

The feast was pushed to one side of the table and Lucia and Bertoldo sat across from each other. Another of the fine Arabic goblets was conjured from somebody's reluctant satchel so the rounds could be fairly judged. Maria and Lorenzo made their way to the front; the beautiful singer and Becchino elected themselves as judges, sitting close to the pair to ensure there was no trickery. Becchino gave Lucia what he must have meant as an encouraging smile, but ended up looking quite frightful on account of his brown and stunted teeth. *Maybe he's not so bad, after all*, she thought, but there was no more time to ponder because the contest had begun.

Bertoldo finished his first drink fast, and leered at her. Lucia did her best to go hurriedly, but she was not used to large sips and also had to take care not to swallow the amethyst. Nevertheless, soon she, too, set down her empty cup to be refilled. Cheers were cheered. Coins were exchanged. Seven, eight, nine, a dozen (two dozen?) pours until Bertoldo's crass taunts became mumbled nothings.

At last, after calling Lucia a "something, something" (nobody could quite hear), he leaned back too far, his bench flipped over, and he lay ruddy-faced on the floor while Lucia remained white and upright and every bit a lady. The whole room erupted in cheers and laughter, and she was hugged and kissed and slapped on the back, for never had anyone been able to outdrink Bertoldo (not that anyone was trying).

"Lucia!" exclaimed Maria, pushing her way to her side. "A woman of your size! How did you do that?"

"Like this!" she said, swept up in her triumph. She picked up a last ceremonial glass of wine, draining it for effect. Oh, fateful moment! In her confidence she forgot carefulness and swallowed the gem that kept her safe from the alcohol's effects. Instantly, every single drop she'd imbibed rushed through her veins. The room reeled, she clutched her hand to her face, willing herself not to vomit.

"Alright, darling," said Maria, watching her sway, "you've proved your point, let's get you home."

"Can't we just put her in some corner?" said Lorenzo, eyeing the food.

"No. Bertoldo isn't the only pervert in the room, and I don't want to be standing guard all night. Here, love, drink up this wine, we'll make our journey more merry."

"But the feast—" objected Lorenzo.

"Will be here when we return," said Maria. "Look at the pig – it's still hours from cooked."

Lorenzo filled his pockets with cheese just in case. Maria put her arm around one side of Lucia, and Lorenzo around the other, and they walked her out the front door, grabbing a lit torch from the entryway.

"Right. Which way to your bed, darling? Lucia? Hey! Focus. Which way?"

They shook her until she nodded vaguely toward a street that exited the little piazza in front of the grand home. Even sober, she wouldn't know the way back. She hardly ever came to Oltre Arno, and hadn't been paying attention when they left Alle Panche. To complicate things, the thunderstorms anticipated the day before were gathering, the already moonless night made blacker by clouds. But Maria and Lorenzo dutifully guided her in the direction of her nod, laughing and joking and recalling Bertoldo's stupid face to cheer her up.

THIRTY-FOUR

MINIATO AL MONTE

Late at Night, July 10th of 1348,
City of Florence

After a decent while of Lucia's aimless pointing, her guides' wine-induced cheer wore thin. "Lucia, I hate to say it but you've been taking us mostly in a circle. You do know where you live, right? Which side of the river?"

She nodded "yes" but that was all she could muster.

"Oh, God, Maria, we're fools," said Lorenzo, smacking himself on the face. "She already told us the night we met, remember? She's in Santa Croce! Mother of God, still so far!"

"No. No. Not there," Lucia slurred. "Santa Trin-i-ta." Her chaperones stopped in their tracks and looked at each other.

"No," said Lorenzo.

"We can't just leave her here, she's plonked."

"Yes, we can. She should be dead already." He let go of Lucia's arm and moved several steps away. "Come, Maria."

"Lucia, in what parish is your home?" asked the woman.

Lucia realized the mistake through her drunkenness, and tried clumsily to correct it. "Shh. Shhhh. S'alright… San – HIC – Croce."

"She lies in her throat," said Lorenzo angrily.

Maria unraveled herself from Lucia, who began to sway

precipitously without her supporters. "You are a dirty, dirty liar," she said. "There is no one left alive in Santa Trinita – well, no one but you. It is filled with pestilence. A *dead parish*. You exposed us all to your contaminated breath. Now we leave, to enjoy what is probably our last evening."

Lorenzo spat on the ground at her feet and called her a whore for good measure, and the pair walked away into the darkness, taking the torch with them. Lucia staggered until she bumped into a wall and finally puked purple all over the front of Antonella's dress. She knelt down and searched with her hands through the vomit, looking for the amethyst, but she could not find it. The street tilted up to greet her, and she lost her balance. She was both terrified to be alone, and glad nobody was there to see her. She vomited again, pushed herself back up, and began to wander through the pitch-dark streets, clinging to the walls of empty houses for balance.

No windows showed lamps, no lanterns were lit in their niches to mark the crossroads. Houses leaned over the roads and blocked the sky completely. Lucia could not see her hand in front of her face. The wind became angry, little raindrops began to fall. Soon the sky spilled forth a proper summer torrent and streams of water rolled down the streets, washing mud and dead things toward her. Lucia wept, huddled in some corner. She deserved all this, she told herself. She had prioritized her own pride, her own vengeance over the all-important search for the thief. In a flash of lightning, she saw the ancient hulking church of San Miniato al Monte, keeping its lonely watch over the city. She must have wandered right through the Porta San Niccolo! All the gatekeepers really *were* dead. She went toward the church, and found it open.

It was blacker, still, inside. She could barely make out the pale rectangles of white marble sarcophagi, laid flush with the floor. Lucia did not want to sleep on the floor among the dead so she shuffled, hands out to see where her eyes could not, until she found the steps leading up to the raised choir.

The choir platform was supported by a columned crypt

that held the tomb of the martyr Miniato. A grate was set in the floor of the choir platform through which the priest could look down to view the holy grave.

Lucia crawled up the stairs on all fours and sat down behind the altar. How would she explain this part to San Tommaso? Being so drunk that she slept in a church. The lonely and frightening walk had brought Lucia a false sobriety, but now that she was sitting down, the church began to spin faster and faster until she thought she might be sick again. She lay down, touching the cool floor with forehead and palms. An attempt to steady the world that was whirling around uncontrollably. Blessedly, she passed out.

Sleep comes easily to the inebriated, but it does not stay long, and Lucia woke some hours later with a spasm of anxiety, still quite drunk. She stayed absolutely still, working out where she was and why. She couldn't believe she'd lost *another* of Ginevra's magic stones – and this one she took without permission! Fool, fool, no wonder her husband left her. She was always taking and giving only frustration.

It was still as black as the bottom of a well inside the church. Fool again! The heliodor, still in her pocket. So drunk she had forgotten the very thing that might have led her home. She pulled it out and held it aloft, a personal orb of light in the vast darkness of San Miniato. But there was another faint glow hovering above the floor, about ten feet in front of her. She stared hard at it, convinced it was a spirit come out of its grave. The sounds of soft scratchings and the chink of metal on stone echoed up – the noise was coming through the grate over San Miniato's tomb.

Lucia stayed still on the floor, terrified that any small noise or movement would make her presence known to whoever (or whatever) was in the crypt. She listened hard, the chinking and scraping continued, and then a melody, hummed as by a carpenter busy at his bench. A person absorbed in their task, not worried about observers.

On fingertips and the toes of her ruined leather shoes, with her invisible light, she crept toward the grate so she might better observe. She reached the hole and peered through.

Below her, she saw the back of a figure kneeling down in a rough wool cloak. A small lantern, a large satchel, and a little bottle just the shape of a spring onion rested on the ground beside the figure. Her heart flipped over in her chest – here was their thief at work! But – Miniato was not one of the Divine Nine. His church was too far from the city center.

There was a faint sizzle and smell of something acrid, like vinegar, that stung her nostrils and throat. Her eyes watered with the effort of suppressing a cough. From below, now a rasping, scraping noise that carried on for a few minutes. A muted exclamation of triumph and a louder clang as she saw metal bars placed carefully to the side of the cloaked figure. Then to her horror, Lucia saw the figure reach into the tomb and ease out the dried old leg of the hermit martyr Miniato. He rocked the leg to and fro and with an unpleasant "crack" and a little puff of dust, it broke free of the body.

She waited for something, anything – the floor to open up and swallow this thief – but there were no sounds besides the clinks of his labor. The thief's hand reached out from his cloak, and pulled the bottle underneath it. Lucia could not see what was happening, only the skeletal foot of Miniato, sticking out from under the cloak at an odd angle, jerking about as he fiddled with it.

She heard the tinkling of liquid being poured into a vessel. A flurry of movement under the cloak, then the thief stuck the holy right leg of San Miniato into his satchel and stood up. Lucia rolled away from her viewing grate. Her wet shoe made a tiny squeak on the floor. The thief looked around, and then blew out the lantern. Lucia had not caught one glimpse of his face. She removed her shoes and slunk away, guided by the light of the heliodor. She crept down the stairs to the crypt door and hid beside it, against the wall. A moment later out came the thief with his lumpy satchel in one hand, the other stretched out in front to feel his way. The hood of his cloak was drawn.

As she strained to see his face, she was hit by a nauseating stench, worse than the sickly sweet scent of rot to which she had become accustomed. Worse than a beard stuck full of anchovies. The thief turned his head in the direction she stood, and she felt cold, deep inside her body, though the air was hot and humid. She nearly puked again. While she struggled to stay silent, the thief went beyond the light of the heliodor. He hurried out of the building, going as fast as the darkness allowed, and into the night, unconcerned with the rain that still came down in sheets. Lucia slumped to the floor and lay with her back pressed against the wall of the crypt, trying to pull warmth into her body from the stone floor. She stayed there until dawn crept through the windows and the storm had passed.

THIRTY-FIVE

FRIENDS & ENEMIES

July 11th of 1348, City of Florence

The next morning, the two women sat across from each other at Lucia's kitchen table, a tiny onion-shaped bottle of violet liquid between them. Ginevra had dark circles under her eyes from yet another sleepless night. Lucia looked like she had crawled out of the river.

"What were you thinking?" asked Ginevra for the fifth time.

"I'm sorry. I told you, I thought I was helping," was all Lucia could answer.

"The selenite – perhaps that was my fault. But my bloodstones – gone due to your carelessness. And still, after all this, you take more of my stones without asking, you lose another precious gem."

"Please, my head aches so. I told you I am *sorry*."

"So you said. You're sure of what you saw at San Miniato, what you felt? What you *smelled*?"

"I told you, I am certain. Please, I must go lie down."

"Tell me again. I want to make sure I understand all the details clearly."

"I told you, a man dissolved the iron mesh of the tomb of Miniato and stole his leg. He poured liquid into this bottle and left it in the tomb. Then he came close to me, and I became overwhelmed by his stench – like a dead dog left in the gutter. It made me so cold I thought I might die."

"You were a fool to approach him. Lucia – this thief is a *jettatore*. I'm sure of it now. The cold you felt confirms it. You are very lucky. The darkness of night protected you from his cursed gaze – I think the plague must be drawn to him. This is why everyone is dead in the parishes he visits, not because the relics are stolen."

"He must have given it to me again. I have never felt so low." Lucia buried her throbbing head in her arms on the kitchen table.

"It's not the plague. It's the wine."

"You might have warned me that would happen, if I swallowed the stone."

"Well, I didn't know you were going to steal it to compete in a drinking contest."

"I told you, I didn't plan on the contest. It just happened."

Ginevra scoffed.

Lucia changed the subject. "What of the little girl, then? Did you go to her? Was there enough medicine to help?"

"I— I don't know if it was enough. She died the night before I arrived, while we sat on your roof, gossiping and eating salami."

"Oh, Ginevra, I'm so sorry. If only I hadn't ruined everything."

Ginevra said nothing, and began flipping through the apothecary's guidebook of saints. "San Miniato is not listed in here."

"Because the book is only the Divine Nine. I told you—"

"Stop saying *I told you*!" Ginevra swept the book off the table in frustration. As it flew, a sheet of accordioned paper unfolded from the back cover and trailed behind the volume like the tail of a comet.

The women looked at each other. Neither of them had noticed this feature. Ginevra picked it up.

"What does it say?" asked Lucia.

"It is a poem." She held the book vertically, so the hidden sheet hung down, and read out loud:

Good Pilgrim
If you have some extra time
After all the Divine Nine
Or should a priest stop you and say
The Baptistry is Closed Today
Or Crowds are too great, for your taste
To these o'rlooked Places, please make haste

"It is a list of more churches!"
"Shh. Of course it is."

If empty peace is what you seek
Find San Paolino, of the Meek
A simple place, but in its store
A relic of San Francesco poor
For goodly walk and greenly trees
To Miniato of the Mountain, will you please

"But the thief has visited these places also!" said Lucia. "Don't you think I know? Shh."

Construction clogs old Reparata
But one parish past, is Santa Margherita
Their church is small but full of charm
And holds San Pancrazio's virtuous Arm

"We must go there—"
"Shhh—"

And for respite, in Good Sisters' Care
Sant'Elisabetta has room to spare
In Oltre Arno you will find
Holy bread, with blood of Christ Divine

"Oh, Ginevra, isn't that where—"

"I must go! I must go at once. Lucia, PLEASE. Just stay here until I am back."

"Ginevra— wait." Lucia reached into her purse, and held out the squashed orange she took from the party. "I'm sorry. *Really.*" Ginevra took the sticky orange and realized how awful it felt to be in a fight with her only friend in the whole world, besides maybe Taddea. How she never wanted to feel this way again. She lifted her eyes to the ceiling, and before she could change her mind, she said, "I have something for you, too." Onto the table next to Lucia's face, she placed a pointed crystal, harder than steel, clear as water: the diamante. A rare and precious thing. Given as a gift, to end all quarrels. Immediately, Ginevra felt lighter.

A tear rolled down Lucia's face onto the table.

Ginevra patted her head. "I must go now, dear friend. Drink water and do not stop until you feel better. I'll be back soon."

Ginevra took the book and flew toward the convent of Sant' Elisabetta, praying that Taddea's locks had held. Once more over the bridge, over the stinking river. *Every other piece stolen is a piece of body. He did not take the crucifix of San Giovanni Gualberto. He did not take the shoe. He would not take the bread.* She prayed this would be true.

She burst through the doors as soon as Taddea opened them.

"Ginevra! What's going on? Have you caught the—"

"Taddea, the book!"

"I told you the books were sold to the merchant from San Romolo. What's going—"

"No, the guidebook – for pilgrims who come to Florence to visit the relics. You're in it!"

"Oh, that thing. Yes, we *are* there, but you'd hardly know it.

They just write us in sometimes in the back as a place for food and lodging. The full pages are always the Divine Nine now—"

"No, no, Taddea, the thief, he knows the book! *He uses it to select his relics.* Tell me your bread is safe! That you have seen it today."

Taddea's face went white.

Ginevra ran to the chapel door.

"Wait!" called Taddea. "I have the key."

But when Ginevra pushed on the door it fell inward with a great clatter, the hinges and lock rusted through, the door propped back up to disguise the intrusion.

"Oh, my God," said Taddea. "It wasn't like this just yesterday—"

Ginevra ran up to the altar, and with trembling hands, she lifted the reliquary out of its cabinet. It was as she remembered: a crystal orb mounted in the center of a cross, where a holy loaf with its dark brown stain should be suspended between two halves of the sphere. As she examined the crucifix, the front half of the crystal fell and shattered on the ground.

"Shit! I'm sorry!"

"What are you doing? Please stop it!" cried Taddea, horror-stricken.

"Look!" said Ginevra, pointing to material that fluttered out from the broken reliquary like a leaf falling from the tree.

"That is not our bread," said Taddea.

"It is *parchment*," said Ginevra. She picked it up from where it landed atop the shards of crystal and the two women looked at it. Ordinary parchment, with nothing upon it but a dusty brown smudge.

"Do you see a bottle? Filled with purple or green?"

But Taddea was not listening. She had collapsed onto her knees, heedless of the broken crystal pieces. "Wh-what will I do now, without even the protection of our relic? Why was I left alone and alive?" She turned to Ginevra. "The door was not like that before you touched it!"

Ginevra's blood froze. "Of course it was – you just did not notice it until now."

"And the relic, it was bread just yesterday, until you came and reached for it."

"Taddea! How could you think I would do anything to harm Fra Simone's bread?"

Taddea stood up. "*Is* it so hard to imagine? You could always work magic more than anyone else. I know you meant to do good back then – I think, at least – but you have been gone years, while we suffered for your misdeeds. I was foolish to think I still know you. To believe your story about the bishop!"

"Please, Taddea, why else would I be here?"

"You – you come to seek revenge on all who shunned you. Take advantage of us when we are weak. To think I let you near Agnesa! What did you do but hasten her death?"

"How can you say such a thing? It is me! The only woman trying to help you. The thief – *he* has exchanged your bloody bread for parchment."

"Stop it. Quiet. Leave and do not return again!"

"You know not what you say."

"I *know* what I say."

"I will be back. Upon my word, if I am alive, I will be back. And I will bring your relic."

THIRTY-SIX

SANTO DEI SANTI

July 11th of 1348, the Inquisitor's Palazzo

Ginevra walked briskly toward the inquisitor's residence.

Never mind that Taddea does not believe you. She would speak to him and then continue on to the neighboring parish of Santa Margherita, the last church in the apothecary's guidebook. *She is scared and alone, but you will fix it.* She reached the Piazza della Santa Reparata; there was the dead mason still on the scaffold. She tipped her head in greeting. Outside the inquisitor's apartment, a dirty monk waited in front of the door, which was slightly ajar.

"Oh! Excuse me. A live woman, how marvelous. Fra Leobaldo at your service – do you know if the inquisitor is still, ah—" Ginevra saw her note from the day before still stuck in the doorjamb.

Oh, God, he's dead, she thought, unsure if that nullified their deal. But then the door swung open fully and there was Inquisitor Michele with red-rimmed eyes and stubbly face.

"You!" he said to her, breath stinking of wine. "Why do you keep me waiting for so many days? It has been... many of them."

"I keep *you* waiting? I was here yesterday! Why did you

not answer my knocks? Wait – why do you open the door yourself? Where is your man Giuseppe?"

His lip trembled. "Dead! Dead. The pestilence... Does anybody die from any of the usual ways anymore? Death was once endlessly creative – all manner of diverse and wondrous accidents – broken hearts, getting stuck in odd places. Now he strikes the same note again and again, no longer creating harmonies. But what he lacks in artistry, he makes up for in tenacity. It's only a matter of time, now that he has entered my home."

Ginevra and Fra Leobaldo exchanged glances. She had expected the same subtle intoxication as before, but now he was downright drunk, the monk's knocking the only thing that had gotten him out of bed. She took his arm, giving him a little shake. "Come now, you've made it this far. Some have hearty constitutions against it naturally."

"Ahem, forgive me for interrupting – Fra Leobaldo, at your service, Ser Inquisitor. I am the record keeper for the church of Santa Margherita. I've come to tell you the results of the inventory you requested in May—"

"Did you say Santa Margherita?" interrupted Ginevra.

"Oh! My brave monk," said Fra Michele. "Noble man, most worthy keeper of records! I'd given up hope that anyone would respond. It took you a while, but still, your faith brings much heart."

"Ah...yes, well, I fled to the countryside months ago, and it wasn't until I returned that I discovered your letter—"

"This is Monna Ginevra, an expert on depraved thievery."

"At your service," said Ginevra with a small bow.

"My dear Leobaldo, please come sit. You must be thirsty from your journey."

"Thank you, Ser Inquisitor, but seeing as somebody just died here—"

"Nonsense! All the precautions *I* followed, keeping

myself apart from people, from my work. It has meant nothing! In or out, it makes no difference, death will come, death will come for us all."

He grabbed the reluctant monk by the arm and steered him through the entryway to an interior courtyard, where there was a table with several open bottles of wine and also a donkey that had come in through the open door to munch on the courtyard's garden. Ginevra followed. The inquisitor wiped out a cup with his sleeve, filled it almost to the brim, and then held it toward the monk.

"I'd offer you something to eat, but you see, it was Giuseppe who—"

"Ser Inquisitor – what I have to tell you is brief. I return to Florence only because everyone at the monastery where I stayed in Frascati died besides me."

The inquisitor put his cup down. "What is the brief thing you have to say, then?"

"That the church of Santa Margherita has been robbed?" cut in Ginevra.

Leobaldo stared at her. "The right arm of San Pancrazio replaced by—"

"An evil-looking glass vial?" she finished.

"I see you truly are an expert in depraved thievery. Here." He took a bottle from his purse and placed it on the table. The liquid inside matched the purple color of the wine. "I know not when the arm was taken, only that it was present when I departed in May."

Inquisitor Michele took out his pomander and inhaled deeply, then took a large sip of wine.

"Ahem – as I have delivered my message and you have no servant, I'll, um, see myself out. I pray you find the person responsible and that they suffer a terrible punishment." Leobaldo left as fast as he could without running.

The inquisitor jumped a little at the sound of the front door slamming, and turned to Ginevra. "And how did you know what he was going to say, late woman?"

Ginevra brought out the apothecary's book, and stretched the accordion pages out on the table. "Because every one of the churches in this guide have been visited by the relic thief. And here, in this bit at the end, it mentions the San Pancrazio arm just reported missing by Leobaldo." Next to the book, she placed the inquisitor's original list and wrote upon it:

San Miniato – right leg of San Miniato.
Robbed on July 10.

Sant'Elisabetta – holy bread.
Theft noticed: July 11. Relic last seen: July 10.

Santa Margherita – right arm of San Pancrazio.
Theft noticed: July 11.

The inquisitor shook his head and moaned as he read through all the additional thefts Ginevra had recorded. Then he paused, and picked up the book, turning quickly through the pages. "Is this...a pilgrim guidebook for the Divine Nine?"

Ginevra nodded slowly.

The inquisitor raked his fingers over his tonsured head.

"Even the finger of San Tommaso in its locked chapel has been taken?"

"Locks mean nothing to this thief. He knows how to turn iron to rust."

The inquisitor drained his wine. "He is versed in alchemy. A man of education."

"There is more – those who encountered him *felt* him. Became cold right down into their souls. Into their bones. Inquisitor, do you know what that means?"

He reached again for the bottle. Ginevra moved it away.

"My aunt spoke to a *jettatore* once," he said. "Then a pile of bricks fell off a building and squished her. No wonder the plague rages so in our city. This *jettatore* draws it to us and then steals our holy guardians. Have you discovered, at least, what he looks like?"

"No, but I know what he smells like."

"But *jettatore* do not have a smell. Otherwise no one would go near enough to be cursed."

"This one does. They say he has a strong and peculiar odor that overwhelms the senses. They say he smells like a dead dog left in the gutter."

"Ah. I know that smell. He is wearing a cilice. A *hair* shirt. Nasty things, woven from horsehairs, worn against the skin. They're for lazy people that need pain to remind them to follow God. But, he wears it as he robs churches?"

"Perhaps it is in penance for his crimes?"

The inquisitor made a face at the suggestion. "Last night... last night was very dark, wasn't it?"

"A new moon and a wicked storm."

The inquisitor clapped himself in the head so hard his palm left a red mark. "I've been a fool, and so have you! It is the simplest pattern: when it is the blackest night of the month – a new moon – he goes about to do his wicked deeds unseen. He has robbed us every month since the start of spring, pulling as much as he can in an evening."

Ginevra realized he was correct; it was possible the thefts coincided with the new moons of April, May, June, and now July.

"This *jettatore*!" continued Inquisitor Michele. "He has not been too clever for us. He has been too simple! Using a cheap pilgrim's guide and waiting for dark nights. I'm surprised he had the brains to get San Miniato down the mountain!"

"He took just the leg."

"What do you mean, just the leg?"

"I mean he broke the right leg off the relic, and left the rest of him in the tomb."

The inquisitor snatched the wine bottle back and refilled

his beaker. "Tell me slowly, Monna, name the parts he has taken."

"If you stopped drinking you could remember them yourself."

"JUST tell me."

"Fine. First, San Filippo's left arm, and San Zenobio's head, then the thigh of San Barnaba, and from the churches of the *Rogazione*, the torso of San Piero, the right and left buttocks of San Paolo—"

"I remember when they decided to divide the buttocks. A most magnanimous solution."

"And the left foot of Santo Stefano. And since we first spoke, to this list are added the shoulder of San Giovanni Gualberto, the finger of San Tommaso D'Aquino, the right leg of San Miniato, the right arm of San Pancrazio, and the bloody bread of the convent of Sant'Elisabetta."

"Did you know," said the inquisitor grimly, "the right arm of San Pancrazio is missing its pointer finger. The king of France requested a bit of him so we broke it off."

"So?"

"Did you know also that the finger relic of San Tommaso happens to be the pointer finger from his right hand?"

Ginevra's eyes widened with understanding. "Oh. OH. This is *so. Very. Strange.*"

"Please – fetch my desk from the front hall. My head aches too much."

She brought it and the inquisitor took pen and parchment and drew a curious figure:

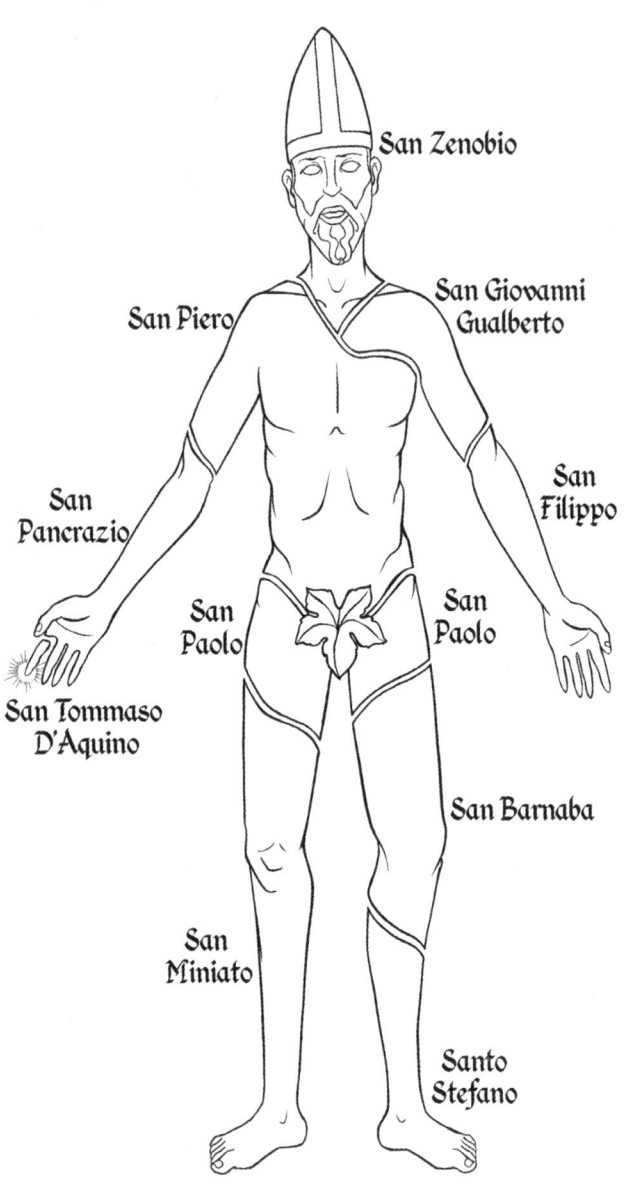

The two of them stared at the sketch in horror. "He is building himself a whole new saint from other saints," said the inquisitor at last.

Ginevra picked up the parchment and examined it. "But what about the bread relic from the convent? This man looks whole. Did the thief mean to give him supper?"

"He is not whole. Not quite. Whoever heard of an evil spell using *eleven* of something? He will need twelve pieces. One for each of the apostles."

"Well, there seems but one part missing and it is not a loaf of bread."

"Not THAT. Perverted woman. And besides, the left buttock of San Paolo is rather more complete than the right if you know what I mean."

"Then what, if not that?"

"What he is missing," said the inquisitor, "is a sacred heart."

"The blood of Christ, preserved in the convent of Sant'Elisabetta's miraculous bread," said Ginevra, understanding. "What will he do, then, with this new saint made of saints?"

"If only we had one of those necromantic books you trafficked, we might know."

"I *told* you, I never trafficked – why do you know what is inside such books?"

"A hazard of my trade. They are all variations of the same. Instructions on how to command demons to fulfill base desires. Empty rituals, things like circles with stars drawn inside them, the sort of thing peasants put about their cowsheds to scare away the spirits of their dead relatives. Burning blood and chanting words in the night to make the peas grow. And to trick the ignorant that it is no heresy, the first step prescribed by these books are rituals of Christian penance so strict no man who was not a saint could succeed at them."

"So our thief wears his hair shirt to prepare for a ritual."

"It must be so," said the inquisitor. "And there is nothing

we can do about it." He raised his wine cup to his lips. Little gold chickens stared at Ginevra from purple and green vines. How she hated those chickens, their blank expressions, the monotonous colors from the kilns of—

"San Romolo!" she yelled.

"What? There are no relics of San Romolo."

"Not the saint, the town… The pottery merchant of San Romolo once bought a secret book!"

"I *knew* you trafficked them!"

"Shh. Look on your cup – the colors come only from there. Purple and green vines! *The same as the liquid in the bottles.* Sometimes it is diluted, sometimes intense, but the hue is the same!"

She took the cup the inquisitor clutched, dumped out the wine, and held it next to the onion-shaped bottle from San Pancrazio. The inquisitor opened his desk again, took out the bottles he had gathered in the early weeks of the investigation. Held purple to purple and green to green, and it was true: the liquid inside, all shades of the intense pigments that rendered twirling vines and grapes.

"And look," he said, "the very shape of the vessels! These are exactly the sort of vials that precious pigments are stored in." He showed his own painting supplies to Ginevra. "The sort of vials that you must keep hundreds of to run a pottery workshop."

"What do you make of this, then?" asked Ginevra, mind racing. "At Sant'Elisabetta the bread was replaced not with a flask, but this scrap of parchment with a smudge upon it."

He held the parchment up to the light, then placed it next to the bottles. The tips of his fingers fluttered against his lips. "He leaves something to replace that which he has taken." He picked up a lavender-colored vial and before Ginevra could so much as utter a warning, he broke its seal and poured a drop onto his finger. He touched it with the tip of his tongue.

"Inquisitor! Stop, drunk fool!"

"Pah. He has added only *water*. Plain water, poured into bottles and stained by chance from their prior use."

"How can you know this?"

"Our thief, our penitent *jettatore*, he needs our relics for his ritual, but leaves third-class relics, created by pouring water over the bones, or in this last case, he must have rubbed a bit of the holy blood onto a piece of parchment. Water would have dissolved the bread."

"I don't understand—"

"It's standard, really," said the inquisitor, growing excited at his discovery. "A way to make many relics from one. If water is poured over a relic, some of the relic's power is transferred to the water, though of course the power is less potent than that of the original. But I'm confused – to leave behind these vials, then, is an act of kindness. He is returning a bit of what he has taken. But never mind that now – what will he *do* with our city's treasures, now that his composite saint is complete?"

"We must find the answer in San Romolo," said Ginevra.

The inquisitor nodded. "I will inform the bishop at once. He must send men to recover them. San Romolo is less than a day's walk from here."

Ginevra's coral grew cold upon her chest. She looked at the inquisitor with incredulity. "You have let me do all the work. You have let me do the work, and now the two of you will claim *you* found the relics, and say I did not fulfill our contract!"

"Don't insult me! You'll get what we agreed on – a pardon on your exile, and a recommendation to start your business. If, of course, they *are* in San Romolo."

Ginevra did not like this one bit – she remembered from her arrival in Florence the Swiss mercenaries the bishop kept at his door. These were not men she trusted to recoup fragile items from a *jettatore*. They were bloodthirsty soldiers-for-hire known for their brute strength, not for their finesse. And her future hopes hung upon the relics' intact return.

"Inquisitor, please. We have come to our most delicate step. We know not what this *jettatore* means to do with your relics. What will happen if soldiers arrive and he is in the middle of his ritual?"

"They will poke him with knives and tie him up, I suppose?"

"But this man is a *jettatore*. He knows how to turn iron to rust! He could probably just look at them and their blades would fall out of their handles."

Inquisitor Michele shrugged. "Then the mercenaries will use their fists to overpower him. This is one man against many. I do not see what you are so concerned about."

"Ser Inquisitor, you must understand that the *malocchio* that is living inside the thief feeds on anger. The bishop's men will be full of it. Surely this twisted creature, in his cilice, must be approached more gently."

"Monna. This is something that requires arms first and compassion later. A show of physical force. Then after, forgiveness. This is how things are done. I *will* tell the bishop to send his soldiers to San Romolo, and he *will* see how wrong he was to think I could not solve this crime."

"So that's it, then," said Ginevra, disgusted with herself for trying to reason with an inquisitor. "THAT's what this is all about? Proving yourself superior to the bishop? He will not take kindly to that."

"Womanish worries only. It is natural for you to be frightened, but don't be. I'll be right back from the bishop's. Wait here. I don't think he likes you very much."

THIRTY-SEVEN

NOT A CHICKEN

July 11th of 1348, the Residence of the Bishop
Bishop Acciaiuoli was staring at his lunch, served on one of his favorite plates. The plate was painted with the image of a young woman riding some sort of fantastical eel-looking creature. A limited edition from the famed kilns of San Romolo. Normally, he looked forward to the moment when his food was finished, the tantalizing image fully visible. Today, though, it was hard for him to eat at all. His plan to recoup funds for his bank had taken a turn for the worse. Autumn was not far away. The plague would withdraw, as all plagues did with the cold, and his shareholders would resume their hounding. All this was in his mind when the beaming and quick-talking inquisitor arrived, wrapped head to toe in fragrant linens. But as the inquisitor went on, the bishop became more and more interested.

"Let me see if I understand: you believe the relic thief is the man who makes pottery in San Romolo?" He pushed aside a bit of his lunch, and eyed the eel-woman's green legs clutching violet scales.

"Yes. And I believe he has stolen all he means to steal, so may be returning back to his home."

The bishop shook his head and resumed eating.

"Well, anyhow, haste is of the utmost import, we must

intercept him before our relics are subject to unholy ritual – we must pray we are not already too late! If your guard leaves now, they can make it there early in the day tomorrow."

"No," said Acciaiuoli between bites. "But, have the woman go on her own. I'll not risk my men on this foolish journey."

"Foolish? There could be no quest more sensible! To rescue the items that protect our citizens, give sanctity to our churches, and a soul to our city!"

"I know what a relic is, Inquisitor. I'll not send my last healthy men on a long journey to an infected town. This theory is rather fantastical, you must admit."

"But…the bottles! The moonless nights! The saint made of saints!"

"Please, Michele, a saint made of saints? You sound ridiculous. But still, I agree your Ginevra should at least go. As inquisitor, you must be thorough. On the small chance she finds something in San Romolo, she can report back, and I promise you'll have my men at your disposal."

"But…we need our relics back as soon as possible! That is the whole point."

The bishop put down his bread. "You don't think I know that? That I do not pray they will return, reveal themselves to the individual they deem most worthy?"

"Yes, such a thing would be the greatest of miracles. But to be stingy with resources now? When we have identified the criminal? Every moment they are in his custody, they are in danger of unholy violation—"

"Enough! Enough." The bishop wiped his mouth and stood up, walking over to the inquisitor. "Michele, let us speak as men to each other: I have indulged you for some weeks now. I helped you bring back a most strange investigator. I understand how it is. It is a hard time and, frankly, you've been drinking too much, so you needed the help. But now, do you see what pathetic result it has come to? You really can't expect me to use my personal resources to solve your problem."

"*Indulge me?* Signore, you insult me! I will not leave until—"

"Control yourself!" said Bishop Acciaiuoli, slamming a fist down on the table so hard that his plate leaped off and shattered on the floor. "You forget it is I to whom you owe your position – and do you know why I nominated you? I chose you because I thought you would shut up and respect your place, unlike your predecessor. But you've been nothing but a fly buzzing around my face. Make the strange Ginevra go by herself. That was your plan, wasn't it? To have her do the job for you? I've extended myself enough on your behalf."

"Why will you not help me, Bishop?"

"Michele, you had better go home before the miasmas get to you. It's only a matter of time, with how widely you open your mouth. You know the way out."

Inquisitor Michele turned on his heel, leaving red and furious. As he hurried out, he bumped into a nun clutching a broken crystal orb.

"YOU—" said Ginevra as the inquisitor burst back through his own door. She had worked herself up. Yelling at an inquisitor would be the only redemption she would gain from this long and futile journey. She gesticulated wildly as she spoke. "You make a fool of yourself, like the chicken who sits at the back of the butcher stall, watching the other chickens get their necks wrung and thinking it will never happen to him. They ran the last inquisitor out of town. They will do it to you—"

The inquisitor grabbed her wrist, which was wagging a pointed finger in his direction. "I am NOT a chicken. And YOU. You were right. The bishop will not help us on our journey, insisted that *you* go alone. And so we must discover the answers for ourselves. Too long I have left my work to others. Woman, we go to San Romolo. Right now. If I die, I die inquisiting."

THIRTY-EIGHT

THIS JEWEL IS MAGIC

July 11th of 1348, City of Florence

Lucia sat alone in her dim palace, wondering if this was what the rest of her life would be like. Her hangover had faded to a dull nausea where both eating and not-eating seemed equally bad. Her spirits lifted at a knock upon her door. Finally! Ginevra had returned. But when she opened the door, there was only a young boy wearing the uniform of the bishop's page.

"Excuse me, Lady, are you a ghost?"

"What? No. I'm not dead! I am alive and this is my house. Why does everyone think I should be dead?"

"Oh...well, then, are you a friend of Ginevra di Genoa, who walks through pestilence but will never be ill?"

"Who has said this of me?"

The boy smiled. "I'm Piero di Piero. I'm her friend, too. But my master, the bishop, he is not – I must speak to her before she leaves for San Romolo."

"San Romolo?" said Lucia. "Where they make the chicken plates?"

Piero shrugged.

"Come in and tell me everything."

They went into the garden, where it was coolest, and Piero

explained it was he that fetched Ginevra all the way from Genoa. The bishop was impressed that he managed to bring her back all by himself without dying, and immediately hired him as a servant. Piero had meant to find Ginevra and tell her, but he hadn't known where she was staying until that very afternoon.

A nun came to the bishop's palazzo, and she complained that Ginevra used magic to try to heal another older nun. But the magic didn't work, and the older nun died and now their holy bread relic was missing. The bishop told the complaining nun that Ginevra had run off to San Romolo, but not to worry, he already knew she was stealing relics and had a plan to arrest her when she came back. He said his guards were stationed at the Porta San Niccolo to get her. Piero knew it could not be true, that Ginevra would not hurt a nun or take their bread, and the complaining nun had mentioned that Ginevra had taken over the house of the Tornaparte, where everyone was dead, which is why Piero took Lucia for a ghost.

Lucia's head reeled. "Why would she go to San Romolo? What else did you hear?"

"Nothing. I snuck out straightaway to warn Ginevra before she left."

"She has not been here since this morning, Piero. I'm afraid she must have gone already."

"But when she comes back, they will take her and put her in the *stinche*!"

"Oh, what do we do?? You must go back and find out more. Find out why the bishop believes that she stole the bread relic, when it was he who asked her to come and apprehend the thief."

"He will never tell me; I only am his servant. I only learned of this by accident. What if you asked him? Your house looks important."

"No. He mustn't know I'm still alive. Or that anyone is trying to help Ginevra. Tell me, Piero, do you sleep in his chamber?"

"Of course," said Piero proudly. "I have my very own truckle bed that rolls out."

"And is he a sound sleeper?"

"No...he tosses and turns until it is very late and then sleeps for just an hour or two."

"That will do." Lucia unpinned a golden brooch from her shoulder and handed it to Piero.

"What is this? It looks very expensive. Is this a spell written on it?"

"Sort of – it says *not my wife, but my life* – Ginevra says this jewel is magic. I need you to take this, and stay awake all night on your truckle bed, and when the bishop sleeps, put this above his heart. Then you ask him to tell his secrets, and why he lies that Ginevra has stolen relics."

Piero went back to his master's home, but the bishop was not there. Nor were the mercenaries who usually hung about, tormenting him. He was too late. They already were camped together at the Porta San Niccolo, waiting with their pointy knives for Ginevra's return.

THIRTY-NINE

THE INQUISITOR & THE STONE WITCH

Evening, July 11th of 1348,
the Road to San Romolo

And then it was just Ginevra and the inquisitor, plus the donkey from the courtyard, who would carry back their holy cargo. Ginevra did not have time to tell Lucia where she was going. She did not want the inquisitor to know about their relationship if things went badly, anyhow. They would be back tomorrow, God willing.

After they passed through the open Porta San Niccolo, empty homes thinned to the refuse-strewn wastelands, and then to fields of whatever unruly wheat had sown itself, threaded through with vines of cucumber and blue morning glories. They heard the loud hum of frogs and crickets in irrigation ditches, the chattering of summer birdsong. The earth did not mind that those who tended it were dead. It carried on merrily. The two individuals walked in silence, uncomfortable in their travelers' intimacy.

The inquisitor went slowly, still bundled in his perfumed, protective linens and huffing through his pomander. "Well, Monna Ginevra. You must be pleased."

"What do you mean?"

"I mean, here is what you wanted. The two of us, off to

capture the thief ourselves with no support from the city." He was still smarting at the bishop's insults.

Ginevra snorted. "This is not what I wanted. To be walking toward a *jettatore*, with an inquisitor, the office that ruined my life, and now asks the most absurd task of me in order to get it back." She didn't like that he had called her worries womanish. That he was with her only because nobody else would help him.

"It was not *I* who passed your sentence. It was my predecessor—"

"It may as well have been you."

"Monna, it is made *so* clear how to avoid heresy. You cannot be angry about your punishment; you must have known you were transgressing."

"Against the rules of men, perhaps. But sinning before God, no. People were dying and I helped them. The methods I used – the secret gemstones? Doesn't the power of all things on the earth come from God?"

"Perhaps. But these powers must be translated through the church, or there would be chaos. You know that."

"I thought only to show Christian charity. I thought learned men could understand what I was doing. But their minds were small."

"Let us forget it," said the inquisitor. "It was long ago, and you are here, doing penance."

"It is not long ago for me. They cut off a piece of my face as punishment for saving children. I think about it every day. Anything I do has the shadow of this cast over it. When Ludovico – when I got that letter, I thought it was perhaps a chance to free myself of this shadow. To sleep without nightmares. To live freely in this place I once held so dear."

"I will pray for you to be relieved of your tortured mind."

Ginevra spit on the ground.

They lapsed into silence until it was dusk and time to make camp: wine, bread, and a fire against wolves. Ginevra did all the work. The inquisitor sat and thought about how to prove to his travel companion that he was not evil. He settled on telling the truth.

"Ginevra, I must tell you something: your Ludovico was dead before the letter was sent."

She looked up from the fire. "I know. You are a terrible liar for a priest."

"Well, it's not something I have much practice in."

She went back to her task.

"You know, you must take comfort in the fact that God especially chastens those whom he loves, visiting them with all manner of trials and obstacles. Such as he has visited you…"

"Humph."

"And you have not had it so bad as you might – your face is only minorly ruined. Still quite lovely, actually. They could have taken a hand, or a foot! Do you know the story of the man who had no shoes?"

"There are many men without shoes."

"I mean the one who was distraught and cursed God, until he met a man without feet…"

"And the man with no feet said, 'Hey, give God a kick in the ass for me, would you?'"

The inquisitor opened his mouth, shut it, and then burst into laughter. He laughed until he fell over and Ginevra could not help but catch it herself, to see this fussy man rolling around in the dirt, and soon the both of them had tears streaming down their faces and the stale bread became the merriest meal either of them had had in months, the inquisitor and the stone witch.

Later, as they sat watching the fire die, the inquisitor spoke again: "I am sorry for what happened to you. I… I do not think it was right."

Ginevra smiled sadly. "You say these words to me now in the wild darkness. Let you say them in the daylight, on the steps of Santa Reparata. Then I might believe you."

"Alright. I shall."

She looked at him across the fire, incredulous, but in the

flickering light, she saw only sincerity. "You would do this thing, truly?"

"I promise before God I will. If I do not die first, from this pestilence that floats all around us." Here he took out his pomander and huffed, but Ginevra could see his heart was not in it.

"Ser Inquisitor—"

"Please, we are here in the dirt together. I am Michele."

"Fra Michele, then – I have with me a small dose of an elixir, and I can't promise it will work, but it may keep the pestilence away. I was saving it for someone, but she died. Now, I would give it to you, if you will take it. It will be at least as helpful as whatever you sniff."

"But, you swore you would practice no—" Fra Michele stopped himself, and placed his hand on his heart. "What I meant to say was it is an honor that you give something to me." He drank the contents down with coughs and sputters. "It tastes like cat piss," he said.

"Yes, it would."

He laughed again and then began to weep and so did Ginevra, and they embraced and cried together for all the misfortune that had come to pass in their time, and the heaviness of bearing it and not just lying down to die. But when they parted and went to their separate chaste sleeps in the sweet-smelling grass, it was the contented rest of those who know they have made a friend of an enemy.

FORTY

SAN ROMOLO

July 12th of 1348, Village of San Romolo

In the morning of the next day, the town that must be San Romolo appeared in the distance. They walked through orchards of peaches, roots littered with the spoiled fruit nobody had harvested, until they came to the bottom of the steep plateau upon which the town was perched. Thick stone walls encircled it, built of mammoth blocks of rough volcanic tufa, and rising vertically, as if a natural extension of the plateau. Mounds of garbage lay on the valley floor, thrown over the edge by the inhabitants.

The pair and their donkey walked quickly, up a steep and slanting path cut in zigzags in the side of the cliff and slick with moss that grew when no footsteps were there to wear it down. Ginevra pointed to the center of the path, where the moss was crushed. "Somebody has walked here recently," she said.

They continued on in hurried silence, the pleasant ease of the early walk evaporating in the late morning heat. The two people wondered what the deranged *jettatore*-potter had in store for them. The donkey wondered when he could sit down. Flushed and more sweaty than was comfortable, they reached the top of the steep pathway.

The stones of the city walls now loomed gigantic as if placed by cyclopes. They craned their necks to see above them, and saw flying swallows jerk this way and that, silhouetted against a yellow sky. The gate presented the now-familiar sight of a precious portal left open and unattended. The heat and the long walk meant that finding a well was the first priority.

Though the trash outside the walls indicated that death had come for the town's inhabitants, swift and brutal, inside the gate there was none of the stench they had grown used to in Florence. And though they saw no one, and doors and windows were open, the homes were not in the chaotic state of the abandoned places in Florence. Rather, doors were left slightly ajar, as if guests were expected and welcome, or to let in a breeze. Ginevra poked her head into one such home: it looked swept and clean with fresh mats on the floors and wood piled in the hearth.

Soon, they arrived at the town's central piazza, the little well they sought at its center. San Romolo was compact; the whole perimeter might have been circumnavigated in less than an hour. The piazza was an elongated triangle, two sides occupied by loggia shops, and the shortest side taken up by the facade of a church that seemed absurdly grand for the tiny town. The original Roman arches had been surmounted, only recently, with an upper pediment and a golden mosaic of Christ Ascended floating above his admiring apostles. Such artwork would not have been out of place in Florence, but to find it in this minor village felt presumptuous. The largesse of the wealthy pottery merchant, Ginevra decided. She shivered as she tied the donkey up to a stone hitching post. The thief was real, and this was his home. The inquisitor lowered the bucket down into the well with a terrible *clang*. Ginevra grabbed the chain.

"Sorry!" he said. "I've never drawn water before."

"It's alright, I'll do it, just shhh…" She pulled it up as quietly as she could, and they took thirsty gulps from the bucket.

"I'm glad I had your elixir," said Fra Michele. "If ever a well was infected, it's this one."

A hot gust of wind blew through the piazza and caught the door of the church, swinging it open. Foul air exited, drifting to the well. Ginevra felt a sting on her breast, and pulled out her coral. It was hot to the touch, an unnatural saturated red. She showed Fra Michele, who looked at her charm curiously as she whispered, "The *jettatore* is near."

The inquisitor pointed to the church. She nodded. They walked toward it together, and slipped through the open door.

The interior of the church featured the standard arrangement: a central nave flanked by two aisles, divided by arched colonnades. The pitched roof was supported by thick timbers, painted in gaily colored stripes and knots. The round columns were decorated with black-and-white stripes, and the floor was of terra-cotta tiles, polished shiny by the faithful feet of the village. But on the walls, the stations of the cross, the birth of Christ, and the torments of hell were painted on new glazed tiles, in colors now too familiar: purple and green. Purple demons in green flames. Green sinners skewered by purple stakes.

Ginevra's assumptions were confirmed: this rich patron in his small town had spared no expense glorifying himself. He had refurbished the church in his own taste, in his own tiles. Would he fill this place with the saints of Florence? But aside from the garish decor, all was quiet and unremarkable. Other than the smell.

Ginevra traveled down the right aisle and Fra Michele the left. In equal intervals, the sun shone through alabaster window panes and cast golden light upon the floor. Nothing stirred, but as Ginevra walked, she could feel something bad was hiding in this church. The stinging coral, the faint foul smell. Behind the altar, she saw it: a lantern left flickering beside a dark square hole in the floor. An iron grate pulled to the side. The entrance to a crypt. She gestured Michele over, and they both knelt down to get a better look. It was too dark to see anything, but the stench slapped them in the face like water thrown from a window. They struggled to contain coughs and retches, and closed their eyes against it. Here, the odor was so powerful it seemed a physical thing.

"Michele, I must go down there. You wait above." She pulled out the heliodor and put a foot on the stairs into the subterranean vaults.

"I'm coming with you," he whispered.

"You will not. I can move quietly, unseen. And the coral protects me from the *jettatore*'s gaze."

"I have my own protection for that," he whispered, pulling a carved wooden crucifix out from his robe.

"That will not work! The *malocchio* is older than Christ."

"I will pretend I didn't hear that blaspheme."

"It will be very awful down there, Fra Michele. You have been cloistered in your house. You have not seen—"

"What is a priest who's afraid of a crypt, hmm? Besides, you will need two people to carry the relics back. I will not make you go alone."

"Fine! Fine. Do you see this?" She pointed to the heliodor. "It emits light, but only to those holding it. You must keep hold of my hand, or you will see no light. If the *jettatore* comes, drop it. If you cannot see his eyes, he cannot curse you."

Before the inquisitor could express his marvel or disapproval, Ginevra tucked her coral away, grabbed his hand, and descended into the black. Down a steep and spiral stair that deposited them into a crypt cut entirely out of the tufa stone. The whole hill that formed the foundation of the church was made of tufa, she realized. Most crypts she had seen followed a typical plan: orderly columned spaces that followed the footprint of the church above. No such architectural conventions were followed here. The room was the shape of a round loaf of bread, with an opening in the center of the floor, a passage that sloped downward.

This unorthodox design was because the crypt was carved long, long ago. Before Rome, before churches, when nothing was on top of the hill but long grass. The archaic builders found the stone of the hill was soft in places and resilient in others, so they carved their chambers and passages as the rock allowed them, with as little order as holes formed in a cheese.

As Ginevra and Fra Michele descended these passages, they came across openings in the walls, doorways that led to amorphous rooms, branched off from their path like organs grown off their central tubes. Into the walls, niches were carved for the dead. But they were not filled with dusty bones. They were squeezed full of new corpses, still clothed in their flesh. Here were the people of San Romolo, laid out not just in the niches but all over the floors of the chambers, like the mottled mosses that cover the forest. Only small paths were left bare between them; it was these Ginevra carefully followed, trailed by the gagging inquisitor.

The deeper down they walked, the stronger the stench and the more intensely the coral stung Ginevra's chest. The golden strings that connected her to ancient magic began to hum and then buzz, the air alive with their vibrations. She felt the antiquity of the chambers, felt how they were made by people so old that nobody remembered them anymore. People so ancient that when the Christian builders of the church had first discovered and cleared out the rooms for use as their own catacombs, they found, embedded in the dirt, ivory statues of women with fat breasts and no heads, and they smashed them because they were afraid. But smashed or not, the ivory goddesses still held some sway over the place, and as punishment to the men who had destroyed them, they allowed evil to come and go from the little town as it wished. As a result, the *malocchio* long ago marked San Romolo as a favorite place to cause mischief and misery.

Ginevra felt these ancient spirits cling to her like naughty children, weighing her down so her steps became labored as she continued through the dark caves. The ground appeared to shimmer and swirl, and she realized that it was covered with thousands of the burying beetles she had seen in the graveyard at San Paolino – their iridescent shells clicking and twinkling, jewel-like in her magic light. At last, the passage seemed to level out and the pair were so deep underground they felt they might hear the heartbeat of the earth. In this very deepest and darkest place, they came to a doorway flanked by columns carved out of the living rock. They stood on its threshold and observed through it a round room with curved walls. Its floor, too, was host to a number of beetle-covered bodies save for a bare circle four feet in diameter. By the light of the heliodor, they saw a stone bier in the very center of the room, the resting place of some forgotten king.

But today, the king's bones had been swept from their bier and shattered into a dusty mess, leaving the spiders who lived for generations inside his ribs scattered and homeless. And upon his stone bed were now, carefully arranged, the desiccated remains of other men. Here the disparate parts of the saints of Florence were laid out like a cadaver at an anatomy lesson. Here, too, was the thief himself, flitting about, in his hooded cloak.

Ginevra dropped Fra Michele's hand before he could protest, leaving him outside the door. Alone in her light now, she moved forward into the room, each step making the coral pulse and burn, like splashes of boiling water. She inched closer, the noise of the beetles muffling her steps, trying to understand what the thief was doing with the relics. He leaned over the bier intently, absorbed in his task. The light of his small lantern cut only inches into the darkness, a glowing orb in a sea of black.

Cruuunnnnnchhhhhh. Ginevra whipped her head around and saw Fra Michele, in his blindness, had stepped off the cleared path and put his foot through some poor person's skull.

She turned back around and the thief was inches from her face. A man of middle age, with eyes that glowed like a dog's in the meager light of his lantern, the rest of his face obscured by dark hair and bristly beard. Her coral burned so hot her eyes watered.

"Good," he said. "You are here, come."

"What?" said Ginevra.

"Not *you*," hissed the thief. *"The priest.* I know he is with you. I watched you walk up the hill together. I opened the gate and unlocked the church for him. The saints must have brought him to me, to save me the trouble of finding one."

"One what?" called the inquisitor.

"Michele, close your eyes! Do not look at him," cried Ginevra.

"Be quiet. You are extra. Go over here." The thief grabbed Ginevra and threw her hard against the wall at the back of the chamber. Her head slammed into the rock, and the heliodor was knocked from her hand, sending her into darkness.

"Foul thing!" cried the inquisitor, who could see nothing at all and was still trying to shake his foot free from the skull. "We have followed you here to your cursed den and in the name of Jesus Christ, the holy Virgin, and all the saints, I command you to cease your work and cede the relics you have taken or be damned to the fires of eternal hell!"

Ginevra tried to shout out a warning, but the wind was knocked out of her and she lay on her back, gasping for breath.

"Oh, potter, maker of painted plates, mixer of secret colors! Your wealth has corrupted you. You take what is not yours," yelled Michele. He held the wooden crucifix before him and flailed blindly.

The thief laughed. "The relics let me take them. They belong to God, not to a city or a man. The people of Florence took them for granted, locked them away in cupboards, so they came with me where they are needed. Come."

"I will not! Where is Ginevra? Give back the relics, save yourself from the fires of hell."

"Do not try to scare me with talk of hell, Priest! Hell has already broken through to the living earth. For months, I have waited and gathered and fasted and punished my flesh and now you must do your part. Come, and do not interrupt me."

In a flash, he was behind Fra Michele and shoved him hard into the bare circle on the floor, forcing him to his knees and binding his hands to an iron stake driven into the stone floor at the circle's center. "Good, now stay. I will tell you what to do." The thief returned to his bier and began lovingly adjusting the relics, but each time he got one into just the right spot, another rolled out of its place and had to be adjusted again.

Ginevra found her air and let out a moan.

"Be quiet, you are extra," he repeated, as he nudged the foot of Santo Stefano up against the thigh bone of San Barnaba for the hundredth time. The scapula of San Giovanni Gualberto tipped over. He sighed, repositioning it.

Ginevra was baffled. What did he mean, *extra*? Right now, it mattered little. What she needed to do was find a way out. Her coral was stuck to her, burned into her flesh. She picked it out, hung it outside her dress. She forced herself onto all fours, and began to search the ground, swiping away beetles and feeling for the heliodor.

"Where is my friend?? Untie me!" yelled Fra Michele.

"No! Do not interrupt me."

"Why do you build a saint made of saints?" he persisted.

"Do NOT interrupt me."

"If you answer my question, I'll stop interrupting you!"

The thief was silent for a moment. "You will think I am mad."

Ginevra paused in her search to listen.

"We already think you're mad," Michele said. "What difference does it make?"

"If it will make you quiet..." said the thief. "The secret of it matters little now. These separate relics will soon be joined together into a new saint, the sum more powerful than the separate parts. He will be called the Holy of Holies and will speak to God on my behalf and compel Him to bring these dead around you back to life."

"It is not possible," Ginevra said from her spot behind the

bier, hands moving frantically through the mire. At last, they closed around the heliodor.

"Are you a virgin?"

"Uh—"

"If you are a virgin, like the priest, I'll put you in the circle instead of hitting you on the head."

"Yes, yes! I am," she lied. With large rough hands he dragged her to the open space where Michele sat, binding her with the other end of the rope to the same stake.

"There," said the thief, "this is easier now."

"It matters not. What you seek is not possible," said Ginevra.

"Yes, it is! I found an ancient spell. *How to make the dead appear again as the living.*" He held up a thin volume. Gold letters winked in the lantern's light: *Liber Iuratus Polydoros*. It was Agnesa's book.

"The spells in such books are false," said Fra Michele. "It is a heresy to believe them!"

"It seems straightforward enough to me, Priest. Listen: *Upon the ground draw a circle of white chalk that is twelve fingers for the twelve disciples of Christ.* Done. *Within the circle draw a cross with its axis in the top half of the circle, in lines twice again as thick.* Done. *Then a triangle with its points all the way to the edges (on account of the three magi) and this is where a virgin, at least one,* (we have two!) *must willingly sit in the center. Around the circle you must write the 180 letters of the sacred name and they are* i.b.n.a.b.n.e.x.a.t.r.o.m.u.m…etc. All done, as you would be able to see, if it were not so dark."

He turned again to the crumbling bits of saints. Ginevra held up the heliodor and saw the words he spoke were, indeed, copied onto the ground beneath them in chalk. They, the "virgins," sitting in the center.

And even though she never believed that spells of this type were valid, she could feel the ancient holiness of the place, and while one relic was almost surely useless here, he had a dozen together and there were some spells that never worked except for when the situation was perfectly correct, and perhaps this was that time?

"Ginevra...you do not believe this ritual is legitimate, right?" whispered Michele.

"No – no, of course not. Do you?"

"No, definitely not. But just in case, we must try to distract him."

Ginevra looked at the bodies upon the floor.

"You have waited too long, friend, look at them, fingers are bones, mouths cannot close. What would it be for them to live again?"

"Be quiet! You said if I answered your questions, you would not interrupt me, and I have answered many! They will be as they were. I have prepared their homes and all will be joy!"

"Even Lazarus, raised by Christ himself, was only dead four days," said Fra Michele. "These poor souls have been dead for months."

"Be quiet! I did not lead you down here to insult me! Now: Virgins, do you say you sit willingly inside the circle? You must say it."

"Never," said Fra Michele.

The thief went over to the columned doorway they came down through, and pulled a rock from its lintel. There was a rumble and a crash, and the air was filled with dust.

"You see?" he coughed. "That was your path out. I've smashed it. Only I know the secret passages. If you do not say you are willing in the circle, I shall seal you up forever and go find some different virgins who are willing and quiet!"

"We are willing, we are willing!" cried Ginevra. Her head ached from where it had hit the wall, and she could not bear the noise of another passage collapsing. The time had come. The person they chased had caught them, and now they must bear witness to his designs. She fought a wave of nausea, rolling down through her from her sore head. The *jettatore*

nodded, satisfied his captives were willing, and untied them from the stake, though they remained lashed to each other.

"Good, now all you do is stay in the center, and do not say one word or I will smash you." The thief turned back to his assembled saint, precariously stuck together. He took off his cloak and there was the hair shirt, wiry, frizzled, and stuck to his raw skin. He placed his hands upon the bier:

> *Oh, angels of the heavens,*
>> *Oh, celestial orbs, lords of the day and of the night,*
>> *I have completed your rituals and so you are bound to me and required to hear my story and make it so and the story is:*
>> *San Miniato was walking through Florence when a soldier cut his head off but he took it back and put himself together again and that is how*
>> *I, Giancarlo di Sporco, who has adhered to God's strictest penance of ninety days, wish you to turn these separate saints into one saint who is called the Holy of Holies and in gratitude he will speak to God and ensure my request is granted NOW.*

He picked up the relic of Christ's blood soaked into bread from Sant'Elisabetta and then paused and flipped through the book. "It does not say... It does not say how to add the blood..." In the end, he decided to stuff it through a hole in old San Piero's torso. Then he kneeled on the ground and made the sign of the cross and said:

> *All this is done in the name of the one true God,*
>> *from whom all blessings flow, whose will shall be done on earth as it is in heaven, forever and ever, Amen.*

And then he waited for something to happen, but the Holy of Holies just laid on his table, dark and still and made of many parts.

"Aha! He moved a little!" said Giancarlo after a while.

"It is the beetles, Giancarlo, who crawl on him and trick your eyes," said Ginevra. She touched the back of her head and pain shot through it. She was getting tired.

"No! He moved and is awake, now it is time to make my request."

Ginevra slumped.

"Ginevra," whispered Michele, shaking her. "Ginevra, stay awake! Do not leave me here!" But she was so tired, so in pain, she could not answer and slid down to the ground.

Holy of Holies I request of You
For these dead in this crypt that
You make their still tongues to talk
Cold feet walk
Shut eyes to see,
Gone souls come back to be—

A great roaring and whooshing immediately filled the chamber and the light from the lantern and even from the heliodor went out. Fra Michele screamed and the *jettatore* whooped with joy and Ginevra passed out.

FORTY-ONE

UP, UP, UP

July 12th of 1348, the Crypt of San Romolo

"Wake up! Ginevra, wake up!!" came Michele's desperate voice through the whooshing and whirring and buzzing and the whole air fluttering and shifting and bumping into her. Ginevra couldn't even tell if she had opened her eyes, so complete was the blackness.

"Michele! The souls. The souls have come back to their bodies!"

"No, woman! It is not the souls. It is the burying beetles! The beasts have taken flight."

"The beetles?"

"Ginevra, they will devour the relics!"

"Forget the relics! They will devour us!"

"Light your magic light, where are the relics, where is the thief ??"

She sat up straight, the pain still pounding in her head, and held the heliodor aloft with her bound hands. The beetles that were touching her saw the light, too, and were upon it in an instant and blotted out its glow. She wiped them from her face and covered her mouth with her headscarf. "Michele, it's no use, I cannot see a way out!"

The frustrated bellows and crashings of the thief reached

them through the shifting blackness as he tried in vain to sweep the swarming insects from his composite saint.

"We must find a way out while he is distracted," Michele whispered to her. "Come! You are a woman who knows things – use your powers, find the alternate passage he spoke of!"

The inquisitor's words cut through the fog of her pain. He was right. She was a woman who knew things. And she knew she did not want to be smashed like a beetle. She exhaled and listened and found, beneath the noise of the insects, beneath her throbbing head, the searing sting of the burn left by her coral *figa*, a gentle tugging upon her left hand. It was Vermilia's Nemesis stone, and it knew the way out.

"Come, Michele. Do not make a sound."

The pair struggled to their feet, bound together at either end of the thief's rope, and slipped through a crack in the wall.

"Virgins!" called the thief. "Do not move! You said you were willing! Do not move or I will smash you as I smash these beetles!"

"Hurry!" whispered Michele.

Ginevra followed the pull of the jasper ring leading them up, up, up through the pitch-black until they burst in a cloud of beetles into the church's sanctuary, and ran past the greenand-purple-painted hell, into the piazza, into the full light of day, where, struck temporarily blind by the sun's brightness, they spun around and beat the shimmering beetles from their faces and hair.

"Has he followed us?" said Michele, coughing up insects.

Ginevra touched her coral, and it burned her fingers. "He is near! We must hide."

But she was too late, the thief was upon them. He grabbed the rope that lay between them and yanked it hard so they fell upon the stones of the piazza.

"Close your eyes or he will curse you!" cried Ginevra to her inquisitor.

"We are all cursed, Virgins!" said the thief, dragging them

across the stones and tying them anew to the well's winch so they were pulled tight against its wall.

Michele cowered with his hands over his eyes. Ginevra, whose vision was adjusting back to the light, saw the thief pick up a lumpy beetle-covered sack. He shook it and out tumbled the arm of San Filippo, the thigh of San Barnaba, and the rest of the relics of the great churches of Florence. In a frenzy, he began again to piece them together into a man. His hands were shaking as he batted at insects with the blessed finger of San Tommaso. He accidentally kicked the sacred head of Zenobio and then had to chase it to the edge of the piazza.

"He has gone even more mad," whispered Fra Michele, peeking through his fingers. "It is that hair shirt – such a device turns even the most pleasant individuals into complete nightmares."

"It certainly isn't helping," agreed Ginevra, "but worse is the *malocchio*. Look." She pointed to the coral that still smoldered against her dress. "It is here and it revels in his misery."

The thief ran back to his pile, clutching the head, and hastily pushed the relics together, giving up his attempts to align limbs to trunk. "Stop whispering!" he shrieked at them. With a piece of chalk he began to draw another magic circle around the priest and the woman but the cobblestones were rough and his chalk broke so he was left dragging the white dust with his fingers to make his marks.

Ginevra said, quieter still, to the inquisitor, "Like the discomfort from his shirt, the *malocchio* pushes him further away from his humanity. We must try to bring back the part of him that donned it in the first place, sacrificed his own body to save the souls of his village."

The thief picked up a loose cobblestone. "With this I will beat you on the head until you are willing."

"Wait!" cried Ginevra. "Giancarlo di Sporco – this is what you called yourself in your spell? Giancarlo, your spell is made up. Written by charlatans. It's a shame you didn't ask me, before you tried it the first time. For I am a witch and could have given you a good spell, a genuine one."

"You lie in your throat. There is no such thing as a witch."

"I will prove it to you, *jettatore*, that I have the magic to change a person from one thing into another."

The inquisitor gasped.

The thief scoffed at her, still clutching his cobblestone. "I am a wealthy and learned man; for months I studied secret texts. A low woman like you could not succeed where I have failed."

"I speak the truth, Giancarlo. And I'll wager you for our freedom that I can change *you* from one thing to another."

"And when you fail, as sure as I wear the cilice, I will beat you and then leave you tied here to bake to death in the sun."

The inquisitor peeked nervously at Ginevra through his fingers.

Ginevra swallowed against the nausea and the sting of the smoldering coral. Laughter to drive away misery. "Cilice? You wear no such hair shirt."

"What?? Do you think I know not what shirt is upon my own body? That I am not every moment aware of its itching and chafing."

"I tell you, you wear no such shirt."

"What is this, then?" He rent apart his tunic and revealed the appalling garment.

"That is no shirt, but your own hairy belly!"

"You mock me! I will not stand these base insults. Look, obnoxious woman." He dropped the cobblestone, and, for the first time in months, peeled the cilice from his skin and held it out, shaking it at her. "See, see-est thou!"

Ginevra choked at the stink of the garment, and replied, "And see-est thou – I have changed you from itchy to comfortable. A worthy spell, all can agree."

The *jettatore* let out an involuntary "ha," then clasped his hand over his mouth. And whether it was Ginevra's small play of wit or simply the physical relief of being free from the tortuous hair shirt, Giancarlo suddenly recovered the small bit of himself that was not owned by the Eye, and the violent fiend plopped down upon the ground and began to sob.

"I did everything right," he wailed. "I purified my mind and punished my body, followed every specification the book required. I prayed and prayed, but it mattered not. I am forsaken by God."

"What is *happening*?" said Fra Michele, still covering his eyes with his hands.

"I wore the shirt! I had not one, but two virgins. Woe, woe to me!"

"Um – there, there, it is not your fault," called Ginevra. "Only God decides who is living and who is dead, and we cannot sway it."

"It was not God, but *I* who brought death here. The plague came to San Romolo, potent and vicious! My whole life I have brought only misfortune! I heard what you called me – a *jettatore* – you are not the first. Before the plague struck anywhere else, it came here, in the late winter. My whole village, dead in a day! My mother, my father, and neighbors! All dead besides me... This is why your bishop would not help me in the end. I am cursed."

"Wait, what did you say?" cried Fra Michele, still covering his eyes. "What about Bishop Acciaiuoli?"

"I went to him with my spell. Asked him to share the relics. He said it was a good idea! Gave me his blessing. Showed me a safe place to keep them, while we were gathering them together."

"This is impossible," said Fra Michele. "Impossible. I cannot believe it. The bishop is a learned, sensible man. He does not believe in such spells."

"If the bishop said you could take what you needed, then why all the sneaking?" asked Ginevra.

"He said the people would not understand, that they would not approve."

"Of course they wouldn't! I don't," retorted an indignant Fra Michele.

"He said our relationship must be kept secret, that I must do it all on my own, so I had to go around and slink and ask for directions."

"If you were to keep it secret, why did you shout your thefts from the *ringhiera* platform for all to know? Why if not to shock and scare Florentines? To cause panic and disorder?"

"I know not what you speak of. I did no such thing. I love all people. I left saint water in place of everything I took so nobody would be without divine protection."

"Lies, lies from a thief. A *jettatore*! You have failed, so you seek to cast blame on someone other than yourself. A typical sinner," said Fra Michele.

"No! I am many things, but I am no liar. Here is proof." The thief took something out of his tunic and moved toward the bound prisoners at the well.

"Stop!" said Ginevra. Her coral glowed like a coal. It had never been exposed to a *jettatore* for so long before. The fabric of her dress beneath it was black and singed. "The *malocchio* still does its vile work through your eyes... Come no closer or you will burn me up!"

"Enough of my cursed gaze!" he wept. "If it is my eyes that bring this misfortune, then it is time I put out my eyes! I would rather be blind than see the misery I have caused."

"Stop it!" said Fra Michele. "Stop crying! If your eyes are causing all this misery, then just put on a blindfold. That should work, right?" He turned toward Ginevra.

"I— I don't know...but...I suppose it's worth a try... before you go through the trouble of putting out your eyes, at least?"

Still weeping, Giancarlo nodded and ripped a piece off his tunic, binding it around his face. Immediately, Ginevra's coral stopped burning and she felt as if a weight had been lifted in her chest.

"Did it work??" asked Giancarlo, spinning around in his new blindfold.

"I— I think so," she said, gasping in relief at the release from pain. "Make sure it is tight, that you can see no daylight through the cloth."

Giancarlo fumbled with the blindfold, pulling it down farther around his face, then strode toward the well, smacking right into it. He fell into a seated position, clutching his shins, then groped forward and at last untied the ropes that trapped Ginevra and Fra Michele.

The inquisitor gave a little squeal and leaped away, toward the jumble of relics, and prostrated himself before them.

Ginevra got up and stood over the thief, her strength returning. "Where is your proof, then?" He held up a silver key, surmounted by a lion rampant. The crest of the Acciaiuoli.

"Michele, do you recognize this?" Ginevra brought the key to him.

"It cannot be! The *jettatore* speaks the truth. That is the bishop's personal key to the Baptistry!"

"It is where we kept the relics, the bishop and I. They needed a dignified hiding place."

"You said he would not help you in the end," said Ginevra. "Why?"

"He did not like when I broke the leg off San Miniato. He said that God had changed his mind, that it was no longer a good idea to make the Holy of Holies. He told me to return his key, but instead I shoved him, and ran to the Baptistry, took the relics that we hid together, and brought them back here with me to San Romolo. I never told the bishop where I lived, so I knew I had time before he would find me. You must understand: I had to complete the spell! It was the only way to save us all. God has not been listening to normal prayers."

Ginevra looked again at the intricate object in her hand and with a new shock of fear realized something: Fra Michele had unwittingly revealed to Bishop Acciaiuoli the true identity of the relic thief and his likely location. But the bishop could not simply have his mercenaries journey to San Romolo. If he did, he risked others learning that Giancarlo had been acting with the bishop's permission! But if Ginevra retrieved the relics *for* the bishop, if she was the only witness, he could easily dismiss the testimony of a woman and a convicted heretic. Still, he would not have counted on the inquisitor traveling with her...

"Alone, alone, blind and alone, I will wander the world," cried Giancarlo.

"Stop wailing," said Ginevra. "I am tired of all you sad men. You will not wander the world alone: you have made a mess, and you will come back to Florence with us to fix it."

Fra Michele stopped praying to the relics and looked at her in horror.

"If I go with you, the bishop will chop my head off and string up my body on the *ringhiera*," said Giancarlo.

"You don't have a choice. We need you as a witness to the bishop's involvement. And besides, this man here is the inquisitor – he can promise you will not be strung up, right, Michele?"

"Well, erm, it will be—"

Ginevra stared hard at him.

"I mean, that sounds rather difficult, but I will see what I can..."

"See, there you have it. We will all go together."

"I will not. Not after stealing the bishop's key."

"Giancarlo, look – you are not the only person the *malocchio* watches. Since I was a child, it follows me closely – I punctured it long ago and it waits always for a chance at revenge. Come with us, and once all this is settled, I will try to find a way to rid you of the Eye."

"I do not like being a *jettatore*," he admitted. "But my village! My poor mother, my dear father. My servants and the laborers of my kiln! I cannot leave them here."

"You've buried them in the crypt of their own church. This is more than many kings and lords could wish for now. Would you stay here alone, talking to skeletons?"

"I must stay and pray for them, for who else will do it? Old people and little babies stuck in purgatory."

Ginevra was impatient to be away, now. "Michele, can't you intercede for them?"

So Fra Michele, under Ginevra's stern gaze, managed to bring himself back to the entrance of the crypt and said a blessing over all the dead and said it counted retroactively since they had no chance to call for a priest and that they were all in Heaven.

Giancarlo was finally convinced, then, to come back with them. Ginevra's promise to break the curse the Eye had on him sounded much better than wandering the world, blind and alone. The relics, with a few beetles still crawling over them, were loaded onto the donkey, who was fitted with a rope, the other end given to Giancarlo so he could follow along even with his blindfold. This is how they left San Romolo, and they were the last living people there for many years.

FORTY-TWO

THE PORTA SAN NICCOLO

July 12th of 1348,
the Road Back to Florence

Fra Michele and Ginevra walked some distance ahead so they could speak without being heard. "It just doesn't make sense," said Ginevra. "Do you really think the bishop believed the spell would work?"

"Not for a moment."

"Then why would he go along with it?"

Fra Michele shook his head. "His family is in serious money trouble. Perhaps he means to sell the relics, and just wanted Giancarlo to do the dirty work for him?"

"Then why leave the golden reliquaries?"

"I don't know. All I know is I wish we had come here without informing him."

"Now it is done – what are we going to do about it?"

"We must announce the presence of the relics as soon as we reenter the city. The people will rally around us, and I will gather a contingent of men and we will confront the bishop. But first our witness – we must put him somewhere safe."

Ginevra nodded. "Let us go to Sant'Elisabetta. It is close to the Porta San Niccolo – return their bread. Sister Taddea will be relieved to have it back and will watch Giancarlo for us."

"Ginevra—"

"Yes?"

"I— I am not a virgin."

"Nor am I," she admitted.

They passed the rest of their journey in silence, each wondering what might have happened in the San Romolo crypt if Giancarlo hadn't been so trusting of their virtue.

Late in the day, they reached the Porta San Niccolo and were surprised to find it had been closed. Fra Michele gave the gate a little push. Ginevra heard the distinct sounds of men's voices and clinking metal.

"I suppose it's good that the gatekeepers are back," he said.

"Wait, Michele—" But the door was swinging open.

Ginevra stepped back and whispered frantically to Giancarlo, still standing obediently at the donkey. "Hide, you! If something happens to us, find Monna Lucia, the fine palazzo on the Piazza di Santa Trinita. Do NOT remove your blindfold, you must find your way somehow." Ginevra pressed something into his hand, then shoved him against the city wall so he was hidden to those who stood in the gate. The door was opened and there stood the bishop himself, flanked by guards with fine clothing and too many knives.

"Michele?" he said with surprise. "What are *you* doing here?"

"Since you would not help Monna Ginevra, I went myself—"

"Fool. You have inserted yourself into a dangerous plot."

"What do you mean? Why are you here at the gate with your guards?"

"Arrest both of them," said the bishop to the mercenaries.

"Arrest ME? You have gotten it backward. It is I who arrest *you*, for committing the worst of heresies. Guards, do it! Tie him up!"

But the guards were loyal only to the man who paid them, and were upon the travelers in an instant. The bishop made his way to the donkey, and palpated the bundle that was tied to its back. He smiled and patted it. Then took the donkey's bridle in his own hands.

"Do not lay your hands on that sack!" said Michele.

"Guards, gag their mouths quickly, or they may say evil spells at you."

"No, no, this is wrong!" cried Ginevra as she bobbed her head this way and that to avoid the gag. "Bishop, we have done as you asked, I am no heretic—"

"Then what is that pagan thing you wear around your neck?"

Ginevra looked down and realized that she had never tucked her *figa* back inside her garments.

The bishop nodded to the nearest guard, who came behind Ginevra and held her arms behind her back, thrusting himself into her and leering as another guard cut the coral from her neck. So numb with fright was she that the protestations she meant to shriek came out only as a whisper and they hardly needed to gag her. "Oh, please, oh, please, I have worn it since I was a child! It's a harmless thing! You do not know what will happen to me without it."

Fra Michele sputtered in protest through his gag until somebody smacked him.

"There, now off to the *stinche*. The jailkeeper lives yet. I'll mind the donkey myself. I need to make sure there is nothing corrupt in their luggage."

The guards shrugged, annoyed. They had hoped to keep the donkey for themselves.

The bishop scrutinized the surrounds, but Giancarlo stayed still and silent, and soon the gate was shut upon him. Once he was alone, Giancarlo peeked into his hand to find the heliodor. He was not worried the gate was closed. He'd been sneaking in and out of the city for months. He wished they'd have told him there would be trouble. He could have shown them any number of discreet entrances.

FORTY-THREE

THE *STINCHE*

Evening, July 12th of 1348,
City of Florence

Lucia stooped to pat the little cat who followed her pacing. Piero had not come to her with the bishop's secrets, nor had Ginevra returned. She had spent one night alone and now another was approaching. She was afraid to leave her house lest she be discovered as not dead by the bishop. A gentle rapping at the door brought short-lived relief, but she opened it upon a blindfolded stranger.

"Who are you, then?"

"Dama Tornaparte? I am the relic thief, at your service. Monna Ginevra sent me." He knelt and held up the heliodor.

Lucia slammed the door in his face. Then opened it a crack. He *did* have the heliodor. And he didn't smell anymore.

"Where is she, then?"

The thief frowned. "Your bishop—"

It was all Lucia needed to hear. "Come inside. Quickly." Lucia sat rapt as Giancarlo told her all that had come to pass, of how Ginevra had taught him to bandage his evil eyes, how he had failed at his spell, and how the bishop of Florence had betrayed him and stolen the relics for his own self. Lastly, he told of his escape and how Ginevra and Fra Michele were now locked up together in the *stinche*.

A song floated on the evening air through the window, pausing their conversation.

King and miller, priest and nun
Last night they supped and drank their wine
Now bones are whitening in the sun
On dirt unturned, 'neath untamed vine

"I do not like that song," said Giancarlo.

"Becchino!" cried Lucia, who leaped up and waved her arms from the window.

The gravedigger stopped his cart. "It's Dama Dionysia! Pleased to see you alive and well – I thought you'd have drowned in a wine barrel by now."

"Aha – yes, that was an interesting party. Listen, does your work take you to the *stinche*?"

"Sure, I go in every day or so to get the dead ones."

"Can you carry messages as you carry the dead? To somebody held within the walls?"

"That depends—"

"I will pay for your discretion."

"In that case, I am the trusted squire of your secrets. They're expecting me tomorrow morning. What lucky debtor is getting a love letter?"

"Don't be rude!" said Giancarlo from inside the house.

"Shh, it's alright, it's his way." Lucia turned back to Becchino. "It's my friend with the scar on her nose."

"Interesting pair, you two. Sneaking around church altars and getting all drunk as monks. It's no wonder she's in the *stinche*. Only surprise is you're not there with her!"

"Yes, well, my freedom depends on your discretion. You will come here first thing in the morning?"

"As it pleases you and, Dama, you might want to pack some food and drink for her as well. Those who sell food to the prisoners in regular times are all dead. There is but one guard and he doesn't get around to cooking every day. A pie, if you can make one, is a good place to hide a message."

On the splintery wooden floor of the *stinche*, Ginevra curled up and waited to die. It would come for her now, and it would be unpleasant. Without her coral, she was no more protected from plague than anyone else. From the smell and the dark stains on her straw pallet, she guessed the current plague was but one among many that contaminated the cell.

Giving her only dose of medicine to an inquisitor would be the last bad decision she made in a life full of nothing but. Why had she involved herself in this ridiculous scenario? To try and join a *guild*? She was a fool with a far-fetched plan and an impossible goal; she saw that clearly now. As if the truth of it was written on the moldy stones of her jail cell.

Already she felt unwell. Her stomach cramped, her head ached. But perhaps it was only despair she felt, not pestilence. Ah, well, if plague did not find her, she would be convicted as – what had the woman on the docks in Genoa been called, so long ago? – a *witch and unrepentant heretic*, and burned up. The *malocchio* had been lurking in the shadows since she was a child, and now it was close, and ready to pounce. She closed her eyes and remembered Vermilia asking her so long ago, *What do you know?* But her mind was blank. Her world was silent. The Nemesis stone did not tug at her hand. No golden strings played their notes of truth. Her luck, such as it was, had run out.

Fra Michele was allowed, on account of his status, to roam the whole giant cube of the prison building, and stood in front of the locked door of Ginevra's cell, speaking to her through the bars. "Ginevra, Ginevra, forgive me, I've brought this whole mess upon you."

She answered from her place on the floor. "It's alright, Michele. Death comes for us all." She held no ill will for him. She was too tired.

"Don't die yet," he tried to joke. "We still have work to do."

She rolled over and remained stoic with her back to him.

Michele continued to speak, anyway. "I never liked the bishop but I didn't think he was *evil*. Disagreement in politics is a healthy thing, for the commune. I know times are strange but to collude with a thief...and what will he do with our relics now that he has them?"

He muttered like this all night outside Ginevra's door, talking about how he would write a letter to the Pope and all would be settled, even though he knew it would take weeks to get there, and that the Pope had sided with the bishop in the expulsion of the last inquisitor. After hours of monologizing, he grew tired of Ginevra's silence, but when he drew breath to admonish her properly he saw that she was not being obstinate but was overtaken by great black swellings rising at her throat.

The jailer gave Fra Michele access to her cell, so he could perform last rites. He who had been too afraid to serve his constituents now rested Ginevra's head on his lap as her breathing became more labored, and helped her as the spasms of vomiting came and went. This is how Becchino found them in the morning.

"Ah— Ser Inquisitor, bad luck, eh? One day, you're sending sinners to the *stinche*, the next day you yourself are a sinner in the *stinche*—"

"What do you *want*?"

"I've come for the lady Ginevra."

"She's not dead yet. Perhaps tomorrow."

"In that case, she might like this? Sent from her friend, the Dama Tornaparte."

Fra Michele placed Ginevra's head gently down upon the filthy pallet. He went to the bars, and was passed a lumpy pie, the burnt head of an eel poking through the crust, and a bottle of wine.

"I don't think she can eat much."

"Well, if I was you, I'd still open that pie *immediately*, best fresh, you know."

"I don't need a gravedigger telling me about pies," he said, uncorking the wine with his teeth and taking a big swig.

"What I'm *trying* to say, dense sir, is there might be more than eels in this pie."

"OH. *Oh.* I see. I see. I will eat it right away, then. Carefully."

"Now you've got it. Enjoy. I'll be back the day after next to collect the lady."

The jailkeeper walked by on his rounds, and Becchino hurried away.

Fra Michele knelt back by Ginevra and inexpertly poured wine down her throat, which made her choke and sputter but raised her from her stupor a little bit. "Look!" he said, breaking the pie apart once the jailkeeper was out of earshot. "You have a message from a Signora Tornaparte – do you know her? She says that Giancarlo is with her."

Ginevra smiled weakly at the news. It hurt too much to talk. The inquisitor read the letter in hushed tones, one eye out for the jailer. It detailed how Piero was to spy on the bishop. Ginevra stirred at Piero's name – he had not left her! He had been trying to find her! Fra Michele took a huge bite of the pie. He yelped in pain and spat out a mouthful of eel bits, a broken tooth, and two little green stones speckled in red. He held them out in wonder.

"What sort of eel part is this?"

Ginevra's eyes opened: How could she have forgotten? It was a plain truth that fish dearly love to eat magic jewels. Lucia's eels must have swallowed the bloodstones when the medicine jar exploded over their well! She forced herself up on the rough boards, took the stones from Fra Michele, and pressed them against her throat until the golden strings hummed and the air filled with vibrations. But her hands were too weak and she kept dropping them. Fra Michele put them back and held his own hands flat against hers, all the way through the spasms and twitching that followed. This way the bloodstones stayed in place until their magic forced the sickness out and she puked up a great black glob and fell asleep. He whispered into her unconscious ears that if this was not the magic of God, then nothing was, and swore he would do everything in his power to see that she was admitted to the Guild of Doctors, Apothecaries, and Grocers.

FORTY-FOUR

THE SLEEPING BISHOP

Night, July 12th of 1348,
the Bishop's Chamber

Piero's master returned from his night away in a *very* good mood and with a brand-new donkey. After supper, as was usual, Piero lay down on his truckle pallet on the floor of the bishop's chamber. As was not usual, in the dark hours of the early morning, he crept over to the grand platform bed and eased back the curtains, staring hard into the dark until the shape of a person could be discerned upon the silk sheets. The bishop lay on his back, his face stern in sleep. Piero started to be afraid, but then stopped. He'd been frightened so much already that he'd grown used to it. He leaned over his master and placed the gold-and-amber brooch on his left chest, just as Monna Lucia instructed. Immediately, the bishop's eyes opened wide, their whites glinting in the faint light from the window.

Piero ducked down and covered his face with his hands. When there was no noise, he rose up and peeked through his fingers. The bishop stared out into the darkness, but his body did not move. The amber jewel glowed soft and golden, as if lit from behind.

"Bishop…are you awake?" he whispered.

"No…" answered the bishop, a soft slur in his voice.

"You're sure?"

"I am sure. I am. Asleep."

"Then – will you really tell me your true secrets, any that I ask of you?"

The bishop's mouth trembled, and a tear rolled down from his unblinking eye.

"Oh! Why are you crying?"

"B-because I do not wish to tell you my secrets."

Piero began to doubt his mission – this man had been kind, taken him in, and now he was using a spell to make him cry. "Just tell me one thing, then, and I won't ask anything else – why did you put Ginevra in prison, after she came all this way to find our relics for us?"

Tears now streamed down his cheeks, but his voice was hard and angry. "It must be *me* who finds them... It is all arranged. Our Lady of Requisiti will reveal them to me... choose me in front of a crowd of believers."

Piero forgot his promise to ask only one question. "The Lady of Requisiti? Do you mean the gilded statue that is sent through the streets when there is trouble?"

"Her, none other."

"How do you know she'll reveal them to you? Did she tell you in a dream?"

"No—" choked the bishop, fighting hard to stay silent.

"Then how do you know??"

Struggling against the power of the jewel, the bishop spat out quickly: "I hid them inside her, just this afternoon. I took them off Ginevra's donkey and put them there."

"But, everyone is worried about them! And Ginevra is in *prison*."

"Of course they are worried. I *made* them worried. For months, I have seen to it that news of the relics' disappearance has spread. Paid vagrants to shout the news from the *ringhiera*. It is the talk of the town, for those who still have tongues in their heads. Word has even reached the Pope! Think how pleased he will be with me when he learns I've recovered them. What relief to the citizens to know their relics are back safe; what adulation they will heap on me, their savior."

"If you have them, why not put them back now?"

"No. No. Not yet. It must appear as a miracle with many witnesses – the relics will pop out of the statue, as the relic of San Marco showed itself to the Venetian bishop. Then I will have the support of the people... The Pope will make me a cardinal. His only Italian cardinal is dead, you know."

Piero did not feel bad for making the bishop cry anymore. "You stole relics to be made a cardinal? Cardinals are supposed to be GOOD. You are already rich and powerful. Look at how fancy your sheets are! Why would you do this?"

The bishop ground his teeth, struggling to stay silent.

Piero gave him a little shove. *"Why??"*

"Because – the fortune of my family is depleted. We are ruined, our name is mud, our properties seized, unless I can restore it. The cardinalate brings wealth, allies, immunity. My creditors would be made to kiss my ring. It is the only way."

"So you hired a thief to do your dirty work and steal our relics for you?"

"Hired? Ha. I didn't even have to pay him. A broken man. He would not even look me in the eye. He followed a ridiculous book. Did whatever I told him...until he didn't. Until he took them for himself. But it does not matter now. God, in his infinite justice, leans on the side of the Acciaiuoli. Your Ginevra has returned the relics to me—"

A rooster crowed, the bishop's words ended in a terrible snore, and like lightning Piero jerked back the jewel and lay upon his own pallet.

The bishop sat up with a start, a tear-wet face, and a strange sense of urgency. He had intended to wait a bit to hold the "miraculous" procession, so it might by chance coincide with the plague's natural end as the weather cooled. But something told him – if he was going to go through with his plan – it had better be as soon as possible.

He pushed his lazy servant Piero awake, and then gave him instructions and made arrangements for the trial of Ginevra di Genoa and the Inquisitor Michele di Lapo Arnolfi to happen in one day's time.

FORTY-FIVE

THE LADY AND THE JETTATORE

*July 13th of 1348,
the Palazzo Tornaparte*

Lucia and Giancarlo the Relic Thief sat in her home, wondering what to do with the latest news brought by Piero.

He had hurried it to them, in between tasks. The trial was to be tomorrow, in the central piazza upon the *ringhiera* platform. Lucia understood what would happen immediately: the trial of a heretic was the perfect place for the missing relics to "reveal" themselves to the bishop. He must be planning to smuggle them onto the platform inside the blessed statue. The false miracle, witnessed by many, would elevate the bishop's holy reputation, putting him forward as a primary candidate for the vacant cardinalate.

With Becchino nowhere to be found, Lucia could send no warning pie to the *stinche*. As long as the bishop held the relics, nobody would believe their story, that of an abandoned wife and a blind man. Filled with dread, time seemed fast and slow all at once. Lucia thought again and again of going to San Tommaso for assistance, only to remember his relic was stolen and she already owed him many candles.

Lucia looked at Giancarlo and sighed. She meant to be frightened of the *jettatore*, and upset with Ginevra for sending her such a dangerous guest. But because she now held Ginevra's diamante, it would not let her be angry, and compelled her to become friends with this strange creature. Even without the influence of the diamante, Giancarlo so dutifully kept his blindfold on, and loved so much to lie on the floor and let the kitten walk on him, it would not have been long before she forgot his crimes and perceived him a gentleman. She chastised him for his heinous acts now as one would tease a dear friend who had done something foolish.

"And *what* were you thinking, taking our relics at a time like this? It was not enough that everyone in your town died, you had to go and destroy the protection of *our* saints?"

"But, Dama, I did think of it! I was trying to stop death, not give him an invitation. This is why I asked your bishop to lend them willingly."

"But instead he made you steal them, let the rest of us believe we were forsaken."

"I did not like that idea. I refused, at first, to go along with the bishop's request that I steal them away in the dead of night. But then he told me to leave the bottles of water – he said that if I poured it over their blessed remains, the water would hold the same power as the relics, and I would not be taking anything from anybody. And at Miniato, I took only the last bit I needed! I left practically the whole relic there!"

"Well, whatever you did, I don't think it worked," she said.

Giancarlo wiped away a sniffle under his blindfold.

Lucia reached and took hold of his hand. After tomorrow, this strange man might be her only friend left in the world. She would not press him. "It's alright, Giancarlo. I have been lonely here, but to be the only living person in your town... What was it like?"

"Terrible. I went a bit mad, I think."

She politely refrained from comment.

He told her how after he had gotten everyone he could find into the crypt, he spent his days looking through books in his library. One day, he found a book hidden within a book, and it was full of magic spells.

"And that is how you learned to turn iron to rust?"

"Oh, no – that is but a secret of my shop – a trick taken from alchemists. I applied a burning liquid known as *Aqua Regia*, it dissolves metal but not glass and creates the shimmery gold glaze used for the little chickens on our pottery."

"Those chickens are my favorite part."

"I wish I never had seen the book, for it is the source of my deranged behavior. The spells were all nonsense, and for this, your Ginevra and Fra Michele are in prison. I thought – I thought since the bishop agreed with me, it was sure to work! But he is a liar, and I am a fool. A blight. A curse. Doomed to a sad life, a…"

"A what?"

"A *jettatore*," he whispered. "I am loath to say it. Even though my mother told me, even though I bring destruction to everyone I know. But Monna Ginevra knew. She knew before she met me; her magic coral told her."

Lucia was fascinated. "Do you know why the *malocchio* chose you?"

The mouth under the bandages frowned. "I was cursed before I was born."

He told how his parents were poor and lived on the valley floor, outside the walls of San Romolo. When his mother was pregnant, a party of free lances came to their village, eager for plunder. Giancarlo's mother found a clever hiding spot, and from her place, she watched the terrible things that were done to her neighbors. Because she was too stunned and frightened to look away, the abominations she witnessed were seen also by her fetus, and this was when the Eye marked him a *jettatore*.

From the beginning, other babies cried if Giancarlo was placed among them. When he was old enough to work at farming, the milk of cows would dry up and any plow he used would hit a rock and break. His mother knew what had happened and told him so, told him what he was but cautioned him to keep the secret or he would be shunned wherever he went. So after he failed at farming, she begged a ceramics master to take him as an apprentice. The master took pity on her, and took Giancarlo as his own son, teaching him the trade and to read and write. For ten years, Giancarlo labored under him and the Eye lay dormant, biding its time.

When Giancarlo had at last learned all the secrets of the factory, the Eye made it so the master and all his sons died, one right after the other until Giancarlo, as apprentice, was next in line to inherit the business. It thrived under him; the Eye saw to that, too. A shiny lure that drew people close and then ruined them. Employees suffered terrible accidents – kilns exploded, acids spilled onto hands, men tripped and paintbrushes jammed up their noses. But the people of the valley were poor, so they always came back to work for him.

Still, no matter how much Giancarlo paid them, they never got any richer. Coins fell from holes in their purses, they grew ill and spent all their money on doctors, and the free lances returned to burn their fields. Even as Giancarlo wept and prayed for his people, glorified the humble church in their town with gold and glazes and towers, and did his best to be a good and generous man, he carried inside him a terrible guilt, knowing that the good he did could not outpace the bad – and that it was *his* curse that had brought about all the misfortune. When the plague came to San Romolo, terrible and strong and early, he knew, he *knew* it was all his fault, and he had to make it right somehow.

Through his story, so enraptured was Lucia in listening and Giancarlo in telling that they did not notice how a bit of his blindfold had come unwound and the kitten was playing with the end. All of a sudden, the cat had it off completely and man and animal stared into each other's eyes for a brief moment. The poor cat puffed up into a giant ball and bolted through the open window. Lucia covered her eyes and screamed at Giancarlo to fix his blindfold.

"What have I done, what have I done??" he cried, frantically wrapping his head.

Lucia ran to the window. "Cats are good at falling, I'm sure she's— oh. Oh, no."

Maybe if it were a normal fright, the cat would have remembered her tricks and landed on her feet, but it was the stare of a *jettatore*, so she landed instead on her back, and when Lucia looked down, she lay still, four little paws straight in the air.

"Tell me she is alright!" wailed the thief.

"She is dead, Giancarlo," Lucia said, wringing her hands.

The *jettatore* pulled at his hair and began to weep anew. Never had animals trusted him, and now he killed the first one that ever came near him.

Lucia ran out to the street to pick up the dear little body, but as soon as she touched it, the cat gave a funny twitch and rolled over. Then she did a sort of shiver that began at her nose and ended at the tip of her tail. She arched her back, rubbed up against Lucia's leg, and walked back into the house. Lucia stood still a moment and then she laughed and bounded back up the stairs – "Giancarlo! Our cat! She has used but one of her nine lives! She is well, she is well, give her some cheese."

Still weeping, Giancarlo felt around and picked up the last remaining cheese end from the table, breaking it into crumbs and admonishing himself for his carelessness. The cat jumped on the table, eating the cheese crumbs and purring, butting her head against him. Tears streamed from under his blindfold. "What— h-have— I— done to deserve such kindness from this creature?"

"Giancarlo, stop crying," commanded Lucia. "Our kitten's fall has given me an idea. We must make you a hood."

"A hood?" he choked.

"Yes. A hood so you can see neither right nor left but only what is right in front of you. And you will wear it to the trial tomorrow."

FORTY-SIX

THE PLAGUE SAINTS

July 14th of 1348, City of Florence

Our Lady of Requisiti was a wooden statue, slightly larger than a real woman, carved by the Apostle Luke. She was passed to San Romolo (for whom Giancarlo's town was named) in ancient times, and the saint hid her in a cave in the woods outside of Florence so she would not be destroyed by pagans. She remained hidden for centuries, until a farmer and his wife became lost in a storm. The wife was about to give birth, but it was all rain and lightning and there was nowhere for them to go. The farmer prayed to the Virgin and suddenly his oxen knelt down in adoration before the entrance of the Virgin's hidden cave. The little party entered and were dazzled by the beauty of the statue. The farmer's wife gave birth to a healthy boy who lived to be one hundred years old.

The Madonna was carved as one piece with her throne, and the Christ child upon her knee. She was painted in polychrome with a veil of blue and gold stars. Inside her was a large cavity – just big enough to fit twelve of the most revered relics of Florence.

On July 14 of the year 1348, the bishop ordered her placed on her palanquin of red silk brocade and paraded through the streets on the shoulders of his Swiss mercenaries. A curious crowd of citizens came out of their houses to follow and pray. They had not seen her since her initial refusal to stop the plague. Perhaps she was ready, now, to reconsider her stance. Their bishop seemed to think so, anyhow.

They stopped as one in front of the *stinche*, where with hands bound behind their backs, and leather straps tied across their mouths, Ginevra di Gasparo and Fra Michele di Lapo Arnolfi were dragged onto the street by the soldiers. The procession of the Virgin continued now to its destination, the *ringhiera* platform. The Madonna was placed reverently atop a cloth-covered altar to oversee the trial. Tiered wooden benches, dusty with disuse, were also placed upon the platform. The mercenaries then dragged out a smaller separate platform with a hole in the middle to steady a tall gallows tree. Bundles of kindling to burn the bodies after they were hanged were politely kept out of sight around the corner. The Swiss soldiers picked their teeth, satisfied with the work they had done.

Ginevra and Fra Michele were not given seats on the bleachers, but would stand on view for the growing crowd. Ginevra was still weak from her illness. The filthy, steaming jail cell and an inquisitor for a nurse had not made for an easy recovery, and it was painful to stand in the hot sun.

She looked out at the piazza. Dust devils, trash. Scared faces. Those damn daytime rats. And here was the Madonna of Requisiti, staring at her, lovely and judgmental. She regretted curing herself of plague now. She had been motivated by the immediate physical pain, but hanging to death would be worse. Without her coral, she was unprotected. She felt the *malocchio*, feeding on the emotions of the gathering crowd. The bishop had let her live, once. He would not again. Still, she did not wish to make it easy for him, and bit hard into the leather strap that kept her from speaking.

She looked at Fra Michele, who caught her eye and nodded.

A tug at her dress, and there at last was dear Piero.

"Ehmmphphhm," she said to him.

"Do not worry," he said. "Monna Tornaparte will save you, I think."

"Hommphummeth?" she asked.

Bishop Acciaiuoli arrived and took his place, in crimson robes and a pointy white hat. He sat at the highest part of the bleachers, and scowled at the soldiers when he noticed all the dust and cobwebs still upon the boards that stuck to his clothes. He saw Piero with the prisoners and scowled again.

"Come, boy. You should not stand so close to nasty people."

Fra Michele tried to yell at the bishop through his gag.

"Michele, for once, be quiet – I'm sorry it's come to this, really. I told you not to concern yourself further, but you did, and now here you are, with only yourself to blame."

Michele continued, anyway, but even if he could speak properly, the din of the piazza was loud now and drowned him out. Word of the procession and trial had spread, and people came, standing far apart from each other in little groups, to pray to the Lady of Requisiti and view the treacherous criminals who had... Well, nobody was really sure what they had done, but whatever it was must be terrible for the bishop to call a trial like this in the middle of a plague.

For many, it was the first time they'd ventured from their own home in weeks, months. There was giddy anger from some, trepidation from others. The revelers and looters of peoples' houses stood in their own knot, in brightly colored clothing too festive for the occasion. Others were swaddled up from head to toe, only their eyes visible. Many carried large bunches of leaves and flowers and stuck their faces in them, filtering the air. In this strange crowd, Lucia and Giancarlo positioned themselves, she with a veil over her face and he in a deep dark hood, eyes still bandaged, their unusual garb blending in with the unique plague fashion of their fellow citizens. The conversation was getting louder and the Swiss soldiers were making a game of guessing which ladies were beautiful under their silly outfits when the bishop walked to the center of the platform and raised his hands before the statue of the Virgin. The crowd became silent.

"Benevolent Mary, Mother of Jesus Christ, the King of glory, help us to make the right use of all the suffering that God sends, and to offer to Him the true incense of our hearts; for His name's sake. Amen."

"Amen," said the crowd.

"We begin," said the bishop.

"Ginevra di Genoa, in the year of our Lord 1340, you were found guilty by this court of *heretical depravity*, consisting of the trafficking of necromantic books; possession of notebooks containing witchcraft; destruction of property; practicing medicine without a license; and disrespecting a member of the Guild of Doctors, Apothecaries, and Grocers. Is that not so?"

"Mmphh."

"That is a yes. Florentines: here we have a woman – allowed back into our city on the most Christian principles of forgiveness. But! She takes advantage of our kindness, of the absence of our protective relics, and is here again accused of attempting to spread plague further through witchcraft; of practicing medicine without a license; of causing the death, through said means, of Sister Agnesa of the Convent of Sant'Elisabetta delle Convertite; and of *seducing* our own inquisitor again by means of sorcery, entrancing him so he might be an accomplice to her terrible designs and who now must stand next to her accused of all the same." He looked over at the stunned crowd with satisfaction.

Ginevra's head snapped to the bishop. She had been accused of many things in her life but seducing an inquisitor was surely the most insulting.

Fra Michele did not appreciate it, either, and grew very red in the face.

"Are you sure, Bishop?" yelled a voice from the crowd. "If ever a man was afraid of a naked lady, it's that one. He's red as a rooster at just the suggestion." There were some cackles from the square. Ginevra looked out, and saw it was Becchino.

"His embarrassment is only that he is found out," said the bishop. "There are *witnesses*."

"Hnnnen?" said Fra Michele incredulously.

"Who's been watching our inquisitor go at it? And why wasn't I invited?" yelled Becchino.

Another murmur of laughter from the crowd.

"Brother Leobaldo, you will come forward," exclaimed the bishop, ignoring the laughter.

The Swiss soldiers escorted the reluctant monk onto the stage. Nobody liked to be a witness at a trial. Especially of someone accused of witchcraft.

"Ah, there's the great pimp! The friar who found a whore for the inquisitor!" yelled Becchino.

"I've never pimped except for your sister!" retorted Leobaldo.

A few gasped at the monk who would speak so in front of the Virgin, but most of the crowd erupted into laughter, proper and loud. This trial was going to be *fun*. Ginevra herself smirked, even all tied up as she was. *Laughter to drive away the Eye*, she thought, willing Becchino to keep at his jokes. *It saved Giancarlo and can save us again.* Here was the one magic possessed by all people, one that required no jewels to work.

"Monna Ginevra," said the bishop, eyeing her smile. "You wouldn't make light of your situation if you understood its gravity. Now, Fra Leobaldo: You say you went to the home of the inquisitor, and interrupted a visit that was meant to be just the *two* of them? Man and woman?"

"Well, a donkey was there also."

The crowd roared with laughter.

"QUIET!" yelled the bishop. "Brother Leobaldo, would you say that their company had a familiarity and intimacy to it?"

"I saw her place her hand upon his arm, Ser Bishop."

"But what happened with the donkey?" yelled Becchino.

"QUIET," said the bishop, and to his soldiers, "Somebody get that guy out of the crowd!"

The Swiss soldiers pantomimed agreement, but they were enjoying the spectacle too much. A few marched toward Becchino, though none had any intention of actually detaining him.

The bishop nodded again, and other soldiers brought up the apothecary of the Twin Janus. The anchovy was gone from his beard, and he had been dressed in a clean new robe.

"Here is Maestro Guido del Garbo, a respected member of the Guild of Doctors, Apothecaries, and Grocers. Maestro, tell us of your encounter with Monna Ginevra."

The maestro (who *was* a guild member, but not really a respected one) told of how she came with another woman, how they had bewitched him.

"Do you deny knowing this man?" the bishop asked Ginevra.

Ginevra shook her head "no" and chewed at the leather. It was getting softer and her mouth was filled with the bitter taste of it.

"She threatened me, stole my medical books," said the apothecary, leaning into his role, "sneezed and a befuddling potion flew from her nostrils and onto my face." The audience was in his grip until Becchino's voice sang out from the same corner as before:

Grave Robber, Grave Robber
He breaks the fingers off the dead
Pulls the hair out of their heads
Ties them up with silken bow
And calls it San Sebastian-o

The crowd hissed, fingers formed horned gestures and pointed into the earth, and hands made crosses in the air. They did not question the allegations against the greasy apothecary – if anybody knew the truth about grave robbers, it was a *becchino*. A few who'd acquired relics from the man in the past removed the pouches from their necks and crushed them under their feet. The bishop yelled at his mercenaries to shut up Becchino once and for all. One of them finally complied and chased him off with a stick. The apothecary, feeling the horns pointed toward him, jumped off the side of the platform, bumping into the bishop in his haste. The bishop stumbled and Ginevra saw something fall forward in front of his robe – a black cord strung with an ancient coral *figa*. *Her* ancient coral *figa* was tied around *his* neck. She could not help but laugh anew at his hypocrisy.

"QUIET," said the bishop, against the grumbling and shouts that kept rising with the temperature. The buzzing of voices was lessened only slightly by his admonishment. This was all proving too exciting: sorcery, grave robbers, an inquisitor who made love to both a heretic AND a donkey!

The bishop pressed forward. This was already taking too long. He needed to get to his point, to his miracle. He stepped to the front of the platform and thought of how soon he would be cardinal, rich once more, and never have to do anything this annoying ever again. He looked out into the crowd, held out his hands, and began to pray to Our Lady of Requisiti.

Oh, Blessed Virgin, who helps us in our hour of need

"Here," whispered Lucia, who had been waiting and watching for him to stand exposed at the front of the platform. She grabbed Giancarlo and maneuvered her way to the front of the crowd, putting the *jettatore* in a direct line of sight with the bishop.

We have allowed the wicked to walk among us and rape our city
The devil has infiltrated the holy office of the inquisitor
The devil has disguised himself as a base woman
We have been punished but remain faithful
Have mercy on us and let our suffering end

People were listening to him now. They began to weep and pray; they knelt down in the square.

God wants us to rid our city of sinners

"Yes!" cried the people.

And we have found the two wickedest among us

"We have found them for you, Madonna!" cried the people.
Lucia squeezed her *jettatore*'s arm.
"Now?" he whispered.
"Now," she said.
She adjusted his hood to create a tunnel of vision directed toward the bishop.
"Alright," she said, "go ahead."
Giancarlo pulled the linen from his eyes and stared hard at the bishop who was speaking, eyes to the sky.
On the platform, Ginevra, who had not taken her own eyes off her stolen amulet, saw the coral begin to glow on the bishop's neck. She ground her teeth into the gag.

Give us a sign, Madonna. Give us a sign that I have done right

The bishop began to step backward toward the statue.

In bringing these criminals before you
Give me a sign that you are pleased with my righteousness
That you favor our city and will intercede on our behalf
with the Lord God

"He will not look at me," said Giancarlo.

Give us a sign that we have discovered the source of evil
Return to us our relics, tell them we are righteous

Lucia did a gigantic, ridiculous fake sneeze, her trick from the apothecary's shop, that echoed off the walls of the piazza. The bishop looked down at her. Giancarlo locked eyes with him. The bishop gave a little shiver and a puff of icy breath left his lips. He shifted his eyes skyward again.

Hear us, oh, Madonna, hear me, your bishop of Florence, and come to my aid!

The people writhed on the ground, complete in their supplication.

"Damn, I thought he would fall off the stage and die, like our poor kitten," said Lucia.

"Lucia," said Giancarlo. "He is smoking."

"He is not just smoking. He is on fire. Hey! The bishop is on fire!" she shouted.

The crowd looked up.

The bishop looked down at himself and screamed as flames licked across his chest. The *figa* had grown so hot from the *jettatore*'s stare that it lit his robe on fire. He ripped it off his neck and threw it. Ginevra watched it bounce off the throne of the Virgin and land on the gilded brocade at the statue's feet

As the bishop slapped out the fire on his chest, Becchino ran back into the square, brandishing the stick that the soldier had been chasing him with, dancing around the shocked Florentines. "The soldier tried to catch me, but the plague caught him!

Dropped dead in the middle of a step. That's what you get, taking pay for dirty deeds! I would know!"

The bishop, now just lightly smoking, yelled for his mercenaries to kill Becchino, but now they would not. The Madonna had struck their comrade dead and lit their boss on fire. The mercenaries who had been minding Ginevra and Fra Michele walked over to the bishop to tell him that they were quitting his employ, that they wanted what was owed them today. All eyes were on the ensuing argument, so nobody noticed at first that flames grew upon the Madonna's wooden skirt. Nobody besides Fra Michele, the inquisitor.

Yelping, he leaped upon the statue, and Ginevra jerked behind him on the ropes that bound them together. The flames shot along the ropes; Ginevra snapped her hands free of the burning fibers and began to swat at the fire that now attacked the inquisitor's perfumed linen wrappings. When his garments died down to a smolder, she turned to the Virgin, and helped the inquisitor beat the flames from her painted robes. At last, Ginevra pulled the gag from her own mouth. She spun around, searching the platform for her *figa*.

"She has saved the Virgin!" yelled somebody in the crowd. A fold of the Virgin's wooden robes, weakened by the flames, fell aside.

"No, she has defaced her!" yelled somebody else.

Ginevra crouched, certain she was about to be stoned to death.

"BEHOOOLLLDDD SINNNERSSS," screeched Fra Michele. He pulled Ginevra into a gesture of supplication before the Madonna, and raised one arm above his head, pointing.

The crowd went dead silent. And then they began to point at the stage and whisper. Not sure they could trust their own eyes. The wooden panel of the Madonna's skirts had fallen in such a way that it was clear to them the Virgin had pulled aside the burnt robe herself for the benefit of her audience. And staring out at them from the folds of her garment was the skull of San Zenobio.

People started to cry out, "It is the relics! The Virgin has brought them back to us! She revealed them to the criminals!"

"NO!" said the bishop, fighting his way through the mercenaries. "No. No. No." Never in his life had a plan gone so badly.

Giancarlo smiled and wrapped the blindfold back around his eyes.

Fra Michele and Ginevra began to remove twelve relics from the statue and place them at her feet.

The bishop stepped between the statue and the crowd.

"These are counterfeit! Counterfeit relics, put here to trick you! They would not reveal themselves to sinners such as these!"

"That is Zenobio, I swear it on the graves of my children!" It was Lady Girolami, who made her way to the front. "He is my ancestor, I would know him anywhere."

"No!" said the bishop. "You are wrong, a widow mad with grief."

"But there is the bread," said another woman's voice. "The bread that I have guarded these weeks. I would know it anywhere." Taddea collapsed at the front of the platform, weeping.

"No!" said the bishop, yelling down at the top of her head. "You are wrong, a silly nun who knows nothing of the world."

"She is not silly!" cried Lucia. "That is the finger of San Tommaso, who I pray to in Santa Maria Novella! I know it down to the fingernail."

"No! No, no, no!" said the bishop. "Foolish women, who believe anything they see! These are false! Bits of ordinary men, pulled from our own graveyards!"

"But smell the air," cried somebody. "The odor of sanctity! The relics cannot be false."

Ginevra sniffed and realized that the inquisitor's smoking clothes gave off the sweet and musky odor of his pomander.

"It is a miracle! A true miracle," cried Fra Michele in all earnestness, who was so used to his own perfume, he could not recognize it. He had not seen the *jettatore*, and truly believed the Virgin had interceded on their behalf.

The crowd believed this also, and fell down on their knees as one and crossed themselves and then began to clamor to touch Ginevra and Fra Michele.

Bless Me
Save Us
Forgive Us

The Swiss soldiers also knelt down, wept, and begged to see the North again, told the relics how they had been tricked and didn't know for whom they worked. They crawled to Ginevra and the inquisitor and kissed the bottoms of their garments.

Bishop Acciaiuoli stood alone now, on the other side of the platform. In shock over the short ruin of his long ambitions. "Bishop," called Ginevra. "I have found your relics, as you requested of me. Will you not kneel before them?"

So the bishop knelt in front of the relics he had hoarded for months, for what else could he do? But as he knelt, he found his robes had grown tight and itchy. When he put his hand on the planks, somebody stepped on his fingers by accident, crushing them, and splinters dug into his palm. Then another person stepped on him, then another, in their eagerness to touch the relics of their saints, and it was all he could do to slink away through their feet and fall off the edge of the platform.

He limped toward his palazzo, but on the way, a pack of dogs that normally kept to themselves chased him. He only just managed to keep them at bay by throwing his expensive bishop hat at them, the one with his family crest embroidered in gold and pearls, which they tore to shreds. When he reached his palazzo, he slipped on a letter that had been dropped on his doorstep. It was signed by ten of his creditors, powerful dukes of the countryside. If he did not return their investments immediately, they would be sending forces to recoup what they could from his personal property, plague be damned.

As he was reading, the Swiss mercenaries caught up to him and demanded again their own payment. He started to yell how he owed them nothing, how they had voided their contract by abandoning their posts, but he stopped when they held him down and ran a long knife from the top of his forehead to the bottom of his chin. The bleeding bishop crawled into a corner and the mercenaries ransacked his palazzo, taking what they wished and fighting among themselves as to who would claim the plates with the shimmering purple eel women.

Back atop the *ringhiera*, Ginevra di Genoa picked up her coral from the feet of the Virgin and tied it back to its rightful place around her neck.

FORTY-SEVEN

A CHANCE TO BE KIND

Late in August, 1348,
City of Florence

A close sun baked dusty streets, and thin lines of shadow outlined open doors and empty fountain heads. On their beds, upon their floors, and in the dirt of their gardens, the bodies of dead Florentines had begun to dry out into hollow husks. The city was silent, as if respecting the dead on their arduous journey from soft flesh to hard bone. Except for one place; behind stone walls and locked doors, the convent of Sant'Elisabetta hummed with activity. Here the still living gathered together. Visitors shuffled slowly through the halls, quiet and purposeful. They stopped first in the chapel, where they whispered prayers to sacred bread enclosed in a new crystal orb. They were there because it was said that here, at last, the plague's secrets were discovered and could be unraveled. The methods were unorthodox, but effective. So, that August of 1348, Sant'Elisabetta became again a bit of an open secret in Florence and the surrounds: the sort of place everybody knew about but nobody talked about.

In what had been the women's ward, there was Taddea, spooning porridge into the mouths of peasant, priest, and lord. In the kitchen was the noblewoman Monna Lucia Tornaparte, sweating over eel pies that were only slightly burnt. And in the courtyard where gossiping nuns once spun golden threads, Ginevra di Genoa made a soup from secret stones and ladled a noxious broth, tasting of honey and smelling of ammonia, into any bowl that was proffered.

Running about, tripping over cats and people with his hands full of clean sheets or dirty bandages, was the still-blindfolded Giancarlo di Sporco, merchant of luxury ceramics, would-be necromancer, doomed lover of his people. Though Ginevra had made him poke many needles into many bowls of olive oil, made every traveler who came to the convent tell him every joke they knew, the Eye still clung stubbornly to him. If he so much as peeked out of his blindfold, all the cats in the place yowled like demons until he put it back on. But still, his blindness did not trouble him. He was elated, at last, to be bringing true help instead of harm. Lucia sewed him a new mask that had no danger of slipping. She made it so it fit the contours of his face and laced securely up the back of his head. It was embroidered with special prayers to San Tommaso, to make doubly sure the *malocchio* would find no way to escape. San Tommaso, pleased with the many candles Lucia eventually delivered to his shrine, was only too happy to guard the *jettatore*'s blindfold. A helper to all was the boy Piero, who had taken his leave of the bishop's household immediately following the Miracle of the Virgin of Requisiti, as the incident came to be known.

Those recovering in the beds and waiting in line told stories about the bishop – how he had found himself relieved of all personal properties by his creditors, that he had been chastised by the Pope himself for shouting in front of a crowd that genuine relics were only replicas. Some said you could see him now, wandering behind the windows of his palazzo (church property), with a bandaged face, eagerly awaiting his next salary installment (which, of course, was delayed). It was advised that if you attended a mass or a procession led by him, you'd better keep a hand pointed into horns behind your back. Mothers whispered to each other that if the bishop baptized your child, you had better take the baby straightaway to a healer who knew about needles and olive oil because it was understood that the bishop of Florence was badly cursed by the *malocchio*.

Ginevra stepped away from this gossip, outside of the efficient little cloister, for the first time in many weeks to walk over an empty bridge and through empty streets and meet with the Inquisitor Michele di Lapo Arnolfi at the steps of the half-built cathedral. He had asked her to come, to say goodbye. He was on his way to Avignon, summoned by the Pope. It was rumored he was to be made cardinal, as the Virgin of Requisiti clearly favored him.

He took both her hands in his. "Monna Ginevra, our sacred bones are back in their homes. A miracle, witnessed by many, occurred. You will be known as a most holy woman."

Ginevra looked down at the ground. She hadn't the heart to tell the inquisitor it was no miracle, but the battle between the *figa* and the *malocchio* that had started the fires. "It will be a refreshing change to be thought of as holy," she said at last. "Though after all I have seen of your bishop, I do not think I need the church to tell me what is holy and what is not."

The inquisitor sighed. "Here, we are in agreement. I have seen that God works great things through you, your little stones and strange ways. Without you, we never would have had our relics back. But besides that – I shall – I shall miss you dearly."

"Will you?" asked Ginevra, suppressing a smile. "Well, I suppose I shall miss you, too."

"That is pleasant to hear… I don't think anybody has ever missed me before. Ginevra, here – the letter that expunges your prior charges and rescinds your banishment. And here is my letter of recommendation and promise of finances for the Guild of Doctors, Apothecaries, and Grocers. It includes my own eye-witness account of how you expelled the pestilence from yourself in prison, applying the powers of stones in such a way that no guild physician ever has."

"Thank you, Michele," said Ginevra, with a half-hearted smile.

"What's this? Is that all the emotion you can muster? Is this not the very reward you asked for?"

"Michele – when we first met, you told me that your recommendation would not matter – the guild would never let me in, anyhow. I didn't believe you, but now I see – even with your protection and blessing, again I was hauled before a violent crowd. I thank you for completing the terms of our agreement but I fear even so I must keep my work in the shadows."

Fra Michele put his hand on her shoulder.

"Have faith, woman. I give you this letter now not as my final act, but so you have proof of my intentions: I will share all you have accomplished with His Holiness, and secure his blessing for your request. It is but a small favor you require, in return for great service."

Ginevra was stunned. An inquisitor was making her case before the *Pope*. It was the ultimate endorsement, guaranteed to secure her admission to the guild. She had done it, *really* done it. And she didn't even have to marry a rich man. She smiled fully now, and Michele returned her joyful gaze.

"And there is one last thing, dear Ginevra: I have not forgotten what I told you in the meadows." He went up the front steps of Santa Reparata. "Hear me, Citizens," he shouted so loudly that pigeons flew out from under the dilapidated scaffolds. "I, Michele di Lapo Arnolfi, Inquisitor of His Holiness Pope Clement VI, declare that Ginevra di Genoa is a righteous woman of God."

Though there was no one to hear it besides the dead mason on the scaffold, now all but a skeleton, Ginevra was grateful.

"May we meet again, God willing," he said, coming off the steps. "And until then, may the for-hire messenger donkeys clop with purpose, straight and true, with letters between you and me." With these words, the inquisitor took his leave, and began the long journey north to Avignon. He did not bring his pomander.

Ginevra looked around at the piazza, just as desolate as when she had first arrived. The plague still raged, outside their convent. Perhaps it would forever. She could not cure the whole world. But in the midst of this overwhelming blackness, she was just glad for the chance to be kind inside the walls of her own dear city.

EPILOGUE

1925, New York City

Belle da Costa Greene looked at the stack of correspondence on her desk and sighed. She counted at least two dozen letters, all from eager dealers of books and antiquities, hoping to entice her employers into a purchase. Responding to these tedious inquiries was her least favorite responsibility as head librarian for one of the most important public collections in the world.

She picked up her silver letter opener, admiring for the thousandth time its handle: a branch of Mediterranean coral, red as oxblood.

Slice. The envelope offered a first edition of *The Lamplighter* by Charles Dickens.

We already have at least two of those. No, thank you.

Slice. A terra-cotta idol, from Cyprus, or maybe Tunisia. Perhaps sixth century BC, or maybe seventh? The dealer couldn't say.

Sounds suspect. Next.

Slice. This letter was addressed to a *Mr.* B. Greene. Belle threw it in the wastebasket without reading further.

Slice. As Belle's eyes scanned the next letter, a welcome and familiar feeling overtook her. It felt as though the air hummed with faint vibrations, as though the coral letter opener grew warm in her hand. It was the feeling she got whenever she came across something extraordinary. She read the letter again, slowly.

JACQUES SELIGMANN & FILS
GERMAIN SELIGMANN & CIE SUCCRS
57 RUE SAINT DOMINIQUE
(ANCIEN HOTEL SAGAN)

Miss Belle Greene, July 12, 1925
Morgan Library,
33 East 36th Street,
New York City

My Dear Miss Greene:-
I have just arrived in New York and my first thought was of you. How wonderful to hear that Mr. Morgan's library will now be open to researchers!

I have brought back with me a rare trecento manuscript of Florentine provenance that I hope you will find a worthwhile addition to the library's collection.

The volume is a lapidary text containing verse on the magical properties of gemstones, and is unique in that the author is a lady called Ginevra di Gasparo. Her name appears as one of the rare female members in the registrars of the Florentine Guild of Doctors, Apothecaries, and Grocers.

Would you allow me a moment of your time, so I may show you the work in person?
Yours very sincerely,
Germain Seligmann

Belle folded up the letter and closed her eyes. There were hardly any medieval manuscripts attributed to women, and even fewer references to female physicians. But she'd always felt that this couldn't *possibly* represent the truth. She picked up the telephone, and asked the operator to connect her to the offices of Seligmann & Co., art dealers. As she waited, she looked at the letter again and smiled.

"Well, Ginevra di Gasparo," said the librarian, "let's show the world what you knew."

AUTHOR'S NOTE

I am a gemologist and a jewelry historian by trade, which means I get to evaluate all sorts of weird and beautiful old things for a living. Ten-carat diamonds, mourning jewelry made of human hair, ancient cameos – you name it, it's been on my desk. It was this work that inspired me, a number of years ago, to begin writing what would become *The Stone Witch of Florence*. I had been studying the uses of gemstones in the Middle Ages, and I became fascinated by medieval lapidaries – books that describe the magical and medicinal powers of gems. This was when the idea of Ginevra, a woman who could get these purported powers to actually work, came into my mind. I couldn't stop talking about her. I talked about her so much, in fact, that my nice boyfriend (now husband) said something along the lines of "Sounds like you have to write this book." He was right. So I quit my job, and he took a leave of absence from his, and we went to Italy (where I'd never been) for three months on tourist visas and visited Florence and all sorts of other wonderful places that became part of *Stone Witch* in big ways and small.

As I fell deeper and deeper into Ginevra's world, I learned that in the fourteenth century, magic, medicine, and religion were all tangled up with each other; it could be difficult to tell where one ended and the other began. In this work of fiction, I have similarly interwoven history with fantasy, because it is more fun that way. And medieval Florentines, despite everything they lived through, did like to have *fun*.

It is true that ancient writings on gemstones by the likes of Pliny the Elder and Theophrastus survived through the centuries and were referenced by later healers. These classical works also became source material for medieval scholars, like Albertus Magnus and Bishop Marbode of Rennes, who wrote their own lapidaries. Sister Agnesa only had access to the classical works, but I looked at everything, and then made some things up besides. In both ancient times and during the period in which this novel takes place, some people really believed that coral protected against disease and changed color depending on the wearer's health; that an amethyst under the tongue prevented inebriation; that the urine of a lynx hardened into a stone called lyngurium; and that toadstones not only came from toads' heads, but also sweat in the presence of poison. It really was written that diamonds were harvested by eagles in the canyons of India, and that they had the ability to end conflict. The supposed powers of the bloodstones, hyacinth (sapphire), smaragdus (emerald), amber, heliodor, antipathy, eaglestone, milkstone, Nemesis stone, selenite, and others were exaggerated or invented anew in keeping with the spirit of the historic texts. *A Lapidary of Sacred Stones* by Claude Lecouteux is a helpful compendium of dozens of these sorts of works.

I took care to model any actual jewelry after designs that were worn at the time – close examples of Ginevra's *mano figa*, Ludovico's sweetheart brooch, Fra Michele's pomander, and Vermilia's Nemesis ring can all be seen in museums. Go to one now! Yay, museums!

Folk healers, like Monna Vermilia, were frequented by all levels of society, as any child who has read Tomie dePaola's *Strega Nona* will tell you. People who practiced these arts could be punished if they clashed with established church or guild hierarchies, though *Stone Witch* takes place prior to the witch-burning frenzies of the later Renaissance. All the Florentine churches visited by the relic thief are real, most of them still standing. A number of the relics mentioned really were located in Florence. San Miniato still lies in his ancient church on the mountain; the arm of San Filippo is in the collections of the Museo dell'Opera del Duomo; and the head of San Zenobio, in its silver reliquary, is still at Santa Maria del Fiore (Santa Reparata has long since been leveled to make way for the current duomo).

A few other bits of fact inserted into the fiction: Sant'Elisabetta really was a convent where former sex workers spun golden threads. Two of them were named Agnesa and Taddea. Fra Michele really was hired to replace overzealous predecessors that annoyed the city of Florence. The Guild of Doctors, Apothecaries, and Grocers was established in the year 1293. Medieval Italians did keep eels in their water cisterns, both to control insects and to bake into pies. Giancarlo's magic book is based on the famous *Liber Iuratus Honorii*, which does contain elaborate spells requiring strict penance, though none of them mention a "saint made of saints." (I used Joseph Peterson's illuminating translation as reference.) The Black Death famously did lay waste to Florence, and *becchini* roamed the empty streets singing dreadful songs. Marchione di Coppo Stefani said of the city's burial grounds: "they put layer on layer (of bodies) just like one puts layers of cheese in a lasagna."

And then, some fiction inspired by fact: though the Acciaiuoli bank was caught up in a broader financial collapse, the timeline has been stretched for this story, and recent scholarship has shown that the king of England was not *entirely* to blame. The bishop's imagined end was inspired by the nineteenth-century Pope Pius IX, who was known far and wide as a *jettatore* that you really did NOT want visiting your town because a natural disaster was sure to follow his blessing. (For more on the *jettatore* and the Evil Eye, see *The Evil Eye: An Account of this Ancient and Widespread Superstition* by Frederick Thomas Elworthy.) I have played with timelines surrounding feast days and surely have omitted many important saints and celebrations that took place during the time span of this story. I have bumped up the date of the astrological report from the University of

Paris. I have exaggerated the absence of government and church officials during those first months of plague. I have used our own Gregorian calendar instead of the unique Florentine calendar that was in place during the fourteenth century. I ask for grace from medievalists, ceramicists, historians of art, architecture, and theology, and anybody fluent in Italian. Also, if any entomologists have made it this far: forgive me the liberties I have taken with the life cycle and morphology of burying beetles.

To try to capture what it was like to be alive at this place and time, I focused my research on writings that are contemporary-ish to the story, including the usual suspects of the brothers Villani, Petrarch, Dante, and of course, Boccaccio's *The Decameron*. For the latter, I relied on Wayne A. Rebhorn's clever translation, and did my best to give my own characters a similarly modern parlance. I also took great inspiration from *The Merchant of Prato* by Iris Origo, and the merchant's long-suffering wife, Margherita. Writings by the Pope's physician, Guy de Chauliac, and many others provided firsthand accounts of the Great Mortality. *The Society of Renaissance Florence*, a collection of translated records edited by Gene Brucker, illustrated the daily trials and tribulations of Florentine life. The religious works of Fra Simone Fidati da Cascia, translated by Sister Mary Germaine McNeil, and the famous medical treatise by Trotula of Salerno brought additional context. From these works and others, I borrowed delightful old idioms like "men who could not govern three snails" and "you lie in your throat." The manifestos of Margery Kempe and Christine de Pizan gave precious and rare insights into the minds of late-medieval women. This is by no means a complete bibliography, but I hope it provides a glimpse of the diverse and fascinating records that exist for those who are curious to learn more.

Into this mixed-up, beautiful, and calamitous world, a world just on the cusp of a renaissance, I placed Ginevra, who, like me, was just trying to do her best.

ACKNOWLEDGMENTS

Thank you to my agent, Stefanie Lieberman, and to her team, Adam Hobbins and Molly Steinblatt, for their unwavering dedication, vision, and kindness. I am so grateful for our partnership and friendship. To my editors, Laura Brown for her initial insights and enthusiasm, and Erika Imranyi for bringing everything together in the most beautiful way. To Nicole Luongo for keeping me on track. To Emer Flounders, Justine Sha, Rachel Haller, Lindsey Reeder, Kathleen Oudit, and the rest of the Park Row Books/HarperCollins team for bringing this book to life. To Kathleen Carter for lending her expertise. To AC Canup, Sam Rasche, Manasa Donaghy, and Becky Sandler, who provided invaluable early feedback when I sent them a giant pdf filled with typos. To Laura Hayner for her support during the submission phase. To Larissa Hayden and Hannah Baram for listening. To my writing group partners, LK Lohan and Courtney Knight, who have read this manuscript approximately one billion times and have had something helpful to say each time. To Elise Canup for her assistance with Italian. To Kate Rasche for her assistance with illustrations. To Dr. Gillian Jack, who generously shared her research on the women of Sant'Elisabetta delle Convertite. To my parents, siblings, and the rest of my family and friends for their interest and enthusiasm throughout this endeavor. To Cricket and Noms, the most companionable of cats. To my wonderful husband and partner, William Canup, who never misses a chance to be kind, and our baby, Bea, for showing up to the party.

And of course, all my thanks to you, dear reader, for making everything possible.

THE BOOK SOCIAL

Where stories meet community.

The Book Social is an imprint of independent publisher Legend Times, publishing both engaging fiction and thought-provoking non-fiction.

Our mission is simple: to connect great books with passionate reader communities and celebrate a shared love of reading.

 @_thebooksocial   @_thebooksocial

 thebooksocial.co.uk   @thebooksocial on Substack

Praise for *The Stone Witch of Florence*

A Book Riot Recommended Read

10 noteworthy books for October 2024 Washington Post

'Sparkles with suspense and the magical power of women... I devoured this novel'

Laurie Lico Albanese

'Perfect for lovers of witchy fantasy'

Historical Novel Society

'An interesting look at the intersection of folk magic, medicine and religion in the 14th century'

Washington Post

'A twisty, historical witchy escape'

Entertainment Weekly

'Magical in every sense of the word'

Katy Hays

'Magnificent'

Sarah Penner

'Get ready to be transported'

Mary O'Malley, Skylark Bookshop

'Captivating and original'

Maxwell Gregory, Madison Street Books